WHEN LIFE CARTWHEELS

WHEN LIFE CARTWHEELS

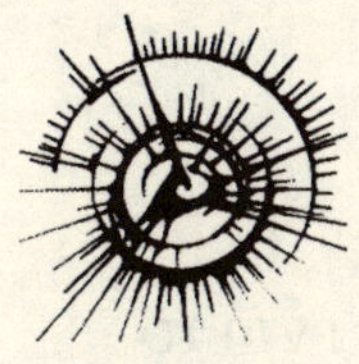

TUMULTUOUS LOVE STORY OF A SANNYASI

RAJ SUPE

PLATINUM PRESS

ISBN: 978-93-52011-91-9

Cover design: Aniruddha Mukherjee & Ashwini Jadhav
Layout: Ashwini Jadhav
Printing: Thomson Press

Published in India 2019 by
PLATINUM PRESS
An imprint of
LEADSTART PUBLISHING PVT LTD
Unit 25/26, Building A/1, Wadala (East)
Mumbai 400 037, Maharashtra, INDIA
T + 91 96 99933000 E info@leadstartcorp.com
W www.leadstartcorp.com

To my Gurus
Sri Sitaramdas Omkarnath and Kinkar Vitthal Ramanuja

ABOUT THE AUTHOR

RAJ SUPE (aka Kinkar Vishwashreyananda), is a poet, story-teller and novelist. An MBA by education, he had a career in advertising, research and creative consulting, before turning to literary and spiritual pursuits. Some of his literary works include the prequel to this work, *When Life Turns Turtle*; the novella *Big Bappa*; the spiritual memoir, *Pilgrim of the Sky*; the anthology *Hundreds of Shells*; and translations of *Cloudburst of A Thousand Suns*, and the Sahitya Akademi award winning *Rainbow at Noon*.

He has also worked on film scripts and plays. His writings convey the passionate intensity of a spiritual seeker, and one who strives to merge traditional mythicism with the urgencies of modern life. In the words of a leading poet, 'he has the anonymity of the saint-poet on the one hand and the self-expression of the modern writer on the other'.

Raj is Editor of the spirituality e-magazine, *The Mother* [www.themotherdivine.com], and co-founder of the Foundation for Contemplation of Nature [www.foundnature.com]. Initiated into the Order founded by Sri Sitaramdas Omkarnath, he met his Guru in the person of Kinkar Vitthal Ramanuja. Raj leads a simple life on the banks of the Ganges.

He can be reached at: rajsupe@gmail.com

FOREWORD

by Kinkar Vitthal Ramanuja

An ideal follower of Sri Sitaramdas Omkarnath, our beloved spiritual brother, Kinkar Vishwashreyananda, Sri Raj Supe, is a unique combination of seeker and artist *par excellence.* He lives on the banks of the Ganga and relentlessly preaches the *vaani* of Omkarnath Dev, and the words of our sacred scriptures.

We have been overjoyed and overwhelmed by his most recent spiritual romance—*When Life Cartwheels*. Here, we come to know about the most critical spiritual journey of Shaman, a high-profile seeker whose career is full of ups and downs, ambitions and frustrations, attachment and detachment, renunciation and illusion—finally leading him to scale a spiritual height which he verily deserves. Then, after a somersault, like a cartwheel, he comes back to his own.

This work is also a splendid romance, full of suspense at every turn. You never know exactly what the future holds for the much tired and tried hero. But in the end, after many trials and tribulations, he gets a taste of divine nectar, giving him eternal bliss and peace. This reminds us of the Vedantic truth: *Shrinvantu Amitasya putraa* (Do please listen to me! Offspring of the Deathless!) Shvetashvatara Upanishad- 2/5.

The most brilliant feature of this realistic novel is the artistry with which the narrative is cleverly woven to disclose the bare truth that even an ascetic and strict celibate like Shaman cannot sidetrack the lures of the *samsara,* which are impassable. Practical life is no fairytale; flesh and blood has its own demands. Only the siddha-saints can override this onslaught. It is not a possibility for any ordinary man—not even an extraordinary man like Shaman.

Readers will find their own thoughts and struggles echoed in the characters in this book. This novel tells us that every individual will inevitably reach his or her destination for this lifetime. The upheavals in one's life serve only to lighten one's burden, clear one's sight and illuminate the path to one's destination. However, not knowing the nature and distance to the destination is the test; a part of the intricate plot of Divine Leela.

We hope this book will reach a large number of readers and through the fascinating tale of Shaman and others, bring a ray of illumination and better understanding to their own lives.

PART I

I renounced until I had renounced everything.
I even renounced food and clothes.
When I renounced renunciation,
I found spirituality in worldly life.

~ Swami Muktananda

PROLOGUE

Sudden showers had turned the warm muggy day into an incandescent evening. Shaman looked out of the large picture window of the anteroom of his bookshop, El Dorado. The waters of the Ganga rippled like glowing ribbons in the last rays of the setting sun.

Shaman was a fit man, 55 years of age, of medium height and wiry build. He had piercing brown eyes. His salt and pepper hair was trimmed close to his head and he was clean shaven. He had pronounced laughter lines at the corners of his eyes and mouth, which deepened every time he smiled.

He had earned his PhD from Harvard and ran a flourishing bookshop in Rishikesh. The bookshop, now a local landmark, was on the to-do list of every tourist. People from every walk of life, from popular Hollywood celebrities to well-known Indian writers, visited El Dorado.

Shaman was clueless about clothes. To keep his wardrobe simple, he consistently chose to wear jeans, a white *kurta*[1] and Kolhapuri slippers, along with a large-faced watch on his right wrist.

Shaman looked at his mobile phone expectantly as it beeped. *Nearly there,* read a message from Indraneel.

He had met Indraneel Barua, an accomplished filmmaker from Bombay, in this very shop, little more than two years ago,

[1]Kurta: a loose shirt falling either just above, or somewhere below the knees of the wearer, worn traditionally by men. However, women do also wear the straight-cut kurta or its shorter version, the kurti.

when Indraneel was going through an extremely low phase in his life, following a break up with a beautiful actress.

Shaman checked the time. Though it was 7 pm, the lingering summer twilight created magical light conditions, perfect for photography. Shaman recalled how Indraneel had been inseparable from his camera during his stay in this quiet town.

The tinkling of doorbells indicated someone at the entrance. Payal, his assistant, went to the door and greeted Indraneel with a warm '*Jai Guru*[2]'.

Indraneel was a tall, lean and handsome man. Almost 42 years of age, he wore his long, curly, black hair tied back. Who would have thought an engineer from Massachusetts Institute of Technology would turn out to be a successful mainstream Hindi filmmaker, mused Shaman, as he watched Indraneel walk into the store.

"Sir, they are like dolls!" Payal exclaimed in a whisper as she admired the napping babies in the double-stroller Indraneel wheeled into the shop.

The elderly British couple browsing through the many books that lined the shelves turned to look at the infants.

"Little angels!" the lady remarked. "Yours?"

"Yes indeed," Indraneel replied with a smile, wheeling the pram into the anteroom.

"Indraneel Bhai! How are you doing?" Shaman asked with genuine warmth and affection.

"Shaman! So good to see you," the younger man replied as he hugged his mentor.

"See the babies…bless them Shaman…"

Shaman knelt beside the stroller to take a closer look at the infants. "Baba has already blessed them. What more do you

[2]Jai Guru: Greeting to say Victory to the Guru!

want?" he remarked. "And he has given them such lovely names – Dakshayani and Katyayani – both powerful names of Ma Durga."

"Yes, Baba has been most gracious and kind. By the way, the Nagaprayag *ashram*[3] is beautiful!"

"Well, it is beautiful, but my heart has been claimed by the beauty of these two now," Shaman replied, admiring the darlings in the stroller.

"The babies need your blessings," Indraneel said.

"My love and blessings for them will always be there!"

"You were the one who picked me up from ruin and put me on this path," Indraneel said, gratitude clear in his deep voice. "But for you, I could have been just another loser without moorings."

Shaman simply smiled. "I am only a tiny cog. It was your fate and destiny that you took shelter in *naam*[4]. But thank God your children look like Vasundhara! In fact, they are the spitting image of their mother," Shaman said with a laugh, looking at the plump and fair, sleeping infants.

"Yes, they also have her green eyes! You'll see once they wake up."

"Can you tell them apart?" Shaman was curious.

"Not when they are sleeping, but it's easy to identify them when they are awake; they have such different personalities."

"Where is Vasundhara?"

"She has gone for the Ganga *arati*[5], leaving us to babysit. She

---

[3]Ashram: place of religious retreat

[4]Naam: The name of God. But the word Naam refers more particularly to the Mahamantra Hare Krishna Hare Krishna Krishna Krishna Hare Hare, Hare Ram Hare Ram Ram Ram Hare Hare

[5]Arati: a Hindu religious ritual of worship, a part of puja, in which light from wicks soaked in ghee (purified butter) or camphor is offered to one or more deities.

has fed them, so we are sorted for at least two hours."

"How come you didn't go for the *arati*?" Shaman asked.

"I sorely miss the Shivji statue. I find it hard to go to the *arati* without seeing the majestic Shiva. The singing is good, as always, but the vacuum of His absence is overwhelming."

"I understand, but are you confident of looking after the babies by yourself?" Shaman asked, his eyes glinting mischievously as he looked at his friend.

"To tell you the truth, I *can* look after them, but there are two of them and only one of me! The nannies are sitting outside. I didn't want the shop to get crowded."

"They can wait inside, Indraneel," Shaman said. "It's no problem at all!"

"No Shaman, they are fine outside. They can come in if one of the babies wakes up."

The aroma of freshly brewed coffee filled the room as Shaman offered a cup to his friend.

Indraneel took a sip. "Great coffee, Shaman!"

"Thanks. Good to read so many positive reviews about your film. There is a huge buzz around *Incandescence*."

"Thank you, that's just one of the things I am grateful to you for putting into perspective for me. But for you, I may not even have married."

"Marriage is too big a change, Indraneel. If it has to happen, it does. I can't take credit for it."

"Sometimes, I seriously wonder how it would have been had I not married and taken *sannyasa*."

"Why, Indraneel? Are you not happy as a householder?"

"No, I am very happy. It's just a stray thought that crosses my mind on and off. How would it have been if I had taken the road less travelled? You know how it was at that point… I was ready to renounce the world. Now look at me—Daddy to not one, but two daughters!"

"There are things that make us feel like we are making the choices, but it's far beyond that. These are significant waves of *praarabdha*[6] or destiny," Shaman observed quietly.

"I agree Shaman, these are life-changing forks in the road. Tell me honestly, have you ever contemplated renouncing everything, donning the ochre robe, and leading the life of a *sannyasi*? Did the thought never touch you?"

Indraneel could think of no person more worthy of the life of a *sannyasi* than Shaman, and wondered why he wasn't one.

~

[6]Praarabdha: The unfolded destiny. The part of the collection of past karmas, which are ready to be experienced.

1.

The smell of strong petrol fumes made her gag. Her shivering body was drenched in it. She could not move. Her body was so heavy, it seemed to be weighed down by wet concrete. Her eyes felt heavy too; she could not keep them open. She wanted to scream but could not; with a dirty cloth in her mouth. Her hands, she realised, were bound behind her back. She felt a hard poking sensation in her back. With great difficulty she opened her eyes and discovered she was lying on a pile of firewood.

The awful smell of petrol unleashed in her a miasma of dark fear.

That helpless fear unspooled so fast and so strong, it caused in her a huge wave of panic. She made a valiant effort to sit up and as she tried to free her hands, she fluttered like a pinned butterfly.

She thrashed against the bindings that trapped her delicate wrists; to her great relief, her feet were free and unbound.

Suddenly, she heard a male voice and stilled herself.

"Has she woken up?" a gruff voice asked.

"She has been drugged, you know that..."

No wonder her limbs felt so heavy she could not move.

Another voice replied with a jeer. "No. I heard something rustle."

"Must be the wind..."

A strong gust of wind muffled the rest of his words.

"We will burn her soon. Let the drug take effect..."

"We must remove all her jewellery before burning her... Alas! There

is no fun in touching a sleeping woman!" another voice said with a wicked laugh.

"She is not a woman, she is a child. We took money to burn her. So let's just stick to that!"

"A female is all I care about. Child or woman, doesn't matter and this one is very beautiful..."

Raucous laughter followed.

Upon hearing these words, she suffocated with strangulating terror. But it was not the time to panic. She needed to escape. She took slow deep breaths and forced herself to think calmly. Carefully, she twisted her hands; the bindings from her wrists finally yielded. Though they had been loosely tied, the rough rope cut into the delicate skin. She worked them free with stealth, removed the dirty cloth in her mouth and fought the overwhelming urge to retch.

Her mouth was chaffed and her throat parched. It took all her strength to stand up quietly. Her heavily embellished red ghagra[7], *now drenched with petrol, made movement difficult.*

The men who were squatting around a small fire and drinking, saw her. They immediately made a dash for her. She started running, her gold anklets tinkling in the wind. Several thick bangles clanked against each other. Her large uncut diamond earrings moved wildly as she ran, pulling on her small earlobes painfully. One of the men shouted – "Don't try to catch her!" – and threw a burning twig from the fire onto the trail of petrol that leaked from her ghagra.

She ran as fast as she could. Sheer terror fuelled her legs and freed her from the debilitating effects of the sedative. Being a trained dancer, she was in very good physical condition. But the fire snaked and roared rapidly towards her.

Within minutes, her ghagra *was engulfed in flames. The heat was unbearable! She opened her mouth to scream...*

---

[7]Ghagra: A tradition Indian long full skirt, often decorated with embroidery, mirrors, or bells.

She bolted up, a soundless scream locked in her throat, soaked in sweat. Her fingers were curled into tight fists, the bedsheet twisted round her tiny waist. The acrid smell of smoke burned her lungs, leaving her breathless. She looked around, her heart still pounding like a crazy drum.

She took deep breaths. 'I am safe,' she told herself. It had been a recurrent nightmare for the last ten years.

A slight breeze carried the heady scent of jasmine past the fluttering curtains and the creeper draped across her window. She looked at the glowing arms of the clock on the bedside table. It was just after 5 am. A pale pink dawn was emerging and the previous evening's rain had left a trace of moisture in the air. 'Bangalore is a beautiful city,' she thought to herself.

In the quiet morning stillness, she heard the sound of rhythmic footsteps coming from the room above. The 64-year-old Chandrahasini, Head of the Nrityanupur Dance Academy, was up by 4 am every day for her dance practice.

It was the first day of summer break. Shambhavi was leaving that morning to visit her beloved *guru* at his *ashram* in the distant Himalayas. His health had deteriorated and she longed to see him. She rose quickly, made her bed and hurriedly got dressed.

Fifteen minutes later, looking into the mirror to comb her long and beautiful, thick, black hair, all she saw was a woman whose eyes seemed too large for her face. But what the world saw was a stunningly beautiful woman of medium height, with an exceptionally proportionate body, who moved with the feline grace of a professional dancer. She was 24 years of age now, but looked much younger.

Shambhavi quickly braided her hair and locked her room, wheeling her suitcase through the empty corridors. She had already bid goodbye to her dear teacher, Chandrahasini.

It was time to go to the airport.

2.

Shaman slowly emerged from his evening *japa*[8]. He could hear the faraway sound of bells from the small Shiva temple, nestled at the *sangam*[9] of the Mandakini and Alakananda.

The *ashram* of Naam Yajnananda Maharaj was located high on a cliff of the Himalayas. Directly below, the jewel-green Mandakini rushed towards the azure waters of a calmly flowing Alakananda. Almost every room in the *ashram* overlooked this little known *sangam*, called Nagaprayag; its name born from the two serpentine rivers that twisted and turned many times before they met.

The green Mandakini jumped over the rocks with great force. Her waters were frothy and full of power as she squeezed into the narrow, confined gorge, which she had carved out of the mountains. The seemingly calm Alakananda was very deep, hiding the treacherous eddies and currents that swirled within her depths.

The steady roar of water could be heard clearly at the *ashram*. It was like living with a large conch pressed to one's ear. But, like everything else that one gets used to over time, the occupants of the *ashram* had got used to the loud background score.

Shaman sat quietly for several seconds, tuning his mind to the sound of the rivers below. He then rose and prostrated before the deity before him – Mother Gayatri.

The idol was beautiful – about four feet tall and exquisitely carved from the purest white marble. She was seated on a

---

[8]Japa: The meditative repetition of a mantra or a divine name

[9]Sangam: A confluence of rivers

large swan and had five faces and four hands. In one hand, she carried a *kamandalu*[10], the Vedas in another, and a rosary in the third. The fourth hand was lifted in blessing. She radiated bliss and peace. The Gayatri Temple was the nucleus of the *ashram*, with the rest of the structures built around it.

As the sun sank below the mountains, a chill descended upon the tiny Himalayan hamlet. Bird calls punctuated the tranquil silence as they prepared to roost for the night. Shaman picked up sounds of commotion coming from the kitchen wing. He folded his *asana*[11] with great care, touched it to his forehead and put it away, hoping the serenity would last. But the sounds of clanging pots and raised voices continued.

He adjusted his ochre *dhoti*[12], put on his wooden *chappals*[13], and went to the kitchen. He had a wheatish complexion and stood 5 feet 10 inches on his bare feet. The wooden sandals added at least another two inches. His thick, black, shoulder-length hair was twisted neatly in *jataas*[14]. Over three decades of hard yoga had honed his wiry muscles. He looked at least a decade younger than his biological age. His features were even and balanced; his brown eyes being the most striking feature. His gaze had the piercing quality of an eagle. Shaman just stopped short of being handsome.

As he stepped out of the *ashram* temple, the view made him pause, as it always did. The cool air of the hills caused gooseflesh to rise on his bare chest. The craggy and snow-capped Himalayan peaks around the *ashram* rose like twisted spires, reaching out to the orange-grey twilight sky. It was the standard view throughout the year; only the amount of snow varied, depending on the season. Snow-capped or snow-clad,

---

[10]Kamandalu: Oblong water pot made of a dry gourd (pumpkin) or coconut shell, with a handle and a spout, used by Hindu ascetics or yogis

[11]Asana: Meditation mat

[12]Dhoti: Traditional Indian lower body garment for men

[13]Chappal: A pair of sandals, usually of leather, worn in India

[14]Jataa: Matted hair/ locks

that was the only difference. The weather was always cool, except for the bitter cold of the harsh winters.

Shaman joined his palms and lifted them high above his head, offering his salutations to the holy peaks. Even before he neared the kitchen area, he could smell the aroma of food, hanging heavy in the still air. There could be no doubt that whatever was being cooked was delicious. He spotted the three *sannyasis*, Venu Da, Madhav Da and Keshava Da, sitting on the steps outside the kitchen. As soon as they saw Shaman approach, they stood up to receive his blessing.

"*Pranaam*[15] Dada," they said, even though Venu Da and Keshava Da were at least two decades older than Shaman. Everyone was aware that Shaman was slated to be the next pontiff of the Order, and the inmates respected him greatly.

"You finished cooking so soon, Venu Da?"

"Yes, yes…You know Shambhavi Didi[16] is coming. I finished quickly so we can be at the gate to receive her." Venu Da was a fair, plump and short man with a round belly.

"The best thing that happened to this *ashram* was the day that child, I mean Shambhavi Didi, came here," opined Keshava Da, a tall, dark *sannyasi*, usually a man of few words.

"I have never seen Didi, but she must be special indeed. Maharaj looks so happy. He hasn't even taken his nap; he is waiting for Didi to arrive," said Madhav Da, a young *sannyasi* in his mid-twenties, who had transferred from the Rishikesh *ashram* a few months ago.

"Even Shaman Da has not seen Didi," Keshava Da informed the others.

"You must see Maharaj and Didi together. He treats her just

---

[15]Pranaam: Salutation. A respectful greeting made by putting one's palms together and often touching the feet of the person being greeted.

[16]Didi: An older sister

like his daughter."

Krishna Da, the personal assistant of the Master, came down from the Master's chamber. "*Pranaam*, Shaman Da," he said, bending his head to receive Shaman's blessing.

"Venu Da, Maharaj is asking whether the food is ready."

"Oh yes. You can tell him it's all done!"

Krishna Da hurried away to inform the Master.

Shaman was really curious now. True, he had never met Shambhavi, but he could not wrap his head around the frenzy of anticipation she had generated amongst the normally staid *sannyasis*.

The *pundit*[17], Partha, was arranging fresh mauve lotus flowers at the feet of Ma Gayatri. When he saw Shaman, he answered the unasked question, his face wreathed in smiles, "We are all happy that Shambhavi Beti[18] is coming... And she loves flowers."

Leela was busy tracing a beautiful *rangoli*[19] at the entrance to Maharaj's room. Without looking up, she asked, "Has Didi's taxi come?"

Shaman, who felt like the only one not invited to the party, did not answer. Instead, Krishna Da replied from Maharaj's room, "I am standing near the window, overlooking the main road. No taxi has come." The disappointment in his voice was palpable.

"What's the time?" Maharaj asked in a feeble voice.

Before Krishna Da could answer, Shaman jumped across the large *rangoli* and said, "Seven o'clock, Maharaj."

[17]Pundit: Priest

[18]Beti: Daughter

[19]Rangoli: An art form native to India in which patterns are created on the floor in living rooms or courtyards using materials such as coloured rice, dry flour, coloured sand or flower petals

He proceeded to remove his wooden footwear, still confused by the drama occurring around him. He bowed to the Master and was surprised to find him sitting in his chair instead of lying down. His pale features were radiant with joy and anticipation.

"You should be resting. Why are you exerting yourself?" Shaman asked gently.

"Ah! How can I sleep or rest? The child Shambhavi is coming..." the old *guru* said in his asthma-stricken voice.

3.

Shaman went to check if Krishna Da had given the Master his evening medication. He made a mental note to replenish the multivitamin tablets. Only three days' supply remained.

There was a sharp chill in the room. Shaman looked out of the window, but all he could see was Krishna Da's silhouetted form. The younger *sannyasi* was continuing his vigil for Shambhavi's taxi; his neck nearly sticking out between the iron bars in an attempt to get a clearer view of the winding road that led up to the *ashram*.

'This kind of excitement, I have never witnessed before,' Shaman thought, as he turned to another window. A thick layer of mist had slunk from the craggy peaks into the surrounding areas, blurring everything in its path. He picked up the red shawl from the foot of Maharaj's bed and draped it around the frail *guru*'s shoulders.

The Master once again asked for the time. Shaman said it was nearly 7:30.

"Please close the windows. The cold mist is slipping right into the room," Shaman instructed Krishna Da.

Before Krishna Da could do so, the Master whispered hoarsely, "Let this window remain open; how else will we know the child has arrived?"

Shaman sat down to meditate in one corner of the room.

Shortly afterwards, Madhava Da arrived and told the Master, "Chandni is here."

Even as the Master nodded, Shaman heard an off-key rendition of the film song, *Humko Humise Churaa Lo*.

Hearing the song, the *pundit*'s wife, Leela, laughed softly and asked in a whisper, "How many more people are going to rob you from yourself?"

Chandni giggled and replied, "More the merrier!"

The women thought they were whispering, but in the evening silence, every word of their exchange could be heard clearly.

"How is your fourth husband? Or is it the fifth?" Leela asked humourously.

Chandni responded in a conspiratorial tone. "He is a young stud. So I am happy…"

Hearing this exchange, Shaman became irritated. This was further aggravated by Krishna Da's smile. The Master had slipped into meditation, and so the entire conversation had eluded his ear.

Shaman did not like Chandni. She was a loud and garrulous woman from the village below. She used to sweep the *ashram* every day before her aching knees made it difficult for her to climb the narrow steep path to the *ashram*. Presently, she entered the Master's room and prostrated before him. Fair, short and plump, she was about 50 years of age. She was dressed in a bright blue *salwar*[20] *kurta* , her thick unruly hair tied in a messy bun on one side of her head.

Shaman saw her as a woman of loose morals who openly flirted with everyone. He particularly detested the innuendos in her conversations with the *sannyasis*, though they did not seem to mind. That annoyed Shaman even more.

The Master blessed the woman. "As usual, you will stay in the *ashram* as long as Shambhavi is here," he said.

---

[20]Salwar: a pair of light, loose, pleated trousers worn by Indian women, usually tapering to a tight fit around the ankles

Chandni respectfully draped her *dupatta*[21] over her head. "Of course, Maharaj. I will be at her service."

Shaman did not like that at all. "But why Maharaj? Why do you want her to reside here?" he asked.

Before Maharaj could reply, Chandni said with a faint trace of arrogance, "I always stay when Shambhavi Didi is here. Maharaj knows this; it's been the practice ever since she came here as a thirteen-year-old girl. Is it not Krishna Da?" She turned to the *sannyasi* who was still stuck to the window.

"Yes, you are always here," Krishna Da concurred.

Maharaj silenced Krishna Da with a look and lifted his hand, gesturing to Chandni to be silent. "Go, get her room ready. You'll find everything she needs there, in her cupboard."

The Master struggled to remove the key from the oversized keyring on the table beside his chair. Shaman stepped forward, deftly removed the key and handed it over to Maharaj. Chandni gave him a smug smile before she left the room, key in hand.

The old *guru* called Shaman close and explained, "See Shaman, Shambhavi came here when she was just thirteen years old; an extremely traumatised child who had gone through horrific experiences. She was just an empty shell when she came. Not eating, not talking…" There was a faraway look in his eyes as he recounted, "She had lost everything…everything." He paused as a severe bout of cough wracked his weak body.

"Maharaj, do not talk." Shaman handed him a glass of water and massaged his back gently.

The Master sipped the water and continued nevertheless. "The child needed generous love and affection, more than anything else. We were just a bunch of *sannyasis* here, incapable of

---

[21]Dupatta: A length of material worn by Indian women, arranged in two folds over the chest and thrown back around the shoulders, typically with a salwar kameez.

meeting Shambhavi's emotional needs. Leela was not at this *ashram* back then. It was Chandni's love and affection that soothed the child; she slowly blossomed under her care."

Shaman listened quietly.

"Chandni is a loud mouth. But a good woman."

Shaman still thought it was a bad decision to have Chandni in the *ashram*. He couldn't fathom how a woman living with Husband No. 5 could be a good woman. But he didn't say anything. The Master knew best.

Chandni returned in a cacophony of jingling sounds. She called to Krishna Da that she needed toothpaste for Shambhavi. Krishna Da reluctantly stepped away from his post near the window and opened a small supplies cupboard. "Take what you want," he said simply.

Chandni took what she felt Shambhavi might need and was about to close the cupboard when Krishna Da interjected, "Take soap for Didi."

Chandni clucked her tongue and shook her head. "No soap. Didi only uses body wash," she said, pronouncing *body* as *bawdy*.

Shaman thought this was rather too much. Maharaj handing him the key to another cupboard, only added to his displeasure. To his shock, the cupboard was cramped with an exotic range of perfumes, body washes, face washes and other skin products. A distinctly expensive and feminine aroma pervaded the room. From Yves Saint Laurent and Christian Dior to Gucci, it was all there.

Having spent a lot of time at Harvard, Shaman knew roughly how much they cost. The label on one bottle that Chandni picked up read, *Fragrance of Clear Springs*. Shaman wondered for a moment what clear springs smelled like. His mind drew a blank. He noticed the tagline read, *Made from the purest extracts of patchouli and macadamia*. 'Manipulative marketing gimmicks,' he thought with a grimace.

Chandni picked up several bottles and tubes casually, like she had an intimate knowledge of these top brands, and left with a bounty of high-end toiletries.

Shaman locked the cupboard, barely able to contain his curiosity. "If I may ask, Maharaj, where did you procure all those things from?" His tone was casual, but his feelings far from it. He was annoyed that this mysterious Shambhavi had made the *ashram* spend so much on exorbitant indulgences.

Maharaj evaded answering directly. "The child is used to these things," he said with eyes shut and head resting on the back of the chair for support.

Krishna Da added in a matter-of-fact voice, "Anyone coming from outside India normally gets five or six things that Didi uses. Sharmaji, Shuklaji, even Meenaji, brings." He continued to look out into the thickening mist as he spoke.

Shaman was infuriated by this information. How could Maharaj accept gifts of that kind? It was against everything he believed in. He decided he needed to talk to Maharaj about this some time.

Just then, Chandni came running in. "Didi has come! Didi has come!" she cried joyfully and ran back towards the gate.

Leela ran down with her, laughing. A faint smile of delight appeared on Maharaj's face; there was a glow in his eyes and his features visibly relaxed.

"Oh ho! Damn mist, it made me blind. How could I miss the taxi?" Krishna Da mumbled to himself.

Shaman heard Venu Da and Keshava Da greet Shambhavi, but her voice was too low for him to hear her reply. He did, however, hear the high-pitched greeting of Chandni.

The landline rang in the other room. Shaman hurried to attend to it. It was a trunk call. He waited for the line to be connected. He still had a clear view of Maharaj's room.

When he saw Shambhavi for the first time, he was speechless. Why had no one mentioned that she was staggeringly beautiful? And that she was not a child, by any stretch of the imagination? She was a slim woman of medium height, with curves that accentuated her latent sensuality. Her complexion was like a polished pearl. Her eyes were a striking grey, and radiated an unmistakable fire. A small mole just above her upper lip drew attention to her perfect mouth. She was dressed in a pale pink Mysore silk sari with a thin gold border. She looked fresh, hardly like a person who had been travelling for the whole day.

Putting down her bag, she bent down with extraordinary grace and touched Maharaj's feet. "Baba..." she mumured affectionately.

Maharaj drew the *Om* symbol on her forehead with the ring finger of his right hand. The holy man looked at Shambhavi with such love that Shaman was speechless. The *guru* gestured for her to sit on the chair beside him, but Shambhavi sat down on the floor, at his feet.

She reached for her large handbag and took out a small garland of golden *champa*[22] flowers. A sweet smell flooded the room as she gently placed the garland on the Master's feet.

He smiled as he whispered, "My favourite flowers..." He bent and picked up the garland and put it on his sidetable.

Shaman found this very odd. Thousands of devotees came from all over the world and garlanded the Master. The Master invariably removed the garlands immediately and gave them away to Krishna Da or garlanded other devotees with them. What he did here with Shambhavi was certainly out of the

---

[22]Champa: Magnolia

ordinary. Shaman observed all this with knitted brows.

"Baba, you should be resting," Shambhavi said. "Why are you sitting up?"

Krishna Da, who was standing little away, smiled and answered, "He was waiting for you, Didi."

"You must make sure he rests," Shambhavi told Krishna Da in a tone of great familiarity and asked, "How are you doing Da?"

Shaman wondered how Shambhavi seemed to have won everyone's hearts. Somehow, she looked oddly familiar to him as well. 'If I had met someone as gorgeous, there is no way I would forget her,' he told himself.

He heard Shambhavi ask Maharaj in a soft voice, "Why didn't you inform me when you were hospitalised? I was so worried." Her eyes glimmered with unshed tears.

"Now that you have come, I will be fully okay," he said, effectively ending the topic.

"Where is your shawl?" he asked.

"It's not so cold, Baba," Shambhavi reassured with a smile. Her voice held a musical quality.

Maharaj called to Chandni, his feeble voice finding renewed strength. "Get Didi's shawl," he ordered. As Chandni ran to fetch it, he said, "I want you to meet Shaman Da."

Shambhavi looked around. "Where is he? I, too, wish to meet him."

Maharaj called to Shaman. Unable to get through, Shaman hung up and stepped out from the other room.

Shambhavi came to her feet nimbly. She was about to greet him with a *pranaam* when the warm smile on her face faded and a look of strange distaste gathered in her eyes.

Shaman realised where he had seen her. It was at a lecture-dance demonstration where he had got into an argument with Chandrahasini, Shambhavi's *guru* and mentor. That lady Chandrahasini thought too much of herself, Shaman had concluded.

"This is my dear Shambhavi." Maharaj's voice brought him back to the present. "And this is my right hand, Shaman Da," he said to Shambhavi with pride. "Shambhavi Beta, do *pranaam*," he urged.

Shambhavi immediately did the Master's bidding, bending to touch Shaman's feet. But her dislike flashed clearly in her beautiful eyes.

Shaman blessed her with a '*Jai Guru*', and she quickly stood up.

Chandni returned with two shawls. "Didi, which one do you want, the white one or the pink?"

"Any will do."

Chandni was so short, her head barely reached Shambhavi's chest. "The pink one will match your sari," she declared, handing it over.

"It is getting late," Maharaj said. "Go and have your dinner Shambhavi. It's been a long day for you… Come to my room to have your breakfast," he told her as she left, with Chandni in tow.

Shaman was astonished. Maharaj always ate alone. No one ate with him. He could see the Maharaj was caught in the throes of *maya*[23] – the web of filial love.

As they walked away, Shaman could hear the women's waning voices. "You are thin like a stick. People will think you are a boy! Will men like you? You don't even have a kilo of

[23]Maya: the illusive or delusive power by which the universe, which is essentially divine, appears as the phenomenal world

flesh on you. Men want women who fill their arms. Like me…" Chandni said with a loud laugh.

"I don't want men to like me. It would be enough if just one man loves me passionately," Shambhavi replied, her voice fading away.

There was no way anyone could mistake Shambhavi for a boy. She was all woman, Shaman thought, as he bid the Master goodnight. His mind flew back to *that* day. He had not recognised Shambhavi immediately because back then, she had been wearing heavy stage make-up.

4.

The weather in Bangalore was clement. A slight drizzle accompanied the cool breeze. But the traffic was an ugly and chaotic nightmare.

Dr Shamantak Srivastava took a cab to the Centre for Indian Art and Culture (CIAC), the venue of the conference, along with his colleague Kumud Roy, a research assistant from Cambridge. They made an odd pair. Shaman with his shoulder-length *jataas,* in his ochre *dhoti* and wooden sandals, and a simple orange cloth bag that contained his laptop and books, slung over his bare shoulder; and Dr Kumud, with his bald head and plump frame, a dark blazer over his blue full-sleeved shirt, black trousers and polished black shoes, carrying a briefcase.

Dr Kumud pointed to a life-sized picture of Jayadeva holding a palm-leaf manuscript of *Gita Govind*. "What is it about this guy Jayadeva? Is he a saint? Or is he just a writer? I'm sorry to sound so ignorant, but apart from the fact Jayadeva is the master of *shringara kavya* etc. I don't know anything else," he said frankly.

"Well, Jayadeva is a celebrated poet," said Shaman. "He was a *sannyasi* who studied the scriptures and became a great scholar. Subsequently, he renounced the world and wandered as an ascetic, *kamandalu* in hand."

"Oh! So he is like Kabir, a saint-poet?"

"No, not like Kabir. Actually, his life was quite mysterious. He was a *sannyasi* who embraced the worldly life again."

"I am sure many of these guys go back to being householders, don't they?" Dr Kumud observed rather sceptically.

"No, they don't. It's a serious vow," said Shaman.

"But you admit he was a great poet?"

"Of course, he was," said Shaman. "But his writing does not seem divinely inspired to me."

"Is there a problem with that?"

"With what?"

"I mean, what's the problem if a particular text is written by a *samsari*[24] or *sannyasi*—good work is good work, is it not?"

"Not really. A physicist is a good physicist whether he is a debauch or a drunkard; it doesn't take away his scientific ability. But a holy man must practice what he preaches. If you are a householder, you cannot give tall sermons on renunciation."

"I see." Dr Kumud seemed to agree.

They walked to the room where the conference convenor, Chandrahasini, had an office.

"Good afternoon, Madam," Dr Kumud greeted her, while Shaman merely nodded.

Chandrahasini was a slim, dark-complexioned woman in her sixties, with grey hair that she wore in a neat bun. She wore a dark maroon *kanjeevaram*[25] cotton sari with a yellow woven border. A large green *bindi*[26] adorned her forehead and she wore large silver *jhumkas*[27] which pulled down her earlobes.

---

[24]Samsari: Worldly person

[25]Kanjeevaram: Kanjeevaram silk sari is a magnificent creation of the craftsmen living in a small town, Kanchi (Kanchipuram), situated near the Bangalore city of South India.

[26]Bindi: A decorative mark worn in the middle of the forehead by Indian women, especially Hindus.

[27]Jhumkas or Jhumkis: Striking and exotic large-sized chandelier earrings in circular or conical dome/bell shape.

Her voice had the clear bell-like quality of good teachers. She sat behind an enormous desk, surrounded by scholars and artists, like sycophants in a King's court.

"Oh Kumud, come, come! How are you? Please sit down." Chandrahasini gestured to the chairs before her. "I must complain; you did not stay for the sound-and-light rendering of the *Vishnu avatara ashtapadis*[28]." She was surprised to see Shaman dressed like a *sannyasi*, but she hid it well.

"I am sorry, but I had a personal call," Professor Kumud Roy said apologetically.

Realising that she was ignoring him, Shaman broke in. "Listen, can we speak about the abstract?"

"I thought you were leaving the abstract with the secretary," she said glibly. "Am I needed?"

"You are needed. You have to approve it, don't you?"

"Oh, it's approved. What's there to discuss now?" she asked.

"Thank you. I wanted to suggest that the *Gita Govinda* session be shifted to post-lunch. My piece should come with the Kalidasa group of speakers in the first half," he said.

"No, Mr Srivastava, absolutely not! *Gita Govinda* cannot be moved to the second half."

"But chronologically, Kalidasa comes first."

"No, Jayadeva will come first…" Chandrahasini insisted.

Shaman realised Chandrahasini held a grudge against him.

"Madam, Jayadeva straggles behind Kalidasa by a full nine centuries," he observed irritably. "Anyone will tell you Kalidasa's *Kumarasambhava* should have precedence over Jayadeva's Radha-Krishna dalliance of the latter day."

---

[28]Ashtapadis or Ashtapadi: Sanskrit hymns of the Gita Govinda, composed by Jayadeva in the 12th Century. Literally, ashtapadi is 'eight-steps', refers to the fact that each hymn is made of eight couplets (eight sets of two lines).

Chandrahasini did not give up. "Are we fighting over dates?"

"No, I am not fighting at all. This is pure academics. Unlike you, I never hung out with politicians, Chandrahasini…"

"*Doctor* Chandrahasini…" she corrected.

"Sure. *Doctor* Chandrahasini. The name is too much in the media to be missed," remarked Shaman.

These exchanges sent a ripple of disturbance through the people in the respected lady's office. They held her in high regard, and the exchange made them feel uncomfortable.

"I have worked on *Gita Govinda* for 41 years, and in all that time, I have not come across one person who has objections to Jayadeva's pre-eminence," she stated.

"It all depends on where you are setting your post. Einstein isn't pre-eminent among wrestlers, is he?" Shaman remarked.

"What are you talking about?" Chandrahasini was angry. She felt that Shaman was being condescending.

"I am merely saying that Jayadeva is an extraordinary poet, but an ordinary human being."

"So?"

"So, nothing. You song-and-dance people have unnecessarily raised him to the heavens."

"Mr Srivastava, did you just say 'song-and-dance people'?" The lady was livid.

"I did. I was merely drawing your attention to the difference between philosophers and divinely gifted literary figures," Shaman replied coolly.

"Sir, please do not resort to personal affronts," a man standing next to Chandrahasini snapped.

"You are not invited to the discussion, young man. I'd advise you to stay out of it," retorted Shaman.

"Yes, you keep out of it," Chandrahasini concurred. She turned back to Shaman with apparent repugnance. "We are here for an art and culture convention, Srivastava. I don't want your Benarasi *pundit* talk."

Her assistant sniggered at this, but stopped short when Shaman threw him a stern glance.

"I come from Harvard, as you know," Shaman said criptically. Her mention of Benares was a hit below the belt.

"Mr Srivastava, we all know you are a celebrity in philosophy circles, but I am surprised you find a luminary like Jayadeva ordinary. Do you think the Nimbarka scholars, Ramanuja's wise companions, and a host of Vrindavan Goswamis do not know what they are talking about when they considered Jayadeva a divine being?"

"Those great people knew what they were talking about, I am sure. But perhaps you don't," said Shaman. He was about to go further into his argument, but stopped when a group of foreign delegates arrived at the door.

Dr Chandrahasini smiled at them warmly. "Welcome to the lecture demonstration. Sorry, we are running a little behind schedule." She took the opportunity to dismiss Shaman, saying, "Thank you, Mr Srivastava, for your suggestions. The Secretary here will address your concerns."

Shaman's first reaction was one of anger, but he made a strong auto-suggestion, breathed deeply and calmed down. He had succeeded; Chandrahasini was out of his mind.

When he left the room, he saw a beautiful girl dressed in *kuchipudi*[29] costume and makeup, looking at him with a stricken expression on her face. She glared at Shaman as he

---

[29]Kuchipudi: One of the eight major Indian classical dances, with origins in a village named Kuchipudi in Andhra Pradesh

left, her striking grey eyes filled with anger and hatred. Great beauty and extreme anger can exist in the same person without one compromising the other, Shaman thought to himself as he walked away.

5.

The most wonderful fragrance wafted to Shaman as he walked towards the Gayatri Temple the next morning. He rang the big brass bell outside and entered. The aroma emanated from a single *agarbatti*[30] that burned in the sanctum sanctorum.

The *pundit* was offering fresh flowers at the Devi's feet. "*Pranaam* Dada," he said. "Wonderful *agarbatti,* isn't it? Didi got it from Bangalore," he said, pointing to the open box.

"Yes, it's indeed a captivating fragrance," agreed Shaman.

He offered his obeisance to the Mother and then looked at the box. It was an expensive looking package, wrapped in yellow tissue, with a label that read *Raindrop*. Yes, Shaman thought with surprise, the fragrance exactly captured the sweet smell of Mother Earth when the first rain hit her parched soil. He decided he must ask Shambhavi where she had bought it.

He headed towards Maharaj's room and found him seated on his easy chair. Shambhavi sat at his feet on a small stool, cutting an apple into neat narrow wedges. She wore a black and white *khadi*[31] silk sari with a red and green patchwork blouse. Shaman quietly sat in the outer room, waiting for Maharaj to come out. Mr and Mrs Ramakant from Delhi were scheduled to visit the Master that morning.

He listened as Shambhavi tried to persuade Maharaj to eat just one more piece of the apple. "Baba, how will you get strong if

---

[30]Agarbatti: Incense stick

[31]Khadi: handspun, hand-woven natural fibre cloth from India, mainly made out of cotton

you don't eat? You have knowledge of the past, present and future, but when it comes to your own well-being, you refuse to be wise. Please eat just one more piece. You were always only bones, but now your skin has also become like paper."

The Master smiled, patted her head and took the piece from her outstretched hand.

"Maharaj has eaten half an apple only because it is you. He would have simply dismissed anyone else with a look," Krishna Da complained.

Slowly chewing the fruit, Maharaj asked Shambhavi, "Are you comfortable? Did you sleep well?"

"I am more than fine, Baba. In fact, I am very happy I can spend this time with you." She turned to Krishna Da. "Has Baba taken his medicine?"

"Shaman Da will come and give it, Didi," he answered.

"It is almost 9 am. Please give me his medicines and the prescription. I'll give it to him myself." Her voice had a hint of irritation.

Maharaj sipped the water she handed him and swallowed the tablets with some effort.

"Baba, you have become frail. You will have to bless yourself to get well as there is no one I know who can bless you!"

Maharaj laughed at this. But it only made him cough profusely. He sipped more water till the bout subsided.

"Beta, I want to tell you something. You need not wear saris here every day. I know you don't wear them in Bangalore."

"Baba, I like wearing saris. I wear them at the institute too."

"This is your home; it incidentally happens to be an *ashram* too, so wear whatever you are comfortable wearing. The rules of the *ashram* do not apply to you."

"All right, Baba... Thank you..."

Shaman was surprised. Though he was usually open-minded and forward-thinking, he believed in the virtue of women wearing traditional outfits when they visited the *ashram*.

The Master asked, "I hope you brought your winter clothes? It gets very cold here. Where is your shawl?" He looked at Krishna Da. "Where is Chandni?"

Shambhavi interjected, "Baba, my shawl is in the room, but honestly, it's not too cold. Please don't worry about me."

"Okay, but don't think you can be like Shaman and spend winter without warm clothes."

"Why would I want to be like Shaman Da? He really doesn't wear warm clothes in the winter?" she asked, surprised.

"Yes, Didi. He wears next to nothing even in winter," Krishna Da answered.

"Shaman is a highly accomplished *sannyasi*," the Master said. "He is ordained for big things."

Shaman felt immeasurably blessed and mentally offered his *pranaam* to the Master.

"Yes I know, Baba. You've been telling me this for many years," replied Shambhavi.

Madhava Da came to announce that Mr and Mrs Ramakant had arrived. Shaman told him to bring them upstairs.

Krishna Da helped Maharaj into his seat in the visitors lounge.

~

Mr and Mrs Ramakant prostrated themselves before the Master. They also sought Shaman's blessings though he was at least three decades younger than them.

"Dada, Maharaj has recovered so quickly only because of your excellent care," Mrs Ramakant said.

"Don't say that, Mrs Ramakant. I take it as my greatest blessing that I am able to serve the Master."

"Dada, my daughter Shubha, your student at Harvard, sends her regards. Her friends from Harvard had come to India for a holiday. They said it is a loss to Harvard that a professor of your calibre and passion has quit. I don't know if you remember them—Dheeraj, Sushma, Nivedita and Hari? They all speak highly of you and how they always looked forward to your lectures."

"Yes, I remember them," said Shaman. "They were amongst my best students."

Shambhavi sat in a corner on the carpeted floor, reading the discharge summary of the Master and other notes from his medical file.

Mrs Ramakant turned to her husband. "Now ask Swamiji all your questions."

6.

"Maharajji told us to write *Ram naam* and we surely will, but when we asked him about its importance, he said Swami Sharanananda would explain that to us. Could you please enlighten us?" Mr Ramakant asked.

"Of course. *Ram naam* is the oldest and simplest way to greet and meet God," said Shaman.

"How old is it?"

"The chant *Ram naam* began in the reign of Raja Ram, following his victory over the forces of evil and unrigheousness. Not a moment passes now without someone chanting his name in some part of India."

"You are right!" observed Mrs Ramakant. "People chant *Ram Ram* everywhere, all the time."

"In India, Ram is a *mantra,* a greeting, a punctuation mark." Shaman said in a matter-of-fact way.

"Maharaj asked us to write *Sri Ram Ram Ram*. But why 'Ram'? Why not some other name?" Mr Ramakant asked.

"Well, there is a scientific reason for that. Each letter in Sanskrit has a unique vibration; some have high vibrations, and some low. 'Ra' and 'Ma', in that order, account for the optimal spiritual power that can be packed in two letters," Shaman explained. 'Ra' is considered the point of origin of the power of the *kundalini*[32], and 'Ma' is the destination. Hence, when *Ram naam* is chanted in the right tone and manner, the spiritual

[32]Kundalini Shakti: latent spiritual energy believed to lie coiled at the base of the spine in every human being

power, like a divine serpent, rises to the head and helps release *amrit*, the nectar of immortality."

"That is interesting. Someone told me *Ram naam* also effectively controls *prana*, the vital breath. Is that true?" Mr Ramakant asked, curious.

"Let's check that out," replied Shaman. The couple looked back at him in surprise. "I ask you both to do a simple exercise," he said, "Say 'Ra' without opening your mouth."

The couple attempted to do so, but could not.

Mrs Ramakant gave up. "Sorry, can't do it..."

"Okay, now try to say 'Ma' without closing your mouth."

The couple tried, but failed again.

Shaman laughed. "When you say 'Ra', you open your mouth; when you say 'Ma' you close it. This is in the very phonetics of the word 'Ram'. 'Ra' and 'Ma', 'Ra' and 'Ma'. Open the mouth and close it, open the mouth and close it. This way, *pranayama* or breath control happens automatically. And through that power, you can solve all problems."

"That is wonderfully direct!" Mr Ramakant exclaimed, elated.

"I never knew there was so much science behind chanting *Ram naam*. Swamiji, you explain these things so beautifully. I feel enlightened," said Mrs Ramakant, her voice soft with gratitude.

"I merely tell you what my Gurudeva taught me," Shaman replied humbly.

7.

Shaman sat with Maharaj, savouring every syllable the Master spoke. He understood he was specially blessed to be able to interact so closely with this living luminary of the spiritual world.

The Master sipped some warm water and continued. "I have been reading the *Bhagavad Gita* for over 55 years, but each time I do, especially now, I find new meaning. It's like the text is revealing itself to me. If I had known what we just discussed when I was younger, the gravity of it may not have dawned on me."

Shaman made notes as the Master spoke.

"I have written commentaries on many things over the years. Now when I re-read them, I feel they could have been done much better. But then it's all a question of time… That reminds me, what's the time?"

"Almost 4:30," said Shaman, consulting the clock on the wall.

"Okay, that's it for today."

Shaman shut his notebook and prostrated himself. He rose and said, "Maharaj, when you were resting earlier, Nagaraj called from Anand Ashram. He said there was a squall last night and a big branch of the peepul tree fell on the Ganga *mandir*, damaging a part of its roof. He wanted me to inform you. I told them to use a thick tarpaulin to cover the roof immediately. It will prevent rainwater from directly entering the temple."

The Master thought for a moment. "Shaman, they will not be able to handle this on their own. Go there first thing in the morning. Check the extent of the damage and commission the repair work immediately."

"Yes, Maharaj. Should I use our regular contractor, Agarwal?"

"Do as you deem fit. I know once you take up a job, it will be done."

"I'll leave early in the morning, Maharaj. *Jai Guru*." Shaman bowed to receive the Master's blessings and turned to leave.

"Baba, I am going for a run," Shambhavi said from the door.

"Come and sit with me for while, child," the Master said affectionately.

"I am wearing shoes. I'll be back in an hour and join you."

She was dressed in grey track pants and a neon green T-shirt; her long hair tied tightly into a high ponytail.

"You are already late," remarked Shaman, walking towards the door. "Here in the hills, it gets dark quickly. It's not safe to run in the forest alone."

Shambhavi was not in a mood to concede. "I have to go alone since I cannot take Chandni. Besides, it's only 4:30."

"Shambhavi, you must listen to Shaman Da. He is right. The forest is not safe. Darkness falls quickly," Maharaj said.

"All right, Baba. I will not go to the forest. I'll take the dirt track that goes up towards the tribal settlement."

"That's too steep. You cannot run on that path," Shaman warned her.

Shambhavi's eyes flashed with irritation. "I'll figure it out, don't worry! *Jai Guru*, Baba," she said as she left.

~

When Shaman went to the temple for his evening prayers an hour later, he found beautiful bright orange roses at the

Mother's feet. He knew those flowers grew wild near a natural spring above the tribal settlement. He looked at his watch. Shambhavi must have returned. She had obviously taken the steep path to get back soon. Shaman was impressed. Most people found it difficult to even walk fast on that path, much less run, unless one was a local or had superb stamina and cardio fitness.

8.

Eight days later, Shaman returned to Nagaprayag from Anand Ashram, leaving only after the repair work on the temple roof was well on its way to completion. It had been an extremely busy trip. He had plenty on his plate with assessing the damage, getting competitive quotes for the repair, and supervising the actual work itself. However, he squeezed in the time to browse through the book shops there; possibly the thing he missed most in Nagaprayag.

Shaman enjoyed driving on these roads. There were mesmerising views of the snow-capped Himalayas as they played hide-and-seek with the butter-soft, puffy clouds. Though he had been driving for the last seven hours, he was not in the least bit tired. He parked the car, took his duffle bag, and ran up the few steps that led to the *ashram* building.

He spotted Shambhavi walking to the Gayatri Temple and was surprised to see a strange animal following her. Was it a dog? Upon closer inspection, he realised it was a young fawn. He couldn't believe his eyes. The fawn followed her like a pet as she did the *pradakshina*[33]. When she prostrated herself before the deity, the fawn nuzzled her neck.

She started to giggle. "Naughty child… That tickles me. I told you that before," she said, kissing the creature's forehead. The fawn snuggled close to her, licking her fingers. She hugged him close, saying, "Come, its feeding time." She caressed the small body. "You are missing your *mama* aren't you? I know exactly how that feels."

---

[33]Pradakshina: circumambulation, consists of walking around in a 'circle' clockwise as a form of worship in Hindu ceremonies in India.

The fawn was small; it had red silky fur with a few white spots. Its large beautiful eyes looked like they had been outlined with *kajal*[34]. 'Hence the term *mriganayani*[35],' Shaman thought to himself.

It was only after she had left that Shaman realised he had been standing rooted to the spot. 'Where did a fawn come from?' he wondered.

He went to his room with its view of the *ashram* and unpacked his bag. He noticed Shambhavi sitting outside the kitchen, bottle-feeding the fawn. Madhava Da, Keshava Da and the others sat around her. Leela and Chandni were asking for a turn to feed the fawn. He noticed Krishna Da looking down from the window outside Maharaj's room, watching what was going on.

Shaman quickly had a bath and performed his afternoon prayer. There was a special magic in Nagaprayag, he thought yet again. He instantly felt a deep connect with the divine. The sound of the Ganga was a continuous background score. Shaman had missed it in the silence of his room at Anand *ashram*. He picked up the books he had got for the Master and went to see him.

The Master was reclining in his chair while Shambhavi sat at his feet. The fawn slept peacefully in her lap. She was reading out a devotee's letter.

"*Pranaam* Maharaj..."

"*Jai Guru*, Shaman. Good you are back. How was your trip? Shambhavi, do your *pranaam* to Shaman Dada," the Master instructed.

"*Pranaam*," she said, not meeting Shaman's eyes.

---

[34]Kajal: Collyrium A black paste mostly used by women as a cosmetic around the eyes for adding lustre and enhancing beauty

[35]Mriganayani: woman with eyes as beautiful as that of a doe/ gazelle

Shaman gave his blessing and then sat down. He recounted his trip in detail and gave the *guru* the books he had brought.

"Very interesting," Maharaj commented, reading the blurbs.

Shaman was surprised no one was talking about the fawn in the room. He decided to wait and see.

The cook came to ask Maharaj what he would like to eat for dinner. Noticing Shaman, he said, "*Pranaam* Shaman Da. When did you come? Do you want something to eat?"

"No, thank you. I came an hour ago and I'm not hungry."

"Maharaj, what would you like?"

"Whatever Shambhavi decides. Don't ask me about these things anymore. She will decide for me," Maharaj said.

The cook looked at Shambhavi and noticed the sleeping fawn. "So he is sleeping now. Must be tired after playing all afternoon. The goat milk he drinks is finished."

"Chandni and Leela took money from Maharaj and have gone to the village to buy some," Krishna Da informed him.

"In that case, it's fine," replied the cook.

"I will tell you what to cook later," said Shambhavi.

"Alright, there is no hurry…"

Just then, Chandni and Leela returned with the milk. "*Pranaam*, Shaman Da," they greeted him.

"Oh, look how sweetly he is sleeping in Didi's lap!" Leela squealed.

"He loves Didi," Chandni said. "In fact, Shaman Da, Didi wakes up in the night to feed this greedy fellow."

"Why is the deer here?" he asked.

No one answered.

"It was injured… So I brought it here," Shambhavi said.

"You should have given it to the forest rangers. Why bring it here? It's a wild animal. Do you know what size he will grow to in just a few months? He will want to sleep in your lap even as a grown animal. I think it should be sent to the forest authorities immediately. Besides, it is illegal to possess a wild animal. We could get into trouble," Shaman said, voicing his disapproval.

"Baba gave me permission," Shambhavi said defensively.

"Maharaj, you gave your permission?" Shaman asked, incredulously.

"Shambhavi, tell him exactly what I told you," the Master replied.

She was silent for a second before saying, "You said you have no problem if everyone in the *ashram* was okay with it."

"We're all fine with it. I say this on behalf of everyone," the cook said and everyone nodded.

"Even the *pundit* is okay with it. He told me," Leela said.

Shaman looked at Shambhavi. "What happens once you go back to Bangalore?"

She did not answer. Eyes downcast, she just caressed the velvety ears of the sleeping fawn.

"We will all look after it. We look after the cows anyway," said the cook.

Everyone laughed at her matter-of-fact words.

"So, all of you want the deer," said Shaman with a sigh. He was surprised. "We are *sannyasis* trying to lead a life where we can cut off attachments. But I see that all of you are falling deeper and deeper into the trap of *maya*. Don't you all know the story of Jada Bharat? The story is a warning…a wake-up call to all of us."

Shambhavi's eyes glowed angrily at Shaman's words, but she said nothing.

9.

"Like the story of Ajamila, Jada Bharata's story in the *Srimad Bhagavatam* is important for all of us," Shaman said.

Though Leela and Keshava Da did not say anything to suggest they were uninterested, their faces betrayed it. Leela looked away, out the window, only half-attentive.

"Bharata was an ascetic who ruined his evolution by growing attached to a fawn," said Shaman. "All his life, he had kept away from *samsara*. He had led a solitary life, never growing attached to family or anything worldly, but the little fawn aroused *maya* in him—the same affection filling your hearts."

"Actually Da, you've told us this story before," said Krishna Da politely.

"I know that you know it. We must abandon these things in spiritual life," said Shaman.

"Like abandoning a hurt and helpless fawn?" Shambhavi asked, still fuming.

"Will you let me speak?" Shaman snapped.

Shambhavi fell silent, but Shaman saw anger flash in her eyes.

"*Jada* means gross or dull-witted. Bharata was dull-witted, but what's wrong with us?"

Though everyone listening was against Shaman narrating the story, in an oddly ironic way, they could not help but identify with Bharata. They were all attached to the fawn.

"So years passed and he looked after the fawn in his hermitage," Shaman continued. "When Bharata died, his last thought was of the deer. Due to his concentration on the deer at the time of his death, he was reborn as a deer.

"You all know what the Bhagavad Gita says: *Whatever thought one remembers or entertains in the mind at the time of passing, is the state you will attain in the next birth*. There is a direct correlation between desire, thoughts, and the body. This law operated even on the great ascetic Bharata. Who can tell what will bind each of us? Attachment sneaks into our minds like a serpent slitheing into a hole, without our even knowing that it has entered."

Shaman paused. Everyone was silent. "So you people still want the deer here?" he asked.

No one answered.

"Didi wants the fawn, so let her keep it. Moreover, she saved it, so it belongs to her. It's for her to decide," the *pundit* said a little reluctantly.

'Yes, yes, that's true!' the others said in unison. 'She should keep it!'

Shaman realised Bharata's story had had no effect on them. He posed a more direct threat. "I am saying it's illegal… We could all be arrested."

"The range officer already came and saw the fawn. Didi called him immediately after she found him. Naikji is a devotee of Maharaj. He didn't think it was a big issue. He said it can be managed," said Krishna Da.

Shaman was truly amazed at the lengths to which everyone had gone to keep the fawn.

"Dada, looking after it is not a problem at all. Once it's bigger, it will be in the cowshed," said Keshava Da.

The Master watched all this without saying a word.

Shambhavi lifted the fawn in her arms and stood up. "Baba, let me organise your dinner."

Everyone left except Krishna Da.

"Get some warm water for me to drink," Maharaj said to him.

When Krishna Da left to get water, the Master was left alone with Shaman. "Shambhavi is a young girl," Maharaj began. "It is boring for her here in this remote place. Let her amuse herself with the deer."

"But Maharaj..." Shaman protested, "It's wrong! We can't have a deer here!"

"Women have a strong maternal instinct. That's why she is drawn to the deer," the Master replied. "You don't understand women, Shaman."

"Maharaj, I absolutely agree that I don't understand women. But I know the law and this is illegal. Let me speak to Shambhavi; I will convince her."

"No, Shaman. Leave it alone. I will talk to her. You call Naik and ask him to send the van to pick up the fawn."

Krishna Da returned with the water. "Ask Shambhavi Didi to come here," the Master said to him.

~

Shambhavi emerged from the Master's room as Shaman finished speaking to Naik. Her eyes were red-rimmed and she did not speak a word to him.

It was not long before the van arrived. Chandni handed over the fawn to the ranger. Everyone in the *ashram* was sad. They stood at the gate long after the van had disappeared. Shaman felt like a villain.

At dinner, the only person eating was Shaman.

Chandni carried the big cardboard carton lined with hay, an old blanket and two feeding bottles, and threw it into the trash can. "Now there's no need for all these things," she said, washing her hands.

"Where is Didi?" Keshava Da asked.

"Didi has closed her door. She said she was not hungry."

The cook sighed. "If we are all feeling like this, imagine how she must be feeling. But for Didi, those wild dogs would have eaten the poor little thing."

"I don't know how she chased away the dogs. I could never have done it. Even after she brought the injured deer to the *ashram*, they were still snarling at the gate!" said the *pundit*.

"Ferocious dogs!" Leela agreed. "Chandni, at least persuade Didi to have some milk. It's not good to sleep on an empty stomach. You know Shaman Da, she was like a mother to that baby deer. She stayed up the whole night feeding it and applying medicine to its wounds. She went to the village and got the feeding bottles. She found out that goat's milk is ideal for it. Left to us, we would have given it cow's milk and killed it with our ignorance. She will miss the deer."

"Yes, Chandni, give Didi a glass of milk," the cook agreed. He handed Chandni the glass after putting oodles of fresh cream into it. "Didi likes *malai* in her milk," he said with an indulgent smile.

"Oh Dada, give it in Didi's cup. How will she drink hot milk from this steel glass? The cup is washed and kept right behind you," Chandni admonished.

It was a large bright yellow cup with a peacock feather imprinted on its handle. The cup had *Krishna, My Divine Lover* printed on it.

So Shambhavi was a Krishna devotee, Shaman inferred.

10.

The stench of petrol made her gag. It had drenched her shivering body. She felt immobile, her body so heavy, it seemed to be weighed down by wet concrete. She could not keep her eyes open. She wanted to scream but could not; she was gagged with a dirty cloth in her mouth. Her hands, she realised, were bound behind her back. She felt a hard poking sensation in her back. She struggled to open her eyes and discovered she was lying on a pile of wood.

A baby fawn lay next to her, also tied to the pile of wood. The mouth of the poor creature had been tied shut with wire. She felt terrible that the deer shared her fate.

Shambhavi forced herself to think calmly. Carefully, she twisted her hands; the bindings around her wrists finally yielded. She pulled the dirty cloth from her mouth, fighting the urge to retch. Her mouth felt chaffed, her throat parched. She untied the poor fawn and hugged it close to her body. She could feel its heart beating rapidly in fear. She left the wire on its mouth, fearing it would make noise and attract attention.

She struggled to rise despite her drugged state. Her heavily embellished red ghagra, *drenched with petrol, made movement difficult. The small fawn in her arms felt heavy.*

The men drinking and squatting around the small fire saw her. She started to run, her gold anklets tinkling. Her bangles clanked against each other. The weight of the fawn slowed her down. One of the men shouted – 'Don't try to catch her!' – and threw a burning twig from the fire into the trail of petrol from her ghagra.

The man's voice sounded so much like Shaman's. 'Why was he here?' she wondered in horror. She ran as fast as she could. Sheer terror freed her from the debilitating effects of the sedative that had been administered to her. But the fire snaked and roared rapidly towards her.

She threw the fawn as far away as she could to save it from burning, regretting not having opened its mouth. 'How will it survive?' she thought guiltily.

Within minutes, with a whoosh, her ghagra *was engulfed in flames. The heat was unbearable! She opened her mouth...*

Shambhavi woke with a soundless scream, soaked in sweat. Her fingers were curled into tight fists; her heavy blanket twisted round her body. The acrid smell of smoke burned her lungs, leaving her breathless. She opened her eyes and looked around, her heart still pounding like a crazy drum.

She took deep breaths. 'It was a nightmare. I am safe,' she told herself. She looked around. She was in her room in Nagaprayag *ashram*. Chandni snored peacefully on a mattress on the floor. She wished she had brought her bedside clock from Bangalore. Dim light from the window heralded the coming of dawn. The sharp chill made her shiver.

In the quiet of the morning stillness, she collected her thoughts. The poor fawn. She wondered how it was doing. She missed carrying its small warm body and the unconditional love she felt when it came running to her as soon as it saw her. She recollected with a shudder how the wild dogs had surrounded the poor animal and almost torn it to pieces.

Shaman could have allowed it to remain in the *ashram*, but he was so stuck on rules he couldn't understand what it felt like to be helpless and almost devoured. Thank God Baba was not a man bent on petty rules, she thought, deeply grateful.

She wondered why Shaman had been part of her nightmare. She shook her head in an effort to push the images away. There was no point dwelling on it. When she looked into the mirror to comb her long hair, she could see the early morning light reflected in her light grey eyes. She had dark shadows under her eyes. She had been told that her great-grandmother was an Afghan or English woman, she couldn't remember which.

She had a performance scheduled at her old school. She told herself she didn't have the time to mull over memories that were just faint murmurs, and quickly braided her thick hair. It was time for dance practice.

11.

Someone knocked urgently at Shaman's door. His first thought was that it was some complication in Maharaj's health. He quickly opened the door.

"Maharaj is calling for you," Krishna Da told him.

"What happened? All okay?" Shaman asked, running towards the Master's chambers.

"Master is fine. Shambhavi Didi fell down," Krishna Da said.

Shaman stopped running. "Anything serious?" he asked.

Krishna Da was clearly worried. "She fell while teaching Chandni how to ride a TVS Luna."

"Luna? Where did these women get a Luna from?"

"From the village. Shambhavi Didi was trying to teach Chandni to ride it and Chandni fell on Didi, along with the Luna. Didi fell down a small slope and ended up in a thorny bush. Her clothes were torn. She was bleeding but nothing happened to Chandni. Didi is hurt on one leg, from the thigh to the ankle. She was bleeding when she came back to the *ashram*."

"Obviously, Krishna Da. Shambhavi took the impact of the fall and cushioned Chandni from injury."

"It should have been the other way around. Poor Didi, she is so small and fragile and that pumpkin fell on her!" Krishna Da said, clucking his tongue. "By the way, I was knocking on your door for a long time, but you didn't respond."

"I was doing my *bhramari*[36] meditation," said Shaman.

The Maharaj had been waiting anxiously for them. "Shaman, take Shambhavi to the doctor immediately. She is hurt," he said.

"I will, Maharaj. Where is she?"

Shambhavi came in, freshly showered, in a calf-length peacock blue silk skirt and dark pink sleeveless blouse. She limped a little as she walked, holding the skirt away from the injured leg.

"Is it hurting a lot, Beta?"

"No, Baba. It is just irritating when the cloth rubs against the abrasion, that's all," she replied.

"Go with Shaman Da. He will take you to the hospital."

"Baba, I don't need to go to the hospital. It's not that bad!"

"You need a tetanus shot, Shambhavi. Chandni told me you were bleeding a lot… Shaman, take—," Guruji said, coughing.

Shaman said to Shambhavi in a low soft voice, "Don't create a fuss. Maharaj is getting agitated on your account."

She glared at him for a second before giving in. "Baba, I will go. Please do not worry."

"Take her to Dr Sudarshan, not the government clinic in the village."

"But Baba, that's an hour away. I only need a tetanus shot," Shambhavi protested.

Shaman too, thought that going all that way was unnecessary.

But Maharaj was emphatic. "Shaman, please take her to Dr Sudarshan. And take Chandni with you too."

---

[36]Bhramari: A type of pranayama, breathing technique, in which one plugs one's ears, derives its name from the black Indian bee called Bhramari.

"Shaman Da… I have severe motion sickness, and that clinic is on top of the next hill," said Chandni.

"Don't worry," Shaman replied, opening the medicine cabinet in Maharaj's room. "Take this tablet… The motion sickness will not bother you."

Shambhavi climbed into the Qualis with a little difficulty. Chandni fell asleep in the back seat almost immediately.

"I think you are driving too fast," Shambhavi said after a few minutes.

"Fast and slow are relative terms. I think I am driving safely," Shaman countered.

"You are the most exasperating individual I have ever met," she said, shaking her head.

"You seem to have a lot of problems with me," Shaman said, negotiating the big car round the narrow bends expertly.

"I don't know you well enough to have 'lots' of problems with you. I just think you are an extremely arrogant man. I realised how impolite you can be when I saw you interacting with Chandrahasini, my *guru*. I was aghast."

12.

"I remember your argument with Chandra Ma. I was so livid with the way you spoke to her. What was the need for you to be so touchy about *Gita Govinda*?" said Shambhavi.

"Oh, come on. I wasn't touchy... *She* was touchy! She was making it seem like the composition is an ultimate prayer to God."

"But it *is* divinely inspired."

"No, it's not! It's just a two-day drama with three characters—Radha, Krishna and the messenger. I don't even think Lord Jagannath or Krishna inspired *Gita Govinda*," Shaman said in a defiant tone.

"That's a first! If it was not Jagannath, can you tell me who it was?" Shambhavi asked, shrugging her shoulders disapprovingly.

"His beautiful wife, Padmavati," Shaman observed in a matter of fact way, as he took the sharp hairpin bend with ease.

"You're a cynic and a sceptic," she griped.

"Well, I'd call myself curious..." said Shaman. "Your Jayadeva was actually a *sannyasi* before he met Padmavati. He fell for her and simply got married. And just to vindicate his funny situation, he chose to preach *grihastha sannyasism*—the householder brand of asceticism! How convenient for a person who fell into a trap!"

"What trap? You just don't realise what a classic he wrote."

"Sure! This is a woman's thing. All women love *Gita Govinda* because it's mushy stuff! Spring-time love play, erotica…"

"Erotica? God! How can you talk like that? *Gita Govinda* is dripping with devotional *rasa*…"

"Shambhavi, don't talk to me about *rasa* and all."

"I should be telling you that… A *sannyasi* preaching about *rasa*… Look at the irony!"

"If *rasa* is the same as erotica, you got that one in him."

"You're just obsessed with erotica, aren't you? And what's wrong with the genre, anyway?" Shambhavi exploded. "Even poets like Kalidasa, Bhartrihari and Amaru have unhesitatingly described some open portrayals of erotic sentiments…"

"Yes, but they have done it contextually. Your *Gita Govinda* is blatantly an erotic love-poetry."

"No. It is *shringara rasa*. And if you were so learned, you'd surely know that *shringara* is the main *rasa*—it leads to creation."

"Are you giving me a Freudian lesson?"

"Can't you see *Gita Govinda* speaks of sacred love between Radha and Krishna?"

"Listen, Radha is a liberty. In the original *Bhagavatam*, the character of Radha just doesn't figure. Radha becomes larger and larger when the poets step in. And Jayadeva makes her so central that you forget she is just not there in the original."

"Frankly, I don't really care for your original. Be reasonable, can you imagine amorous things in that age?"

"Jayadeva lived in the 12th century, an age in which sex was not taboo. Buddhist tantric practices may have contributed to this open language."

"You have great imagination," Shambhavi remarked sarcastically.

"I have no imagination," said Shaman. "I just have a bit of a flair for fact finding. Your Jayadeva is the one with great imagination. I salute him. Imagery of spring season clouds, mango-blossoms, rivers, gentle zephyr, cuckoos, lotus, and black bees… sweet smile, amorous glances, kisses, moving of brows, maddening gestures."

"Oh, you seem to have learnt much more about this than a *sannyasi* should."

"I was an academician, a student of philosophy. I learnt Sanskrit poetry and I know *rati*[37], *shringara*[38] and the whole nonsense about Eros being the main instinct of life of mundane beings…" he said.

"Well, the reality for you is that *Gita Govinda* has 24 melodious songs, 100 commentaries, 132 imitations, adaptability to sing in all *ragas*[39] and it is enacted in dance forms like the Odisi, the Manipuri, the Bharatanatyam, and so on."

"Read it carefully, Shambhavi. Read it a few times and you will realise that the part about ten incarnations is a separate piece, simply added to give the work some divine credibility."

"I have never met a greater fault-finder than you. Who do you think you are?" she exclaimed exasperatedly.

"I'm zero… Nobody. Surely not worth your anguish," he said.

"Zero it seems…" Shambhavi muttered, they took the last bend to reach the top of the hill. The hospital came into view.

---

[37]Rati: (from Sanskrit root ram, meaning "enjoy" or "delight in.") Although the verb root generally refers to any sort of enjoyment, it usually carries connotations of physical and sensual enjoyment

[38]Shringara: one of the nine rasas, usually translated as erotic love, romantic love, or as attraction or beauty

[39]an array of melodic structures with musical motifs, considered in the Indian tradition to have the ability to "color the mind" and affect the emotions of the audience

13.

The hospital was a small, neat, white-washed building that sat on a small tableland in the mountains. The tribal folks had easy access to the twenty-bed medical facility. Shaman stopped the car where it would be easiest for Shambhavi to go inside the hospital.

Chandni was still sound asleep.

Shambhavi stepped down slowly. It was evident to Shaman that she was in pain. Sitting immobile for an hour in the car had caused her leg to become stiff. After shouting her name aloud several times, Chandni woke up and followed Shambhavi. Shaman quickly parked the car and went inside.

The nurse at the counter greeted them. "The doctor has asked you to come in."

He knocked on the door and entered the large, airy consulting room.

Shambhavi sat on the stool, next to the doctor. "That's how I fell…" Shaman heard the tail-end of her sentence.

Dr Sudarshan was a small, active, cheerful man with a bald head. The only hair that was left on his head were like wisps of cotton that surrounded the back of his head in a semi-circle from ear to ear.

"*Pranaam*, Swamiji," he greeted Shaman. "We were expecting you. I got a call from the *ashram*. Good to see you… How is Maharaj doing?"

"Good to see you, Doctor! Maharaj is getting better day by day."

"Let me examine the patient..."

Shaman went outside and started doing his *japa*. Chandni sat opposite him. The waiting room was full, but there was little noise.

When he opened his eyes, he realised nearly forty-five minutes had passed by. He was surprised that it was taking the doctor so long. He got up to find out.

Just then the consulting room door opened and the doctor came out.

"Good you got her here, Swamiji! There were many thorns that had pierced her skin and had broken inside. I think the maid tried to remove the ones she could reach, but there were many embedded deep inside. She must have slipped on a slope and that has caused deep abrasions. These thorns were inside the wound. I had to take them out one by one in order to avoid it festering. It must have been excruciating, but she didn't wince even once. I must say, she is a very brave girl with a high pain threshold!"

Shaman immediately remembered how the Master had insisted that she be brought to Dr Sudarshan's hospital. He did a mental *pranaam* to his *guru's trikaal gyaani*[40], vowing never to question his words.

"The nurse is tying a bandage... She should not have bath for a day. She will need a dressing change in two days' time. When I come to check on Maharajji, I will do the needful in the *ashram* itself, there's no need to bring her here."

"Thank you so much doctor..." said Shaman.

"It's my duty, Swamiji," the doctor said. "It's because of Maharaj's blessings that this hospital is doing so well. We are getting generous funding, which helps us reach out to so many

[40]Trikala Jnani: one who has the knowledge of past, present and future—knowledge of the highest order

poor people."

"But what you are doing is very noble. You've given up your flourishing practice as a surgeon in London. Very rarely do people pursue these kind of things."

Shaman really meant it. He thought his parents, who were successful cardiologists in America, would never have taken a call like this.

"God has been kind to give me an opportunity to serve these people, and I am grateful for that," said the humble doctor.

Shambhavi came out, slowly limping with the help of a nurse.

"You will be fine in two days' time. Have your painkillers and antibiotics on time," said Dr Sudarshan as he handed over the prescription to Shaman. "Pushpa, you get the medicines from the dispensary. Let Swamiji sit with my patient."

Chandni helped Shambhavi sit down. As they waited, a small child of about three stared at Shambhavi. Slowly, the child wriggled out of the mother's arms, stood in front of Shambhavi and continued to stare at her.

"Are you a fairy? You are so pretty," the child asked.

"No, I am not… Look behind me; I have no wings," Shambhavi said, laughing. She picked up the child on the uninjured side of her lap.

The child was not convinced. "But you're like the fairy in my story book!" he said.

Shambhavi kissed the child. "You are very pretty too!"

"I love children," she said turning to Shaman. Her eyes were glowing with genuine happiness, but suddenly she looked uneasy. She didn't mean to share that with Shaman.

"Children are direct reflections of God," Shaman said in order to put her at ease.

While on their way back, Shaman drove at a slow pace. "I am sorry I drove so fast when we came. I didn't realise that you still had the thorns. It must have been very painful."

"Even I didn't know the thorns were still there. I thought Chandni had removed them all," said Shambhavi.

Hearing her name, Chandni woke up from the backseat with a start. "You called me, Didi?"

"No, no. Go back to sleep."

"Tell me one thing, Shambhavi. What were you doing on a Luna with her?"

"Chandni is constantly complaining about her knees hurting, so she is unable to walk. I thought if she learnt how to ride a Luna it would give her the freedom to move around without pain."

"She is fat and her knees can't take her weight. If I were a doctor, I'd advise her to lose some—that's the only way her aches and pains can be reduced," said Shaman.

"She is short, that's why she looks fat."

"You seem to be very protective of her. By the way, Krishna Da was calling her a pumpkin this morning!"

She laughed; it was melodious and full of mirth. "That's so mean… Poor Chandni!"

When they reached the *ashram*, Shambhavi couldn't get out of the car. Her injured leg throbbed with pain. Shaman offered his hand and she took it after a moment of hesitation. Shaman was surprised that though her hand was small and soft, it was strong and firm.

Once she stood on her feet, Chandni helped her to her room. She turned around and said, "Dada, thank you for everything! Could you please tell Maharaj that I am fine? I just want to lie down for a bit."

"Have your painkillers immediately. They will make you feel better."

She nodded in agreement and walked to her room with difficulty, despite Chandni's support.

Shaman parked the car and quickly went to Maharaj's room to update him on everything.

14.

Two days later, Dr Sudarshan arrived to check on Maharaj. He felt the Master was a lot better now.

"Doctor, his appetite is still very bad," said Shaman.

"Swamiji, we have pumped Maharaj with so many antibiotics. It will take time for his appetite to get back to normal. Besides, if I recollect correctly, Maharaj has always been a small eater. As one gets on in years, the process of recovery takes much longer."

"Sudarshan…" the Master called from his room.

The doctor went back inside. "Examine Shambhavi properly. She is finding it difficult to climb the stairs."

"Maharaj, that's because of the dressing. It's been tied over her knee which is a moving part. Let's see if her wound is healing well, and we can do away with the bandage."

"Shaman, take the doctor to Shambhavi's room," the Master commanded.

"Yes, Maharaj."

On the way, he saw Chandni and told her to escort the doctor to Shambhavi's room. He waited for the doctor to finish.

The doctor returned in ten minutes. "Her wound is healing well. She does not require a bandage anymore. She will be fully all right in another week's time. In fact, the wound will heal better if it's exposed to light and air."

"Thank you, Doctor."

"My pleasure, Swamiji. If you need me for anything, don't hesitate to call me," he said before driving off in his Jeep.

~

For the next two days, the *ashram* witnessed a continuous stream of visitors. A group of pilgrims stopped at Nagaprayag on their way to Badrinath to take the Master's blessings. Shaman busily mingled with them and made sure that the Master didn't exhaust himself in the process.

He realised he had not seen Shambhavi for more than four days.

As he made his way towards her room, he spotted her on the stone steps leading to the Prayag. She sat on the steps and stared at the majestic scene below.

Her long hair was untied, moving in the breeze like a waterfall. She wore denim cut-offs and a thick black woollen top. There was a big book open in her lap.

"*Jai Guru*, Shambhavi!"

She looked up in surprise. "*Pranaam*," she said with a slight smile.

"How come you are here?"

"I just wanted to see how you were doing. How come I don't see you around the *ashram*?" he asked.

He walked closer and saw that the large wound had almost healed; it was still red and angry in parts. There was a delicate scab over the rest of the injury and large bruises all over her legs.

Shambhavi sighed, "Actually, after the doctor removed the dressing, I've been unable to wear anything other than shorts and skirts. I had to cut off two of my jeans to turn them into shorts. The fabric chafes the wound and tears off the scab. The healing is going to take forever at this rate. I have a dance performance in my school. I need to get well and start practicing as soon as I can."

"What are all those black and blue bruises? They look like very interesting tattoos."

"Oh these..." she said with a laugh. "That's where Chandni fell on me. It's not her fault. It's just that I bruise easily."

There was a moment of comfortable silence, before the Shanbhavi continued on. "I love the view from here. I came here to read, but could not manage more than half a page. The rivers are so different from one another – in colour and in character. They meet in a crash of turbulent water, but watching the Prayag fills me with peace."

"Yes... To look at the flowing water itself is a spiritual practice. It's called *Jal Darshan*. Scriptures say, as your eyes follow the flowing water, in a river or a stream; as it observes the waves coursing and surging forward, your mind automatically starts to still itself. Maharaj used to recommend gazing at the Ganga as the quickest remedy to still the mind. In fact, not just to still it; he said one can even attain *samadhi* by just looking at the flowing Ganga... Anyway, you still didn't answer my original question... Why are you not seen in the *ashram*?"

Shambhavi looked uneasy for a second. "I didn't want to come in front of everyone wearing shorts. See, you have travelled the world and you have seen people wear all kinds of things. But here, it's still very conservative... This place is full of elderly *sannyasis*."

Shaman nodded. "That's a fair point... You know, I have never noticed what people are wearing. But strangely, I always notice what people are reading."

"How interesting!"

"When I wait at airports, in trains, even at hospitals, I try to make up a back story for people depending on what they are reading. I tend to categorize people based on their reading choices."

"Okay, tell me what sort of a person am I?" she asked, smiling.

She closed the book she was reading so that he could see the cover. *An analysis of Aesthetics: the Dance, the Dancer and the Spectator*, it read.

Shaman laughed, "This is just way out of my expertise. I can hardly make an observation other than the fact that I already know…that you are a dancer."

15.

The alarm on Shaman's bedside table rang. It was 3:45 am. For years Shaman had been getting up at this hour to catch the *brahma muhurta*[41]. The warmth of the quilt silently invited him to spend more time in bed but he broke from his comfortable cocoon and headed for a bath.

Even though it was chilly outside, Shaman did not put on a sweater. He never did—even in the peak of winter. He quickly wore his *dhoti*, picked up his torchlight and *asana*, and left for the steps that lead to the water. His shoulder-length *jataas* swayed on his bare back as he made his way in the steady beam of the torchlight.

The roar of the meeting rivers was loud in the deep silence of pre-dawn. He held his torch in one hand and the rolled *asana* tucked safely under his other arm as he negotiated the stone steps cut into the rockface. The steps were precarious, steep and almost perpendicular, like a ladder. There was no railing for support. Shaman made his way in the dark carefully. The closer he got, the louder became the roar of the rushing water.

Once he reached the rocky bank of the river, he bowed down to Ma Ganga with great reverence. He touched some water to his head and then sipped it. Though he could not see the water, he could feel the sharp bite of its cold water.

He spread his *asana* in his usual place—a large smooth rock, away from the spray of the water, and performed his *japa*.

---

[41]Brahma muhurta: Time of Brahma, is a period (muhurta) one and a half hours before sunrise or more precisely 1Hr 36 Mins before sunrise. It's conducive to meditation.

An hour and a half later, his morning *sandhya*[42] was done. He opened his eyes slowly. The birth of a dew-fresh day greeted him as the night sky left behind only streaks of pink. He could see the waters clearly now.

Suddenly, he heard a low moan. For a moment he thought it was the wind. He looked around and saw a group of men dressed in white, sitting on the bank downstream, their figures shrouded in a light fog.

A pyre was set close to the leaping water. Shaman assumed it was a cremation. He could vaguely make out the shape of a man carrying a burning staff. Within seconds, the pyre was on fire. The mourners gathered close, watching it burn. Shaman spent a few minutes praying for the departing soul.

The mourners slowly began to disperse. Soon there was no one. The breeze blew the smoke from the burning pyre into all kinds of impossible shapes. The scene took Shaman back to Varanasi, where he had grown up.

In Varanasi, death was a given; looked upon more as a daily occurrence than a tragic event. It brought income to the city. Shaman lived with his grandfather, a widower by the name of Manohar Srivastava. They lived near the Manikarnika *ghaat*[43] where burning pyres were the order of the day.

'Manikarnika,' he remembered his grandfather's deep gravelly voice telling him, 'is where Ma Sati's earring fell.'

Shaman was raised by his grandfather, a retired college principal. Both grandfather and grandson practiced yoga at dawn and went for *Ganga Snaan*[44] every day. Shaman inherited his grandfather's deep reverence and love for the Ganga. The

[42]Sandhya: Literally "the transition moments of the day" (namely the two twilights dawn and dusk). Sandhya is mandatory religious ritual performed in the transitory moments, traditionally, by Dvija communities of Hindus, particularly those initiated through the sacred thread ceremony referred to as the Upanayanam and instructed in its execution by a Guru

[43]Ghaat: a flight of steps leading down to a river

[44]Snaan: Ritual bath

old man was a disciplinarian, but also fun to be with. He shaped Shaman's childhood with the right mix of love and severity. Everything about the old man was about balance and checks.

Every day after school, they would go out to eat street food in the narrow bazaar lanes leading to the famous Kashi Vishwanath temple. Each season had its own specialities - creamy thick *lassi*[45] and *aam panna*[46] in summer; crispy fried *pakodas*[47] in the monsoon; *gajak*[48] in the winter. And *jalebi*[49] and hot milk all year round.

When the sun rose, his grandfather would join his hands in salutation and look at the burning orb with affection.

"Dadaji, why do you look at the sun so lovingly?" Shaman asked.

"Because the sun, Surya Bhagawan, is among the four Gods you can behold with your naked eyes, my child. God cannot be seen, yet we have the luxury of seeing four living forms."

"And which are those?"

"The sun, the river Ganga, the *tulasi*, and the cow."

He taught Shaman the *tulasi vandana*—the practice of giving water to divinity in the form of a plant, and taught him the 108 names of the Ganga, and the 12 names of the sun as part of *Surya Namaskar*.

"If you can do this much, it's enough to start with," Dadaji had said. "And all these things are easy."

---

[45]Lassi: a sweet or savoury Indian drink made from a yogurt or buttermilk base with water

[46]Aam panna: a tangy summer cooler made from raw mangoes, cardamom powder, salt and jaggery

[47]Pakodas: a piece of vegetable or meat, coated in seasoned batter and deep-fried

[48]Gajak: a dry sweet made of sesame seeds, and ground nuts, as they are known in Hindi, and jaggery

[49]Jalebi: sweet made of a coil of batter fried and steeped in syrup

Whenever they passed a cow, the old man offered his *pranaam* with affection and reverence, and Shaman learned to imitate him.

During the summer holidays, he taught Shaman to fly kites. And when the Sankranti festival came, both proved to be champion kite-flyers. Manohar had the zeal and energy to outrun all the youngsters of the locality as he chased the cut kites along the wide *ghaats* of the Ganga, laughing and calling to Shaman to catch up with him. The scene of thousands of differently coloured kites in myriad shapes, flying in the air from every conceivable and inconceivable nook and cranny, was etched forever in Shaman's mind. They rose into the sky, their tails slithering like snakes, as they bobbed in the breeze and gained height in the expert hands of the flyers.

"Dadaji, why do so many people fly kites on *sankranti*?" Shaman asked.

"During winter, our body suffers from cough and cold, and the skin becomes dry. When the sun moves into *Uttarayana*, its rays act as medicine for the body. During kite-flying, the human body is continuously exposed to the sun's rays. It eradicates infection and insanitation," Dadaji explained.

Apart from kite-flying, Manohar also taught his grandson to spin wooden tops, play with marbles, and perform card tricks. He was exceedingly competitive and gave Shaman the taste to excel in everything he took up.

Manohar was a well-built man with dark hair that had not greyed. He was an authority on the *Yoga Sutras* of Patanjali and the *Bhagavad Gita*. Scholars came to their house in the evenings to debate and discuss matters of high spiritual import. Shaman loved to listen to these discussions. What he did not understand, he would make a note of and ask later. And his grandfather explained it to him with great patience and interest. In time, Shaman was able to discuss complex concepts with great scholars with ease and confidence.

"You are my gem!" an immensely proud Manohar would say as he put Shaman to bed at night.

Manohar's library was a veritable archive of books on every discipline. They ranged from literary classics to astronomy and astrophysics, from the works of Zen Masters to the *Kamasutra*. Manohar urged Shaman to read and discuss. This inculcated a great love of books in the child. He taught him that books should be organised and kept neatly, no carelessness. He fumed when he found book corners curled up. Dadaji hated the practice of folding down page corners and used his exotic collection of bookmarks instead, some made from paper, others from feathers and sandalwood.

They would frequent the second-hand bookstores. If they found a good book, Manohar would take the child on a boat ride at night on the Ganga to celebrate the prized acquisition. Shaman simply loved those boat rides. But for the rhythmic sound of the oars slapping the water, everything else would be drowned in dark silence. Manohar always trailed his hand in the water as the boat slowly moved on.

"Why do you put your hand in the water?" Shaman asked.

"This is Ma Ganga, my child, a celestial river. You are seeing her here, but where is her origin?"

"Gomukh glacier?"

"No, no. That's not where she originates; that's just her mouth on earth. She falls from the heavens."

"Falls?"

"Yes, right now her top end is in the heavens. She is twirling in Lord Shiva's matted locks and pouring down to earth. If I touch her, I actually touch the divine locks of Mahadeva. I touch heaven."

"Actually?"

"Yes, my child, actually."

Shaman had also tried to bend over the side of the boat to touch the water, but Manohar had said gently, "You are too small. You'll fall into the water. Do it when you are older."

Years had passed since then, but even now, Shaman touched the Ganga whenever he could. He remembered those book acquisition celebrations with fondness.

Both of Shaman's parents had been successful cardiologists, with a thriving practice in Boston. They had gone away to do their Masters in America, leaving young Shaman in the care of Manohar Srivastava. When the time came for Shaman to join his parents after they finished their education, the young boy refused to go. He had grown attached to his grandfather. He shared a good relationship with his parents but he had nothing in common with them or their Western ways.

Manohar took young Shaman to meet his *guru*, Naam Yajnananda Maharaj, during Shaman's school breaks. A deep love for the *guru* developed in Shaman's heart. He was fiercely drawn to the Master—rather unusual in a child. He looked forward to the visits and the warm exchanges with him. Thus began the relationship between the Master and the child Shaman.

The sharp call of the peacock brought Shaman back to the present. It was bright daylight now. He stood up and walked to the river to offer water to the infant orange sun that adorned the sky. He picked up his *asana* and torch, and ran lightly up the treacherous stone steps. Yoga kept him in excellent shape, thanks to his grandfather.

16.

A *Daridra Narayan* Seva was organised at the *ashram*, when a simple wholesome meal was served to the poor. The entire village came to the *ashram* to partake in this sacred meal as it was considered auspicious to eat the food cooked by the austere *sannyasis*.

The *ashram* was a beehive of activity. Piles of golden *puris*[50] were to be served with delicious *matar paneer*[51], accompanied by hot, ghee-laden *sooji halwa*[52]. Shaman greeted the villagers with great warmth, serving everyone with his own hands. Other *sannyasis* brought in the large platters of food from the *ashram* kitchen while Shambhavi ensured the supplies continued without a break, replenishing the food constantly. The Master sat in his chair and watched from the window of his room.

The hectic activity went on till almost 3 pm. Finally, the village Head, Sharad Juliyal, arrived with his family. When he finished eating, he requested a private audience with the Master. Krishna Da escorted him to the Master's chambers upstairs. The Master sent word for Shaman to join them.

Maharaj was seated in his usual chair while the old village Head sat on the floor.

"Shaman, Sharadji has something to say," the Master said. "Now tell him what the issue is…"

---

[50]Puris: small, round pieces of bread made of unleavened wheat flour, deep-fried and served with vegetables

[51]Matar paneer: a curry made from a type of milk curd cheese and pea

[52]Sooji halwa: a sweet Indian dish consisting of semolina (sooji) boiled with milk, almonds, sugar, butter, and cardamom

"Swamiji, we are having great trouble with a rogue elephant for the last few weeks. It comes, destroys our crops and damages our houses, and we are just helpless. Last week, at Champalal's daughter's wedding, the elephant came to the sugarcane field behind the marriage hall and was frightened by the fire crackers. It ran amok and attacked one of the *baaraatis*[53] who had come to attend the wedding."

"That's most unfortunate," said Shaman.

"By God's grace the man survived, though he was seriously injured," said the village Head. "Maharaj, we approached our Naikji, the forest range officer, but he said that till the tame elephants come from Rajaji National Park, this fellow cannot be captured. I have been going to him almost every day for the last three weeks, but in vain. Please help us, Maharaj. Naikji will listen to you; he is your disciple."

"Let me see what can be done," replied the Master.

The village Head bent his head to receive the Master's blessing and left.

The Master turned to Shaman. "What do you think we should do? The villagers are suffering."

"Maharaj, we should write a strongly worded formal letter to the forest department, requesting them to look into this matter urgently and follow it up with a few phone calls."

"Yes, do it immediately, Shaman. I know that if you take up something, you will not rest till it's completed."

Bowing to take the Master's blessings, Shaman left to draft the letter.

~

A fortnight had passed since Juliyal's visit to the Master. The old *guru* sat erect, lost in the depths of meditation. Krishna

[53]Baaraati: Members of the marriage party

Da tiptoed into the room with the day's mail. Shaman, sitting on the floor, sorted through it. There were literally hundreds of letters. Maharaj personally read almost all, and dictated answers to most. To a few, he replied in his own hand.

'If I could ask the senior devotees for a copy of their correspondence with Maharaj, it would make a great book,' Shaman thought.

There was a letter from the Shankaracharya of Vyomakesh Peeth. It required the *guru's* immediate attention and Shaman put it to one side.

Though it was a dull day, the sky was peppered with clouds of varying shapes, one moment a tortoise, the next a graceful swan. Shaman watched the constantly mutating cloudscape from the window with awe. The immense power and versatility of the Creator blew him away every time. The same force that created dark, heavy, menacing clouds also created these delicate candyfloss shapes, he reflected.

The Master slowly came out of his meditation and clasped his hands in silent prayer.

"*Jai Guru*, Shaman," he said, after a long moment.

"*Jai Guru*," replied Shaman. "Maharaj, many letters have come as usual. This one is from Shankaracharyaji." He handed it over to Maharaj, who reverentially touched the envelope to his forehead.

"Shaman, I am unable to make out his handwriting. Perhaps his hand grows unsteady with age. Can you read it out loud?"

Shaman too, found the narrow and looped handwriting hard to decipher.

"Shaman Da, sit by the window where there is better light. Low voltage is a big problem," muttered Krishna Da.

Shaman sat on the broad window sill and perused the letter. "Maharaj, from what I can make out," he said, "His Revered

Self, Shankaracharyaji, has accepted our invitation to come for the celebration of the *Param Guru's* birth anniversary."

Maharaj was delighted. "*Jai Guru*, Shaman! It is a great honour for all of us."

Just then, Shaman heard sounds and looked up, out of the window. He saw hordes of people coming up the snaking *ghaat* road towards the *ashram* in an unending stream of humanity. Shaman figured they were local villagers.

"Maharaj, the villagers are coming to the *ashram*," Shaman said. The Master merely nodded.

Krishna Da and Shaman watched the crowd enter the gates. There were men, women and children of every age. They sat down peacefully in complete silence. The crowd was so large it spilt out of the *ashram* gates; those outside sat where they were. Shambhavi, Chandni, Keshava Da, the *pundit*, and Leela, all came out to see what was happening. Shaman went down to ask what they wanted.

"Sharananandaji, we have come for *darshan*[54] of the Master," an old man whom Shaman knew, said.

Shaman looked up at the Master's window and noted Krishna Da had heard the exchange and left to ask the Master. In a few moments, he returned to the window and indicated that Maharaj would give *darshan*.

The Master slowly descended the steps from his chambers and stood before the crowd. His charisma was unmistakable. As soon as he emerged from the shadows of the *ashram* building into the open daylight, the crowd stood up and in one motion, fell on their knees and prostrated themselves before the *guru*. Maharaj lifted both his hands and blessed them, saying '*Jai Guru*'. Though Maharaj's voice was not loud, the pindrop silence accentuated every syllable he spoke.

---

[54]Darshan: an opportunity to see or an occasion of seeing a holy person or the image of a deity.

The crowd stood up again, standing with joined hands.

Krishna Da came running with the Master's chair. He sat down and gestured for the crowd to sit.

After everyone had settled, Sharad Juliyal, the village Head, stood up to speak. "Maharaj, the elephant that was troubling us has been captured. We cannot thank you enough for making this possible. Without your intervention, we would have been at the mercy of the ranger even now. Our meagre farms and humble dwellings would have continued to be ravaged by the rogue elephant."

'Yes, yes!' the crowd echoed.

"It's all your kindness," said a young man from the back.

"*Jai Guru*! Words cannot express our gratitude," a woman shouted from one side, lifting up her joined palms.

"*Jai Guru,*" the Master replied. "It's good to hear the elephant has been caught, but you must all give your thanks to Swami Sharanananda here." Maharaj pointed to Shaman. "He was the one who enabled it. He made calls to the higher authorities to ensure the elephant was captured. He worked tirelessly until the authorities sitting faraway in Dehradun listened to our appeal and acted on it."

"*Swami Sharanananda ki Jai*!" Sharad Juliyal shouted, and the crowd echoed and clapped in response.

Chandni's husband Balvir, and his friends, stepped forward and spontaneously lifted Shaman onto their shoulders. The entire crowd laughed and clapped, chanting in unison, '*Swami Sharanananda ki Jai*!'

Shaman nimbly jumped off their shoulders, feeling rather embarrassed. "It is due to Maharaj. When he decided to help, things just happened. It is all His grace."

The old village Head clasped his hands, saying, "Swamiji,

you are the instrument the Master chose. So please accept our heartfelt thanks."

'*Maharaj Shri ki Jai! Swami Sharanananda ki Jai*!' the crowd chanted as they slowly walked out of the *ashram*, receiving *prasad*[55] from the cook and Krishna Da at the gates.

Shambhavi watched all of this with great interest.

~

Keshava Da came in with baskets of fruit and vegetables. "No one is accepting money from me for anything. In fact, the vendors in the village market have given so many fruits and vegetables that I had to take a rickshaw. The rickshaw fellow didn't charge me a single paise for ferrying me to the *ashram* either."

"Let's see what they've given," the cook said, excited.

"You must pay them," Shaman said.

"How can I pay them, Dada? They refused, saying they will never take a single *naya paisa* from this *ashram* from now on."

"Rightly so!" opined Chandni. "You have saved their livelihood and homes from the elephant, Dada. Everyone was living in fear of the animal. You are the hero of the village," she declared dramatically.

"And of the *ashram*," the cook added.

"Shambhavi Didi, see what the villagers have given Shaman Dada," Keshava called out when he saw her coming towards the kitchen area.

"Not me; the *ashram*," Shaman corrected.

"It's for you, Shaman Dada," said Shambhavi. "Baba is so pleased he has not stopped talking about how great you are."

---

[55]Prasad: a devotional offering made to a God, typically consisting of food that is later shared among devotees

"Now this is getting embarrassing. I only did my duty. The rest was just the sheer grace of Maharaj," said Shaman.

17.

It was a miracle Shaman woke at his usual time, given he had been working on his research paper, *Kutiyattam and Yakshagana in the light of edicts of Natyashastra,* till 2 am. He kept his eyes closed for a few moments, trying to absorb the sound of the rushing Ganga. To his surprise, the faint sounds of a woman's tinkling laughter accompanied the sounds of the river. Shaman was curious about who it could be. Following the incident of the rogue elephant, the village folk rarely ventured out of their homes in darkness. The village wore a deserted look by as early as 6 pm.

Shaman quickly showered, picked up his torchlight and *asana* and made his way to the steps leading to the *sangam.* As soon as he neared the top of the steps, he stopped. Each step had been anointed on both sides with turmeric. On one side was drawn a small *rangoli* with a marigold flower as its centre, while the other side bore burning *diyas*[56]. In the inky darkness that preceded the dawn, the *diyas* looked like a fiery necklace adorning the stone steps. The little orange flames stood erect, illuminating a small circle of light around them. It was breathtakingly beautiful.

There was still enough space to navigate the steps without disturbing the *rangoli* and *diyas*. Shaman switched off his torch and made his way down.

As he descended, he heard Shambhavi say, "Chandni, finish fast! Shaman Da will come for his meditation any moment."

"Yes, but he is a *khadoos*, a grumpy fellow. He is not going

[56]Diyas: mud lamps

to appreciate any of this decoration," Chandni grumbled, gesturing towards the steps.

"Shh… I decorated the steps because today is *Ganga Saptami*, the day Ganga descended to earth. I haven't done this to win anyone's appreciation. And Shaman Da is a serious *sannyasi*, you cannot call him *khadoos*." Shambhavi paused. "And by the way, you should be grateful to Shaman Da. It's because of him that the elephant was captured."

Chandni realised her mistake. "Sorry Didi, it was thoughtless of me to call him *khadoos*."

They did not see Shaman in the deep shadows beyond the lamps. Once his eyes became accustomed to the darkness, he saw Shambhavi sitting on her haunches, decorating the last step. She was making a beautiful *rangoli* in the lamp light. In a matter of seconds, her experienced hand completed the *rangoli*. Chandni placed a marigold in the centre; she was grumbling that her back hurt from washing the steps.

As both stepped back to survey their work, Shambhavi saw Shaman descend the steps. She gestured to Chandni to quickly pack up the remaining flowers, oil wicks and extra *diyas*. Chandni put them all into an open wicker basket.

As Shaman descended and stood before them, the women bent their heads to receive his blessings.

"The steps look beautiful," he said. "Like a painting."

"Thank you, Shaman Da," said Shambhavi.

"We've been here since 2 am," Chandni informed him. "See Didi, I have put even the used matchsticks in the basket as you asked. I'll throw it all in the trash can upstairs."

Shaman looked at Shambhavi. She wore a sky-blue *salwar* suit decorated with small white embroidered flowers. Her matching *dupatta* was tied diagonally across one shoulder and knotted around her waist to enable her to work freely. Chandni handed her the white shawl she had discarded by the side of the steps, preparing to leave.

"Do you know how many steps there are?" Shaman asked.

It was a casual question, but Shambhavi looked up confused. "No Da, I don't know. But wait, I can tell you... Chandni, how many lamps did we buy?" she asked. Before Chandni could answer, she did her own calculation aloud, "We got 10 dozen, out of which 4 broke and 8 remain. So, 108 steps, Da!"

Shaman smiled. "Yes. But do you know the significance of the number 108?"

Shambhavi shook her head. "I know it's an auspicious number, but beyond that, I know nothing."

"Then let me tell you...there are actually a bunch of things."

"Chandni, you go. I will come later," Shambhavi said, turning to her companion.

Chandni balanced the basket on her head and slowly made her way up, cursing her aching knees.

"What's so great about 108, Dada? Tell me why do *tulasi malas*[57] and *rudraksha malas* have 108 beads?"

"The number 108 suggests total identification of the *Jiva*[58] with the *Paramatman*[59]."

"How?"

"Let me ask you a simple question, Shambhavi... How many fingers is your height?"

"What do you mean?"

"I mean how many index fingers is your height if you were to

---

[57]Mala: rosaries. Rudraksha is the grooved seed produced by several species of large evergreen broad-leaved tree in the genus Elaeocarpus, a rosary made from these seeds is used for chanting

[58]Jiva: individual self/soul

[59]Paramatman: supreme self/soul

place them one on top of the other?"

"I don't know."

"96," Shaman informed her.

"Really!"

"Yes. A person's height is 96 times the width of their index finger."

"For everyone?"

"Yes, for everyone."

"How did you come up with this?" Shambhavi asked.

Shaman smiled. "Well, the *Varahopanishad* gives this math."

"I've never heard of this particular scripture... Never knew scriptures had so much science either!"

"The scriptures are gold mines of information and knowledge. Coming to the math, the height of an individual is 96 fingers. Now, the seat of the *Paramatman* in the human body is just above the navel—a distance of 12 fingers. Hence, the total number, adding 96 to 12, is indicative of the oneness of the *Jiva* and *Paramatman*."

"You said there are a bunch of things..."

"108 represents the daily breathing count in a self-perfected man. According to Tantra, every being breathes 21,600 times on average. Of these, 10,800 are for solar energy and 10,800 for lunar energy. If you practice *pranayama* and meditation and achieve perfection, your breathing stabilises at 108. That's the point at which one realises the Self."

Shambhavi thanked him and turned to leave. She ran up the uneven steep steps with the surefooted nimbleness of a mountain goat.

Shaman was impressed. He sat down in his usual place and began his meditation.

18.

Shaman sat in Shyam Kanoria's office at the Jwalaji Press in Dehradun. He had come to iron out a few details before the Master's book went into print.

"Don't worry, Swamiji, the book will be in your hands in a week's time," Mr Kanoria assured him. "It's a good thing you came because all things cannot be sorted out on the phone."

Mr Kanoria was a fair man in his 60s, and a great devotee of Maharaj. He always insisted on printing for free, but the Master somehow found ways to pay him. The phone on his table rang and he answered it briefly before handing it to Shaman saying, "It's for you."

Shaman was surprised. Who could be calling him?

It was Krishna Da. "Dada, Maharaj wants to talk to you."

Shaman stood up. "*Jai Guru*, Maharaj."

"Shaman, Kanhaiya, the driver we hired from the village, has taken Shambhavi for a school function. His father-in-law just called; his wife has been rushed to the hospital. The doctors are saying she may need surgery to deliver their child. It's the first child, so the family is quite worried. Could you please pick up Shambhavi from the school? Ask Kanhaiya to go to his wife's village immediately. You and Shambhavi can drive back in the car."

"Yes, Maharaj. I will also give him some money. It will come in handy. *Jai Guru*."

"That's exactly what I was about to tell you also. *Jai Guru*."

Shaman hung up.

"All well, Swamiji?" Mr Kanoria asked.

"Yes, but I need to get to the Infant Jesus Convent."

"I am going there anyway," replied Kanoria. "The school is celebrating its 75th anniversary and my daughter is taking part in one of the skits."

Shaman must have looked surprised for Mr Kanoria hastened to clarify, "My youngest one... She is still in school. My fourth daughter actually," he added with a laugh.

Shaman told him he had to pick up Shambhavi.

"Oh Shambhavi! I know her. She and my daughter, Matangi, were classmates. In fact, Matangi mentioned that Shambhavi is giving a dance recital today. Swamiji, come with me. It'd be just the two of us in the car. Matangi is getting married in a couple of months. You may perhaps know—it's a match suggested by Maharaj."

"Congratulations!" Shaman said.

"My wife and my other daughters, along with my future son-in-law, have already gone to the school," Mr Kanoria said and then stopped, as if he'd suddenly remembered something. "I am so sorry Swamiji, I didn't offer you anything. I'm becoming senile and absent-minded, as my wife always keeps saying. If she comes to know this lapse, she will have my hide. What can I offer you? Some milk...fruit..."

"There is nothing to apologise for. I am fasting for *navaratri*. I just have some fruit at night and am carrying some apples in my bag."

"You fast all nine days?"

"Yes, but honestly, it's no big deal. I break my fast with milk and fruit at night."

"If I am not mistaken, today is day five, yet, after five days of fasting you are still so full of energy… It's great."

"The Mother's *murti* will be installed tomorrow at the *ashram*. The next few days will be hectic. And when one is busy, food is not a priority."

Kanoria laughed. "It may be so for you, Swamiji, but people like me are always fantasising about their next meal!"

Shaman laughed, amused. "On a serious note..." he said, "everything is enabled by the grace of Maharaj."

"I agree with you on that," said Kanoria.

They finished the work on the book and then drove to the school. It was a big school, situated on more than 60 acres of land, with a picturesque view of the valley below. The majestic and imposing stone building served as a fine example of colonial British architecture. When Shaman and Kanoria arrived, the campus was buzzing with people—parents, grandparents, students, photographers, nuns and school support staff. The lone watchman had a torrid time trying to hold together the veneer of order and a semblance of discipline.

Shaman thanked Kanoria, saying, "I need to locate the *ashram* car and send the driver off. You carry on, Mr Kanoria."

"I will reserve a seat for you. You get the keys and come in," Kanoria replied, walking into the school premises.

The parking space outside the school was full with an endless stream of cars splilling onto the road. It took Shaman almost half an hour to locate the *ashram* car. Kanhaiya had parked it a little away from the others, under a tree on a grassy knoll. The driver's door was wide open. Kanhaiya was sound asleep inside, the pleasant evening breeze blowing over his face.

Shaman knocked on the windscreen. "Kanhaiya… Kanhaiya…" he called.

The driver woke with a start. "Shaman Dada!" He quickly bowed his head for his blessing. "How come you are here?"

"Kanhaiya, go to your wife's village at once. You are going to be a father very soon."

"But Dada… It's not yet time! More than a month is left. I hope the baby will be fine?"

"Don't worry, Kanhaiya. Maharaj will take care of everything. Start right away," Shaman said, handing him some money.

Kanhaiya looked up from the packet in his hands. "Dada, more than money we need your blessings. We have already lost one child. My wife was heartbroken the last time it happened. Please pray that everything goes well. My wife is very young, Dada. I want her to be happy."

Shaman did not have the heart to tell him his wife was scheduled for a caesarean. As Kanhaiya set out for the bus stand, Shaman locked the car and walked back to the big auditorium. One of the Kanoria girls spotted him and guided him to the empty seat next to her father.

"Your daughter found me easily," remarked Shaman.

"To spot a man in an ochre robe at a school function is not difficult," chuckled Kanoria. "You are just in time for Shambhavi's performance."

The lights dimmed. Shambhavi walked onto stage in a white and red *kuchipudi* dress. She gave a stunning performance of Yashoda and baby Krishna. Her expressions of maternal love and exasperation at his naughtiness effortlessly transported everyone to Gokul. It was followed by a splendid piece where she danced on a moving brass plate by gripping it between her toes. Simultaneously, she balanced a pot of water on her head and held two burning *diyas* in her hands. It was a scintillating performance, with lightning-quick footwork and immense grace. The entire auditorium gave her a standing ovation when she finished, the loud applause continuing long after the curtain had fallen.

'She is truly a great performer,' thought Shaman. In watching her perform, he had forgotten she was Shambhavi, believing her to be Yashoda. She had enthralled everyone in the audience effortlessly.

"She is like a goddess," Mrs Kanoria said, in awe. "What beauty! What charm!"

Shaman's mind returned to Kanhaiya. He thanked Mr. Kanoria for the lift, saying it was time for his evening prayers and that he would wait for Shambhavi in the car.

19.

Shaman sat cross-legged in the driver's seat. He prayed that Kanhaiya's child would be born safely, and that his wife would be free of complications.

He heard voices approaching the car.

"Shambhavi, when are you going back to Bangalore?"

"Nothing decided...I'll go only when Baba has recovered."

"I wanted to introduce you to Rohan, but God knows where he has disappeared."

"Another time, Matangi. It's getting late."

Shambhavi wore charcoal grey jeans and a deep plum-coloured knitted top that moulded her form softly. A black pashmina stole was wrapped around her neck. She looked very different from her stage persona, Shaman thought.

"Wait, I think they're looking for us. Rohan!" Matangi called.

Two young men in their late 20s hurried towards them.

"Where did you guys disappear?" Matangi asked.

"We went for a smoke," replied Rohan.

"This is Shambhavi. I was telling you about her. Shambhavi, this is Rohan, my fiancé, and his brother, Rahul," Matangi said, making the introductions.

"Jeez... You're beautiful!" said Rahul, openly staring. "Sorry, I didn't mean to stare, but you're really beautiful. Matangi, you did not tell me your friend is a stunner!"

"But you just saw her on stage," Matangi reminded him.

Shambhavi smiled. "Hi Rohan and Rahul… Nice to meet both of you."

"We make ad films," Rohan told her. "This is my card. You should seriously give modelling a shot."

"You are embarrassing her!" Matangi protested, giving Rohan a push.

"Thank you, but I must go now. Goodbye. I'll see you at the wedding," Shamabhavi walked away with a wave and a smile.

Shaman was surprised that no one had commented or complimented her on her exquisite dance performance.

~

"*Pranaam*, Shaman Da," Shambhavi said as she put her backpack on the rear seat. "Sorry I kept you waiting. Kanoria Uncle told me you had come and were waiting for me here; that Kanhaiya had to leave."

"I lost track of time. There is no need to apologise," Shaman replied.

Since the car was parked away from the others, they could easily leave the place without getting stuck behind other cars and school buses. Soon they were on the road to Nagaprayag.

It was a night full of stars and silence.

"I saw you dance. You were splendid. The fact that you got the audience to believe there was really a baby in front of you proves you are a remarkably talented artist."

"Thank you, Da. My *guru* has trained me painstakingly."

"Yes, Chandrahasini did a damn good job, I must admit. But you have the talent to translate her vision on the stage. I really felt that if I saw Ma Yashoda, she'd be like you!"

"Thank you, Shaman Da. That means a lot to me. And I will tell Chandra Ma you said this. It will make her very happy."

"Somehow I doubt that," Shaman remarked, laughing.

A family of four mongooses were crossing the road in a straight line, their golden fur glistening in the headlights. Shaman slammed on the brakes and the car came to a screeching halt. At the same time Shaman felt something bite him on his shin. The pain was so intense that he involuntarily cried out "*Hey Prabhu*!". He felt a sharp sting as if someone had stabbed him with a red hot knife.

"Dada, what happened?" Shambhavi asked, worried.

"Something bit me. It hurts terribly."

His whole leg throbbed with pain. Shambhavi switched on the inside light to have a better look. His leg already looked swollen. Shambhavi scrambled out of the car and hurried to open the driver's door. When she bent low to look, she heard an angry hiss.

"Dada, I think it's a snake!" she cried in alarm.

She looked carefully into the dim car interior. A slim and shiny reptile, the width of a thick pencil, sat near the brake and accelerator pedals. It had bright yellow glowing bands on its skin. Its head was raised, ready to strike again.

Shambhavi quickly threw her stole over it and the hissing stopped. She tied the ends of the stole around the confused snake and put it into her backpack, zipping it up.

"Did you just catch a snake?" Shaman asked, shocked.

"A snake once bit a friend of mine in a farm near Bangalore. When we took her to the doctor, they said they had to identify the snake before starting treatment. We had a tough time trying to describe the snake, which, in our panic, none of us had noticed properly." She stopped short. "Dada, how are you feeling?"

"My vision is blurred." Shaman's voice was slightly slurred.

"Move Dada, sit in the other seat. Let me drive."

Shambhavi took the wheel once Shaman had shifted across with difficulty.

"You are sweating profusely, Dada. Stay calm; you'll be fine."

Shaman's leg felt like it was on fire. Thick black curtains of crushing pain began to smother him. He could not keep his eyes open. It felt like someone was burning a hole into his leg with a blowtorch.

"Talk to me, Dada. Don't close your eyes!"

"When they said you fought wild dogs to rescue the fawn, I thought everyone was exaggerating. Now you just caught a snake with such ease." Waves of biting pain squeezed the breath from his chest. "I cannot breathe. I am floating Shambhavi… I can see Ma Durga…"

"Shaman Da! Shaman Da, wake up! I am taking you to a hospital just down the road. Talk to me… Don't sleep…"

"I am not sleeping. I can see the Divine Mother, Shambhavi. She is sitting on a lion. I can see how sharp her sword is; blood is still dripping from its pointed tip… You think I am blabbering? No, no, she is right in front of me… Ma, my leg is hurting so much… Please just cut it off with your sword… Relieve me from this agony, Mother!"

Shambhavi glanced at his leg. It was swollen to twice the size of the other.

"Where are we going, Shambhavi?" Shaman asked in a feeble voice as he shifted in and out of consciousness.

"There is a missionary hospital run by my school, Dada. I am taking you there. Don't worry…"

"What is there to worry?" Shaman mumbled. "Ma will take me with her on her lion, Shanmukha. I am not at all worried."

Suddenly Shaman was lucid. "I know what must have happened… Kanhaiya was sleeping with the car door open. The snake must have entered the car then. When I slammed the brakes, it must have been scared or injured, that's why it bit me…in self-defence."

He stopped for a moment. "My world is spinning. I am falling down a pit," he said, his voice fading.

~

He felt strong hands lift him and carry him away. Bright light forced his eyes open. Someone was calling his name, "Mr Srivastava…" but he was too tired to answer. Shaman welcomed the dark peace and silence that engulfed his being as he let himself flow away.

20.

Though Shaman could hear voices, they sounded far away. His eyelids felt like they were encased in heavy concrete. When he finally opened them, sharp bright light pierced his dark cocoon of comfort. Quickly, he closed them again.

Time passed…

Someone was shaking him with determined vigour. He opened his eyes. This time, his eyelids did not feel so heavy.

"Hi! I am Doctor Samuel…"

Before him stood a man with remarkable resemblance to the famous cricketer, Vivian Richards.

"How are you feeling?" he asked in a booming voice.

"I don't know…" said Shaman, his voice scratchy and barely audible. "I just want to sleep."

"You've been doing exactly that for the last 48 hours," Dr Samuel told him, glancing at his watch. "All right, you sleep."

Darkness enveloped him again.

The next time Shaman woke, it was evening and no bright light stung his eyes. He saw a female form. After some concentration, the form crystallised into Shambhavi. She was reading. He strained to see what it was, but his blurred vision refused to let him focus on the title of the book.

"What are you reading?"

"Dada! You're awake! Let me call the doctor!" She ran out of the room, leaving the book on his bed.

Shaman tried to pick it up but noticed that an IV line had been attached to his right hand. He picked up the book with his left hand instead. It was a copy of *Durga Saptashati*[60]. He touched the book to his forehead. It felt unusually heavy. Shaman realised he was very weak. When he tried to move his right foot, bright fireworks of pain exploded in his brain. He decided to keep still and wait for the pain to abate.

Soon the doctor arrived with Shambhavi.

"Good to see you awake." Dr Samuel placed his stethoscope on Shaman's chest and listened.

"You're very lucky to be alive. This angel saved you."

"My leg hurts a lot," complained Shaman.

"It is but natural. You were bitten by a King Cobra."

Shaman frowned. "It looked like a small snake, maybe a foot and a half in length; black and yellow. I've seen King Cobras; their colours are very different." The effort to speak exhausted him and he lay back with eyes closed.

"Don't tire yourself," Dr Samuel advised. "Let me explain. It was a baby King Cobra. Their colouring changes as they grow into adults. But these baby Kings are born with poison as lethal as an adult's. So even if an immature King Cobra bites a fully grown elephant, it will die in three hours. A single bite is enough to kill twenty men. Sometimes, they strike their victims more than once."

"It almost did," Shaman said. "That's when Shambhavi put her stole on it."

"You were certainly lucky! Everything worked in your favour. Since she brought the snake, we knew it was a King. And the

[60]Durga Saptashati: Also known as Devi Mahatmya and Chandi Path, it is a Hindu religious text containing 700 verses describing the victory of the Goddess Durga over the demon Mahishasura. It is part of the Markandeya Purana, written by sage Markandeya.

fact that you were already in a car, helped; you didn't have to walk. Usually, for people who are bitten in the fields or forests, finding transport is a challenge. And then the possibility of finding a hospital nearby is remote. Thirty minutes is considered fatal as the poison spreads and paralyses the respiratory system," the doctor said.

"Luckily, the hospital had just received a stock of anti-venom from the Central Research Institute," said Shambhavi. "God has been most kind!"

"Despite administering the anti-venom, your respiratory system was under severe strain. We had to assist your breathing to stabilise you. It took you a long time to return to wakefulness," Dr. Samuel told Shaman.

"How long has it been?"

"More than two days."

"Two days! I don't remember a thing..." Shaman murmured.

"You kept repeating *Sati Sadhvi Bhavani, Bhavapreeta Bhavamochani,* and many other names," said a plump nurse who had just come into the room, a warm smile on her face. "I am Stella. I was on duty the night you were brought in. You said these names over and over again. So much so, I too, have learnt a few of them!"

She lifted the bedsheet covering his leg and observed, "The swelling has reduced considerably."

Shaman saw he was in a green hospital gown. It felt odd not to be in his ochre robes. "When can I put on my regular clothes?" he asked.

"As long as you are a patient, you will be in hospital robes," said Sister Stella with a small smile.

"Once he starts taking food orally, you can disconnect the IV," Dr Samuel instructed Stella. "You can start with small sips of water. I'll see you tomorrow. Sister, I will write a prescription for a painkiller injection. Give it through his IV."

Stella followed the doctor out. Shambhavi handed Shaman water in a small paper cup.

His mouth felt parched and he slowly took a sip. The water tasted heavenly and he instantly felt better.

"Just lift your head. I placed your *mala* under your pillow. Once you wear it again, you will feel more like yourself."

Shaman touched his bare neck. It truly felt strange without his ochre robes and *rudraksha mala*. He pressed the *mala* to his forehead and wore it using his left hand. "Now, I really do feel better," he agreed with a faint smile.

"Dada, now that you're awake, let me call Baba and tell him. He has been so anxious. Your grandfather and parents too, have also been very worried."

"My parents? Who told them?"

"I assume Maharaj informed your grandfather, who must have called your parents," said Shambhavi. "In fact, your parents have been in constant touch with Dr Samuel regarding the line of treatment."

"Please offer my *saashtaang pranaams*[61] to Maharaj."

Shaman closed his eyes once Shambhavi had left to phone the Master. 'Poor Dadaji, he must be worried stiff,' he thought. He decided to ask Shambhavi to phone him, but was fast asleep by the time she returned.

---

[61]Saashtaang pranaam or dandavat: a symbol of complete submission made through lying prostrate on the ground so that the 8 parts of your body touch the floor (1.forehead 2.nose 3.right hand 4.left hand 5.right knee 6.left knee 7.right feet 8.left feet)

21.

The next morning, Shaman felt much stronger. The pain in his leg had subsided to a dull throb. Now that the tubes had been disconnected from his body, he felt more like his normal self. But it would take him at least another week to sit cross-legged again. He meditated in the chair. It filled him with deep peace and quiet.

Sister Stella arrived to check his blood pressure. It was normal.

"We will monitor you today, and if all is well, the doctor will discharge you tomorrow."

Shambhavi came in. "Shaman Da, *Pranaam*! Good to see you sitting in the chair. Did you sleep well? How is your leg?"

"*Jai Guru*, Shambhavi. I am much better. The pain is quite tolerable now."

"Let me see your leg. See the two puncture holes? That's where you were bitten. The swelling is much less, Dada. It was very bad when we came here. Even the blueness has reduced considerably."

"The nurse said that if my blood pressure is stable today, they will discharge me tomorrow."

"That's great. Baba will be so happy to hear that."

"I forgot to ask, did Kanhaiya's wife deliver the child safely?"

"Yes indeed! They have a daughter. His wife did not require surgery and since the baby was born on *panchami*[62] during

[62]Panchami: the fifth day (tithi) of the fortnight (paksha) in Hindu lunar calendar.

navaratri[63], Baba has named her Lalita."

"God is kind. Poor Kanhaiya, he was so worried."

"Actually, he felt guilty about what happened to you. He phoned several times from the village. He said the snake was meant to bite him but you took it on instead."

Shaman shook his head, smiling. "Only highly accomplished *siddha mahatmas*[64] like our *guru* can avert or take on such things. I did nothing. Whatever happened was the will of the Almighty." Looking up at Shambhavi, he said, "You're looking different. But I am unable to say how."

She laughed in response. "I look different because I am dressed in boy's clothes. I had not anticipated staying on in Dehradun, so I had no change of clothes. Matangi's youngest sister, Maheshwari, is the same size as me; she dropped off some of hers. Unfortunately for me, she prefers boys' clothing. Does that explain my red and black checked shirt and black pants?"

"Nevertheless, that was kind of her."

"Matangi is my friend, Dada. Kanoria Uncle has been coming every day to check on you. He wanted me to stay at his house, but I didn't want to leave you here by yourself."

"Where are you staying?"

"The hospital is not running at full capacity, so they have given me a room across the corridor. The Mother Superior who runs our school holds immense respect for Baba. When I explained the situation to her, she organised the room for me. Baba was keen on sending Madhava Da to look after you, but I convinced him there was no need. Besides, there has been a landslide 10 kilometres from Nagaprayag. There was no way anyone could have come from the *ashram*."

---

[63]Navaratri: a nine-day festival dedicated to Durga and the nine forms of Goddess Shakti which falls in the lunar month Ashwin (around September), during Sharad or the early autumn season.

[64]Siddha mahatma: an ascetic, a high soul, who has achieved enlightenment

"How did you spend your time?"

"I've been reading. Baba wanted me to read from *Durga Saptashati* every day and to sing *naam* beside your bed, which I have been doing. And, of course, I also did my regular *japa*."

"So it was you who was singing. I did hear someone singing *naam*, but thought it was all part of my hallucination. It's good that you are doing your regular *japa*. Just a question: At what age did you take *diksha*[65]?"

"I must have been fifteen."

"How much do you do every day?"

"I do 5000 *ishta japa*[66] every day. I want to increase it though. In Bangalore, I find it difficult since my days are packed and I'm exhausted at the end of the day."

"Chandrahasini is a hard taskmaster?"

"No, not at all! It's a challenge to keep up with the inexhaustible energy of young children. Another thing, now I have started writing *Ram naam* with full awareness, it takes time. I was impressed with the way you explained the significance of *Ram naam* to Mr and Mrs Ramakant."

"I thought you disliked me…at that point."

"I did hate you, I must admit, especially when you had the fawn sent away. I knew it was illegal to keep a wild animal as a pet but my attachment clouded my judgement."

"I know how hard it must have been for you. You even skipped dinner that day."

They were silent for a few moments and then Shambhavi said, "No matter what I felt, I couldn't help but be impressed with your teaching. You were clear and concise in your communication, simple yet highly effective. You are a good

---

[65]Diksha: translated as a "preparation or consecration for a religious ceremony", is giving of a mantra or an initiation by the guru in Hinduism.

[66]Ishta Japa: chanting of the mantra of one's favourite deity

orator. No wonder Baba keeps telling everyone what a great asset you are to the organisation!"

"Thank you, Shambhavi. Spreading the Name of the Lord is my duty," Shaman replied quietly.

"You look tired. Maybe you should lie down."

"No, I am fine."

She touched his forehead. "Thank God, no fever!"

The ward boy brought in some porridge. Shambhavi left the room and returned with two washed *tulasi* leaves. She added them as garnish and handed the bowl and spoon to Shaman. "I know you'll prefer to eat it this way."

Shaman was touched by her thoughtfulness. Thanking her, he ate the bland porridge slowly. "I feel odd in this green robe. I'm waiting to put on my *dhoti*," he said.

"I know. Actually, you look funny in this hospital outfit. Anyway, it's just another day before you are restored to your ochre glory!"

"The porridge tastes like gooey cardboard, but I want to get well soon," he murmured, emptying the bowl.

"Rest now, Dada. I'll come back in an hour."

22.

Shaman was discharged the next morning. He was happy to be back in his ochre *dhoti*. Shambhavi brought his wooden sandals. His foot was still swollen and he put them on with difficulty.

"Shall I help you?"

"No… I can manage."

Shambhavi handed him an oval hand mirror with an ornate silver back, and a small packet.

"What is this?"

"That's just my mirror for now. But the packet is for you. Open it, Dada."

The packet contained materials to make the small *Vaishnava tilak*[67] he drew every day on his forehead.

"Where did you buy all these things?" he asked.

"I went to the market when you were sleeping. I know it matters to you."

"Yes, even though they are only external symbols."

"Let me get your discharge summary; then we can go."

Shaman was deeply moved by Shambhavi's gesture. He drew the *tilak* and looked at himself in her small mirror. Sunken eyes stared back at him; his complexion held a pale unhealthy tinge. It was apparent he had been very ill. Nevertheless, he felt

[67]Vaishnava Tilak: A mark, worn by devotees of Vaishnava tradition, made of gopi mud, considered equivalent to sandalwood powder

better having all his familiar things—his *mala, dhoti, tilak,* and wooden sandals. He felt less vulnerable and more like himself.

Shambhavi returned and picked up his orange bag. Slowly, they walked to the car. Memories of the snake bite and that fateful night came back to him.

"What a night that was!" Shambhavi said, as if reading his thoughts. "Now I cautiously inspect the car before I get in."

"Do you know what the snake represents?" asked Shaman.

"I know snakes are deities called Nagas, but I don't know what they symbolise in Hinduism."

"You have heard of Ananta Naga right?"

"Yes, the one on which Narayana or Vishnu reposes?"

"Correct. *Ananta* means 'infinity'. The snake represents infinity. The *Kundalini Shakti* or spiritual energy flows in us like a snake, through a coiled channel moving upwards, from the base of the spine to the crown of the head, reaching out to eternity. Ananta is just one of the nine *nagas,* the others are Vasuki, Shesha, Padmanabh, Kambal, Shankhapal, Dhrutrashtra, Takshaka and Kalia."

"Dada, what is this strange connection between *yogis* and snakes?"

"Yes, there's a mysterious connection between spiritual practice and snakes. *Yogis* and snakes both live in caves, often happily. Several Swamis have found snakes visiting them during their intense *sadhana*[68], and consider it a blessing. Maharaj once told me of a six-feet-long cobra that used to come to his meditation chamber for 16 consequetive days; every night at midnight, at the same spot. At the time, Maharaj was engaged in a rare *kriya*[69] which he did with a special *pranayama.* With every breath

---

[68]Sadhana: Spiritual practice

[69]Kriya: technique or practice within a yoga discipline meant to achieve a specific result

he exhaled, the serpent, coiled before him with its hood raised, hissed in response. It never harmed him. When he finished his practice, the cobra simply disappeared."

Shambhavi listened intently. "I had heard about the visit of the snake but never knew this detail. Perhaps Maharaj never shared it with anyone except you."

They drove on in silence.

"Shambhavi, you seem quiet today. Is something the matter?"

"No, Dada, all is well."

"But you are so silent."

"This may sound weird, but to tell you the truth, you somehow seem aloof and unreachable in your robes. It creates a barrier between you and the average person."

"So you prefer me in that hideous green hospital gown?" Shaman laughed.

"No way, Dada! I prefer you in the saffron *dhoti* any day."

Shaman dozed off. When he woke, Shambhavi was singing *naam* softly as she drove. He looked out. A stunning view of the majestic Himalayas greeted him, lifting his spirits.

"Dada, you're awake. We are just 30 minutes from the *ashram*. How is your leg?"

"Sorry I fell asleep. My leg seems good."

"Don't apologise. You are recovering from a life-threatening trauma. You need all the rest you can get."

They passed a small Krishna temple. Shaman saw Shambhavi do *pranaam*. "Do you want to stop?" he asked.

"No, Baba is waiting for you. He asked me to call him before we left. I'm sure he's watching the clock for your arrival."

"Shambhavi, I have something I want to read to you." Shaman

fished out a paper from his bag and read out a beautiful verse in praise of Krishna.

"Exquisite! It flows, like the waters of a stream," she said.

"Glad you liked it…"

"Liked it? I loved it! Whoever wrote it is a genius. Besides, the word *shambhavi* was in that prayer. I felt an instant, personal connect."

"Shambhavi, I composed it for you. You'll be the only one in the entire world who will be using this prayer. Every day, when you say this prayer, the Lord will recognise your voice among millions of other voices. You mentioned yesterday that you are finding it hard to increase your *japa;* that's when I thought of writing this. An intense and exclusive prayer like this will make good for the lack of time to do more."

She stared at him for a moment before saying, "Thank you Dada, it's really very kind of you!"

"You are most welcome. And Shambhavi, thank you for saving my life."

She smiled as they entered the *ashram* gates.

23.

An unusual silence greeted Shaman as he entered the *ashram*. Ascending the front steps, the first thing he noticed was the empty *pandal*[70] where the Devi must have been worshipped. It was full of lotus flowers, hibiscus and marigolds, the plates of fresh fruit offerings still there. The incense sticks were nearly stubs, but their fragrance still wafted around. He heard faint sounds of *naam* being sung and the distant blowing of a conch. He climbed the steps as fast as his injured leg would allow.

There, he saw all the *ashramites* carry Ma Durga down for her *visarjan*[71]. He wanted to run down the steps and have Her *darshan*, but knew he could not. Incapacitated, he just sat on the steps, looking longingly at the goddess being carried away in a procession. 'If only I could catch a glimpse of Her beautiful face,' he thought. He knew that even if he called out, they would not be able to hear him over the conch, the *naam* and the drumbeats, not to mention the loud fire crackers.

Shambhavi came to his side, having parked the car. "Here you are! I was looking for you inside."

"Ma is going, Shambhavi," he said softly, his eyes following the procession greedily. "This year I have not seen the face of a single Devi," he said in a whisper.

"Wait, Dada…"

Shambhavi nimbly ran down the steep steps. Soon, she reached

---

[70]Pandal: a fabricated structure, either temporary or permanent, that is used in a religious event such as a wedding or a festival.

[71]Visarjan: Immersion of the consecrated and worshipped idol into the water to symbolise going back the element

the procession and made them turn the majestic idol of Ma Durga so Shaman could have a perfect *darshan*.

The mother was clad in a blazing red sari; she sat on a huge lion and her trident pierced the chest of a dark curly-haired *asura* who had fallen to his knees. The sound of the loud crackers and frenzied drumbeats ceased; only the sound of mellifluous *naam* and the conch remained. As soon as he saw the face of the Devi, Shaman fell to his knees. Tears rolled down his cheeks. So great was his longing for her *darshan* that he felt she was close enough to touch. He prayed, willing away the tears blurring his vision of the Mother.

Some time passed before he realised the *sannyasis* were waiting for his signal to continue the *visarjan*. He gestured to them with a deep bow that he was done. The firecrackers and drumbeats resumed. He turned away from the river, not wanting to see the immersion.

Facing the *ashram*, he saw Maharaj had witnessed the entire exchange from his window. Maharaj smiled at Shaman. The young *sannyasi* lifted both hands above his head and did a *pranaam*. He wanted to touch the Master's feet with no further delay and dragged himself to his chambers despite the increasing pain in his leg.

When he reached the Master's room, his leg was burning with pain, but he paid no heed to it. "Maharaj, please bless me," he said, falling at the Master's feet.

The Master caught his shoulders. "Don't do *shaastaang pranaam*; your leg will hurt more. "Come, sit on the chair."

Shaman was moved by his words but shook his head. "Maharaj, I cannot sit on a chair in front of you."

"Then sit on that small stool."

Shaman sat down on the stool and tearfully touched his forehead to the lotus feet of his *guru*.

"Show me your leg..."

Shaman's leg was swollen and bluish.

"It's *praarabdha*... God saved you."

"With your grace, Shambhavi saved me, Maharaj."

"Yes, you owe your life to her. Our entire *sampradaya*[72] is deeply indebted to her for saving you."

"She looked after me like a parent takes care of a child."

"Shambhavi is a very caring girl. I am glad she was there with you. I am happy to see you unharmed and back in Nagaprayag with me."

"Maharaj, I too, am happy to be back. But this year I did not observe the *navaratri* fast. I didn't pray or undertake the *Durga saptashati* recitation. In fact, I didn't even see Devi properly. These things are really distressing me from within."

"These are all external things, Shaman... You know that. The Mother is inside you, as discernible as the idol that was installed. She is in your mind, in your heart, and in every cell of your being. That is why even when your life force was ebbing away, you called to Her. Very few people can do that... I'd go to the extent of saying the entire purpose of *sadhana* is to be able to do just that – to remember God continually."

Maharaj paused for a moment before saying, "Shambhavi told me how, when you were delirious with pain, and even when you were semi-conscious, you still chanted the names of the Divine Mother. You are imbued with Ma Durga, Shaman. What more do you want? You are truly blessed."

"It's all your grace, Maharaj. Bless me that I will always be able to pray in all circumstances."

---

[72]Sampradaya: An Order, a tradition or a religious system. It relates to a succession of masters and disciples, which serves as a spiritual channel.

Once he had received the Master's blessing, Shaman slowly made his way down. His leg throbbed with excruciating pain. He sat down on the temple steps to rest before continuing to his room.

In due course, the *ashramites* returned from the *visarjan*. The pink *gulaal* powder smeared on their bodies made them almost indistinguishable. It was an amusing sight.

'Shaman Dada! *Jai Guru*!' they shouted in unison.

"We thought you would be resting," said Krishna Da.

They ran to him. Shambhavi warned them about his injured leg, and they immediately quietened and sat down around him.

"Show us your leg, Dada," said Venu Da.

As soon as Shaman did, there was a collective sigh.

"It's so swollen and blue!" said Leela in amazement.

"This is nothing. It was double the size when he was admitted," Shambhavi told her.

"We missed you a lot, Dada. Even Didi was not here. Every year, you recite the *Durga Saptashati,* tell us stories of the Mother, and come with us for the *visarjan*. It felt so empty without you," Keshava Da said, feeling emotional.

'Yes, yes, yes ...' everyone echoed.

"Thank God, you are all right. Many people die from cobra bites," Partha, the *pundit*, said with a shudder.

"Maharaj made me call the hospital every hour throughout the time that you were unconscious," Keshava Da disclosed. "We had never seen the Master so agitated. When Didi called to say you had regained consciousness, Maharaj made a *mala* with his own hands and garlanded Ma Gayatri."

"*Jai Guru*!" Shaman's eyes were moist. He felt overwhelmed.

'What good deeds I must have done in my previous life to get such love and blessings from the great Guru,' he thought gratefully.

"Do you all know that Shambhavi caught a King Cobra?" he asked to lighten the atmosphere.

"Yes, Maharaj told us," Chandni replied.

"But that we can easily believe," Leela added. "You should have seen the way she chased those wild dogs away when they were attacking the baby deer."

"Didi is not scared of anything," stated Chandni proudly.

"Well, I think you're right about that," Shaman laughed.

"Shaman Da, it's time for your medication," Shambhavi cut in. "I will get them; they are in my bag."

As Shaman struggled to stand up, Shambhavi immediately said, "Madhav Da, please help Shaman Da to his room and then come down to take the medicines from me."

"I will send the food to your room, Dada. You just rest and get well soon," Venu Da added.

"*Jai Guru*," said Shaman and slowly hobbled towards his room, holding onto Madhav Da's shoulder. He was deeply touched by the simple warmth and affection of the *ashramites*.

24.

It was late in the evening. Shaman sat in the Master's chambers, busy writing the monthly accounts of the *ashram*. He looked up to inform the Master that he needed to go to the bank the next day, but Maharaj was lost in meditation.

Shaman waited. He had completely recovered from the snake bite. He was happy he could once again perform his morning prayers at the Prayag. He felt healthy and strong.

Krishna Da stepped into the room saying, "Maharaj, Ramdas, the priest from the Shiva temple, has come to see you. I told him it's late, and to come tomorrow, but he said it's extremely urgent and that he must see you now."

The Master opened his eyes and nodded.

The priest was a tall man in his late thirties, wrapped in a brown shawl. Deep worry lines were etched on his forehead. His black eyes had sunken into his face and he looked unwell.

"*Pranaam*, Maharaj," he said in a soft voice, seeking the Master's blessings. He greeted Shaman as well.

"How are you, Ramdas?"

"Not good, Maharaj," he sighed.

There was silence. Maharaj didn't press him, giving him time to open up.

Ramdas collected his thoughts and said, "It's about my daughter Munni. She is acting strange. I don't know what to make of her behaviour." Ramdas' eyes filled with tears.

"What has happened?" asked the Master.

"Maharaj, let me tell you from the beginning." He took a deep breath. "About two months ago, she went on a school trip to a place near Mussoorie… I am unable to recollect the exact name of the place. When she returned, she had high fever for about three days. She was afraid of everything; she refused to go to school; didn't even want to go to the bathroom on her own. My mistake! I should have realised something was wrong, but I didn't take it seriously.

I thought she would get over it, but she didn't. In fact, that unnatural fear grew into frightening proportions. She refused to bathe and she woke up at all odd times. The worst was that she began inflicting cuts on herself. I hid the knives and scissors, anything that was sharp. But she would scratch herself and talk gibberish. She would even shout and howl loudly.

Fearing the neighbours would hear, I locked her in the room behind the cowshed. These days I take food to her there. I have been telling everyone that she has a fever and is unwell. Today, when I went to the room, she had thrown food everywhere. When I reprimanded her, she grasped my neck and pinned me to the wall in a second. I couldn't wriggle out of her grasp! I was breathless, but she wouldn't let go. I really thought I would die. By the grace of Mahadeva, she let go as suddenly as she had caught me.

I came straight here. I am afraid, Maharaj! I cannot go back there. She is a thin girl, but she held me like a strong man, with just her left hand! It's impossible to imagine the strength she had. It was not her, it was not her…"

"How old is your daughter?" asked Maharaj.

"She will be fourteen soon. Maharaj, it was you who named her Mandakini. You may have forgotten that my wife Shalini died while giving birth to this child. She used to come to your *ashram* regularly. When Shalini died, everyone in the village said the newborn girl was unlucky because she had killed her mother. I would have abandoned her had you not said she was pure like Mandakini."

"Yes, I recollect now."

"What is wrong with the child, Maharaj? I am scared!" Tears flowed down Ramdas' cheeks.

"Whatever is wrong with her can be fixed. Do not worry. Shaman Dada will do the needful," Maharaj said.

"Thank you, Maharaj, but I am not going to my house tonight. Please let me stay in the *ashram*."

"Return home," the Master said. "You will be fine. Your daughter cannot be left alone. She is your child."

Shaman spoke up. "Ramdasji, I will come to your house the day after tomorrow, at the crack of dawn. Please arrange for pure *ghee* and mango sticks—that's all. Where is your house?"

"Right next to the bridge that leads to the *sangam*, Dada."

25.

Two days later, Shaman went to Ramdas' house, a little before 4 am. Ramdas was waiting for him at the door. He bent down to touch Shaman's feet and then, without a word, led him to the small room behind the cowshed where a brown cow munched peacefully on grass.

The room itself was nondescript. But for the dank smell, there was nothing to suggest anything unusual. The girl was asleep on a cot. Shaman studied the girl closely. She was pretty and slim, on the cusp of womanhood. She lay on her back with her hands on her stomach. She appeared tall for her age. A mass of soft curling brown hair framed her face. She wasn't fair like the hill girls, but had a smooth complexion, marred only by the raw self-inflicted cuts on her forehead and cheeks. One cut was dangerously close to her left eye, Shaman noticed. A thin bedsheet covered her. What was strange was that though the girl was sleeping, her body appeared rigid.

Shaman opened the window and looked out. He calculated the north-eastern corner of the room and drew a *Shri Yantra* with rice powder.

"Let the window be open," he told Ramdas when he saw him move to shut it again.

He arranged the mango sticks in the *havan kund*[73] and lit the fire. It was nearly 4 am. Shaman spread his *asana* and was about to do his *japa* when, with a loud wail, the girl stood up on the bed,

---

[73]Havan Kund: A sacrificial pit made of clay or metal used to make the ritual fire

staring at him angrily. Her clothes were in tatters and her hair swayed in the breeze coming from the open window.

Ramdas shouted in fear and almost tripped over his own feet trying to run away. He was shaking with terror. The girl looked right into Shaman's eyes, staring with sultry allure.

"Ramdasji, go out and lock the door. When I knock, open it."

Ramdas was relieved to leave. He rushed out, locking the door firmly from the outside.

The girl jumped in front of Shaman, landing on all fours, muttering gibberish. There was something ominous about her. Shaman closed his eyes and began his *japa,* concentrating his energies between his eyes. Soon the gibberish, moaning and wailing faded and Shaman was lost in meditation.

He lost track of time, focussed on the white energy the syllables of the *mantra* unleashed within him. After what seemed like many hours, he felt a damp smelly whiff of air pass his face and go towards the open window. He waited for a few minutes before he opened his eyes.

The *havan*[74] was just embers now and it was bright day outside. The girl slept peacefully, curled on her side on the bed. Shaman covered her with the sheet and knocked on the door.

Ramdas opened it, trembling with fear.

"It's over. Mandakini is sleeping. When she wakes, she will be fine."

Ramdas entered with trepidation. When he saw his daughter peacefully asleep, he fell at Shaman's feet. "You saved her!"

"It's the grace of Maharaj, Ramdasji," answered Shaman. He checked his watch: 11 am.

"Dada, you have been in here for more than a day… Nearly 30 hours," Ramdas told him.

---

[74]Havan: a ritual burning of offerings such as grains and ghee

It had seemed like three hours to Shaman. He felt no fatigue, thirst or hunger. He did a *saashtaang dandavat pranaam* to Maharaj mentally. It was all his grace.

"Have everything in this room burnt. Every little thing," he told Ramdas. "And another thing… Mandakini is such a beautiful name, given by an evolved *satguru*. Call her by that name. Great power comes to our children when we call them by such powerful names."

"I will, Dada."

As Shaman walked out, he was greeted by a large gathering of villagers. They were waiting patiently, sitting cross-legged or on their haunches. When they saw him, they immediately stood up.

"It's all over." Ramdas told them, his voice trembling with emotion. "Shaman Da has set my daughter free."

26.

"Swamiji, we were anxious when you did not come out for so many hours," the village Head told Shaman.

"You were in there for more than a day," Chandni's husband, Balvir, said.

"This Ramdas is so secretive, he didn't tell us anything! He only said that he was worried something had happened to you," said the Lala who ran the town's biggest grocery store, looking at Ramdas in contempt.

The priest was silent, his head hung low.

"We want him to leave this town with his daughter," said an old woman. "Who wants a *pujari*[75] like this? People will lose faith in the Lord himself!"

"I think Ramdas did not want all of you to get worried, that's why he didn't tell you," replied Shaman in a measured tone.

"He wanted to hide it, Dada! He is guilty. I am sure he has done something to incur the wrath of Lord Shiva, that's why he is being punished," said the wife of the village Head.

"Do not blame him, please. These things happen by chance. They can happen to anyone," Shaman told the agitated villagers.

Another woman asked, "Why would these evil things come into homes where prayer is done regularly? There must be something Ramdas has done wrong. His prayer should have protected him and his daughter."

"Our prayer is like a wall. Let me explain," Shaman said.

---

[75]Pujari: Officiating priest for Hindu ceremonies

Someone brought him a chair to sit on. Taking his seat, he began, "Every lamp that is lit around the house works like a three feet compound wall. But a thief can easily scale that wall. If you sing *naam* for an hour every day, it's like having a six feet wall that is difficult to scale, but not impossible for a determined thief. So our prayers protect us, but sometimes the difficulties that come our way are so formidable that ordinary prayers cannot tackle them. So don't be quick to find fault with Ramdasji. He has been through a lot. It is your duty to be empathetic towards him."

There was silence. The mood of the crowd had changed.

"Do these evil spirits really exist? What do they want with us?" asked the village Head.

"What should we do to protect ourselves?" Balvir asked.

"Yes, evil spirits do exist. The evil is in a *tamasic*, a dark condition. The same thing becomes good when it comes under the sway of *sattva* or light," Shaman explained.

"But Swamiji, I am asking about ghosts... Do they exist?" the village Head asked again.

"Yes, ghosts do exist. There are several words for these beings. The life-force escapes this gross physical body and takes up another birth in another gross body. It's like discarding old clothes and wearing new ones. But sometimes, due to excessive sin or unnatural death such as suicide, the life force does not get a new body to continue its journey. It hangs around, like vapour. It is a being with a mind, ego and intelligence; it just doesn't have a body."

"You are saying ghosts exist but nobody really sees them?" Lala asked.

"You do not see the breeze or vapours, but does it mean they do not exist?" Shaman asked. "Ghosts too, exist but we can't see them. They are beings that are stuck with desires they cannot fulfil because to fulfil any desire, you need a body. So this disembodied mass of unfulfilled desires is in anguish, like a frustrated animal in a cage. Some people can feel its unnerving presence."

"Yes, some places seem so creepy," the *dhobi's*[76] daughter remarked, shivering.

"Have you ever been in the same space as an extremely angry person?" Shaman asked. "Even if that person doesn't speak a word, the rage in him somehow makes you deeply uncomfortable. His very presence unsettles you. It's the same with the presence of a ghost; just that its negative energy is a million times stronger."

"Swamiji, you have explained it so well. Can you tell us how we can tackle these ghosts?" the Krishna temple *pundit* asked.

"Vedic religion has made provisions. *Shraddha*[77] ceremonies, *tarpan* and *pinda* oblations for the dead, etc., all help these spirits. Of course, the all-powerful vibration of *naam* can hunt down any haunting thing. But the most important remedy is the presence of holy men; this can diffuse the ghost-state and help the trapped *jiva* resume its journey," Shaman clarified.

"Swamiji, last year, the ironsmith Lakshman died by suicide; he hanged himself. Can he be saved?" asked the Lala's mother. "He had such a terrible life. Sometimes we wondered if suicide was actually a good thing for him, to be free of all his woes."

"Lakshman can be saved. But it is foolish of you to speak of suicide as a good thing. Just because the body is gone, do you think the trouble has ended? They have not. There is no escape—our *karma* and our life are inescapable. We must face it and get through. Besides, the pain of suicide does not subside… It increases," Shaman remarked sombrely.

---

[76]Dhobi: Washer-woman

[77]Shraddha: Shraddha, tarpan and pinda are ceremonies performed in honour of dead ancestors

"Increases? How?" Balvir asked, surprised.

"It's like this. At the time of suicide, you go through physical and mental pain. Death impressions are powerful, particularly those of suicide. Once you are dead and become a ghost, the same pain comes to you again and again. If you have allowed yourself to be run over by a train, thinking it will all be over in one shot and you will be free, you are sadly mistaken. Thereafter, every day, at the same time, the same train goes over you; you feel the same pain a million times and you can't do anything about it."

'Oh my God! That's horrible!' a group of women exclaimed.

"Suicide is worse than horrible. There is no greater offence than self-destruction. Human life is *very* precious. You earn this human body after working hard for several lives. But with suicide, the work of many lifetimes is ruined in one moment, with just one reckless act. The road to evolution is blocked and you are truly doomed," he warned.

The crowd was stunned into pensive silence.

"Swamiji, you have told us something new today. We did not know suicide was such a bad thing. We will tell everyone in the village," the village Head said, joining his hands.

Just then, Keshava Da came running. "Dada, you have come out! We were all so worried. Chandni was waiting here; she just came to tell us you have come out!"

"I am fine by the grace of our Guru. Don't worry."

Keshava Da turned to the villagers. "Swamiji hasn't eaten or even taken water in the last thirty hours; now let him go…"

"Yes, yes Swamiji. We were so caught up in what you were saying that we didn't realise you must be tired."

Everyone bowed for Shaman's blessings.

~

Shaman bathed in the *sangam* and put on the new *dhoti* Maharaj had sent with Keshava Da.

Ramdas waited till Shaman had finished his bath before saying, "I can't thank you enough. Not only did you save my daughter, you also saved us from getting thrown out of Nagaprayag."

"It's all due to the grace of Naam Yajnananda Maharaj. Please burn this *dhoti* when you burn the rest of things in that room," Shaman said.

Ramdas once again fell at Shaman's feet. "I will bring Mandakini for Maharaj's *darshan* as soon as she wakes." His voice was choked with gratitude.

As they walked to the *ashram*, Keshava Da asked Shaman, "How did you stay in *dhyana*[78] for over 30 hours? The only person who was not worried that you had not returned was Maharaj. Everyone else was most concerned. In fact, Maharaj was also in *dhyana* for most of yesterday, day and night."

Shaman smiled. "That's because he was connected with me through meditation. Without his power, it would not have been possible."

"True, but we are all lucky that Maharaj has found the correct medium in you to channelize his power," said Keshava Da.

"It is just his grace," said Shaman.

---

[78]Dhyana: Meditative trance

27.

The next morning, when he came up from his prayers at the Prayag, Shambhavi asked, "Shaman Da, *pranaam*. How are you doing?"

"*Jai Guru*. I am well."

"You were meditating for 30 hours non-stop. I just cannot get over that. All of us were very worried."

"It takes a whole lot of grace, Shambhavi. Sitting in meditation for that long is near impossible otherwise."

"Shaman Da, before I forget, your friend Teddy Jefferson, called last night to say he is coming to see you today. I was about to come and call you, but Baba said you need your sleep and were not to be disturbed."

"Oh, Teddy is coming? That's great! You will really like him, Shambhavi. He is a witty man, full of anecdotes; an excellent raconteur."

"How do you know him, Dada?

"He used to teach at Harvard. Now he is a well-known documentary film-maker."

Before Shambhavi could reply, the arrival of a car caught their attention. Two men emerged from the cab.

"Madhu Da!" Shambhavi called, waving to Madhusudan.

"You know Madhusudan?" Shaman asked, surprised.

"Yes, for many of his visits to Nagaprayag have coincided with mine."

"I see… Well, Teddy and Madhusudan are close friends."

Both men were in their forties. There the resemblance ended. Teddy was a short man with sharp blue eyes and blonde curls. Though somewhat overweight, he had a charming demeanour. Madhusudan, on the other hand, was well-built and had the fit body of an exceptional yoga practitioner, which in fact, he was.

Madhusudan ran up the steps, his large travel bag casually slung over his shoulder. "*Jai Guru*," he said to Shaman before hugging Shambhavi. "How is my *guru behen*[79] doing?" he asked warmly.

"I am fine, Madhu Da. Why didn't you tell me you were coming?"

"It was a last minute decision." Madhusudan pulled out a large bag from his backpack and presented it to Shambhavi. "This is for you."

"Lindt!" Shambhavi exclaimed, delighted. "My favourite chocolate! Thank you so much!"

"You're welcome. When I spoke to Maharaj, he told me you were here. I know you love these chocolates."

Teddy climbed the steps after he had paid the cabbie and hugged Shaman. "Great to see you, Shaman! You're looking fit and handsome."

"You are looking good too," said Shaman affectionately.

Teddy introduced himself to Shambhavi saying, "Hi, I'm Teddy, and whoever you are, you are a beautiful sight for these sore eyes."

"I am Shambhavi," she laughed.

"May I take the liberty of saying you have the most unusually coloured eyes? People may have told you they are grey. But that doesn't quite capture how unusual that grey is. Have you

[79]Guru behen: A sister co-disciple

studied a candle flame?"

"Seen, yes… Observed, no..."

"The part closest to the wick is a spectacular bluish-grey. Your eyes are exactly that colour. There is a smouldering quality in your eyes that is very rare."

"Thank you, Teddy. That's such a lovely compliment," said Shambhavi. "Now I must observe a flame more closely."

Madhusudan peered at Shambhavi's eyes. "Teddy man, you're right. Sometimes you exaggerate, but this time you are spot on."

Teddy laughed in response.

"I am going to Gangaji for a dip," said Madhusudan. "I'll be back soon. I must have *darshan* of Maharaj as soon as he comes out of his room."

"I'd die if I tried taking a dip in the freezing rapids down there," observed Teddy morosely.

"Come, let me show you to your room," said Shambhavi, pointing in the direction of the *ashram* guest rooms. "You'll get plenty of hot water to shower in the bathroom."

~

After *darshan* with the Master, Teddy wanted to explore the town, so the four of them walked down to the tiny village. They strolled about for over an hour and finally sat outside Cafe Moon Beams, at a table overlooking the Prayag.

Teddy took out a pack of cigarettes and asked Shambhavi's permission before lighting one.

"How is your work going, Teddy?" asked Shaman.

"Very well. I am directing films that I love. My documentary on the boatman of Varanasi gave me a lot of satisfaction."

"I am glad you took the bold decision to pursue your passion full time," observed Shaman.

"I respect you for the same reason," Teddy said. "You gave up a strong academic career to follow the path of being a renunciant; you are truly inspiring. I quote your story to many people; they find it difficult to believe that a Harvard Professor can give it all up in the quest of self-realisation."

"Well, I have done nothing. Just gone along… By the way, how was your documentary received?"

"It received critical acclaim and a few awards. *Gopal on the Ganga* was screened last month at the International Film Festival in Bombay."

"*Gopal on the Ganga*? Now, who is Gopal?"

"A boatman who was of immense help to me. Actually, I wanted to give him some of the prize money. I shot the film on a less-than-a-shoestring budget, but I received funds after it was produced. He helped with the language, getting permissions to shoot on real locations, and in so many other ways. He was a happy, cheerful, chirpy guy; he would cheer me up whenever I was down. In fact, he even shared his food with me many times. I owe him big time. I feel it's only fair to give him some of the money. "

"That's a good idea. Gopal deserves it," said Shaman.

"But the problem is, I don't know his address or full name or anything. I just know him as Gopal. And I'm flying back to New York day after tomorrow; I just don't have the time for it right now. I've requested Madhu to go to Varanasi and give the money to him."

"I'm thinking of leaving for Varanasi the day after as well," Madhusudan said.

"That's good. I too, am going to Varanasi two days later on some work. We can go together if you like," said Shaman.

"Wow, that would be super!" said Teddy. "You are so much more sorted than Madhu and you're from Varanasi. You can speak the lingo. I'm confident the money will reach Gopal."

"Thanks for the vote of confidence," said Madhusudan, dryly. "You were literally dancing when I agreed to go to Varanasi… Never expressed the slightest doubt!"

Shambhavi smiled at their easy camaraderie.

"Teddy, tell Shaman the real reason you are running back to America," Madhusudan said.

Teddy merely grinned, rather embarrassed.

"Tell him! Enough with the dramatic pauses."

"All right… Shaman, do you remember Meera?"

"Meera Iyer? The statistics professor?"

"Yes. I wooed her for many years. She finally agreed to marry me. She wants me to meet her parents this weekend."

"That's fantastic!" said Shambhavi. "Congratulations!"

Shaman started laughing. "Congrats man! Finally, the eternal bachelor is getting married! But really Teddy, you fell for someone younger than you by more than a decade?"

Madhusudan joined in the laughter at Teddy's expense. "Cradle snatching," he hooted.

Teddy blushed a fiery red. "Hey guys, yes it's embarrassing, but it just happened."

"I think love can happen to anyone, with anyone," said Shambhavi. "I don't think there's a template for falling in love."

"Well said, Shambhavi," Teddy cheered.

"Actually, you do have a point there. One cannot determine these things," Shaman observed.

28.

The weather in Varanasi was starkly different from Nagaprayag. At 6 am, the sun was already a dazzling red jewel in the sky. Shaman and Madhusudan had finished their morning *japa* and yoga. They sat at the *ashram ghaat* and watched the Ganga flow by, the boats plying on the river full of tourists.

Madhusudan broke the silence. "Shaman, it's been four days and we've pretty much spoken to every boatman at all the *ghaats*. We've checked the names of all the boatmen from their association, but we seem to have hit a dead end. It's incredibly frustrating. No one has even heard of Gopal!"

Shaman nodded in agreement. "It will be Diwali in two days and tourists are already swarming in by the thousands. Everyone is insanely busy and no one has the time or inclination to help locate this guy."

"True."

"I wish my grandfather was around. He knows so many of these local folk. He could have really helped us," Shaman said wistfully.

"When is he back?"

"He went to visit my parents in Boston just last week, so I guess he'll be gone for at least a month or so."

"Just bad timing…" Madhusudan sighed, shaking his head.

"Let's try once more."

They walked along the *ghaat*. Even though it was still early, the sun was strong. People were already thronging the markets to do their Diwali shopping.

As they approached a cluster of boats, a boatman cleaning his boat asked if they had found Gopal. They replied in the negative and walked on.

They saw the priest of the small Kali temple taking a bath in the river. He greeted Shaman. "Ram Ram… You're still here? You didn't find the boatman you were looking for?"

"He seems to have just disappeared," Shaman replied.

"You will find him when the time is right," the priest assured them. He turned away and started taking dips in the Ganga.

As they walked on, Madhusudan said, "Shaman, now people are asking us if *we* have found Gopal. There are no more people left for us to ask! How ridiculous is that!"

All along the *ghaat*, everyone asked them the same question: 'Did you find Gopal the boatman?'

They sat in the shade of a towering peepul tree outside a bustling *anna kshetra*[80] that was frequented by boatmen. 'Do you know a boatman called Gopal, who helped a foreigner shoot a film?' they asked again and again. No one had heard of Gopal, though several boatmen had helped foreigners with their films. Madhusudan was clearly frustrated. He cursed Teddy for sending them on a wild goose chase.

Shaman said his afternoon prayers sitting still amidst all the hustle and bustle. After his prayers he said, "Let's ask Teddy to fax a picture of Gopal, then start our search again, armed with the photo."

"Brilliant idea," agreed Madhusudan.

They returned to the *ashram*.

---

[80]Anna kshetra: Community kitchen distributing free food to travellers, pilgrims and renunciants.

That night, after talking to Teddy, they printed out a photograph of Gopal at the STD centre. It was a picture of a man in his late twenties. He was of medium height, fair, with a smiling face and bright eyes.

"It's too late to take the picture around for identification. Let's do it first thing in the morning," Shaman suggested.

"Yes, it's almost 11 pm. Teddy takes too long to do anything!"

"It's also the time difference. We have to be patient, Madhusudan."

It was Diwali the next day. Shaman woke at 3 am and performed his prayers. He deeply missed the Nagaprayaga *ashram*. By 7 am, they set out with Gopal's photograph. They approached the cluster of boats at the *ghaat*. The boatmen moved away as soon as they spotted the two men.

"Shaman, this is most embarrassing. They are avoiding us," said Madhusudan.

But Shaman only laughed. "Yes, they are. This is hilarious."

They went to the Boatmen's Association, but it was shut.

"Do you think they heard we were coming and shut the office?" Madhusudan wondered.

Shaman laughed again. "No, it's shut because of Diwali. Today is a holiday."

They returned to the *ghaat* where the boatmen were plying their business. No one wanted to look at the photograph or stop to talk. Everyone had had enough of them.

Dejected, they sat outside a *lassi* shop. They noticed an unkempt beggar staring at them.

"He looks like a drug addict. He has a wild look about him," Madhusudan commented warily.

Shaman gestured for the beggar to approach.

Madhusudan freaked out. "Are you crazy? He looks like he would stab us for a few bucks!"

Shaman showed the photograph to the beggar. "I want this man. Do you know where he is?"

"He is Kishenlal," the beggar mumbled.

"No, he is Gopal," said Madhusudan.

"Will you take us to him? I will give you 500 rupees," Shaman said, offering an enticement.

The beggar instantly agreed.

"But Shaman, he says the guy is some Kishenlal, and we need Gopal. You are wasting your time and money."

"Shh… Let's go and see," said Shaman.

The beggar had a bad limp, making their progress slow. They followed him for nearly two hours to the outskirts of Varanasi.

"This is not looking good to me at all. I think this guy is going to kill us…" Madhusudan whispered.

"Hang on," counselled Shaman.

Another half hour later, they arrived at a large, abandoned cement pipe. The beggar pointed inside. They could see a dark human shape in the darkness.

"Kishenlal," the beggar said simply and held out his hand.

Shaman gave him the money and the beggar limped away.

"How will we get out of this place? Do you know the way back?" Madhusudan asked apprehensively.

Shaman bent down and called into the pipe, "Gopal..."

The dark shape turned towards them. "Who are you?"

"Are you Gopal?" Shaman asked.

The man inside the pipe said, "I am Kishenlal. Only one mad foreigner called me Gopal. He couldn't pronounce my name, idiotic fellow!"

Shaman breathed a sigh of relief and silently thanked his *guru* for helping him find Gopal.

"Who are you and what do you want?" Kishenlal yelled.

When he emerged into the light, they saw a figure ravaged by time. He looked nothing like the man in the photograph. His eyes were vacuous pits of bottomless darkness. His body had shrunk to just skin and bones. Though it was certainly the same man in the photo, he seemed to have undergone a disastrous transformation.

Madhusudhan and Shaman explained why they had come. Shaman tried to hand him the money.

"I will never touch that money!" Kishenlal exclaimed, vehemently. "I needed money so badly last year. My wife was unwell; I sold my boat to treat her but she didn't survive. And my newborn child died a few a days later." He wept bitterly. "I could not save them... What will I do with that dirty money now? It is of no use to me. When the timing is wrong, even diamonds have the same value as mud. Take your money and buzz off! Just leave me alone."

Shaman tried to persuade him to keep the money.

"You don't get it, do you?!" he yelled. "I have no need for money. Now get out!" He cursed his fate and stormed off.

The two men left with heavy hearts. They walked towards the main road in complete silence.

"What made you ask that beggar, Shaman? He seemed the most unlikely source, but we eventually found Gopal or Kishenlal..." Madhusudan wondered aloud

"Just a feeling; pure instinct, nothing more."

They made their way back to the *ashram* in pensive silence, contemplating the complete devastation of the boatman's life. All of Varanasi was lit with fairy lights and people thronged the streets in new clothes.

For Gopal, however, sunk in misery, it was a dark Diwali. His empty eyes would remain etched in Shaman's memory forever.

29.

As they made their way to the *ashram*, Shaman and Madhusudan passed Manikarnika *ghaat*, jostling their way through the throng of tourists dispersing after the evening *arati*.

Madhusudan noticed several foreign tourists taking pictures and videos of the funeral pyres. "This is the macabre death tourism Benares is famous for, right?"

Shaman was so lost in thought that it took him a second to comprehend what Madhusudan had said. "Macabre death tourism? Wow! How do you guys invent these terms?" he asked. "You see, the West is shit scared of death, so death is macabre to them. But in India, death is nothing, just a breeze. In fact, it is auspicious. The Lord of Death, Yama, is also Lord of Dharma. He is not a bad guy. As for Benares… Well, this city is indeed connected to death, but the truth is it's a death-crossing city, not a death city."

"But I've heard people come here to die," said Madhusudan.

"Isn't that ridiculous?" Shaman responded brusquely.

"Maybe, but it is true. People do go to Benares to die!"

"Well…there's more to it. In the *Mahabharata*, Bhishma tells Yudhishthira, 'Don't let anyone convince you against dying in Kashi (Benares)'…"

"There! He's said *dying* in Benares; that's why people come here to die," stated Madhusudan. "I'm told 300 odd bodies are burnt here every day. And at one of these *ghaats*, there are 10 or 12 bodies burning at any given time."

"See those fires..." Shaman pointed ahead. "The *ghaat* you're talking about is where we are standing right now. It's called Manikarnika *ghaat*. And it is not death that Bhishma is talking about. What he actually means is that by dying in Kashi, as against other places, you will head towards immortality."

"That's interesting. Not death, but immortality! It gives a whole new spin to Benares."

"Exactly! The scriptures say the holy city of Benares will not be destroyed during the *pralaya* or cosmic dissolution of the world. Any departed soul that has its last rites performed in Benares attains *moksha*[81]."

"Wow! I don't mind dying here then!" Madhu said, laughing.

"Wishful thinking. Not everyone is so lucky."

"Can we stop here for a while?"

Shaman nodded. They sat a little away from the *ghaat*, at a height that gave them a view of the activity around them. They could talk without disturbing the mourners.

"This is the world's greatest place for funeral pyres. They say Vishnu dug a well for Shiva and Parvati to bathe in, known as Manikarnika Kund. When Parvati was bathing there, one of her earrings fell into the well. Since then, it has been known as Manikarnika—*mani* refers to the jewel, and *karnam* to the ear."

"*Mani-karnikaa*... What a beautiful name!"

Yogis sat in meditation within a hundred meters of the pyres, where the dead were being consigned to the flames.

"Why do they meditate in cremation grounds?" asked Madhu.

"The cremation ground meditation is a special one," Shaman explained. "You sit for hours on end, contemplating the burning bodies. Death spares none, be they children,

[81]Moksha: liberation from the cycle of birth and death

youngsters, adults, or the old. They are all here and you see their bodies burn right in front of your eyes. One minute it is a human form and then just hot ash. That's life. Slowly, as you keep seeing this, your attachment to the body, and to life itself, leaves you. You become free. A man who is not afraid of death has conquered the greatest fear. Do you see?"

"Oh yes, it's rather profound," acknowledged Madhu, gazing into the distant horizon across the Ganga, through the bellowing smoke of the funeral fires.

It was late and the crowd had dispersed, save for a few local wood sellers and florists who were part of the thriving death business. A biting chill had descended upon the *ghaat*.

Shaman looked to where the *yogis* sat meditating next to the burning bodies. "I want to go and meditate there for some time. You go back to the house," he said, handing Madhu the room keys.

"How long will you be?"

Shaman thought for a moment. "Maybe half an hour; an hour at the most."

"I'll stay in that case," Madhu decided.

Shaman walked down the *ghaat*. As he got closer, the stench of burning human flesh became unbearable. The thick smoke billowing from the pyres stung his eyes. A few *sadhus* sat meditating in perfect stillness, covered in the flying ash.

Shaman sat down on the step nearest the burning corpse. The heat emanating from it was almost intolerable. Shaman regretted not bringing along his *asana* and prayed to Mother Earth to purify the space occupied by him before slipping into meditation.

As he went deeper into his meditation, his mind filtered out the outermost sounds. He could no longer hear the quaint old Hindi song playing on the radio at the *puja*[82] store. Then the chants of *Ram naam satya hai'*[83] and the soft weeping of the bereaved family faded away. Gradually, the harsh sounds of the crackle and hiss of the fire, the stench, and finally the sensation of heat on his skin, also melted away.

Shaman floated in a calm place of nothingness. Suddenly, the nothingness cleared into an image of a long queue of beggars, in tattered clothing, walking towards the most beautiful Goddess sitting on a golden throne, dispensing freshly cooked *kheer*[84] with a ladle from a golden bejewelled pot. She radiated such effulgence that the dark night lit up with her shining glow. She was clad in a scarlet sari and every part of her body was covered in heavy gold ornaments – a crown on her head, bangles and bracelets on her wrists, and necklaces around her neck. Her heavy bangles tinkled melodiously as she poured the *kheer* into the begging bowls. Her entire being was housed in a red orb of light.

Shaman, nearly swooning in the power of his vision, recited the 1000 names of Devi. The beggars, Shaman noticed, came in every possible shape and size. Some were dwarfs, some had misshapen limbs. One's face was hidden. When Shaman looked closely, he saw that it was the hood of a snake. In that second the snake moved; he saw the beggar had the crescent moon tucked into his matted locks. It dawned on him that Lord Shiva was in the queue of beggars.

Shaman's breath caught in his throat. Shiva exuded a deep blue light from every pore of his body. When his turn came to receive *kheer* from the Goddess, both the blue from Shiva's

---

[82]Puja: Ceremonies and ritual of daily worship in Hinduism

[83]Ram Naam Satya Hai: a chant uttered by one person and repeated by all those carrying a dead body on a bier. It means that in this world, where everything is born to die, only the name of Ram is to stay.

[84]Kheer: a rice pudding made by boiling rice, broken wheat, tapioca, or vermicelli with milk and sugar; it is flavoured with cardamom, raisins, saffron, cashews, pistachios or almonds. Typically served during a meal or as a dessert.

body and the red from the Devi, merged and burst into a spectacular shower of golden spangles.

Shaman was jolted out of his trance. The view of Manikarnika *ghaat* blurred before him for a few seconds. Remnants of the golden spangles floated like lazy tendrils in the periphery of his vision. Slowly, everything returned to the sharpness of everyday reality. 'What a vision!' he thought to himself.

Collecting his bag, he looked around. The *sadhus* sitting nearby were now talking animatedly. When they saw Shaman, one of them asked, "Did you also get the strong smell of freshly made *kheer*?"

"*Kheer*?" Shaman asked confused. Then he realised that his vision had been so powerful that it had spilt from the realm of super-consciousness into tangible reality. The enormity of Shiva and Annapurna having granted him a glimpse of their celestial selves hit him like a sledgehammer. He was overwhelmed by the scale of his experience.

Like a man possessed, he ran to the Annapurna Temple nearby, crying uncontrollably. But the temple was closed for the night. He fell on the ground and there, at the gates of the temple, wept boundless tears of gratitude.

'O Mother, what did I do to receive your divine vision?'

Madhusudan found him still lying there several hours later.

30.

The slow taxi ride to Nagaprayag exhausted Shaman. The thick mist rendered commuters nearly blind. Although the cab driver was experienced, navigating the treacherous roads was a nerve-wracking experience.

Shaman could not relax; the image of the frighteningly empty eyes of Gopal refused to leave his consciousness. He had a clear understanding of *praarabdha*, the karmic roll-out of destiny, but the dark hopelessness of the boatman's face filled him with a sense of inexplicable bleakness.

When he finally reached Nagaprayag, he paid the cabbie, took his duffle bag and headed towards the *sangam*. It was so much colder than in Varanasi. He took a deep breath and lifted his head to see the towering snow-capped mountains standing like sentinels all around. The clean pristine mountain air was refreshing. The sight of the water jumping and frolicking across the massive rocks lifted his spirits immediately. He prostrated himelf before Ganga and felt blessed when a random icy spray fell upon him.

'Alakananda and Mandakini – the two forms of Ganga. How beautiful they look,' he thought, admiring the twisting rivers.

Ma Ganga appeared so different in different places. Though he had seen the river every day in Varanasi, this Ganga felt different. Maharaj had once told him that even in the same town, Ganga had a different feel from *ghaat* to *ghaat*.

It was past 2:30 in the afternoon. He slowly climbed up the steep stone steps that led towards the *ashram*. When he was halfway up, he heard Shambhavi's clear voice counting, "... 5,

6, 7, 8...."

As he walked on, he heard the strains of a song, though he could not make out the lyrics. From the muffled sounds, he understood she was teaching someone to dance. Who was it, he wondered... Chandni or Leela perhaps? An image of Laurel and Hardy popped into his mind and he smiled in amusement. Could it be their motley bunch of *sannyasis*? He couldn't imagine any of them in a dance pose; Shaman laughed aloud at the mere thought. It was the first genuine laughter he had experienced in days.

He wondered what had changed in just 15 minutes. It was nothing but the perspective and lens with which one viewed the same world. The world hadn't changed, only his attitude.

Soon he could clearly hear the song: *Aaadha hai chandramaa raat aadhi*... He knew it was from the famous film, *Navarang*. He genuinely couldn't imagine the inmates of the *ashram* swaying to this classic song and could hardly wait to see what was happening. But instead of following his impulse to run up the last few steps, he climbed slowly and stealthily, wanting to glimpse the action without disturbing them.

To his surprise, he found Shambhavi teaching a group of young schoolgirls, no more than 7 years of age. They were in yellow and brown school uniforms while Shambhavi wore a pair of jeans and a soft navy blue sweater. Shaman was quite impressedwith the skill with which they performed. No one noticed him.

"Sarita, don't stop if you miss a beat or make a mistake. Only you know you have missed something, the audience does not. Just continue from the next beat," Shambhavi instructed. She walked between the dancing girls, correcting their postures as she went.

"Girls, always smile at the audience. Unless we are telling a sad story, I want to see a bright smile on your face. And are we telling a sad story?" she asked.

'No…' they chorused.

"So let's take it from the beginning again. Leela, music!"

Once again the song began to play. They were seven children in all. One stood in the centre while the remaining six danced around her. They danced with grace, in perfect sync with each other. When Shambhavi twirled around to show them how it was done, she saw Shaman.

"Shaman Da! When did you come?" She rushed to him swiftly and took his blessing. Genuine happiness radiated in her eyes.

All the kids came running too, for his blessings. After the ghost-busting incident, everyone in the village knew Shaman, better known as Swami Sharanananda.

The youngest child asked, "Swamiji, you saw us dancing?" She looked adorable with her two front teeth missing.

"Yes I did. You were standing in the centre."

"Yes…" the girl giggled, happy to have been noticed.

"Okay girls, take a five-minute break," Shambhavi said. "Drink some water and rest." She turned towards Shaman. "How are you, Dada? You look tired. Do you want something to eat?"

Shaman sat down on the steps. "I was tired, but the sight of these dancing girls has instantly refreshed me. I just want to see Maharaj before I unpack. Is he resting?"

"Yes, but I think he should be awake in another hour or so."

Leela switched off the music and did *pranaam* to Shaman. Shambhavi told her to bring some fruit. "There is an apple and an orange that I offered as *prasad* at the temple. Please cut them. Or shall I send it to your room, Shaman Da?"

"Actually I'm not hungry," Shaman said.

"But its *prasad*; you cannot refuse," Shambhavi insisted.

While Leela went to get him the fruit, Shambhavi said to Shaman, "It was so boring without you in the *ashram*. I missed you, Da. Glad you're back."

"I'm glad to be back too. Did I miss anything?" Shaman asked casually.

"A Canadian couple, Robert and Lisa, arrived yesterday and spent a lot of time with Maharaj. They have gone to the town and nearby temples for some sightseeing today. They regretted missing you. They said they had met you at the Peabody Museum of Archaeology & Ethnology, at a Harvard Conference."

"Yes, they're a very nice couple."

"I forgot to ask you… Did you find Gopal?"

"Yes, but he was not interested in taking the money." Shaman narrated the details of his meeting with Gopal.

"How unfortunate! Such loss! And yes, timing is so important," Shambhavi replied reflectively.

"I thought you taught only *kuchipudi*," Shaman said, changing the topic.

"At the institute yes, but it would take years of dedicated, full-time practice before these children would be ready for a stage performance. But they can easily learn a semi-classical dance in two weeks. They are to perform at their school's Annual Day. Given their tender age and the school hours, I thought this would be a lot simpler. I'm just focusing on visual appeal."

"Shambhavi, you have trained the girls well. They are dancing with great confidence. I can see you are not only a good choreographer, but a clever one as well," Shaman said admiringly.

"Clever? Why do you say that?"

"You made the weakest dancer stand at the centre as Krishna, with minimum movements reqired."

Shambhavi laughed. "That's a great observation, especially given the fact you watched the dance for only a few minutes! It helps that the weakest dancer is the cutest."

Shaman loved what she was doing. This world seemed like a breath of fresh air after Varanasi. "You have chosen a nice song," he commented.

Shambhavi looked surprised. "You know the song? I thought *sannyasis* did not watch movies."

"I watch classical films and *Navarang* is one of my favourites. I think Sandhya is one of the finest dancers."

"I agree. Do you remember the visual of the song?"

"Yes. It's pretty unforgettable because she dances with seven pots on her head. Now, let me ask you, is that even possible?"

"Yes, Da, it's very much possible. It's a type of *raas* called *bedaa-raas*, performed during *navaratri*. Dalit artists from the city of Rajkot are experts in this dance form. My *guru* told me that Sandhya flew to Rajkot to learn it and that she practiced with the experts there for several weeks before shooting."

"I've learnt something new today, thank you."

"You're most welcome, Da."

The children called out, 'Didi, we are ready.'

"I'm coming," Shambhavi called back, smiling.

"Shambhavi, you are good with kids. You are also patient. It's a pleasure to see you with them," Shaman said.

"Thank you Da, but working with children is easy because they have no egos and they're full of enthusiasm; receptive to anything they are taught. I'm glad you think they are dancing well. Their final performance is day after tomorrow."

Leela arrived with the cut fruit as Shambhavi returned to the children.

"Tomorrow will be the full dress rehearsal at your school hall. Come in your costumes. Get your mothers to come to help you dress," Shambhavi instructed. "Now, get into your starting positions. Leela, music please…"

Shaman watched as he ate the fruit. It was borne upon him yet again that Shambhavi was really good at what she did.

31.

Shaman waited until Krishna Da had left Maharaj's chambers after dinner before knocking on his door. The door was open and Maharaj was sitting on his chair.

"Shaman…what is it?" he asked, pleased to see him. "I thought you would be retiring early today. After the heat of Varanasi, this cold needs acclimatising to."

"Maharaj, I had something important to tell you." Shaman prostrated himself before the Master. "I wanted to share a spiritual experience I had in Varanasi and was waiting for some privacy."

Maharaj motioned for him to sit. "Shambhavi…" he called.

"Baba, I'm almost done, just dusting the last bookshelf," she answered from somewhere within.

"Leave that and come here."

When Shambhavi appeared, Maharaj commanded her to sit. Shaman was surprised. The Master was particular about not sharing spiritual experiences. Yet here he was asking Shambhavi to be present.

Shaman narrated his vision to Maharaj in great detail. The Master did not interrupt him, but sat erect, listening. Even when the narration had ended, the Master continued to sit motionless with his eyes closed. Shambhavi, on the other hand, sat in one corner of the room, tears pouring down her cheeks. She too, did not speak a word.

Finally the Master opened his eyes. "You are greatly blessed!"

he said. You have seen the Divine Mother… Red is the colour of the Mother Goddess… and blue is Shiva's colour. You know that Mother is Fire and Shiva is Earth."

"Yes."

"That's exactly what you saw. The red of Fire and blue of Earth. Shiva and Shakti came together in that spectacular shower of golden spangles."

Maharaj paused and closed his eyes for a moment, and then opened them again. "I want to ask you a question. Did you experience any strong feeling immediately after the vision?"

"I felt exhausted, and for some strange reason, hungry."

"That's exactly what I wanted to know. It's not strange for a child to feel hungry when his mother is around, especially Annapurna," the Master said.

"I never connected the two…"

"Annapurna inflamed the navel. It's the place of fire. And fire is wherever food is, in the kitchen, in the human body."

"This is so enlightening."

The Master spoke no more and went into meditation. Shaman and Shambhavi waited for his eyes to open, but he merely gestured for them to leave.

32.

The next day dawned with only one colour in nature's palette – grey. Heavy clouds hung low, blocking the stunning sight of the snow-capped Himalayas sprawled across the horizon. It was dull, dreary and very cold. The only positive was that it was a still day with not even a hint of breeze. Wind would have made the cold unbearable. There was no rain, but dampness penetrated even the thickest layers of warm clothing.

Shaman decided against going to Prayag. Instead, he prayed in his room. Even at 9 am he needed the lights on to do his chores. It was a dark day. There was no hint of the clouds lifting.

Shaman spotted Shambhavi while on his way to the Master's room. She was wearing a bright yellow fleece jacket, black jeans and black running shoes. A hair band held her long hair in place.

"*Pranaam* Da," she greeted him. "Please pray the weather clears. The poor kids will find it hard to dance in this cold."

"Isn't dancing in the heat more tiring?"

"Heat or cold, it's hard in any extreme condition. In fact, even wind disorients the performer if it's an outdoor event. I'll have to make sure they warm up first doing stretches before the rehearsal. I must go to the school now. *Jai Guru*, Dada."

Just then Chandni came running from the kitchen. "Shambhavi Didi! Shambhavi Didi! You have not eaten anything and you are already running off?"

Shambhavi sighed. "Why are you shouting? The entire *ashram* will hear you."

Unperturbed, Chandni said, "At least eat an apple."

Shambhavi finally conceded when Shaman too, urged her to eat first. Chandni marched to the kitchen to fetch the apple.

"Have you taken the car keys?" Shaman asked.

"No."

"That's what I was telling her also. Let's go by car! But Didi wants to go walking," Chandni complained, returning with two apples.

"Dada, I'm not confident about driving in these mountain roads with so much mist. Going by the looks of it, it promises to intensify rather than clear."

Shaman looked around. "Yes, you're right. But you drove me confidently to the hospital."

"Those were extreme circumstances. Besides, it was a crystal clear evening."

"It will take you forever to reach the school on foot," Shaman said, concerned.

"We'll take the short cut through the forest. Chandni will be with me."

"Be careful," Shaman said. "Stay on the walking track. Chandni, take that big stick with you, the one near my door."

Chandni nodded and left to fetch the stick.

"Be careful Shambhavi, and do make some noise when you are in the forest. That way you will not catch any wild animal unawares."

"Chandni will have to fight hard to keep quiet. Even her normal speaking voice is excessively loud."

"Yes, I know it well," Shaman laughed. "Let me know once

you get back. I'll pray the weather clears."

Shambhavi waved as she walked away, Chandni following with a stick that was taller than herself. It was a comical sight. Shambhavi in her bright jacket was the only splash of colour on this dull day, Shaman thought as he watched them walk down towards the forest.

In the Master's room, Lisa and Robert were waiting for him to emerge from his inner chambers. They were both tall, blue-eyed and blonde. They shared a passion for mountaineering and both were amateur fashion photographers. They were dressed in blue jeans and thick black sweaters.

"You guys seem to be in coordinated outfits. Twinning, is it?" Shaman said, smiling.

The couple laughed, saying it was a coincidence. They were very happy to see him.

Robert got up to hug Shaman. "Man, you're growing younger by the day! Not a strand of grey, and you have the body of a man half your age!"

"Must be the result of all the yoga he does," Lisa remarked.

"How do you like Nagaprayag?" Shaman asked.

"It's fantastic. Shambhavi kindly showed us around the *ashram*, Prayag, and the beautiful forest trails."

Robert showed Shaman some of the images he had captured with his large DSLR—majestic peacocks dancing and jungle fowl, deer, elephants, lone and in herds, and a lovely close-up of the feet of Naam Yajnananda Maharaj. Shaman instantly decided to ask for a copy of that. There were several candid pictures of Shambhavi giving dance lessons to the children. The camera had captured her in different poses.

"Where is Shambhavi?" Lisa asked.

"She has gone to the school for a rehearsal," Shaman replied.

"She's a lovely girl," Robert remarked. "Shaman, I'd say she is a rare combination of great beauty, untouched innocence and magnetic sensuality. Add to it the fact that she is extremely photogenic...the camera loves her. You saw her pictures. She photographs beautifully from every angle. She has a face that could launch a thousand brands. I photograph many people, and I can say she is a rare find."

"We spoke to her," Lisa said, "but she's not the least bit interested in modelling, fame or making money. In fact, she's interested in little other than dancing and teaching dance. A truly dedicated artiste."

This new perspective on Shambhavi had Shaman thinking. He had registered that she was stunning, but he had not really qualified her attributes in his mind.

Robert's voice drew Shaman out of his thoughts. "We spent the whole of yesterday with the Master. He thinks very highly of you. Not only does he have great affection for you, he also has great respect. He even said, 'Shaman is my sounding board and a reference book. Devotees of the Order eagerly await his articles and love his writing'."

"It's just the Master's exceptional humility. I am less than the dust under his feet. He is a fully realised soul, so there is no question of my ever being of any assistance to him."

"Shaman, the Master is a fully realised soul, no doubt," Lisa said, "for the aura of transcendental power simply pours forth from his being. But you, as his disciple, have grasped much from him. Look at us. We have come thus far on the spiritual journey thanks only to you and your guidance."

Robert cut in. "We're both truly grateful to you, Shaman. For all the time you have given us, for answering every little spiritual query on the path to self-discovery. You have enormous patience and interest in seekers like us, and we are very lucky to have met you."

"Now you're embarrassing me," Shaman replied. "I do not deserve this. What I have passed on is all from Maharaj. And every little nugget of wisdom I appear to dole out is from the scriptures. Nothing is mine."

"How can you say that?" Robert argued. "Without the intervention of people like you, the words and teachings of *gurus* remain locked secrets. You have kindled our curiosity, rendered and interpreted the ancient truths and legends in a contemporary voice. That's a great job, Shaman. Access is everything in spirituality, and you have given us that."

At that moment, Maharaj emerged from his room and stepped into the *darshan* area. All three immediately prostrated themselves before him.

"Maharaj, we had so many questions regarding the inequalities in human society," Robert began. "Like why some people are rich and some poor; why some good people are maimed while evil people enjoy immense success. You beautifully explained the theory of *karma* to us, giving us a much deeper understanding of human life and clearing so many mysteries."

Robert stopped and bent low before Maharaj. "Master, please convert us to Hinduism."

"Convert you to Hinduism? You are Christian, why do you want to convert?"

"Because I find my answers in Hinduism."

"If you find your answers in Hinduism, it's a good thing, Robert. Even I have found some answers from Jesus Christ, some from Mohammed, some from Buddha. But how does it matter where the answers come from?"

Robert hesitated, then said, "Doesn't it matter? I feel I should belong to the faith I get my answers from."

"Well said, but we do not belong because we get answers. We get answers because we belong. Whatever you belong to, whatever you follow, will give you answers sooner or later. You just have to stay the course."

"Then is it really true that all religions are equal and they can give you answers? To me, it sounds more like a platitude."

"No, it's not a platitude. It is the truth. The roads are many, but they all reach Rome, so to speak. Have you read the *Gita*?"

"Yes."

"It says: *O Partha! Whosoever worships Me through whatsoever path, I verily accept and bless him in that way. Men everywhere follow My path,*" the Master recited.

"Yes, I remember that. It's a universalist attitude."

"God is universal. So it's logical that universal is his only approach."

Robert still had doubts. "But what if the religion you are born into does not serve your best interests?"

"How can that be? Culture and social rites can be limiting, even stifling at times, but the central truth in every religion certainly gives you freedom and solace."

Maharaj paused. "We can change our food, our clothes, our language, our job…" he said, emphasising each thing.

"People change wives, nations, religion too," said Robert imitating him.

"Yes, they do. But how long and how far can you run from your own self? Can you ever outrun your shadow?" The Master was solemn. "Religion is fundamental. It is an aspect of our being. It is not something you can take on or give up."

"Why not?"

"Because religion is not about what you can do, it's about *who you are*. And whoever you are, you will attain the goal. A blind man does not need to attain sight to see God, a lame man does not need feet to walk to God. God is within. To take on some religion to find God is to look for your glasses when you are wearing them."

"Oh, so you're saying God can be found in any religion, automatically."

"No, not automatically," Maharaj corrected him. "You have to follow your own religion to find your own self. There has been a lot of running around to find oneself these days, but just as the bottom of the pond can be seen only when the water becomes still, you can find yourself only when you stop running and stand still."

"So Maharaj, you are saying conversion won't help?"

"Well, if a crow changed its name and started behaving like a dove, does it become a dove?"

"No… I understand. But I have one more question: How does one reconcile the differences in religions?"

"The differences are many and fundamental. Such differences are inevitable."

"What is sauce for the goose is not sauce for the gander?"

"Exactly. Differences will be there. They are part of God's scheme. It is silly to level them."

"So is there no possibility of a merger?"

"Why do you want religions to merge? Why mix things? You merely have to find a meeting point. Like rivers meeting at a confluence, like Nagaprayag. All faiths meet at the core of their teaching. We should all meet there and shake hands with each other."

"I'm sorry, but what about the differences?" Robert persisted.

"Robert, the first and last lesson in spirituality is unity, not difference. All the trouble you are seeing around you is because of your search for difference. Our job is to find a point of *unity* within the prevailing diversity. There, we can meet without losing our distinctiveness."

Grateful for his guidance, Robert gave heartfelt thanks.

33.

Shaman hummed *Hare Krishna naam* as he leisurely trekked through the forest. He yearned for some time alone and with the Master's permission he had left early that morning for a small and isolated mountain lake three hours from the *ashram*. Aware it would be a difficult trek, he had put away his signature cotton bag and packed a lightweight haversack with his *asana*, two bottles of water, a torch, biscuits, and his foldable walking stick. It wasn't much, but he was satisfied.

He knew the mountains around Nagaprayag intimately. Due to his exceptionally fit condition, he accomplished the steep trek with minimal effort. The view of the snowy peaks and little cascades of water were breathtaking. Vast valleys of flowers provided enchanting vistas as he walked along. He sang *naam* the entire way, pausing only to drink water.

Soon, he was at the lake. It was eight in the morning and the magnificence of the scene made him pause and thank God for such beauty. The blue lake's still water mirrored its surroundings. It lay nestled in the hollow palm of the craggy mountains. Unless one knew it existed, it was difficult to come upon by chance. There were absolutely no tourists. Shaman liked the privacy it offered.

He took off his haversack, and splashed some water from the lake onto his face and neck. The water was icy cool on his hot skin. He stood on his toes and lifted his hands high above his head and stretched, turning slowly from side to side, to ease his neck and back of any cricks. Then he sat beside the small lake and meditated.

For hours Shaman sat unmoving, absorbed in the *mantra*. He felt a deep sense of contentment descend upon him. When the angle of the sun changed, he opened his eyes.

He ate a few biscuits and then made his way down. He felt peaceful and rejuvenated after the extended *japa* session. He took his time to return, pausing to admire the work of the greatest artist of all—God.

When he was 45 minutes from the *ashram,* he found Chandni and Shambhavi on a popular trekking trail leading to another lake. He was surprised to see them in such an odd location. They were equally surprised to see him.

'*Pranaam* Shaman Da,' they greeted him in unison.

Shambhavi was wearing a pastel green georgette sari with a delicate white and gold creeper woven into the fabric. She carried a *puja thali* in her hand. Shaman noticed that Chandni was standing awkwardly on one leg.

"What happened?" he asked, bending to take a closer look.

Chandni immediately hopped away in embarrassment.

"She has twisted her ankle," Shambhavi replied. Turning to Chandni, she said in a firm voice, "Show it to Da."

Chandni gingerly lifted the edge of her *salwar* to reveal a swelling near her ankle. Shaman winced; it looked painful. "But where are you both headed?" he asked.

"There is a temple close by. I wanted to go there," Shambhavi said, pointing in the direction of the trail winding upwards.

Shaman knew Chandni would not be able to take even a single step. Considering that she was portly, they wouldn't be able to lift her either. But he did not say this.

Just then, an elderly Gujjar man came riding on a motorcycle. Seeing the large empty fuel cans strapped to the sides of the bike, Shaman knew the man was headed to the village below.

Shaman gestured for him to stop and requested him to give Chandni a ride to the village. Chandni was so short and plump that she needed the help of all three of them to climb onto the bike, but finally the duo set off.

There was a moment's silence after Chandni left, then Shambhavi said. "Dada, I am going to the temple."

"First thing, there is no temple here that I know of. Secondly, you are not going by yourself into the forest."

"Da, there is a temple here that the locals and tribal folk go to. I have visited it several times with Chandni," insisted Shambhavi as she began walking up the path.

"I'll come with you then," Shaman said, deciding to accompany her.

34.

They made their way in companionable silence. The path took them deeper and deeper into the forest. The character of the forest changed as they ascended the steep pathway between pine trees. A thick blanket of dry pine needles covered the forest floor.

"This is not natural vegetation," Shaman observed. "These trees have been planted in afforestation drives. But the pine needles are prone to forest fires."

Even though it was only three in the afternoon, there was an odd hush in the jungle. Their footsteps crackled loudly on the pine needles. The winter rainfall this year had been meagre.

"It's good that you are wearing shoes," Shaman said.

Shambhavi smiled. "It looks a little strange with a sari, but I figured I needed a good grip to walk these steep slopes."

Shaman was a few steps ahead since the pathway was too narrow to accommodate them side by side.

"Take the left next to the big rock," he heard Shambhavi say.

"Here?" Shaman asked, puzzled. "I see no temple."

Shambhavi laughed. "Trust me, Shaman Da."

After another 20-minute climb, they heard the loud rush of water. Within seconds they found themselves standing near a waterfall. It was more than six metres wide, and fell from a rocky overlip 14 metres above.

"Wow!" Shaman exclaimed. "It's beautiful! But where's the temple?" There was a frown on his face.

"Patience, patience…" Shambhavi sang as she walked towards the waterfall.

She found a path by lightly stepping on the exposed stones in the flowing water. She held up her sari pleats in one hand with rare agility, and balanced the *puja thali*[85] in the other as she hopped on the unsteady stones across the water, without getting her shoes wet. Shaman followed on the same stones.

She stopped at the waterfall, bent low and walked in behind the cascading water into a fairly large cave, its entrance hidden behind the curtain of water falling from above.

Shaman was speechless. He had never seen anything like it. The sound of the water was loud in the dark cave. Shambhavi took off her shoes and walked in confidently. Shaman called out to her, "I can't see a damn thing! I can't even see you!"

"Patience, Shaman Da…" Shambhavi said with a laugh. The acoustics of the cave distorted her voice, as though it came from within a deep well.

He walked in slowly and saw a huge carving of Lord Shiva in the *Ardhanareeshwar* form. It had been carved into the wall of the cave, like a beautifully detailed fresco.

Shambhavi knelt and began applying vermillion from her *thali* to its feet. "Now, can you see me? Do you agree now that there is a temple?"

The carving stood about six feet tall. Half of the body was that of Goddess Durga, clad in a sari, while the other half was the Lord, covered in elephant skin. Intricate anklets adorned one ankle while snakes adorned the other. The forehead of one half was marked by the *tripundra*[86] while the other half was decorated with a round *bindi*. By the side of Shiva stood the

[85]Puja thali: a tray or a big container in which all the materials for worship can be kept

[86]Tripundra: a Shaivite mark of three horizontal lines on the forehead, usually with a dot made from sacred ash

bull, Nandi, and by the side of the Mother stood the tiger. The rare beauty of the fresco came from the fact that everything was lifesize. It made the figures come alive. It was a beautiful balance of Shiva and Shakti.

Shaman put down his bag and performed a *saashtaang namaskar*. Then he opened his bag, pulled out his torch, and examined the idol closely. "A master craftsman has carved this," he said as he ran his hands along the surface of the fresco. "It's been done so finely that the fresco has the smooth finish of polished wood," he observed with awe. He also noticed that there were niches in the wall of the cave, which provided an ideal platform for placing *diyas* all around the deity to illuminate it. His academic mind wondered how old the shrine was, and decided to read up on the *Ardhanareeshwar* form of Shiva.

"This cave is open for only a few days in the year when the waterfall shrinks in its flow. Only then can we enter. Only the local people know about it," Shambhavi told him. "See, they know its accessible now." She pointed to the lit earthen lamps and fresh fruit offerings.

"Yes, the villagers have even offered a sari to the Goddess," said Shaman, looking at the red sari placed near the idol. "Do you mind if I do my *japa* here?" he asked. She shook her head.

Shaman completed his *japa* in 15 minutes. He opened his eyes to see Shambhavi arranging the *diyas* and flowers. She tidied up the place quickly and lit the *dhoop*[87] sticks.

"Shall we go?" Shaman suggested, picking up his haversack.

Shambhavi nodded in agreement. She bowed low for the last time, put on her shoes and began to walk out of the cave, trying her best not to get wet in the spray.

They had barely walked for five minutes when they suddenly heard a creak and felt the earth tremble under their feet. Within moments the tremor subsided. They stood rooted to the spot,

[87]Dhoop: an extruded incense that lacks a core bamboo stick.

alert, waiting to see if it was safe to move. Shambhavi looked at Shaman. He gestured for her to wait for him by raising two fingers.

All of a sudden, they heard the sound of a hundred thundering hooves. A large herd of deer came galloping down the mountainside. Shaman and Shambhavi ran in opposite directions to avoid being trampled to death. And before they knew it, a huge chunk of earth came rolling down the hillside with great velocity. The very earth loosened under their feet as they ran from the falling debris. Vast clumps of earth, boulders and trees rushed past them. Enormous clouds of dust made it difficult to see.

When the dust settled, Shaman found Shambhavi standing on the other side, holding onto the roots of a small tree that had been pulled three-fourths out of the earth. They were a good 20 feet from each other and the earth still rumbled with debris. Loose soil fell from everywhere. Once in a while, a large boulder bounced down the steps like a ball. It was scary and horrific.

"Don't move! Just stay where you are," he told her with more confidence than he felt.

Shaman prayed they would be able to get out of this landslide. When he looked at the path that led back to the *ashram,* he realised that it no longer existed. A deep jagged wound ran across the green mountainside.

There was another violent outpouring of rocks and loose earth. Along with it came burning tree branches. Soon, they were surrounded by it as the dry, resinous pine caught fire.

Shambhavi who had been brave during the whole ordeal, now burst into tears. "Shaman Da!" she called. "Please save me! I'm terrified of fire." Her eyes reflected raw terror.

Shaman felt helpless. He could not go to her as long as earth continued to fall all around them. He said in a calm voice,

"These are small fires, they won't harm you. Just hold on. I will come to you, just wait."

No sooner did he utter these words than a big burning branch came tumbling down towards Shambhavi. As if in slow motion, she watched it bump against the boulders, releasing showers of sparks as it tumbled. Unable to bear the horror, she closed her eyes.

The burning tree was very close to her, showering her with hot ash. Shambhavi let out a blood-curdling scream and fainted against the tree she was holding onto. It creaked under her weight. Her burnt sari hung in shreds on her body.

Shaman knew he had to act immediately. Seeing how far the tree was leaning into the gorge below, he calculated that it would be unable to support her weight for more than a few minutes. He needed to move quickly. He tightened the straps of the haversack around his shoulders and ran across the loosened earth to Shambhavi. In one fluid movement, he lifted her into his arms and sprinted back towards the cave.

It was like running on a sand dune with the earth continuously shifting under his feet. He concentrated on getting to the cave. It was five minutes away but it felt much longer. Shambhavi lay like a limp doll in his arms. His muscles strained under the effort of running with her. By the time they reached the cave, he was sweating profusely.

35.

Greatly relieved to reach the cave, Shaman gently laid the unconscious dancer on the ground. Taking out his water bottle, he splashed water on her face.

Shambhavi woke to consciousness and began to cry hysterically. "I'm terrified of fire, Shaman Da!" she sobbed, her slender body shaking with fear.

Shaman hugged her, whispering gently, "You are safe… See, nothing happened to you." He cradled her close to his chest as she continued to cry piteously.

Shaman held her a little away and wiped her tears. "Don't cry, Shambhavi," he urged her, and in an age-old gesture of comfort, kissed her on the forehead.

Shambhavi opened her eyes and looked at him closely. With more instinct than intent, Shambhavi placed her lips on his. It was as if the earth had stopped rotating on its axis. Shaman was swept away by a flood of sensations. For the very first time, he became aware of her supple body pressed tightly against his, the softness of her lips, and her subtle, yet intoxicating, fragrance.

Shaman kissed her with a passion unknown to himself. It was a combustion of burning desire, like a bushfire doused with gasoline. Shambhavi wove her hands tightly around his neck and returned the kiss. His bare skin seemed to burn under her touch. Shaman ran his hands over the nape of her neck, her back and the indentation of her tiny waist. He tangled his hands into the thick, straight ebony hair that fell to her hips, marvelling at its silky texture.

Shaman hugged her close to his muscled chest. They sat, holding each other in silence for a few long minutes.

"Thank you for saving my life, Shaman Da," said Shambhavi, her voice choked with emotion.

"Too late to be calling me *Da*," Shaman replied with a dry laugh.

He noticed the slight burns on her neck and upper chest.

"Shambhavi, I think you should wash these burns with water. They are very red," he said, concerned, pulling her to her feet.

But for a few strips that clung to her petticoat, Shambhavi's sari was almost non-existent. She washed her face in the waterfall. It glowed like a pearl in the dim *diya*-light of the cave. She took off the remains of her burnt sari and threw it into a corner. Shaman was distracted by the sight of her in just a blouse and petticoat, but the very next moment his gaze fell on the red sari at the idol's feet. He offered it to Shambhavi, who gratefully took it.

Shaman walked to the mouth of the cave to look out while Shambhavi dressed. He could only see a light drizzle and nothing else.

"Thank God," she said, coming to his side. "Now the fires will be put out." Her voice trembled a little.

"Why are you so afraid? Everything will be alright," he assured her, putting his arm around her shoulders.

Shambhavi hugged him tightly and shuddered. Her small frame only made him feel more protective.

"We may have to spend the night here. It's risky to trek back now," he said.

Shambhavi nodded in acquiescence.

They ate the fruits placed at the deity's feet and prepared to sleep. Shambhavi dozed off, leaning against the wall of the cave. But Shaman was too caught up in a dilemma to fall asleep. He did not know how to deal with his oath of celibacy and his deep attraction to Shambhavi. He was now dealing with emotions and desires that had never bothered him in the 39 years of his existence. His relationship with Shambhavi had undergone an enormous change in a matter of minutes. It was all so new to him.

Shaman paced the cave like a trapped animal for many hours, his mind agitated. Eventually, he stopped and sat down to pray before the Lord, asking for direction. As he meditated, the soft sound of sobbing broke his concentration. It took him a few seconds to get his bearings. He looked around and saw Shambhavi in the throes of a nightmare. She was crying in her sleep. Shaman immediately shook her awake. When her eyes opened, he could see that the dark fear of her nightmare still lingered. She was drenched in cold sweat.

"You are safe, don't cry," he comforted her. He helped her drink some water. It was clear that whatever was tormenting her was not easy to deal with. Shaman realised she was vulnerable and scared, without any defences.

"Please don't leave me alone," Shambhavi pleaded.

"I will not leave you alone," he assured her, making her sleep on his lap. She felt fragile like she was made of spun glass that could shatter into a thousand prisms. A wave of affection surged through him as he watched her sleep. She looked like an innocent child with her fist curled under her chin.

Fatigue from the traumatic events of the evening took a toll on Shaman, causing him to doze off. An hour later, he woke with a start, disoriented for a moment. It was bitterly cold, still, and dark. He realised he had Shambhavi in his arms. And when he tried to move, he noticed that she had taken hold of his *rudraksha mala* as she slept.

Smiling to himself, he slowly unclenched her fingers and looked around.

All the *diyas* had been extinguished. He checked the illuminated face of his watch. It was a few minutes past 5 am. A loud trumpeting startled Shambhavi awake. Shaman held her close and whispered, "Elephants…"

On hearing his voice, she relaxed. "They sound awfully close," she whispered back.

"They are not that close. It's the acoustics of the cave, don't worry," he assured her.

A few minutes later, Shaman ventured to the mouth of the cave and looked out. Beyond the waterfall, he spotted a herd of seven elephants, slowly ambling over the path of the landslide. He was happy to see this.

"See, it rained last night, and now the elephants are walking on the trail we need to take. The soil will settle as they pass. Come, wear your shoes. Let's go," he said to Shambhavi.

Shambhavi washed her face in the waterfall and wore her shoes. Shaman prostrated himself before the idol and put on his own shoes. They walked cautiously on the newly-laid elephant path, arm-in-arm, as the sun shyly peeped from the eastern sky.

36.

The overpowering smell of petrol unleashed in her a miasma of dark fear. That crushing fear unspooled so fast and so strong, it caused in her a huge wave of panic. She made a valiant effort to sit up and fluttered like a pinned butterfly as she tried to free her hands. She thrashed against her bounds. To her great relief, her feet were free and unbound.

Suddenly she heard a male voice and stilled herself.

"Has she woken up?" a gruff voice asked.

"She has been drugged, you know that..."

No wonder her limbs felt so heavy that she couldn't move.

"...We will burn her soon. Let the drug take effect..."

"We must remove all her jewellery before burning her... Alas! There is no fun in touching a sleeping woman!" said another voice with a wicked laugh.

"We took money to burn her. So let's just stick to that!"

"A female is all I care about... And this one is very beautiful..."

Raucous laughter followed.

She worked her hands free with stealth, removed the dirty cloth in her mouth and fought the overwhelming urge to retch. Her mouth was chaffed and her throat, parched.

It took her great effort to stand up quietly. Her heavily embellished ghagra, *now drenched with petrol, made movement difficult.*

The men who were squatting around a small fire and drinking saw her. And they immediately made a dash for her. She started running, her gold anklets tinkling. Several thick bangles clanked against each other. Her huge uncut diamond earrings moved wildly as she ran, pulling on her small earlobes painfully. One of the men shouted – "Don't try to catch her!" – and threw a burning twig from the fire onto the trail of petrol that leaked from her ghagra.

She ran as fast as she could. Sheer terror fuelled her running and it freed her from the debilitating effects of the sedative that had been administered to her. But the fire now snaked and roared rapidly towards her.

Suddenly, out of nowhere, she found Shaman standing in the middle of the wilderness, his jataas *flying in the breeze. She ran into his arms. "Shaman, they are trying to burn me!" she screamed.*

Shaman held her close and, with a lift of his right hand, doused the snaking fire. The men chasing her turned into stone statues – frozen in their chasing postures.

"You are safe," said Shaman, pointing to the extinguished fire. She hugged him tight as they kissed passionately.

Shambhavi woke up, soaked in sweat. Her arms were hugging the pillow next to her – her face buried in it – and her silk quilt was twisted around her tiny waist. She opened her eyes and looked around. Her heart still pounded like a crazy drum... but this time, not in fear, but in longing for Shaman.

She took deep breaths.

It was a nightmare. 'I am safe,' she told herself.

She was in her room at the Nagaprayag *ashram*.

She wondered when she would be free from this nightmare.

From the light, she could make out that it was late, may be around 10 am. She had fallen into an exhausted sleep after they had returned from the cave. She recalled the landslide and how dangerous it had been.

Shambhavi quickly showered, wore a white *tussar* sari and studied her reflection in the mirror. She looked like a woman holding a happy secret. Her eyes glowed. She wondered what Shaman would say when he saw her this morning. Would he regret the happenings in the cave? She was unsure of what to expect.

Shambhavi spotted the faint burn marks on her upper chest and stomach. She was moved by the gentleness with which Shaman had reacted to her injuries. She didn't regret anything. She felt safe in Shaman's arms. Shambhavi blushed as she remembered the way Shaman held her and kissed her. She was gloriously happy.

She needed to get dressed quickly. Baba would be waiting for her and she wanted to be with Shaman as soon as possible.

37.

Despite his best efforts, Shaman couldn't get Shambhavi out of his mind. He longed to be alone with her to the point that his desperation stunned him. There was no thought in his mind but Shambhavi. Sensations constantly played in his head—of how soft she felt in his arms, of how her lips tasted and how she melted in his embrace. He savoured and relived those moments with the secret joy of a miser who counted his hoarded coins with glee.

The craving was so strong that he could not think about where this relationship would take them. He was caught in a giant steel trap of his own desire.

As he left his room after a bath, he saw Shambhavi walk towards Maharaj's room. She looked beautiful in a white *tussar* sari with a deep blue border. He realised she had just showered, her hair was still damp and hung in dark waves well below her hips. He noticed that she too was looking in his direction. She smiled shyly at him, unsure of what to expect.

Shaman nodded to her to come to him. She shook her head and, with a mischievous smile, entered Maharaj's room. Without another thought he followed her inside.

The Master was seated at his usual chair, reading and explaining the finer points of *Soundarya Lahari* to an elderly gentleman who sat at his feet. As soon as he saw Shaman, the Master asked, "How are you?"

Shaman took his blessings and said he was fine. He was so distracted that he did not realize that it was Mr Achari sitting there. The elderly gentleman looked at Shaman and asked,

"You were not well, Shaman?"

Realising his mistake, he quickly collected himself and replied, "I was stuck in the cave nearby last night because of the landslide."

The old man's expression morphed into one of shock. "You are lucky that you were unharmed, it's all his grace!" he said pointing to the Master. "Ram Ram…" he muttered to himself. And then, after a pause, looked at the Master to continue with the reading. On the wall behind the chair was a large photo of Maharaj's *guru*.

Shambhavi came from the inner room with a basket of flowers. She replaced the old garland placed around the photo with a fresh one of tube roses. Their pleasing fragrance flooded the room. They were Shaman's favourite flowers!

As she reached up to adjust the garland, Shaman could see the bare skin of her slender waist. Instantly, his mind was once again distracted as he fought the urge to touch her. As Maharaj read aloud the attributes of the beautiful Goddess from the text, cheeks like the moon and sun, Shaman began to think of Shambhavi's cheeks. He felt that the description suited Shambhavi perfectly.

The *mala* that Shambhavi tried to place around the large photo was extremely heavy. It slipped to the ground twice. Maharaj heard the loud thump and asked Shaman to help her. But Shaman was afraid to get close to Shambhavi. Of course, he wanted to be close to her, yet when the opportunity presented itself, he hesitated. 'What a paradox,' he thought dryly.

Slowly, he moved towards her to take the *mala* from her hands. A naughty twinkle played in her eye as she held it out like she was about to garland him. Shaman immediately looked around to see if anyone had seen her gesture. He was relieved to see both the old men deeply engrossed in the text.

When her fingers brushed his, he felt as if he had been burnt.

Shambhavi placed the *mala* in Shaman's hands and spoke to Maharaj, "Baba, I am going to the cowshed to see the new calf."

Then, as she walked out of the room, she added, "Call me when you are ready to have lunch."

Shaman wanted to follow her to the cowshed immediately. He had never felt like this in his life. He was so smitten that he couldn't put two thoughts together. He was like a teenager experiencing his first crush – intense and all-consuming.

Shaman felt he was caught here in the room with Maharaj and Mr Achari. Just then the phone rang in the next room, and, thankful for the distraction, he left immediately to answer it.

It was a lady calling from Indore to enquire about the Master's health. Shaman quickly wrapped up that phone call and literally ran to the cowshed.

Leela, the wife of the *pundit*, was sitting on the steps leading to the cowshed, eating a corn on cob.

"Shaman Da...?" She said and stood up. "You are here? You need anything?"

Shaman didn't know what to say.

Just then Shambhavi called out from inside the cowshed. "You wanted to see the new calf *na*...? Come inside."

Leela moved aside to let Shaman pass.

In the dim interior of the cowshed, only one stall was occupied. The new mother and the tiny calf stood in the deep recesses of the stall while the rest grazed outside.

In a soft voice, Shambhavi called him over. "Come and see this calf. She was born with a *tilak* on her forehead," she said, pointing to a brown calf that bore a prominent and perfectly formed white *vaishnav tilak* on her forehead.

Shaman could barely hear her. Neither could he see her in the gloomy interiors.

"Why are you whispering?"

"I don't want to startle them," she replied with a laugh.

Once his eyes adjusted to the dim light, he saw Shambhavi sitting on her haunches, caressing the calf's forehead. The calf's mother peacefully ate grass right behind the young dancer. Instantly, he remembered her fingers caressing his cheeks.

"Do you think we should name her Vaishnavi? It will be an apt name. What do you say?" Shambhavi asked.

The mother cow mooed softly. Shambhavi laughed again and said, "I think the mother approves of the name."

Shaman didn't care about the name of the calf or whether or not the mother approved of it.

"Shambhavi, come here," he said in a low voice. He didn't wish to disturb the mother and calf.

She got to her feet and came to him slowly. Shaman embraced her quickly and tightly, and whispered in her ear, "I want to be alone with you."

She felt like warm butter in his arms.

Shambhavi put a finger to her lips and pointed outside. She made a gesture with her eyes to convey that Leela was sitting outside.

She freed herself from his embrace and said in her normal voice, "Isn't the calf exceedingly cute?"

Shaman was intoxicated by her proximity. "Meet me at the Gayatri temple tonight. I pray between 11:30 and 12:30," he whispered.

She thought for a moment and nodded. "Let's see…" she added. And as Shaman was leaving, Shambhavi leaned over and kissed his cheek.

Shaman found leaving the shed difficult.

When they walked out together, Leela was nowhere to be seen. But at that moment, someone called out, "Shambhavi Didi, Maharaj is calling for you!"

Shambhavi turned to go. "Shambhavi, wait a second," Shaman said. "I want to tell you something. You know I felt bad that I didn't immediately go and take the Master's *darshan* as soon as I returned. Maharaj didn't ask me anything when he saw me just now. Isn't it odd?" he said thoughtfully.

"Don't worry on that count," Shambhavi said. "I immediately went and told him about the landslide and the forest fire. In fact, Chandni sent word to Maharaj from the village last evening itself, that she had been injured and that you had accompanied me to the temple. So Baba knew you were with me. As a matter of fact, he was relieved that I had not been alone."

Shaman was happy hearing this, but still a little puzzled. "How come he didn't ask me anything when he saw me?"

"Oh, that must have been because of Mr Achari," said Shambhavi. "You know Baba doesn't like to discuss anything in front of outsiders."

"Shambhavi Didi, Maharaj is calling for you," Krishna Da called out again.

"Okay, I am coming," she answered and turned to Shaman just before leaving. "Don't think too much about this."

~

The day couldn't end soon enough for Shaman. He wondered if Shambhavi would come to the temple. Restlessness and irritability gripped him, so much so that he didn't have a proper lunch. What irked him most was that he couldn't concentrate on what he was reading. He had turned into a mass of longing.

Finally, the day ended. Typical of any mountain town, there

was a sudden chill in the air.

Shaman performed his evening prayers. For the first time, he was unsure of what to ask Ma Durga. A dark guilt stung him from deep inside. Shambhavi was the Master's daughter. She was like his sister. How could he feel attracted to her? He cursed himself.

He saw Shambhavi as she took the plate of fruits for the Master and heard her laugh at something that Leela had said. All thoughts of guilt fled away. Her breath-taking beauty enraptured his mind. He was caught in a fresh surge of longing and deep desire.

Back in his room, Shaman tried in vain to focus on an urgent paper he needed to submit on Appaya Dikshita's commentary on *Brahmasutra Bhashya Parimala.* His mind just wouldn't obey him. He picked up his pen and writing pad for what seemed like the 99th time. But his mind was distracted. Instead, he ended up writing a short love poem.

Shaman was aghast at his own behaviour.

He washed his face in the bathroom in an attempt to clear his head and saw his own reflection in the mirror. A voice from within asked the most piercing question, 'You are a middle-aged man in an ochre robe. Aren't you ashamed to be lusting after a young girl who is like your sister? To what abysmal depths have you fallen?'

Hot tears of shame welled up in his eyes. Yes, he thought to himself, he had fallen and had become a victim to carnal desire. He was like a love-sick teenager in the throes of infatuation. He hated himself!

For the very first time, he understood what it was to fall prey to *kama*[88]. And as he felt this, he suddenly saw the subject

---

[88]Kama: Often connotes sexual desire and longing, but the concept more broadly refers to any desire, wish, passion, longing, pleasure of the senses, the aesthetic enjoyment of life, affection.

of his anguish from his window, collecting clothes from the clothesline. She too saw him and smiled, eyes full of happiness. And in that moment, the voice of reason was completely squashed under the weight of his newfound passion.

Shaman could barely finish his dinner. He was merely a creature, waiting. The present was invalid. His mind raced to the time when he hoped he would be alone with Shambhavi. He wondered what it would be like to wake up with her in his arms every morning. Not being with her was akin to a physical ache.

His mind was full of turmoil when he sat for his *japa* at the temple that night. But due to long years of practice, he was able to still it. He finished his prayers an hour later and prostrated before the Goddess. Then he remembered Shambhavi again, and an avalanche of yearning enveloped him.

He quickly folded his *asana*, kept it away and looked outside the temple for Shambhavi, fervently hoping for her to be there.

She was not. His heart sank with every passing minute. Dejected, he started walking towards his room. It was well past 12:45 and terribly cold. The lamp near the *tulasi* plant was still burning. He bent down to prostrate in front of her out of habit. It was then that he saw Shambhavi. She was sleeping in a sitting posture, her head on her knees next to the *tulasi* plant. He watched her in the lamp-light for a few seconds, his heart beating fast. Her hair fell like a black curtain and she had a black shawl wrapped around her.

Shambhavi's creamy skin glowed like a pearl in the frail light. He ran his forefinger slowly along her forehead, down her nose, to her soft lips. She opened her eyes, startled, and then she smiled. Shaman held his hand out to help her up.

They stood face to face. Shambhavi asked directly, "Shaman, do you want to come to my room?" She had almost called him *Shaman* Da out of habit.

He didn't know what to say or do. He desperately wanted to go with her, but he was deeply afraid of being caught. The question hung heavily in the air for a few moments.

Shambhavi bent down and removed her anklets. He looked at her questioningly. "In the quiet of the night everything sounds loud," she said. Without another word, Shambhavi held his hand and led him to her room. There was utter silence in the *ashram*, but for the thudding of their hearts. It was dark, but Shambhavi knew her way.

Once inside, Shambhavi did not switch on the light. But they could see each other in the moonlight streaming in through the windows. She removed her black shawl and threw it on the bed. She was wearing a beautiful cream coloured *chenderi sari*[89] with small round gold *buttis*[90]. Her room was filled with her fragrance – flowers and perfume. Distinctly feminine! She had decorated it with red and white roses. Perfumed candles were placed artistically around the Nataraja idol.

Suddenly, she turned painfully shy. She stood by the window, looking at the moon with her back to Shaman. He slowly walked to her.

He saw her slender waist and remembered how the sight of it had tormented him in Maharaj's room. He touched the exposed skin and found it as soft as water. Shambhavi shuddered in response. Shaman pushed her heavy curtain of hair away from her neck and took a deep breath. He was like a drug addict snorting a line of cocaine. "You smell like sin," he whispered and kissed her neck. The scent of her skin assaulted his senses. He felt like he was drowning.

She immediately turned around and hugged him, burying her face in his neck. "I don't smell like sin," she told him. "It's the

---

[89]Chanderi: a traditional sari made in Chanderi, Madhya Pradesh, known for their gold and silver brocade or zari, fine silk and opulent embroidery

[90]Buttis: small repeated accents in the sari cloth, these patterns could be woven with gold or silver thread, which is called zari work.

perfume I use," she clarified with a smile in her voice. Shaman did not reply.

He kissed her tenderly. When he felt his self-control begin to slip, he kissed her forehead and bade her good night.

He knew it was this restraint—this *niyam*—that secured the true self through the goad of self-control.

Shambhavi continued to hug him tight. Shaman placed two fingers beneath her face and lifted it. "Enough for today… while I can still let you go," he said in a serious voice. And before she could reply, he left her room and slowly started making his way to his.

The almost illegitimate twist in his relationship with Shambhavi added a raw hungry edge to it. They lived for the few short-lived moments they had with each other alone.

Shaman was torn between guilt and desire. He hated himself for having fallen for Shambhavi. His strong attraction to her kindled in him a fiery guilt that burned his insides. Yet he was helpless before his desire.

Shaman was afraid to look into Maharaj's eyes lest the *guru* come to know his transgression. Shaman could no longer read or study, nor could he eat or sleep. He was an out-of-control vortex, swirling with contradictory feelings and emotions.

PART II

No destiny attacks us from outside. But, within him, man bears his fate and there comes a moment when he knows himself vulnerable; and then, as in a vertigo, blunder upon blunder lures him.

~ Antoine de Saint-Exupéry

38.

The story was interrupted by the shrill ringing of Shaman's phone. He showed the screen of the phone to Indraneel. Vasundhara flashed on the screen.

"I guess my phone ran out of battery," said Indraneel.

Shaman picked up the phone.

"Hi, Vasundhara! Where are you?"

"Hi, Shaman. *Jai Guru*. Sorry I couldn't come to the store, it was getting close to feeding time for the girls, so I wanted them to be brought to the hotel room."

"They look like little angels! Very sweet! Beautiful babies indeed," said Shaman.

"They will be little monsters if they are not fed on time," she said laughing. "I have been trying to reach Indraneel. His phone is switched off."

"Here, speak to him," said Shaman handing over his phone. Indraneel spoke into the phone, informing Vasundhara that he would be late and to get some sleep.

After he hung up, he turned to Shaman. "Shaman! You swung from having a direct divine vision of Ma Annapurna to having fallen from your *sannyasa* vows, all within the span of one week! What kind of a life is that where you are swinging between such extremes! I am stunned," Indraneel said, shaking his head as if to make sense of something unbelievable. "What a situation you found yourself in! It's beyond anything I could imagine!"

"Believe me when I say this Indraneel, the last thing I wanted was to be in such a situation. But I was so helpless—it was like fighting a huge tidal wave or a mammoth rip tide. I was drowning. Forget staying away from her, I couldn't even stop thinking of her every waking moment. The speed at which our relationship changed stunned me, but I was like a helpless leaf caught in a tempest."

"Man, Shaman ... It must have been so crazy!"

"It *was* crazy; what's more, I was a proud man. I had been so confident that I'd never fall into the clutches of *kama*. But lo and behold! I was caught so badly that I hardly recognised the person I had turned into overnight. I had dealt with a lot of women in my past, but it had been at a very superficial level. I had never known attraction or felt even an iota of it ever, so I thought I was immune and beyond it. Never did I imagine, even for a second, how life changes once you become passionately involved with a woman. For me, that one encounter at the cave was like someone throwing a lit matchstick into a petroleum well. It was just a raging inferno; after that, my throwing buckets of water was not going to abate the blaze."

"How did you deal with it Shaman? The Master on one side, your own guilt for forsaking your oaths, and of course the deep attraction. How did you come to terms with all these opposing forces without losing your sanity? I cannot even imagine."

"At the time, I was continuously assaulted by the thought of how things will shape up. Did I have a future with Shambhavi? Was I setting myself up to lose everything....? And then my mind would suddenly switch from concerns of the future to those of the past. I would think of all that had happened in the past—my life before Shambhavi and my life after Shambhavi. I did not know if what was happening was right. This gave me great anguish. I so desperately wanted to fix things. I was alive in the present but not living in the present..."

"Alive in the present but not living in the present....that's a deep one. Go on…" Indraneel urged.

"When I thought deeply, I realised my pain was not coming from here and now; it was coming from another source."

"And what was that source?"

"It was coming from contemplations of the past and the future. One day I was reading late into the night and I happened upon a quote by Arya Chanakya. At that moment, it was a godsend; it dispelled all of my doubts and made my mind clear as crystal."

"What was the quote?"

"Gate shoko na kartavyo bhavishyam naiva chintayet |
vartamaanena kaalena vartayanti vichakshanah ||"

"And what does it mean?"

"The Past is not worth mourning. Don't worry for the Future. The wise advise us to live by the present time."

"Beautiful!" Indraneel exclaimed.

"The clearheaded, *vichakshanah*, as Chanakya called him, resides in the present. And that's precisely what I tried doing."

"Was that difficult?" Indraneel asked.

"It was challenging to implement in the beginning, but slowly I got the hang of it. Living in the present means paying attention to what is around us *right now*, and engaging deeply and wholly with it. To achieve that, I had to destroy a bad habit of many lifetimes."

"Bad habit?"

"Yes, the bad habit of being lost in the past or the future! Think about it, Indraneel. The only life we have is the one we are living *now*. There is nothing more to life than the present. People think that the present moment is just a fraction of a long life—a dot, a small parcel. But that's not how it is. The truth is, the present moment is an eternity. We experience life only in the present. Even the past and the future is felt in the present. We may live a life of 60 or a 100 years, but God gives us only one moment at a time."

"Amazing! I never thought of it that way…" said Indraneel.

"Yes, this is the truth that dawned on me. I realised whatever happens, happens by God's will. I just needed to be true to the moment. But, for that, I had to accept the present."

"'Accept'?"

"Yes, you can't live in the present without being empowered by acceptance. God waits for us to accept our lot without resignation. Once we are happy with whatever we have, the present itself gets better. The present is throbbing with life; all that was, and all that will be, is latent in the river of the present though we can't see it. If we perfect our present, everything will automatically fall into place."

"Wow! So you mean that the present could be the cradle of all possibility, the firm abode of reality? Fantastic… Only a person like you could arrived at this!" said Indraneel in a voice full of awe and respect.

"Actually to tell you the truth, it was not a choice I made. I just ran out of choices… At that point this was my only way to survive and keep my sanity intact. Anybody can practice this philosophy. It's just that one first needs to arrive at this way of thinking; implementation happens slowly but surely. I went through every emotion—from joy, love and desire to fear, guilt, helplessness and even envy."

Shaman stopped for a moment to look at his watch. "Living in the present reminds me… It's almost 9 pm. I think I better send Payal home."

"Yes," said Indraneel. "I heard a lot of thunder. Looks like we may get another heavy downpour."

Shaman told Payal to go home and walked back to Indraneel. "Are you hungry, Indraneel?" He asked. "If you want, we can lock up the store and leave immediately to have dinner."

"Actually Shaman, I am not hungry at all. I am just eager to know what happened next."

39.

Shaman barely found the time to sleep at night. Between his stolen nocturnal moments with Shambhavi and his personal commitments, he had to sacrifice his sleep. But Shambhavi had become like a drug that fuelled and shielded him from the fatigue of sleep deprivation. Though he slept for less than two hours a day, he still felt fresh and energised.

When he finished his prayers at the Prayag and went up to the Master's room, he was disappointed to find that Shambhavi was not there. He wanted to know where she was, but couldn't ask anyone.

In that moment, the Master spoke up, "Shaman, for this year, ask Shambhavi to write the *Tulasi Vivah* invitation. Give her the material today, it is an auspicious day. Once it is written, hand it over to the *pundit*, Vishnu Prasad, or his son. Shambhavi is very excited, she could never attend the *Tulasi Vivah* either because of school, college or her job…"

Any information on Shambhavi was vital to Shaman.

"Krishna Da, ready the basket of fruits and sweets to be given at the temple..." Maharaj instructed. "And where is Shambhavi..? She didn't come for breakfast."

No sooner had he said it than Shambhavi came running. She wore a printed yellow and white chiffon sari. Her hair was damp from her shower.

"*Pranaam* Baba…*Jai Guru*…Sorry, I am late. I overslept."

She panted, as she took the Master's blessings.

"Are you keeping well? You never oversleep," he asked in a voice of concern.

"I... I haven't been sleeping well at night."

Her eyes met Shaman's and she smiled and looked away.

"Don't worry Baba...I am fine."

"Beti...Shaman Da will give you the contents for the wedding invitation to be sent to the Murali Krishna temple. Write and give it today itself."

"Right away, Baba..."

After a moment, the Master spoke up again, "Shambhavi. You didn't take Shaman Da's blessings..."

"Sorry, sorry. I forgot." She approached Shaman and bent down to take his blessings. "*Pranaam*...Da..."

She looked up and smiled at him. Shaman was bewitched by her grey eyes and her radiant beauty. It took all his concentration to look away and get the materials needed for the invitation.

~

Shaman sat on the steps behind the Gayatri temple sometime after lunch. He was proofreading the manuscript of the book Maharaj had written. A cool breeze blew through Nagaprayag. Shaman savoured the peace. All the *ashramites* were taking their afternoon siesta.

He hadn't seen Shambhavi at lunch. He wanted to take the invitation to the temple before his evening *japa*. 'What is she up to?' Shaman wondered.

"It's done!" Shambhavi said as she came. She handed over a packet to him.

"Why don't you sit down?"

She nodded and sat on the step below him. "Open it."

The invitation was written in beautiful calligraphy with red ink on yellow art paper. She had rolled and cut the paper around a small wooden flute. Tiny crystals decorated the flute's blow holes. The invitation was stuck on one end of the flute in such a way that when you opened it, it unfolded like a scroll. Inside the open hollow end of the flute was one spring of dark *Krishna Tulasi*. The invitation was arranged entirely in a rich red velvet cloth and sealed with a peacock feather.

Shaman was blown away by her artistic sensibilities. "I love this! It is so beautiful… I never expected something so unique. You are exceptionally gifted!"

"Thank you, I'm glad you like it."

"I feel like I hardly saw you today. Why are you sleeping so much?" Shaman asked after a moment of silence.

"I am up almost through the night talking to you. Besides, I have to complete my *japa*. I can hardly manage my time. I don't know where you find the energy to be up at the crack of dawn. In fact, I am beginning to think you have some secret superhuman power," Shambhavi said.

Before Shaman could reply, they were interrupted by an irked Chandni. "Shambhavi Didi, come and eat your lunch. Where are you? The whole day you were painting and now you are missing," she muttered to herself as she searched for her charge some distance away.

Both Shambhavi and Shaman, by some unspoken agreement, kept silent until Chandni was out of earshot.

"I should go. Bye, Shaman."

"Bye, Shambhavi. By the way, you're looking beautiful. I couldn't take my eyes off you today."

"I noticed," she said with a laugh.

"I was lost in your eyes. I remembered what Teddy said.

They are the same grey as the one seen at the core of a flame. I practice *traataka* so I know how apt that description is."

"What is *traataka*?"

"It's a *tantrik* practice where you stare at a flame or a dot till your eyes begin to tear up and sting. As soon as that happens, you close your eyes and concentrate on the image which is imprinted in your mind."

"Sounds easy enough, but what's the point of doing this?" asked Shambhavi

"See, by staring at an object for a long time, you still the restless mind. But more than that, you slowly start to control the instinct to blink, which in turn stimulates the third eye."

"This sounds ridiculously simple."

"It is simple on one level, but only a realised Master can teach one how it needs to be done. Otherwise things can go horribly wrong. Sometimes you see people whose eyeballs are moving all over the place. Those are instances where *traatak* has been practiced without the guidance of a *satguru*."

"Oh yes. I have seen people like that... Poor things!" said Shambhavi. "What have you gained from it Shaman?"

"*Traataka* has vastly enhanced my memory, concentration and focus. It has brought my mind to a state of sharp awareness."

"What a great learning it has been, Shaman. I could never imagine that such great leaps can be made from simple practices. Thank you for teaching it to me with so much patience."

"The pleasure is all mine. Now go and eat your lunch. It is already very late."

40.

Shaman's entire being had been flooded with thoughts of Shambhavi. He delayed his submissions and instead, spent his time recounting their encounters. Today, however, he was determined to finish all of his pending work. Just as he was about to get into the flow of things, Madhava Da informed him that the Master had summoned him. "Kanoriaji has come with his daughters," he said.

Mr Kanoria and his daughters Matangi, Malati and Maheshwari, sat before Maharaj. Another lady sat a little apart from the group. All three girls received Maharaj's blessings.

"Where is Shambhavi?" the Master asked Krishna Da. "Ask her to come…"

The youngest stood up. "I will bring Didi."

"Mahesh, at least find out where she is before going," Mr Kanoria said.

"Didi has gone to the village. She should be back anytime now," Krishna Da said.

The Master turned to Mr Kanoria. "So Shyam, why the sudden visit? You didn't call before coming…"

"These girls wanted to surprise Shambhavi. That's why I didn't call. Forgive me Maharaj," he said bowing low. "We came to give the first wedding invitation to you." He placed said object at the Master's feet.

"Not at my feet.... Shaman, place it there, near my *guru's padukas*[91]."

Shaman promptly did as told.

"Maharaj, this is Medha, the lady who runs the NGO which gives substantial donations to Dr Sudarshan's hospital. Malati works there. In fact Medha came to visit Dr Sudarshan and then decided to see Nagaprayag as well."

Medha was a woman in her mid-thirties. She was a thin, dark-complexioned woman who wore thick glasses. She also wore a permanent frown on her face, which made her look much older than she was. Surprisingly, her voice, Shaman found, was pleasant to hear.

"It is good work that Dr Sudarshan is doing. Swamiji, I am glad that even *sadhus* like you are doing social work. Though not directly, you are supporting people like Dr Sudarshan from behind the curtain."

Shaman's blood boiled at the woman's patronising tone.

"Personally, the only thing I believe in is man helping another man," Medha said. "I just don't get all these religious practices. I, in one way, feel that religion itself is created by man to keep women shackled."

Shaman could not keep silent now. "Could you please elaborate on that?" he said in a voice laced with tightly controlled anger.

"What's there to elaborate? We have such a great fixation for having boys in our society," Medha said, "Why are girls not good enough? Sorry for taking your name, Mr Kanoria... but the only reason he has had four girls is because he was trying for a son. To the point that he calls his youngest daughter Mahesh! That's the level of craving for a boy! Why are the girls banned from chanting the Gayatri *mantra*? Women are

[91]Padukas: India's oldest, most quintessential footwear. It is little more than a sole with a post and knob, which is engaged between the big and second toe

inferior, is that it?"

"You've got it all wrong," Shaman explained. "There is a change that takes place in the body of a woman every month. This change is crucial. It is God's way of making her capable of conception. She becomes ready to create new life. That's no small feat. The ability to create new life is as powerful as atomic fission—it's just controlled. During this change, a woman vibrates at a very high energy level and has actual "heat" in her body."

"That's an interesting perspective," Medha remarked.

"Gayatri *mantra* is actually a very fundamental *mantra*," Shaman explained. "It is the *mantra* with which Creation unfolds and the five elements evolve. Chanting the Gayatri mantra produces a strong creative energy. When a man chants it, he builds that energy around him. But a woman produces this energy every month within her own body. The very impact of the *mantra* manifests in her biologically. If she were to chant the Gayatri *mantra*, that energy would double and that can harm her. She is forbidden from chanting Gayatri, because she already has it in her by birth right. No meditation is needed for her to achieve it."

"When you say harm, you mean it can physically harm her?" Matangi questioned.

"Absolutely. It's obvious, when we try to hold more than we can, it backfires. Too much glare can blind us. It's like that…"

"I understand now, Shamanji. Please accept my apology, Swamiji!" Medha admitted grudgingly.

Shaman merely smiled.

"Okay, said Mr Kanoria, "Girls, please leave the room. I have something personal to discuss with Maharaj."

Matangi got up to leave. "I wonder why Shambhavi is taking so much time."

Just then, Shambhavi entered the room in a rush. "Matangi! Why didn't you tell me you were coming?" She hugged the happy girl.

"It was a surprise!"

"Why don't you sit down? Where are you guys going?"

"Dad wants to speak to Maharaj, in private," said Matangi.

"*Namaste* uncle!" Shambhavi greeted him.

"*Namaste* Shambhavi… See you later, Beta," said Mr Kanoria.

Shaman, too, stood up to leave. "You sit with us Swamiji," said Mr Kanoria.

Mr Kanoria sat close to Maharaj's feet. "Maharaj, you know Rahul, my future son- in-law…"

"Yes, I know the family very well, Shyam."

"It's because of your kindness that Matangi's wedding has been fixed with a reputed and wealthy family. Rahul's brother Rohan met Shambhavi in Dehradun. He is completely smitten by her and has told his mother that he wants to marry her."

"He is the younger brother, yes?"

"As expected, you know everything, Maharaj… Yes, he is. A year younger than Rahul, so he must be twenty-seven… ideal for our Shambhavi. His mother, Madhavi Ben, called me and told me this. Actually, she wanted to come and finalise the wedding right then. They are over the moon. Shambhavi is your daughter, what more privilege can there be for anyone! I was thinking we could do a joint wedding for both the girls next month… if you permit."

Shaman felt like a bomb had exploded in his face. He couldn't imagine Shambhavi with another man, especially with that boy. He waited with bated breath to hear what the Master had to say.

Maharaj was pensive. He remained quiet for a few moments, and then turned to Shaman. "What do you think Shaman? Do you think our Shambhavi will be happy?"

Shaman was speechless. He didn't know how to answer him. Finally, avoiding the Master's eyes, he said, "You know best Maharaj. What can I say?"

"I even told them that dance is central to Shambhavi. They are more than willing to set up a dance school for her. Both the girls will be kept in the lap of luxury," Mr Kanoria gushed.

"Shyam, money is not everything... She should be happy. But before that, I need to know if she has someone in her mind already."

Shaman tried to look away.

"But this is a good match. The boy is good looking and educated."

"Yes, Maharaj. He is from the creative field, he is a filmmaker. That bent of mind will suit Shambhavi. Also, if there was someone Shambhavi was interested in, Matangi would have surely told me. I asked her directly..." said Kanoria.

"Nowadays children are becoming increasingly secretive. I will speak to her, Shyam. I don't want to pressure her. I want it to be her decision, entirely."

Shaman felt that Maharaj was indirectly telling him something. Guilt punched him hard in the gut.

"It's time for my afternoon prayers. Shaman, take Shyamji for lunch," Maharaj concluded.

41.

Shaman longed to meet Shambhavi alone. He had to tell her what Mr Kanoria had said.

Medha and the girls were having lunch, laughing at something Chandni was saying as she served them. "Now, I am married for the fourth time. Does my husband seek my companionship? Do you girls think it's for companionship? Medhaji, you are older, you tell me."

"No no, men are like animals…"

"That's exactly what I am saying," said Chandni laughing.

"And men have a weakness for girls like you Shambhavi—those who have faces like angels with all the womanly curves in place! Men will come swarming to you… Don't sell yourself short," Medha warned with a serious look.

"Matangi Didi, do you remember the number of boys who used to follow Shambhavi in school? Actually, it's surprising that someone so slim can have such lush contours," said Malati.

"Girls, shut up! You people are talking rubbish. Beauty and physical attributes are just a collection of genes," said Shambhavi.

"No one is talking rubbish. Shambhavi, actually, Rahul told his parents that he wants to marry you. They wanted to come all the way here to talk to Maharaj."

Shambhavi only laughed. "Marry me? I am not interested in marriage at all."

Shaman couldn't believe that while he was worrying over the

proposal, there Shambhavi was, laughing away.

"Okay, all of you go to my room. I need to check on a few things for tomorrow. I wish you all could stay for the *Tulasi Vivah...*"

"We would have loved to. But you know we have to get back," said Medha.

As they left, Shaman waited for Shambhavi to come towards the kitchen.

"You are amused that you got a proposal? What was there to laugh about?" he said. He looked pensive and confused.

"Shaman, what are you doing here?" she asked, surprised. "And why were you eavesdropping? What's the matter? Why are you looking so dejected?"

"Shambhavi, your room is locked!" Matangi called out.

Before Shaman could stop her, she turned away. "Okay, I'm coming! Shaman, I have to go."

42.

Shaman sat under the expansive banyan tree located on a small hillock on the edge of the *ashram* property. The old tree had a neat cement platform around it. From there, he had an uninterrupted panoramic view of the Prayag below. The hanging roots hid him unless they came closer.

He watched the Alakananda and Mandakini Rivers twist and turn in their curved paths, travelling parallelly for several kilometres – coming close, yet not touching one another. Only at the *sangam* did they meet briefly, only to part once again into individual rivers. Did they mimic his life, he wondered. Was he about to lose Shambhavi? He was beginning to feel anxious. Dark clouds blotted the winter sun. A sudden chill pierced him.

"Shaman Da, are you there?" He heard Shambhavi call out.

He was so confused with his emotions, he thought of not answering her. But then he realised it was childish to avoid her.

Before he could answer, she stood in front of him. She looked beautiful in a tomato-coloured sleeveless top and light blue jeans. Her luxurious hair fell like a waterfall down her back. The light breeze teased the soft tendrils around her face.

"Why didn't you answer me when I was calling you? I looked for you everywhere. I would have missed you if I hadn't looked so keenly. You almost succeeded in hiding from me," she said.

"I was not hiding. I just wanted some quiet."

"Why didn't you have lunch?"

"I was not hungry."

"Shaman, what's bothering you?"

Shambhavi tied a few of the hanging roots together and made a makeshift seat for herself in front of Shaman.

"Nothing is bothering me…" he whispered.

"Okay, nothing is bothering you. But you looked deep in thought. Tell me what were you thinking?"

"Shambhavi, I was wondering if we are like these two rivers …"

"We actually are like them," she replied. "We knew of each other for more than a decade, but we never met. Our paths never crossed until recently."

"We had to travel side by side for many years just like these two rivers."

"And meet at Nagaprayag, the place of the *sangam*. It's fascinating to see the waves of one river embrace those of the other and flow together."

"Only briefly. They travel together for less than half a kilometre…before separating again."

"Oh, Shaman," Shambhavi sighed. "How could you think of something like that while looking at such a beautiful scene? Don't think like that… As far as the proposal goes, I am not the least bit interested in marriage. As to why I laughed when I heard about it, it's because everyone assumed I would be excited that a wealthy man like Rohan wants to marry me. Nobody, including Matangi, thought of asking me what I felt. I found it hilarious that while they had assumed so much on my behalf, here I was, simply not interested."

Shaman just sat there, staring at her wordlessly. "Now don't sit there without speaking a word. Say something."

"I don't know… I'm just confused…"

She took both of his hands and held them tightly. "Shaman, look at me. There is nothing to know. You only need to understand one thing—*I belong to you*. There is nothing more to know or discuss."

Her eyes glistened with a slight glimmer of tears.

Shaman paused for a second and said, "I wish I could think as clearly as you do and just stay in the present."

"That topic is now closed. Come, let's go. I forgot my shawl somewhere when I was running around the *ashram* like a maniac, trying to locate you."

She let go of his hands and stood up. "See, I have gooseflesh on my skin," she said hugging herself.

Shaman continued to sit on the slab.

"Okay, enough of staring at the *sangam*. Forget all of this. Let's get you something to eat. Everyone is worried that you didn't eat."

Shaman laughed. "If you had missed a meal the people would have gone crazy, but no such concern for me. Everyone knows I fast quite regularly."

"Yes, that's also true."

"But now I am hungry," said Shaman.

"Let's go and find Keshava Da or Madhava Da. But first I want to see you without that frown."

"Let's go. Suddenly I am ravenous," he said, smiling.

43.

It was the evening of *Tulasi Vivaha*. The *ashram* had transformed itself into a marriage hall. There were marigold garlands all around the hall outside the temple. Neat buntings of mango leaves decorated the doorways.

The *sannyasis* looked fresh in their new *dhotis* and the neatly applied *vaishnav tilaks* on their foreheads. Chandni and Leela were busy creating the large *rangoli* that would welcome the *baaraat* at the *ashram* gate.

Shaman went inside the temple. The *tulasi* was placed in a beautiful pot before the idol of Ma Gayatri. It had already been decorated with vermilion and turmeric dots. When he did *pranaam* and looked up, he saw Shambhavi in the distance, carrying a big brass plate full of lit *diyas*.

She looked like a heavenly nymph in the collective glow of the flames. Shaman almost forgot to breathe. She was wearing a sky blue chiffon *lehenga*[92] with fine crystals embroidered on it and a short silver blouse that was held together by two threads tied behind, giving a glimpse of her toned back. Her *dupatta* was a fine blue and silver chiffon. When she entered the temple to greet him, Shaman realised he was still sitting on his knees.

"*Jai Guru*, Shaman," she said smiling at him.

"Shambhavi, you look like an *apsara*[93]. It feels as though you have worn a swathe of the sky with its stars on your person."

---

[92]Lehenga: a full ankle-length skirt worn by Indian women, usually on formal or ceremonial occasions

[93]Apsara: (Hindu mythology) a celestial nymph, typically the wife of a heavenly musician

"Thank you, Shaman," she said as she smiled sweetly. "I thought you didn't notice clothes; you notice only books."

"I notice everything about you, Shambhavi."

She proceeded to place the *diyas* all around the temple. The large *chandbalis*[94] on her ears glittered in the lamplight as she bent to arrange them all around the temple. Her hair was neatly braided and fell like a thick black rope down her back.

"You have me completely distracted," he said as he looked at her with pure love in his eyes.

Shambhavi sat and dressed the *tulasi* plant. First, she draped a red brocade sari around the pot, then placed several red and green glass bangles around the stout lower branches. After that, she fixed a small silver mask, shaped like a Devi's face, to the upper branches of the plant.

"How does that look Shaman?" she asked. "Does she now look like a bride?"

"Beautiful," he answered. "Yes, she looks like a bride."

She hung *jhumkas* from the branches near the mask to make them look as if the *tulasi* itself wore the earrings.

"Leela said the ceremony is performed only in the evening. Tell me Shaman, why evening?"

"It is believed that on *Prabodhini Ekadashi*, the soul of Vrinda enters Tulasiji at sunset and leaves by the next sunrise. So we have only that window of time, until tomorrow morning, to operate in."

"Can anyone do the *Tulasi Vivah*?"

"Anyone can do it, but it's typically done by people with daughters who need to get married, and also by those who

---

[94]Chandbalis: (from Rajasthan) Vintage style 'moon earrings', there are two crescent moons set within each other that are studded with precious stones like diamonds and rubies of jewellery

have only sons and want the merit of doing a *kanyadaan*[95]," answered Shaman.

"Didi, you have decorated the *tulasi* beautifully," said Leela as she walked in with Chandni. "We could never get the sari draped around the pot so neatly."

"Tulasiji is really looking like a small child bride, and you are also looking like a beautiful bride yourself. Whoever marries you will be very lucky!"

Chandni and Leela lifted the decorated pot and took her to the hall.

"Shaman, I dressed up for you," Shambhavi said shyly.

"Shambhavi, believe me, you look good enough to eat and at the same time you look good enough to worship. I don't know what to do with you. I am caught in your spell! I have a thousand things to do, but I am unable to leave you and go."

Shaman saw the Master descend from the steps.

"Shambhavi, Maharaj is coming. The *baaraat* will be here any minute now. Come, let's go to the gate."

They made their way to the gate together. They could see the small palanquin being carried up to the *ashram* gates by four men. It was followed by several villagers singing *naam* to the beat of heavy drums. Many men and women danced behind the palanquin. The chief priest of Murali Krishna temple intermittently blew a conch as he walked ahead of the palanquin. When the palanquin reached the *ashram* gates, the *pundit* handed over a marigold *mala*.

The Master garlanded the decorated brass Krishna idol and welcomed the Lord inside.

---

[95]Kanyadaan: "gift of a maiden", a part of Hindu wedding ritual wherein a father gifts the daughter so to speak to the son-on-law, often used synonymously with Hindu wedding

Everyone took a seat in the hall. On one side sat the women with Tulasiji in front, and on the other, sat the men with Lord Krishna. Naam Yajnananda sat in his chair on another side, and beside his feet sat Shaman. "Now what will happen?" asked Shambhavi in Leela's ear.

"Didi, now it will be like a drama. You just wait and see, you will understand. It will all be done just to have fun."

Leela stood up, cleared her throat and addressed the men.

"I am sorry, all of you got dressed in such nice clothes and travelled all the way here, but we have changed our mind. We don't want to give our Tulasi in marriage to your boy Krishna. We are truly sorry; since all of you have anyway taken the trouble of coming this far, we humbly urge you to have food and then leave. We regret the inconvenience caused to all of you, we will serve you A-class dinner and make good for it."

'We are not interested in dinner. Why don't you want to give your girl? Why did you call us then?' the men chorused together.

"Agreed, we had all the intentions, but we had not done our homework on the would-be groom. But now that we've done it, we are sure we don't want to go ahead."

'Why? Why?' The men protested.

"There are many reasons. For one, your Krishna has a dark complexion while our girl is as fair as the moon."

"Don't go by external appearances, his heart is made of pure gold," said one of the men and all the men clapped.

Then Chandni stood up and exclaimed, "He is a thief! He always steals and feasts on our butter, cream and curds—we don't want to give our girl to a thief. We'd rather keep her unmarried at our home."

The old priest answered, "He was a child when he was doing

that. Who is not naughty as a child? Now he doesn't rob anyone. He has changed a lot, I promise." Everyone laughed at this.

Leela again stood up and countered. "Now that he has grown up, he has started stealing other things like women's clothes. He is stealing them at the bathing *ghaat*, which makes him a double thief—stealing both clothes and chastity. So you see, the articles have changed, but he still doesn't cease to be a robber!"

The village women began to whisper amongst themselves. 'Let's see what they say to this?'

Another priest from the Shiva temple at the *sangam* rose in defence, "That is the Lord's way of eliminating our ego, by taking away our external appearances." All the men once again cheered hearing this reply.

Before anything could be said, the old priest spoke up. "So all your arguments are over? Shall we now go ahead with the wedding? We think they will make a divine couple. What do you people think?"

Everyone agreed. "Yes yes... in fact your girl won't get a better groom," quipped one of the men.

The actual wedding ceremony was finally underway. Shambhavi sat with the *tulasi* in her lap while the old priest sat with the Krishna idol next to him. Shaman, who was the officiating priest of the ceremony, started chanting the marriage *mantras*.

When the time came for the *jayamala*[96], the priest told Shaman, "I can't lift the idol and garland Tulasiji at the same time. You put the *varamala* while I lift the idol."

Shambhavi lifted the Tulasi post as everyone began to throw rice. The drumbeats reached a crescendo. When Shaman

[96]Jayamala or Varamala: Part of the ceremony on main Indian wedding day which involves exchange of garlands between the bride and the groom

garlanded *Tulasi* he felt as if he was garlanding Shambhavi. She caught his eye as he placed the *mala* around the plant. He was lost in her eyes and for a moment, the rest of the world just faded away.

Now Tulasiji and Lord Krishna stood side-by-side, wearing the *mala* around them.

Amidst the cheers and dancing, the Master walked up to the divine couple and blessed them. Loud cheers of '*Vrindapati ki Jai! Tulasi maharani ki Jai*!' resonated throughout the *ashram*.

Everyone came forward, one by one, and prostrated before the Lord and his newly wed wife. They blessed them with flowers and coloured rice. The drumbeats, the dancing and the *naam*, were reaching a new crescendo. There was pure joy all around.

Shambhavi looked for Shaman, but couldn't find him in the crowd.

44.

When Shaman descended the steps after *bidai*[97] of Tulasi Ma, the cleaning process of the *ashram* was already well underway.

"Shaman Da, where were you?" Shambhavi asked him. "You are the only one who is yet to have dinner."

"Didi, even you have not eaten." Chandni reminded her. "Shall I get food for the two of you? Sit here on the steps. Madhava Da and the others are washing the dining room area, so you won't be able to eat there." Before they could response, she left and made her way to the kitchen.

"Why have you returned to calling me Shaman Da?" Shaman asked.

"As if you don't know. What else do I call you? How can I call you Shaman in front of everyone? People will wonder," she said, her eyes rolling.

"Okay, okay, I get it. Anyway, Maharaj is very happy with the way the entire wedding took place. I just saw him in his room while he prepared for his prayers… By the way, you should have eaten, it's quite late," Shaman said looking at his watch.

"I thought we'd be eating together. Where did you go? I was looking for you."

"I had a call from one of the HODs at Harvard. There is a guest lecture series that they want me to do…it is good money, but I told him I can't come."

---

[97]Bidai: Literally 'Goodbye', a ritual of Indian bride bidding farewell to her family and leaving of her maternal home.

"Shaman, seriously, I'd have missed you like crazy if you had gone," Shambhavi said. "Now I can't imagine my life without you!"

"Me too… If I don't see you for an hour, I start looking for you all over the *ashram*," he said in a serious voice.

"That reminds me, Chandni will be sleeping in my room tonight… so..."

Shaman immediately said, "You come to mine … no Chandni or Chandu will be there."

"Your room…? Let me see... It's a good thing that Chandni sleeps like a log. I will try…"

"Ah! One more thing, come exactly how you are currently dressed... don't change a thing," said Shaman.

"Like this? You've got to be joking. This *ghaghara* is so cumbersome."

"Well, too bad. Let me tell you clearly, keep whatever you are wearing on your person intact… Come as you are."

Shambhavi shook her head and said no with a smile in her voice.

"Your food is coming," Chandni announced as she balanced two trays of food. She set the food in front of them and went back inside.

"It is delicious," Shambhavi said as she finished the last morsel.

"There is some *moong halwa*[98]; shall I get some for both of you?" Chandni asked from inside

"Yes, yes, please get it. I love *moong halwa*. What about you, Shaman Da?"

"I am done… I can't eat any more," Shaman said. "I am

[98]Moong halva: Indian dessert, especially made during winter months. It's made using moong dal (a lentil) and flavoured with ghee, saffron and cardamom.

surprised a tiny thing like you can consume such a large plate of food! You must be weighing a lot less than even 50kgs."

"Not a lot less, but thereabouts. However that's pretty accurate! I am impressed."

"Don't forget I carried you," Shaman said with a laugh, but in that instant he remembered, with frightening clarity, how close they had been to death.

"Yes, you saved my life," Shambhavi said in a grave voice. She too remembered the ordeal of that day.

"Take it as a favour returned. You saved my life after the snake bite!" he said, attempting to lighten her mood.

Shaman bid everyone good night and went to his room. "Waiting for you," he mouthed silently to Shambhavi as he left.

A good two hours passed. Shaman sat at his writing table, the goose-necked table lamp illuminating a bright circle around the desk. The rest of the room was a web of soft diffused light. He was doubtful if she would be able to get away. He hoped she did.

Finally, he heard his door creak open. There she stood, her cheeks flushed from the cold. She was wrapped in a thick dark shawl, only her grey eyes were visible.

"You sure took your time to come. I thought you wouldn't turn up. And just so you know, you are look like Phoolan Devi!" Shaman teased.

"It was either I come alive as Phoolan Devi or come frozen to death as Shambhavi! It's freezing outside." Shambhavi slowly took off her shawl.

She was still wearing the gorgeous *ghagra* that she had worn for the wedding ceremony. The fragrance of her perfume filled the room.

"I wanted to hold you as soon as I saw you all dressed up. I couldn't take my eyes off you." Shaman hugged her. "God almighty, save me. Do you know how beautiful you are?" he whispered. He kissed both of her cheeks; her skin felt like soft, delicate petals.

"It's only grooming and clever make-up. Some of the *pahadi* girls here are so much prettier than me," she said, hiding her face in his neck.

"Now let me cover myself with the shawl. I don't know how you manage to stay alive in this cold in just one thin cotton *dhoti,*" she said wriggling out of his arms. "My *bindi* is stuck on your neck. Tell me, where is the mirror?"

"There is no mirror here."

"Why do I need a mirror when you're there? Put the *bindi* for me," Shambhavi commanded him and held out the blue and silver bindi in her hand.

He stuck it effortlessly between her eyebrows and kissed her forehead, "Now you look perfect again. Good, you noticed that it was stuck on me. Otherwise that would have been a dead giveaway."

Shambhavi covered herself with the shawl again and walked around his clean room.

"My God! You have hundreds of books," she commented as she passed a cupboard bursting with books. Shaman sat on his chair and watched her.

"Why is your room so far from the other rooms? Granted, it has a fantastic view of the Prayag, but it was so dark on the way, I nearly fell down. In fact, I think I lost an anklet on the way here."

"I hope you are not hurt," his voice was full of concern.

"No, I am not hurt." she assured him.

She looked around his room again. "Do you pray here Shaman? This place has a very peaceful vibe."

"Okay, enough of walking around, just sit down," he said gesturing to the single bed.

She sat down on the bed and tucked her knees under the shawl.

"Yes, I do pray here. I wanted a room away from the hustle and bustle of the *ashram* so that I could meditate without disturbance."

"Yes, the location is perfect for that purpose."

"But your room is frightfully cold. I think it's because it directly gets the cold blast of the winds that come from Gangaji."

Shaman was not interested in discussing anything at the moment. "I have something to show you," he said, taking out a neatly folded paper and sitting next to her. It was the love poem he had written for her a few days ago.

She read it.

I gave up my all, and my hollowed substance
Did not until you came sing
You dropped your heart
In this beggar's kamandalu, and a new hunger bring

I fancied loving my Lord, without knowing what love means!
You loved me like a God, without knowing what God means!

If God is on the same side of love, I lose myself and gain Him and thee
If God is not on the same side, then God loses me and must come looking for me

All along I have sought God and now a new path I see
Was there ever a man who knew not love, but knew God?
Nay…
This can never be!

Shambhavi was speechless. She read the poem again. "Thank you, Shaman. It's so beautifully written. May be you should write professionally. Actually, I never imagined that a monk like you would be so romantic," Shambhavi said, still under the great influence of his beautiful words.

"It's the subject that is beautiful, the poet is only being truthful, that's all," Shaman said. "And just for the record, monks are not supposed to be romantic."

Shaman looked deep into her eyes and asked, "Tell me, who is this beautiful in your family? Who has these stunning grey eyes?"

"I think one of my ancestors was Persian or English, I am not sure. I get my skin tone and my eyes from her."

"That's a pretty exotic mix in your genetic tree!" Shaman started laughing. "You always look like you stepped out of the pages of a glossy magazine even when you trek the hills here. I wonder how you manage that...and the best part is you are completely unaware of the way you look!"

Shambhavi blushed. "You are not bad either... if you smiled more, you would look almost handsome," she said teasingly. "And tell me one thing, I know you *sannyasis* don't trim your beard. So how come your beard is only a stubble after so many years?"

"Mine doesn't grow," Shaman said sheepishly. "What you see now is after more than a decade of growing it."

"That's why you look so young and almost boyish," she said ruffling his shoulder length *jataas* with affection.

"You know, I never thought I'd find myself in a situation like this. I am completely torn apart between my duties and desires. I am unable to do anything, but think of you. To tell you the truth, I tried my best to forget you, but all my resolve just melts away the moment I see you. All I want to do is to be with you, to spend time with you and to talk to you. I feel more alive when I am in your company."

"Me too Shaman! On the one hand, I know you are going to be the next chief. Baba has selected you and you yourself command so much love and respect from everyone in the organisation. I am afraid someone will see us. I am not worried for myself, but it would jeopardise everything for you!"

"I have thought about all this and more—you are equally important to me. It's just that I don't know how to deal with it." Helplessness was apparent in his voice.

Shambhavi's eyes welled up with tears. Shaman wiped them with his thumbs gently and said, "A projection into the future will ruin our beautiful present and this beautiful present of Shambhavi is given to me by God." He ran his hands lovingly over her head. "So, for now, I am just going to cherish her."

Shambhavi rested her head on his chest and closed her eyes. He held her close and wished for time to freeze.

Suddenly Shambhavi sat up, alert.

"Shaman, I heard the sound of a door banging. I think I better go…it's almost 2 am."

"Wait, let me come with you. I know the path well," Shaman said.

"No, it's too dangerous. I will go back carefully, don't worry," she said.

"I wish you could stay longer. It feels like you just came," he said with dissatisfaction in his voice.

She kissed him and silently went away.

He felt completely empty after she left. His room smelt of her. He knew he would never be able to sit on his bed without remembering her.

45.

It was already time for the birth anniversary celebration of the *Param Guru*. A crystal clear day dawned, offering an enthralling view of the snow-clad Himalayas as they shimmered in the weak wintery sunlight. There was an air of muted festivity all around as everyone waited for the arrival of the Shankaracharya of Vyomakesh Peeth.

Shaman looked at his watch. The Shankaracharya should arrive anytime now, he estimated. He was to garland him and receive him at the car. There was an air of expectancy as everyone waited at the gate.

A white SUV with a saffron flag at the front arrived, carrying the pontiff. Many vehicles followed him. The pontiff alighted from the car. He was a round, clean-shaven man who held a saffron staff in one hand and a *kamandalu* in the other hand; around his neck was a big r*udraksha mala*.

He had a moon-like face with a ready, easy smile and twinkling eyes. A big beautiful *tripundra* mark adorned his forehead.

When Shaman garlanded him and fell at his feet, he greeted Shaman with a warm '*Namah Shivaay*!'

"How are you, Shaman?"

"By your grace, I am doing well!"

As he led the pontiff to the small dais, the little girls who had learnt dance from Shambhavi stood on either side and threw beautiful yellow chrysanthemums at his feet.

Shankaracharya took off his *mala* and garlanded the smallest child. She immediately fell at his feet and took the pontiff's blessings. Shaman recognised her as Payal, Chandni's niece, the cute girl who played Krishna. 'Good training by the parents,' thought Shaman. He made a mental note to meet them.

Leela and Madhava Da blew the conch and the *naamkaaris* started singing. The Master came down from the dais and the two spiritual giants embraced one another. They were about the same height, though Naam Yajnananda was so much frailer in comparison.

Both were clad in ochre robes and their bodies radiated a pure energy of their massive penance and unadulterated faith. One was clean-shaven and the other had a crown of *jataas;* one sported the *vaishnav tilak,* while the other, a *tripundra*.

Shaman's eyes grew moist seeing this wonderful sight. Naam Yajnananda led the pontiff by his hand and made him sit on a specially designated seat covered by a rich orange silk cloth. The pontiff's assistant had already spread his *asana* and made it ready for him.

Shambhavi stepped forward with a beautiful garland of pure white roses. She was wearing a rich purple Kanjeevaram silk sari with a gold mango border. The Master took the *mala* and garlanded the pontiff. The pontiff's assistant gave a *tulasi mala* to the pontiff and he in turn garlanded the Master.

The crowd stood up and applauded. '*Jai Guru! Jai Guru*!'

"I know how fragile you are, that's why I prepared such a light *mala* for you. Now don't remove it instantly like you always do," the pontiff said with a smile.

The Master smiled and said, "You too keep yours on!"

"Swamiji, I am greedy for your blessings. You know I never remove the *mala* you give me till I go back..." said the pontiff.

"It's just your greatness that you are speaking these kind words to me," Naam Yajnananda said humbly.

Shambhavi received the pontiff's blessings. "*Namah Shivaay*! May God bless you! Swamiji, this child always was like a *devakanya*[99]. Now she is looking like Ma Parvati herself! How are you, Beti? Swamiji is looking much better with you here," he said.

"I am fine, Baba…"

"Did you make this beautiful *mala*?" he asked, pointing to the garland around his neck. "I love the colour white. It's a colour closest to the ashes, the favourite of Mahadeva!"

"Yes, Baba, I made it."

"God bless you once again. May you always be happy," he said, lifting both his hands.

Shaman came up on stage and asked the Master, "Shall we start the *diksha*?"

"Yes we will start the program with only one little change, *you* will be giving the *diksha*. Shambhavi Beta, please hand me the mic. From now on, Swami Sharanananda will be giving *diksha*. He is a *diksha adhikari* now! I authorise him to give initiations."

Everyone cheered loudly as soon as the Master made the announcement. It was an unreal moment for Shaman.

He stood dumbstruck. "Maharaj, me?"

"Yes, you."

"A wonderful decision," said the pontiff. "You have chosen the right heir! I am so happy that you have such a worthy successor. *Namah Shivaay*! Let the *diksha* program begin."

Shaman still stood rooted to the spot.

"Shaman, the *padukas*[100] are on the table. Take them to bless the people with," urged the Master.

---

[99]Devakanya: Divine damsel

[100]Padukas: Guru's sandals

Shaman recovered from the shock and quickly did as he was told. But he still hadn't registered the enormity of the moment. Long years of assisting the Master enabled him to effortlessly carry out the *diksha*.

"Shambhavi, note down the names of the people getting *diksha* and their *ishta mantras*[101] ," said the Master with a smile.

Some got Krishna, some got Rama, some got Shiva and a few young students asked for Saraswati. Others like the ironsmiths got Hanuman.

Shaman was pleasantly surprised to see Raka, a tribal man sitting in a strange headgear, in the line of people receiving *diksha*.

Shaman asked him, "What is the *ishta* you want?"

"Swamiji, the only God I know is mother Ganga."

Shaman looked at the Master. The request was indeed unusual, but the Master nodded and indicated that Shaman could go ahead and give the Ganga *mantra*.

When the pontiff witnessed this, he said, "Your organisation is indeed a great one. Each one gets a *mantra* of their choice. How wonderful is that! In other Orders, there is only one *mantra*, even in our own *sampradaya*, there is only one *mantra*. So whether one is Ram *bhakta*[102] or a Ganesh *bhakta*, his innate predisposition is never factored in. With time, I have realised, one size to fit all doesn't work very well."

The Master smiled. "Every spiritual tool that we hand over to the aspirants has to be crafted in such a way that the devotee using it reaches his full potential. And what is potential after all? It is nothing but how much the person has prayed and meditated in his previous lives. The only way one can tap into this secret cache of merit is for us to take into account his

[101]Ishta mantras: favourite deities

[102]Bhakti: devotion; a bhakta is one who is devoted to a particular God.

leaning towards a particular deity."

"Maharaj, the initiation process is over. If you could both come down the dais, the newly initiated devotees will take your blessings," Shaman informed them.

"All right… Shaman, another thing, as you know, we have scheduled tomorrow morning for the *sannyasa diksha*. Like today, you will be initiating the *sannyasa* aspirants as well."

Shaman was overwhelmed. He felt enormously weighed down by Maharaj's words. "Maharaj… me..?"

"Yes you! You are ready for this and you are an ideal *sannyasi*; people receiving the *diksha* tomorrow are lucky to receive it from your hands."

"I agree," said the pontiff and both the revered *mahatma*s stepped down the dais and blessed the devotees one by one.

46.

The rest of the day was a blur to Shaman as he functioned on autopilot. The guilt of not following his vows made him bleed on the inside. After duly seeing off the pontiff to his car, he told Shambhavi, "I am going for a walk. Too much happened today, and I need some solitude."

"It's three in the afternoon, you haven't had lunch and now it's suddenly become overcast and windy. Why do you want to go now?"

"I'm feeling suffocated. I need to be on my own; can't really explain the feeling."

"Alright, be careful. Come back if it starts raining," she said with concern.

As Shaman walked away, he could feel Shambhavi's gaze on his back. He turned around, and sure enough, she was looking right at him. She waved to him. Shaman understood that Shambhavi was clearly clued into his feelings. Even though he hadn't said much, she understood that something was bothering him deeply.

His mind was running in circles. On the one hand was his deep attraction and affection for Shambhavi, and on the other, his duty towards the life he had adopted, and his vows. He felt he was being torn apart by this double life. The faith that Maharaj had reposed in him made him feel ashamed of how easily he had strayed from the path.

The afternoon soon turned windy and cold as he walked about aimlessly. Soon he found himself by a natural spring near the tribal settlement.

Even on a dull cloudy day, the bright, orange roses stood out sharply against the grey misty surroundings. The wind blew one exquisite blossom almost right into his hand. He caught it and studied it closely. The vivid colour of the rose reminded him of his *sannyasa diksha*. Shaman remembered the day of his initiation into *sannyasa* with a crystal clear clarity, though it took place a good 12 years ago.

47.

Shaman had to fast in the three weeks prior to the actual initiation. In the first week he ate fruit twice a day, in the second, just once a day, and during the third week, his diet was down to just a glass of milk and water. Shaman had been residing with the Master in Uttar Kashi at the time, but his *sannyasa diksha* was scheduled to happen in Badrinath on the auspicious day of *Akshaya Tritiya*.

A day before the event, Krishna Da, the Master and Shaman proceeded to Badrinath by jeep. It was bitterly cold in Badrinath and the entire town was covered in snow and ice. Shaman had been doing one lakh *Gayatri mantra japa* every day in the three weeks of fasting, in a secluded hut allotted to him in a remote corner of the *ashram*. Though he lost weight during that period, his spirit was in a high state of exhilaration. He was drunk on the power of *Gayatri*. His sense of connect with the divine was almost at its peak.

The night before the *sannyas*, the Master asked him to stay awake for as long as possible. Shaman remembered being so excited that he would not have been able to sleep even if it was expected of him. He spent the night in deep meditation and chanting the Gayatri. The prayerful night passed by in the blink of an eye. That day was a full fasting day, not even a drop of water to drink.

Finally Akshaya Tritiya dawned on Badrinath. The *ashram* was located on the banks of Bhagirathi. Shaman left for his ritual bath in the river at 4 am. It was dark and insanely cold. In the light from the lone street lamp, he could see large table-sized ice blocks floating in the holy river's gentle flow. He didn't hesitate even for a second before entering the freezing water. The energy of the deep divine had gripped Shaman so completely that he hardly felt the lacerating cold of the water. He took off his clothes and let them adrift. He had put a brand new *dhoti* on the lowest step near the water prior to entering the river. Now, after the bath, he wore that *dhoti* and walked up the steps to the *ashram*. Ram Dada, an old *sannyasi*, stood at the gates—he helped Shaman shave his head. "Just keep a tuft," Shaman told him.

Shaman felt his worldly bondages drop away with every falling clump of hair. He felt light as a feather.

"I am surprised. Not only are you not complaining about the cold, even your teeth are not chattering," Ram Dada said. "Look at me…" he said pointing to the several layers of heavy woollens on his own person.

"It is cold Dada," Shaman replied with a smile

The old *sannyasi* handed him another *dhoti*. "Go Shaman, have another bath."

Shaman went back to the river. He felt warm anticipation for the new beginning that awaited him in the icy embrace of the water. It was like living in an altered state of consciousness. His mind was so in sync with the Almighty that the physical conditions didn't touch him at all. The weeks of focussed prayer and fasting had polished his inner being. It was like he had a shield of piety around him, protecting him from the elements.

He stepped out after three deep dips, wore yet another new *dhoti* and went to where Ram Dada was waiting for him. He had everything ready for the *atma shraddha*—three rice balls mixed with *til*, flowers and other items. The *sannyasi's* hands were shivering so badly that he was unable to light the lamp. Shaman took the matchbox from the old man's hand and lit the ghee lamp. "We *sannyasis* have to do this for ourselves because no one will do it for us when we die," Ram Dada explained to Shaman. "One is dead to the world as soon as one takes *sannyasa;* death gets its due ritual. But unlike the passing of others, nobody will mourn our passing because we cut off all ties to society and family. Our death is a happy occasion, now and when we leave our body."

Ram Dada proceeded with the rituals, reading the required *mantras* and helping Shaman through the rites. Shaman loved the idea of cutting off from everything. The sense of imminent freedom was a heady one. At the end of the *shraddha*, Ram Dada gave Shaman another *dhoti* for another bath. He told him with great pain, "The water is freezing, I feel terrible asking you to take a bath again and again."

Shaman, on the other hand, didn't seem to mind at all. So fuelled was he by positive energy that he welcomed every ritual with great enthusiasm. This was one of the most ancient rituals that had remained unchanged from the days of the *Upanishads*. An invisible thread of grace connected with the *sannyasa* lineage filled his being. He felt strong and empowered.

He quickly finished having a bath. The pale dawn slowly cast the surroundings with a grey cloak. With each dip, Shaman felt his shackles break away. He smiled as his very being resonated with pure joy.

When he returned, Ram Dada had readied the *havan* and gestured for Shaman to offer *ghee*. "This *yajna* is called Viraja, meaning 'free from Rajas or passion'. Here, you will offer only *ghee* which symbolises sacrifice. And after that, you will offer all your passions. Now, as you make an offering of ghee, think that you are offering your anger, lust, greed, and even your intellect." Though Shaman had read up on all this, he patiently listened to the happy *sannyasi*.

Shaman was fascinated by the idea of physically giving away these bondages. At the end of the *yajna*, Ram Dada said, "All the impurities are gone... burnt to ashes! What remains now is only pure consciousness."

He gave Shaman his ochre *dhoti* and asked him to have one final bath.

By then it was almost 8 am. The sun slowly peeked over the eastern horizon. Every snow-covered mountain reflected the same colours. Everything was paved in beaten gold. The river itself was like a gilded orange ribbon gliding smoothly over the huge ice blocks. When Shaman emerged in his ochre robe from the water, he glowed like he himself was made of pure shimmering gold.

As he put on his *dhoti,* he felt he was born again. The new beginning in his life made him feel free, like a soaring bird devoid of encumbrances! He was almost giddy with happiness.

When he went to Ram Dada, he directed him inside the *ashram*. A large garlanded photo of Ma Kali was placed at the centre of the room. Incense and lit lamps were placed before her. There, Naam Yajnananda Maharaj sat and gave him his *sannyasa mantra*. It was a deeply sombre ritual as Maharaj and Shaman sat in silent communion for a very long time.

"From this moment onwards, there are no fears for you, Shaman. Only fearlessness is the way forward. No fear of society, no fear of men, no fear of animals! You shall live in *abhaya* from now on." A shiver ran down Shaman's spine at his Master's words.

Then the Master led Shaman to Ma Ganga again. Birds sang in the morning light. Someone blew a conch in the distance. A most glorious day had unfolded.

"As the Sun as your witness, renounce the three *eashanas,*" Maharaj told Shaman. "Love of Family, love of Wealth and love of Name and Fame."

Shaman walked knee-deep into the Ganga, offered water to the infant Sun God and gave away the three primary desires.

With tears of joy, he walked out and fell at the Master's feet. The Master blessed him and placed a *rudraksha mala* around his neck. He also gave him a small *kamandalu* and a walking stick.

"Shaman, you have surrendered yourself to the Cosmic Spirit. From today your old identity is dead, a new person is born and he will be called Swami Sharanananda."

"Sharanananda!" exclaimed Shaman, overjoyed and bending low before his Master.

He felt enthused and energised, the effervescence of freedom from the world electrified his entire being. The pure power of renunciation had lit a flame of service in him. He wanted to make a difference to himself and to mankind.

48.

He sat amongst the rose bushes and meditated for a long time. When he opened his eyes, the world was pitch-black and icy cold. It was past 10 pm. He had finally come to a decision; he was going to tell the Master everything. He couldn't bear the burden of guilt anymore. But he was still quite apprehensive. 'What will I tell the Master?' Everything that came to his mind would be blasphemous and sinful in the Master's eyes. Shambhavi was supposed to be like his daughter. Shaman cursed his predicament.

When he reached the *ashram,* he almost gave up on telling Maharaj. But then the all-consuming guilt threatened to swallow him up. He ran up the steps to Maharaj's chambers hoping he was awake.

The Master was reading.

"*Pranaam,* Maharaj." Shaman said, bowing down to seek the Master's blessings.

"*Jai Guru,* Shaman! This book that you have given me is fantastic. You really have the ability to spot gems. But what are you doing here now? Tomorrow is the *sannyasa diksha,* you will be up from 3 am! You must sleep."

"Maharaj, I don't think I am the right person to give the *sannyasa diksha*... I am clearly not worthy of the honour."

"Worthy? There is no one worthier than you. Don't doubt yourself ... I have full faith in you."

"That's exactly the problem Maharaj. I am not worthy of your faith."

"Shaman, come and sit here."

"Maharaj, first let me tell you what I have to tell you. I just don't know how and where to begin."

"First sit down Shaman, and start from the beginning. What's bothering you so much?"

Shaman sat at the Master's feet.

"Maharaj... I don't know how this is going to sound, but I am just going to tell you the truth. Please don't get angry with me. I was caught in a set of circumstances, which seemed totally out of my control, to the extent that it forced me to believe that it is part of the divine plan... Shambhavi and I have grown extraordinarily close and I am very fond of her. My mind now has become occupied with thoughts of her. I think I have strayed too far from the path..."

The Master was silent.

"I am unable to get over this inexorable attraction that I feel for her," Shaman said helplessly.

"She told me..." the Master murmured. "Shambhavi told me that she is attracted to you. I thought it was one-sided. She spoke for herself, not for you. When I heard her, I never, for even one moment, thought you would fall into this age-old trap."

"I fell into the trap and I have strayed from the path... your faith in me is misplaced ... I have fallen!"

Hot tears streamed down Shaman's face.

"No, my faith in you is perfectly placed. Such temptations are common, it happens to almost everyone when one is on the path. You only need to put on your blinkers and stick to the chosen path."

"I am lost...my path is lost..."Shaman bemoaned.

"Nothing is lost… you only need to avoid her and focus on the vows you've made to yourself. Think of your duty to this organisation. You have an extraordinary purpose in life, don't dilute it by succumbing to common temptations. Temptations come to everyone, everyone arrives at crossroads. But *you* can overcome it. It's just about sticking to the correct path. I am sure you will get over this as soon as you set your mind to it. This *sampradaya* needs you. Don't throw it all away. You are destined for great things. You have the charisma, the education and a deep spiritual drive to become a spiritual leader who will impact thousands."

Shaman listened silently, his eyes full of tears.

"Don't judge yourself so harshly, Shaman. Move on. Stick to your vows from now on. Don't contemplate and reflect too much on what has already happened. Go and sleep now. Tomorrow, you must give the *sannyasa diksha*."

The distraught *sannyasi* left the room. He continued to feel haunted and besieged. He spent a sleepless night in his room. And with a troubled heart, he left at the crack of dawn to initiate the novice *sannyasis*.

49.

There was a biting wind blowing when Shaman stepped out of his room. It was still dark, but dawn was just around the corner. His eyes felt gritty from lack of sleep. A heavy lethargy gripped his body and his heart felt even heavier. He saw the light was on in the Master's chamber and decided to seek his blessings.

Shaman felt uneasy about initiating the young *sannyasis*. In his mind, he kept praying to Maharaj, begging to save him from this situation.

The Master greeted him, "*Jai Guru*. You are right on time."

Shaman bent his head low in prostration and touched the Master's feet.

"Shaman, your hands are like live coals and your eyes are bloodshot. How are you feeling? Come here, let me check if you have a fever."

"I am fine Maharaj, just feeling a little low on energy."

"You are burning with fever. What did you eat last night?"

Krishna Da answered, "Shaman Da has not had anything since breakfast yesterday!"

"Shaman, is that true?"

"Maharaj, I didn't feel hungry."

"Krishna, get him a glass of hot milk and give me that medicine case. Shaman, you will not be able to give *diksha*, owing to your sudden fever. Scriptures do not recommend that either the one who confers initiation or one who receives it is sick. Drink your milk and then have this tablet. I will initiate the *sannyasis*... Take rest Shaman. Don't worry, everything will be all right."

Saying this, the Master left the room.

Shaman felt a great wave of relief. He joined his hands in prayer and thanked the Almighty!

50.

Shaman had fever for a day before he started to feel better. But his spirit was still unwell. More than anything, he had found a companion and friend in Shambhavi, whose presence filled him with joy. The prospect of staying away from her was nothing short of an exile for him. He just didn't know how to break Maharaj's command to her.

He went down to the Prayag to do his morning prayers. The usual sense of well-being was absent. He felt dull and heavy.

The sun was breaking away from the tight clutch of clouds in the east when he finished his prayers. It was a day of sudden gusts of wind.

"Shaman..."

Shambhavi came running towards him from the side of the forest. She was dressed in thick black sweatpants and a fully zipped matching top. She had her running shoes on. She took off her ear phones, catching her breath. The jog had left a sheen of sweat on her forehead that sparkled in the early morning light. She herself felt like a burst of sunbeams to Shaman.

"How are you feeling? Is the fever gone? I didn't see you at all yesterday. I missed you. I wanted to come see you, but Madhav Da was there with you all the time."

"I am better."

"You still look unwell. Did you have the medicines on time?" asked Shambhavi.

"Yes I did."

"You finished your prayers? Shall we go up?" she asked.

"You go, I will do some *dhyana* and come up later," he said.

'It's so difficult to find excuses to stay away from her,' thought Shaman.

"Okay, I will shower and wait for you to have breakfast. Venu Da is making yummy *moong dal chillas,*" she said with excitement.

"I don't know if I'll be able to eat something so heavy, I think I'll just have fruit," said Shaman.

"All right, have fruit, but we will eat it together. You really seem out of sorts. I'll see you in a bit. Come back soon; it's so cold here. And you have just about recovered from the fever," she said.

He watched her with hungry eyes as she ran up the steps to the *ashram*. When she was halfway up the steps, a sudden gust of wind blew the sand used for annual maintenance into her eyes.

"Shaman!" she called out. "I have sand in both of my eyes, please come here."

He quickly went up. "Don't rub them."

He wanted to help her, but decided against it. The Master's words were still ringing in his ears.

"I can't see a thing. My eyes are stinging like crazy. Give me your hand, take me upstairs!"

"You come on your own," Shaman replied, trying to avoid the inevitable. "I'll be by your side."

"Shaman, what's wrong with you? Even with both my eyes open, there is a chance I will fall on these tricky steps. How will I walk up without assistance, especially when I can't see a thing? Just give me your hand."

Helplessly, he gave her his hand. She held his forearm and climbed up the steps. He walked as far ahead and away as he could from her, keeping contact to a minimum.

"There is a big step coming up and then two uneven ones," Shaman warned her.

"You are great at commentary," said Shambhavi, laughing. "But you are behaving oddly."

Shaman wanted to tell her everything, but he just couldn't bring himself to. Her proximity rekindled all of the feelings he had been trying to repress. With determination, he snuffed them once again and focussed on the task at hand.

As soon they reached the top, Shaman called out to Chandni.

"Take Didi and wash her eyes in the eye cup. The eye cup is in Maharaj's room. Ask Madhav Da to bring it."

"Thanks for bringing me up; you are a great guide for the blind," Shambhavi said, laughing.

Shaman sat at the temple for a long time. He was finding it impossible to stay away from Shambhavi. But he resolved to do just that, no matter how difficult the task. He was also mentally preparing himself to tell her the Master's command. He was frustrated, angry and miserable – all at the same time.

Just then, he saw Venu Da, Krishna Da and Keshava Da arrive. Without any preamble they asked, 'Why were you holding Didi's hand?'

"What?" Shaman asked. He didn't understand what they were saying, so lost was he in his own thoughts.

"Why were you holding Shambhavi Didi's hand when you were coming up from the Prayag? Is it correct for a *sannyasi* to hold a young girl's hand?" Venu Da questioned him.

"She had sand in her eyes. If she had come up on her own, she would have fallen," he patiently explained.

"We saw you laughing and talking... We saw you from up here. You could have come up and called one of us," said Keshava Da.

"Why? Aren't you all *sannyasis* like me?"

Shaman was getting irritated.

"That's not the point. The *ashram* has a certain code of conduct, and you violated it. This sort of behaviour is unbecoming of a *sannyasi*," Krishna Da admonished.

"What is unbecoming? Helping her is unbecoming? If you had bothered to look closely, you would have realised that she was holding my arm, I was not holding anything." Shaman was angry now.

"Trying to trick us with words, are you? It won't help. You will bring shame to the *sannyasi* community if you continue like this," said Venu Da with vehemence.

Shaman was furious with their accusatory tone, especially given the fact that he was trying his best to stay away from Shambhavi. His own frustration and guilt unfurled in him a dark rage.

"What exactly is your point? Tell me, what's your idea of who is and who is not a *sannyasi*? Let me hear the definition from *yogis* like you," he said sardonically.

"Education is not everything, Shaman Da! You are proud that you have studied so much. You are also arrogant since Maharaj loves you dearly. We went and complained to him that you were holding Didi's hand. He didn't even want to listen to us. But we are not blinded by affection like Maharaj is."

"Why would he listen to you? Are you greater than him?" Shaman shot back. "Maharaj is not blind, he is a *jnani*, and he knows the truth. He knows I was just being natural; I did what was right for the moment—helping someone who needed it."

"Very charitable indeed!" said Venu Da. "Things should not be so natural for *sannyasis*, at least that's what I've understood. Ordinary folks can do what they like, the natural thing, as you call it. But we are *sannyasis*."

"So what? Why are you feeling so self-important about being a *sannyasi*?" said Shaman. "Yes, we are *sannyasis*, what does that mean? The word *sannyasa* is made of *sa*, *na* and *ayas*—living with no intentional effort (*ayasa*), just surrendering everything to God."

"We don't understand these language subtleties," Venu Da protested again. "We just know that a *sannyasi* has to keep his distance from a woman. The scripture says *naari narakasya dwaaram*, 'Woman is gateway to Hell'. You know that better than us. Woman is fire, Dada… Won't you agree?"

"Are you calling Shambhavi fire?" Shaman demanded angrily. "Are you saying every woman is fire?"

"Well…" Venu Da struggled a bit.

"Yes, I agree, woman is fire," said Shaman. "She is the Mother Fire from whose womb you, I and every other *sannyasi* is born. Why do you have these regressive views?"

"You can say whatever you like, but a *sannyasi* must exercise control and not mix with women," Keshava Da spoke up, defending Venu Da.

"Who can control anything? What is this holier-than-thou attitude?" Shaman said, exasperated. "A *sannyasi* should become like the wind or the water—flowing in whatever direction life pushes him. He has to become empty like space and insignificant like a fallen autumn leaf."

"Very well said, but everyone has to own his actions, don't they?" Keshava Da asked.

"A *sannyasi* owns nothing. All is God's will," Shaman observed calmly.

"How convenient and distorted! I don't think the *Bhagavad Gita* advocates holding women's hands," said Venu Da.

"You speak of the *Gita*? I feel so sad that *sannyasis* are not formally educated... They just don't understand the subtle import of the *Gita* or the *Upanishad*."

"Sri Ramakrishna was not educated..." Keshava Da quickly countered.

"That's not an excuse. If you're not educated, you make a big deal out of external things—the dress, social protocol, outer rites..."

"All right, all right... You have the last word on *sannyasa*, we are all lesser mortals. Come on, let's go, there is no point arguing here. We have *ashram* work to do..." said Venu Da.

Everyone muttered a 'yes' and slunk away, leaving Shaman alone to feel miserable for shooting his mouth off.

Just when he thought his day couldn't get any worse, Madhav Da came to inform him that the Master had summoned him.

Maharaj was standing by the window looking out at the snow-capped mountains.

"*Pranaam*, Maharaj."

"Shaman, did you explain the finer points of being a *sannyasi* to Venu, Krishna and Keshava?"

"Maharaj I..."

"Did you or did you not?"

"Yes Maharaj, I did."

"I want you to immediately go and apologise to them—seek their forgiveness and get their blessings."

"As you say Maharaj!" Without a moment's hesitation, Shaman left in search of the older *sannyasis*.

51.

Shaman watched the water leap on the rocks at the *sangam*. The agitated water crashed against the smooth eroded rocks. Shaman couldn't help but think it mirrored his state of mind. The searing heat of humiliation still burned within him. The angry voices of the *ashramites* continued to echo in his mind. He tried his best to control his anger, but he was barely successful. Fury simmered just beneath the surface and his eyes still held the burning embers of his anger.

He paced on the rocky banks, willing his mind to stop spinning and prayed to Ma Ganga to calm him down.

Shaman heard her light footsteps even before he saw Shambhavi race down the steps to the Prayag. She almost ran into his arms.

"Shaman, I looked for you everywhere," she gasped for breath. "Then I thought I'd find you here."

Her cheeks were pink from exertion. Even in the harsh sunlight, she looked beautiful. She was clad in a black and grey woollen skirt with a pink lace top. Despite his anger, her good looks momentarily unarmed him. His weakness for her made him angrier than he already was.

"I am very sorry to hear that you had to apologise to everyone," she said in a voice full of concern.

Shaman held her shoulders and pushed her away. Unprepared for his rejection, she stumbled a little on the uneven ground before she regained her balance. "What happened Shaman? I'm sorry if I have hurt you in any way," she said taking a step closer to him.

He held out his right hand gesturing for her to stop.

"You *should* be sorry. It is because of you that I am in this situation. You should be very sorry indeed," he added. "And please stay away from me, you have caused me enough trouble as it is." His anger was now a raging fire in his eyes.

Shambhavi looked confused. "Because of me, Shaman?" She asked incredulously. "What have I got to do with your argument with the *sannyasis* here? How do I figure in this whole mess?"

"Good, at least you are acknowledging it's a mess! But remember it's a mess you created," Shaman declared with unnecessary aggression. "It's because of you that I am being accused of so many things. I have been humiliated; my fellow *sannyasis* have lost respect for me. My *guru*, who has only shown love for me, has become angry with me. Do you even know how dangerous it is to invite the wrath of a *guru*? I am ruined because of you!"

"Shaman, please calm down," Shambhavi said in a soft voice.

But Shaman was in no state to listen. "Calm down? Do you know what all I had to go through? Do you have any idea? I had to fall at everyone's feet and apologise to them. I feel like a worm!"

Shaman stopped and again continued. "Shambhavi, it's all because of you. You have ruined me, left me with no self-respect. You seduced me with all your womanly charms and I fell for the magical web you wove around me. I have deviated from my chosen path," his voice was choked.

"Do you even know what you are saying?"

Shaman laughed dryly. "Don't... Now don't accuse me of losing my mind. I lost my judgement when I succumbed to your overtures, but now my mind is clear."

Shambhavi's eyes were full of tears. "I seduced you? How can you even say such a thing?" Her voice trembled.

But Shaman was so caught up in his anger that he didn't care that she was hurt by his words.

"Don't cry Shambhavi, that's the easiest thing a person can do. Your tears once had the ability to melt away all logic. Now I am immune to your tears... So don't waste them," he said callously.

"And yes, you seduced me in the cave temple. Face the facts and live with your guilt, just like how I will live with my guilt for having strayed from my path. You know, Shambhavi, I took an oath of *naishtika brahmacharya*, but you single-handedly side-tracked me. You too have sinned greatly. You enmeshed me with lust," he said with disgust.

"Lust?" she said, her eyes wide with surprise and pain. Shambhavi felt like she had just been punched in the gut. She wept silent tears of shock and despair.

"In my 39 years, I have never been touched by a woman. I barely remember even the touch of my mother, and she left me with my grandfather when I was three years old. Now I am so consumed by you that I am in danger of losing everything that I have worked for," Shaman said as he ran his hands over his *jataas* in frustration.

He paced up and down shaking with anger. "Why did you target me, Shambhavi? Did you want to experiment and see if a *sannyasi* would fall for your beauty? What did you want to achieve? Where did you think this dalliance would take us? You will go back to your dance, but what will happen to me? Did you even care? I should have avoided you like the plague. A woman brings destruction. I should have realised that better than anybody else. Every *shaashtra* screams that as a headline... Serves me right for thinking I was above it."

Shambhavi wiped her tears with resolve. Her body language had changed. In a voice bereft of any emotion, she told Shaman, "I sincerely apologise for all the catastrophic upheaval I have caused you. I will leave the *ashram* and return to Bangalore immediately. I hope I will never see you again in my life. Good luck to you, Shaman. And I hope you will not stray from your path again. But before you sleep every night, just ask yourself one question: that evening in the cave, was I in any state to seduce you?"

Before Shaman could respond, she ran up the stairs and disappeared from sight.

52.

By evening, despite the ripples of frustrated anger still crashing through his being, Shaman realised what a big blunder he had committed. His mind was calmer now and he was full of regret at the way he had spoken to Shambhavi.

He tried to tell himself that it was for the best that she left the *ashram*. But his conscience wouldn't let him live with that line of thinking. Now that he had said and done all that he had, he knew he couldn't rectify the situation. Shambhavi left within a few hours after their argument; that brought out another bout of pure frustration.

His mind rotated between deep regret, frustration, and anger directed at his own self. He couldn't bring himself to eat dinner. He lay through the night, trying to come to terms with what he had done.

The next day, while on his way to the Master's chambers he spotted Krishna Da and Venu Da. But they avoided looking at him directly.

Shaman held the *sannyasis* indirectly responsible for the altercation he had had with Shambhavi. Belatedly, he also realised this conclusion was useless now, he had behaved in an unforgivably boorish manner.

The Master was his usual affable self. There was nothing in his behaviour to suggest that he was angry with Shaman in any way. That soothed Shaman to a large extent, but it didn't help the fact that he missed Shambhavi dreadfully. He sat with Maharaj and chalked out the Master's travel plans. The *guru* was going to visit *ashrams* in the states of Orissa, Rajasthan and

Madhya Pradesh later on in the month.

Though Shaman went through the motions of noting down the dates and thinking through the logistics, his mind continued to wander. He wondered what Shambhavi was doing. It was 10 am. Was she teaching? Or was she practicing on her own?

"Shaman!" the Master called.

"Yes Maharaj!"

"You seem a little lost. I had to call you twice before you responded. All well?"

"Yes Maharaj, all well."

"I was asking you what would be the travelling time between Jagannath Puri and Mahakaleshwar."

"I will check it, Maharaj."

"All right, complete the bookings and then come to my chambers after lunch."

"Yes, Maharaj."

When Shaman went down, Venu Da, Krishna Da and Keshava Da were waiting for him.

'Now what?' Shaman thought wearily.

As soon as they saw him they greeted, "*Pranaam* Dada!"

Then Venu Da said, "We want to talk to you."

Shaman looked at them in surprise.

"Come and sit here," they said, leading him to the temple steps.

Once Shaman was seated, they sat one step lower than his. "Dada, we didn't think Maharaj would take such a drastic action yesterday; we were just hurt that you spoke to us rudely," said Keshava Da.

"Who do we have but Maharaj? We were feeling bad, so we

went and just told him that. That's all," said Krishna Da.

"In fact, it was I who suggested we tell Maharaj," admitted Veṇu Da. "But I didn't think that Maharaj would take it to that level. The three of us have known you since you were a teenager; our ego was hurt when you spoke down to us. We were angry, we just didn't know what to do. Dada, we know you are much more evolved than us. What wounded us was the way you spoke to us."

"We were deeply embarrassed when Maharaj made you seek our pardon," said Krishna Da.

"Each one of us felt bad for you and we were genuinely ashamed of ourselves for putting you in that position. We are older than you, we have been wearing this robe for much longer. We should have ideally just let it go, but the ego does not go. We are supposed to give it up, but it's still stuck to us like glue."

"Please forgive us," said Keshava Da. "We are like a family. I can't live with myself knowing how much hurt yesterday's incident must have caused you."

'Yes *Dada,*' Venu Da and Krishna Da said, shaking their heads.

Shaman was deeply touched by their humility and sincerity.

"We would not have come to speak to you in the normal course of things. In fact, before we came to you, we went and told Maharaj that we found you holding Didi's hand and laughing with her. He didn't pay any attention to what we were saying," said Krishna Da.

"Actually, he threw us all out of the room rather unceremoniously," Keshava Da added.

"We were so frustrated, we decided to speak to you directly," Venu Da added.

"The Master knows everything," said Shaman. "Please don't

say anything further. All three of you are so much older than me. If I fell at your feet, it shouldn't be something to cause me pain. I should have learnt at least one percent of humility from our *guru* after all these years."

"I feel so much better after clearing the air," said Venu Da.

'Me too...' echoed the other two *sannyasis*.

"Let's put this incident behind us and carry on," said Shaman. "It was truly very nice of you all to come and have this talk."

'*Jai Guru* Dada,' all of them said together and took his blessings before going about their day.

Shaman was deeply humbled by the grace with which the three older men approached this incident. But instead of feeling better, he felt worse than before. He understood now, with clarity, that he had to apologise to Shambhavi. He couldn't carry on with this immense guilt. However, he also knew that he had to stay away from her. He was caught at a crossroads and the agitation this conflict created in his mind just wouldn't let him be at peace.

53.

She thrashed against the bindings that trapped her delicate wrists; to her great relief her feet were free and unbound.

Suddenly she heard a man's voice and stilled herself.

"Has she woken up?" a gruff voice asked.

"She has been drugged, you know that..."

No wonder her limbs felt so heavy that she could not move.

Another voice replied with a jeer. "No. I heard something rustle."

"Must be the wind..."

A strong gust of wind muffled the rest of his words.

"...We will burn her soon. Let the drug take effect..."

"We must remove all her jewellery before burning her... Alas! There is no fun in touching a sleeping woman!" another voice said with a wicked laugh.

"She is not a woman. She is a child. We took money to burn her. So let's just stick to that!"

"A female is all I care about. Child or woman, doesn't matter and this one is very beautiful..."

Raucous laughter followed.

Upon hearing these words, she suffocated with strangulating terror. She forced herself to think calmly. Her attempt to unbind her hands by twisting them yielded. The rough rope had cut into the delicate skin of her wrists. She worked them free with stealth and removed the dirty cloth in her mouth.

It took her great exertion to stand up quietly. Her ghagra *was drenched with petrol.*

The men who were squatting around a small fire and drinking, saw her. They immediately made a dash for her. She started running, her gold anklets tinkling in the wind. Several thick bangles clanked against each other. Her huge uncut diamond earrings moved wildly as she ran, pulling on her small earlobes painfully. One of the men shouted – "Don't try to catch her!" – and threw a burning twig from the fire onto the trail of petrol that leaked from her ghagra.

She ran as fast as she could. Sheer terror fuelled her legs and freed her from the debilitating effects of the sedative. But the fire snaked and roared rapidly towards her.

Suddenly, she saw Shaman standing right there, like a knight in shining armour. His toned muscles gleamed in the faint moonlight, his jataas *flew in the slight breeze. She ran even faster towards him and threw herself into his arms. Alas! Shaman had disintegrated into a puff of air. She fell on the rough ground, sobbing. Within seconds, with a whoosh, her* ghagra *was engulfed in flames. The heat was unbearable!*

One of the mercenaries caught her by her hair and pulled her to her feet.

"I will teach you a lesson for running away," he snarled through his yellow teeth as he touched her cheek with his thick calloused finger. She wanted the fire to burn her than bear the touch of this man. She opened her mouth –

She woke up with a soundless scream, soaked in sweat. Her fingers were curled into tight fists, her bed sheet twisted round her tiny waist. The acrid smell of smoke from before burned her lungs and left her breathless. She opened her eyes and looked around, heart pounding like a crazy drum.

She took deep breaths. It was a nightmare. 'I am safe,' she told herself. Her nightmare refused to leave her. She was back in her room in Bangalore. A brisk breeze fluttered the curtain carrying the heady scent of the jasmine flowers. The creeper full of white blossoms clung lovingly to her window.

She had forgotten to take the bedside clock from her cupboard. It is past 4 am, and as expected, Chandrahasini was practicing upstairs. There was no point in trying to go back to sleep. Shambhavi got up quickly, made her bed and got dressed.

When she looked into the mirror to comb her hair, all she saw was a woman whose eyes looked haunted. A deep pain scarred her beautiful features.

'Why did Shaman accuse me of such hurtful things?' she asked herself repeatedly. 'Did I really seduce him?' Hot tears burned her eyes as she recollected that night in the cave. She sighed and vowed not to cry. She knew Shaman's accusing voice would haunt her for the rest of her life.

Why did she ever get into a relationship with a *sannyasi*? she wondered as she quickly made her way to the dance hall. Her only solace now was dance. She was going to dance away her sorrow.

54.

Shaman carried on for many days, but each day became worse for him. The guilt and regret of having hurt Shambhavi, his duty to his Master, coupled with his own intense longing for her company, had turned him into an angry zombie.

Constantly, he wondered how she was feeling, and what she was doing. He picked up the phone several times to call her, but the Master's command stopped him. He only felt at peace during his prayers; otherwise, his waking hours were filled with churning thoughts that left him restless and frustrated. As a result, his work suffered. He didn't feel like talking to anyone. Frustration over his circumstances compromised the quality of his life. Every time he thought of Shambhavi, his mind replayed the horrible argument he had had with her. 'How could I behave like that?' he asked himself with remorse.

Most of all, he missed Shambhavi dearly.

After a month of this sort of existence, Madhav Da came running to him after his morning prayers.

"Dada, your grandfather has come!"

"Are you sure?" Shaman asked in surprise.

"Yes, yes Dada. Manoharji has come. He is sitting with Maharaj in his room."

Shaman went running to the Master's chambers. Maharaj was seated at his favourite chair while Manohar Srivastava sat at his feet. He heard the last scratch of their conversation.

"Those times were different Manohar, it was a more innocent

era," Maharaj said with a smile.

"I fully agree Maharaj, and I really respect and admire the way you are changing your approach with the changing times," said Shaman's grandfather.

"*Pranaam*, Maharaj," Shaman greeted the Master. He took his blessings and turned to his grandfather for the same.

"Dadaji! What a pleasant surprise! It's so good to see you."

"It's good to see you too, Shaman. Though it looks like you have lost a little weight."

Shaman sat next to his grandfather. "How was your trip? How are Ma and Papa?"

"They are fine. I returned two days ago when Maharaj asked me to come to Nagaprayag to discuss something. In fact, I was just going to ask Maharaj what it is."

"Manohar, I will not go into the details. Shaman will talk to you about it if he feels like it," Maharaj said directly. "But the reason I called you was to tell you that the place where Shaman stands today is a precarious one. It is one of the turning points in his life. Recent events have put him in a spot."

"I had a feeling. Shaman has not been his usual self lately; I felt it from his voice the last couple of times we spoke on the phone."

"Do you remember, Manohar, you had asked me, some time before he took up *sannyas,* what was the use of Shaman attending Harvard, if he had to become a *sannyasi?*"

"Yes. I remember. You told me, 'I am not giving *sannyasa* to Shaman; *sannyasa* is calling him'."

"There was another thing I had told you at that time," said Maharaj. "I told you, some choices are made by us, and some by the inescapable force of destiny we call *praarabddha*. Today, Shaman is caught in a whirl of this force of destiny."

Maharaj paused for a moment and said, "I have been thinking about him for the last few days and concluded that his future with our religious Order is over. He has to find another path. I don't want him to be here and have his heart elsewhere. That way he will neither do justice to the *sampradaya* nor to himself. Am I right, Shaman?"

"Maharaj, I surrender myself to you... You tell me what is right for me and I will do it," Shaman said bleakly.

"What is right and what is wrong for us is not always something we can decide with our mind, Shaman. The heart takes decisions too. The heart has to be whole always. Whatever we can do whole-heartedly, there we have a chance to be right. Nothing can come out of a half heart. I had asked you some time ago to stay away from Shambhavi. Now I am asking you to stay away from our *sampradaya, our ashram*."

"Are you asking him to leave?" asked Manohar.

"No, I am not asking him to leave the *ashram* or the Order. I am asking him to not leave himself. If he stays here, he will be unhappy. And no unhappy person has ever attained liberation. We have to make choices; but unless we are happy with what we have chosen, there is no point. Look at Shaman. I have never seen him so trapped. I want him to be free."

"But Maharaj, he can't turn his back on his life with you after all these years. He is a *sannyasi*."

"Manohar, Ganga does not always flow smoothly; she passes some great obstacles. And she changes her course. Life is like that—it has to flow. You cannot vehemently accommodate your life onto any path, that's silly. Life itself is the path. And life leads us, it gives us answers. It's time for Shaman to flow in another way. And who knows, that also may not be the only course ahead."

"This is confusing, Maharaj. What is Shaman's future if he leaves Prasanna Ashram?" Manohar wondered as worry clouded his eyes.

"Life will reveal itself as we start walking ahead. You don't need to have every answer ahead of time."

Their conversation was interrupted by Krishna Da who informed the Master it was time for *bhoga*[103].

"All right, Maharaj. You know best. I will have a chat with Shaman. I'll see you before I leave," said Manohar taking the Master's blessings. "Come Shaman, we have a lot of catching up to do," he said as he walked out.

---

[103]Bhoga: Food prepared and offered to God which is subsequently had as a sanctified fare or blessing

55.

"Dadaji, breakfast?"

"No, I had the prasad Maharaj gave me. I am full. You go ahead. Do you want to have breakfast?"

"No, thank you. I'm not hungry."

Shaman's grandfather felt restless. He needed answers, so he decided to confront Shaman directly. "What was Maharaj saying, Shaman? But first, tell me, what's going on here? Why are you at a turning point in your life? I am just not getting it."

Shaman sighed. "What can I tell you, Dadaji? I am confused myself."

"Okay, just answer my question – why did Maharaj ask you to stay away from Shambhavi?"

"Oh that! That's because I told the Master that I had become extraordinarily fond of her."

"What do you mean by 'extraordinarily fond'? She is the same girl who was with you in the hospital, isn't she?"

"Yes, she is the same girl."

"What is this fondness you developed for her?"

"I don't think I can explain it. I myself don't understand what I feel for her. We had a bitter fight and then she left. I feel extremely guilty that I hurt her. I need to apologise to her."

"That still doesn't explain why you are at a turning point in your life," Manohar said as he observed Shaman with sharp eyes. His grandson was keeping something from him.

"Dadaji, I find myself deeply attracted to her and my mind is always preoccupied with her. Now that she has left, I find myself missing her dreadfully."

"What about her? Is she fond of you?"

Shaman nodded. "But I don't know what she feels for me now...after the way I behaved with her... I feel ashamed of all the things I said to her."

"If you have realised you made a mistake, then you must apologise to her. But more importantly, what are you going to do about your feelings? In our time, they called it love."

Shaman merely stared at his grandfather in confusion.

"I need some time to think. Let me just go to my room."

"Sure. I'll be at the temple. I think you must go to wherever Shambhavi is and have a proper chat with her immediately. How long ago did she leave?"

"About a month ..."

As Shaman walked to his room, the realisation hit him like a sledgehammer—he was in love with Shambhavi! He knew that these intense feelings always existed in his mind. He had just stubbornly refused to see it for what it was. He could not be in denial any longer. He knew right then that he had to go to Bangalore. He would first apologise to Shambhavi and then confess his feelings.

The greatness of Maharaj and his immense sensitivity to the mental state of his disciples astounded him. Maharaj knew of Shaman's feelings even before he had addressed them himself.

56.

There was a knock at his door. It was Madhav Da. "Shaman Da, Maharaj is calling for you."

The Master was seated at his writing desk. He gestured for his disciple to sit. Shaman entered and closed the door.

"Did Shambhavi tell you who she is?" he asked when Shaman was seated on the floor.

"Who she is? Maharaj, I do not understand."

"Did she tell you about her life before she came to Nagaprayag?"

"No, Maharaj. She has not said anything."

Maharaj hummed in thought. "Okay, I will tell you the bare minimum. The rest is up to her... This is a letter I received from Shambhavi's grandmother, 10 years ago..."

He handed Shaman a letter written on expensive paper. It bore an embossed royal crest in red, of an elephant and tiger standing on their hind legs, garlanding the image of Devi. Though the letter was old and yellowed, it was still in perfect condition, the handwriting elegant and flowing. It had been written in light blue ink.

> *Respected Guruji, I lay my pranaams at your lotus feet.*
>
> *As you know, I suffer from an incurable disease. I may not last another week. I ask you to promise me that you will save my step son's daughter, Shambhavi. After the death of her parents, she has been living with me.*
>
> *I have come to know, without any doubt, that my son was responsible for the car accident that took the lives of his step-*

brother and his wife. The child, Shambhavi, by the grace of Ambe Ma, somehow escaped unhurt. But deep avarice will drive my son to take even the life of a child.

I have tried my best to protect her, but with me gone, she will not last long. She is the only obstacle in his path to his inheriting all my step-son's wealth. As the firstborn, Shambhavi's father inherited all the ancestral wealth. She is now the sole heiress.

I have committed many sins in my lifetime, but I cannot have the blood of an innocent child on my soul. Please save the child from the clutches of my son. I have no one to turn to but you.

Seeking your grace, Savitri Devi

Shaman read the letter twice before he could take in the horror of it.

"I preserved the letter carefully, Shaman, for I didn't know when I would need it," Maharaj said. "The day I received it, was fortunately the day we were planning to visit our *ashram* in Faridabad. What I tell you now may sound like pure fiction, but remember it is the unvarnished truth."

Shaman nodded in silence.

"Krishna Da, Venu Da, Keshava Da and the driver Lakhan, who died last year, and I, were going on this trip. We went to our *ashram* in Sitapur as per plan, but I was somehow uncomfortable; I wanted to go to Savitri Devi's village as soon as possible.

We drove through the night and arrived at her village at dawn. She lived in a vast palace-like *haveli*[104] along with her son and Shambhavi. She was gravely ill and frail, but mentally alert and coherent. Happy to see me, she immediately sent word for her son, Suryakanta. He came and received us *sannyasis* with such respect that I wondered if his mother was just imagining

[104]Haveli: a sprawling mansion

half the things that she wrote in the letter.

Savitri Devi told her son that she was going to gift me some things. Suryakanta was more than generous. 'Whatever you want, you give,' he told his mother and went away. Savitri Devi had packed four large suitcases and had her servants load them in our Ambassador.

After they were loaded, she called me aside and said. 'That's for the child, Shambhavi. It's my personal wealth. Even my son doesn't know what I have and what I don't have.'

The lady was wheezing very badly and could hardly speak. 'Now that you have come, I can die in peace,' she whispered. She passed away early that very night.

Now, we *sannyasis* cannot be in a place where a death has occurred, so we left the *haveli* as soon as we came to know. I kept praying. I just didn't know how to rescue the child. First thing, I didn't even know if what was in the letter was true.

We received news of Savitri Devi's passing only at around 3 am, from a servant. We left within fifteen minutes, but we didn't have a plan as to where we were going. After driving away from the village for about twenty minutes, we suddenly came upon a girl who was set on fire, running directly towards our car. A group of men, who were chasing her, fled as soon as they saw our car approach.

To my utter shock, I realised it was Shambhavi whom they had set on fire. Thankfully, what she was wearing was a very thick garment. We managed to save her. I realised then that every word in that letter had been true. I prayed to my *guru*, put the child in our car and drove right back to Nagaprayag. Strangely, no one has tried to find the child or trace her whereabouts."

Shaman's face wore an expression of pure astonishment.

"I know what you must be thinking—why didn't I go to the police? Well, I am a simple *sannyasi*, how could I fight the system? I was pretty sure that Suryakanta had the law and order completely under his thumb."

"It must have been very difficult for you."

"It was, but at the same time, it was not. I knew I was doing the right thing. For the first few months, I kept her hidden. I was afraid for her life. Then I felt the people who wanted her out of their path must be happy that she had disappeared or perhaps they had assumed she was dead. Subsequently, I learnt that Shambhavi was declared dead in a fire accident and her uncle inherited all her property. I heaved a sigh of relief."

"How traumatic it must have been for Shambhavi!"

"She was a tiny thing at thirteen, like a thin boy. She was so traumatised that she barely ate or spoke. By God's grace, she slowly started getting better. Then I requested Mother Superior for a seat in her school. She obliged without asking a single question and even without a bit of paperwork. It was only after she joined the school that the authorities informed me that she is a trained *kuchipudi* dancer. I requested the school for a special teacher to hone her skills. The rest of the story, you know..."

"I am shell-shocked, Maharaj. I have no words," said Shaman.

"People do anything for wealth. That's the rule of *Kali Yuga*[105]," said the Master. "Her finances are handled by a professional CA. She has enough personal wealth to run several *ashrams* for a lifetime. Her money is controlled by Shambhavi herself since she became an adult. She insisted she wanted to donate it to our *sampradaya*, but I told her it was not hers to give, for it belongs to her children as well."

"That's true..."

---

[105]Kali Yuga: Lit. "Age of Kali", or "age of vice", is the last of the four stages the world goes through as part of the cycle of yugas described in the Sanskrit scriptures, within the present Mahayuga. The other ages are called Satya Yuga, Treta Yuga, and Dvapara Yuga.

"Shaman, this girl has been through a lot, but her spirit is incredibly strong and positive. These experiences have not embittered her in any way."

"I respect her spirit, Maharaj, and now I understand many things clearly."

"Good. Now that I have told you, I feel a sense of relief."

57.

After his talk with Maharaj, Shaman wanted to meet Shambhavi immediately. He couldn't wait another moment. He didn't know what exactly he was going to tell her. There was no script in his mind. Things were just too unformed in his head. He knew he had to first apologise to her and then tell her he loved her. He hoped she would not refuse to see him.

Time did not move fast enough. He was on his way to Delhi airport after dropping his grandfather at Haridwar station.

It was like a big jigsaw puzzle slowly falling into place. Shambhavi's seemingly irrational fear of fire and her terrified reaction to it, the deep protective instinct and affection that the three *sannyasis* harboured for her, and of course, the pure paternal love the Master had for the girl whom he had nurtured into a confident and successful woman.

Too many things had happened in the last 24 hours. But it was all steadily settling down in his mind.

Shaman was greeted by a long queue to enter the airport. There, in the parking lot, he saw a man give a large bouquet of orchids to his young pregnant wife. The husband was trying to get his arms around her girth to hug her, but when he couldn't, both of them burst out laughing. It was a sweet moment that made Shaman smile.

Shaman remembered the time when he gave a unique flower to Shambhavi. A flower that rarely a beloved may have received.

58.

Shaman first thought it was very late in the night. But then he corrected himself, it was almost next morning. He looked at his watch and walked up the steep slope. The jeep carrying the other adventure enthusiasts dropped him at the village before proceeding to the bus stop. A cold, merciless wind howled down the valley, forcing even the big trees to bend low on its path.

It was difficult for Shaman to increase his pace against the forceful wind, but he wanted to get to the *ashram* as soon as possible. He had promised Shambhavi he would meet her after dinner and it was past that time.

The *ashram* was shrouded in darkness. He assumed that the power had been cut off by the electricity department—a precautionary measure, given the ferocity of the wind.

The *ashram* gate would be locked, he realised. There was no other way than to approach it from the *sangam* side. Every step seemed to take longer than usual because of the icy gale. He quickly reached the *ashram* but was in two minds. 'Should I see if she is awake? Or should I wait for the morning?' He decided to go to her room. 'If she is sleeping, I won't disturb her,' he told himself.

Silently, he went to her room. To his great surprise she was standing outside, in the corridor. Even before he could say anything she hissed in a low voice, "Where were you? I was so worried. Do you know what time it is? Come inside, it's freezing here!" She literally caught him by his wrist and dragged him inside her room. "Your hand is already frozen," she muttered.

Shaman was glad for the warmth of the room. It was indeed bitterly cold outside. He sat on her window sill. A single *diya* at the feet of Nataraja was the only illumination. A *sigdi* warmed the room. He took a deep breath.

Shambhavi stood before Shaman, her arms akimbo and asked again, "Shaman, where did you disappear? I was going insane with worry. And you have been out on a night like this, with absolutely no warm clothes. You will fall sick. Why are you not answering me?"

"I can answer only if you give me a chance. Come, sit next to me," he said, patting the space beside him.

"No, I am not sitting anywhere. *Where* did you go? You tell me that first. And why didn't you tell me? I would have slept instead of waiting for you."

Shaman was amused by her anger. 'So the poets were right,' he concluded, 'a beautiful woman looks more beautiful when she is angry.'

"Why are you smiling?"

Shaman did not answer immediately. "I got you something," he said instead. "But I'll give it to you only if you sit next to me and close your eyes."

Despite her anger, she could not hide her curiosity, "What is it? If you want to give it to me, give it just the way I am. I am not going to close my eyes."

Shaman smiled. "Okay, at least sit next to me…"

His smile melted her anger. "You are not being fair at all. First, you make me wait the whole night, and now you are just teasing me." Nonetheless, she sat down next to him.

"Patience, Shambhavi, patience… is that not what you told me when you took me to the temple?" He put his left arm around her, closed her eyes and carefully took out something from the bag.

A sweet fragrance enveloped the room.

"What's that smell…? It's so enticing!" Shambhavi exclaimed with apparent delight.

He gently brushed the flower along her cheek down to her neck. The flower left a faint trail of its iridescent reddish pollen that glimmered faintly on her fair skin in the dimly lit room. The sight had Shaman enraptured. He was sorely tempted to trace the same path with his fingers.

"It's a flower for sure," said Shambhavi.

"Come on, you can do better than that," said Shaman.

He handed it over and freed her eyes. It was the most beautiful thing that Shambhavi had ever seen. A creamy white delicate flower with several layers of petals and soft yellow stamens bunched in the centre. The fragrance of the flower was otherworldly.

"This is a Brahmakamal!" She exclaimed. "It's so beautiful, nobody has given me something so gorgeous. Thank you Shaman." She kissed his hand and placed the flower at the feet of Nataraja.

"You must be exhausted. Did you eat anything at all? When did you go? *Where* did you go?"

"I wanted to give you something special, so I went and got it," he said quietly. "It was not a big trek or anything. A group of adventure enthusiasts were driving to the Mohini-tal, so I went with them. If I had gone trekking all the way, the flower would have wilted by the time I got back."

"Thank you Shaman! You make me feel so special," she said hugging him.

A moment later, she gasped as she realised something. A

cloud came over her eyes. "Everyone will know you got the Brahmakamal for me. They will find out about us. I can't keep the flower."

"Don't worry too much," Shaman said. "I got one more flower for the temple in our *ashram*, one for Ma Gayatri and one for my Shambhavi."

59.

The drive from the airport to Natyashala where Shambhavi taught was long and painful. Apart from the potholes and huge puddles of water from the recent showers, the traffic itself was erratic. Tempers of drivers were frayed as they tried to weave their way through the bumper-to-bumper traffic.

Shaman gazed out unseeingly. He remembered their bitter fight and how they had parted. It brought a lump to his throat. 'I should have handled my emotions better,' he reprimanded himself for the hundredth time.

The last thing he remembered of Shambhavi was her beautiful grey eyes filled with tears of deep misery. He could kick himself now for his callousness. After what seemed like an eternity, they arrived at their destination.

The cab driver stopped outside imposing white gates that were shut. A graceful arch on the gates had the name 'Natyashala' embossed on it. A sign at the entrance read in bold writing, *No outside vehicles allowed inside*. Shaman smiled at this despite his miserable condition. Another small gate, large enough for one person, stood slightly ajar.

The cab driver informed him that he would be at the visitor's parking lot and left him at the entrance. Shaman was almost dreading this meeting. He wanted to clear things with Shambhavi, but he was afraid she may never forgive him. Setting aside these unsettling thoughts, he walked in through the small gate. There was a small watchman's cabin and a tiny waiting area ahead.

Seeing a man in saffron walk in, the short Nepali watchman

joined his hands in *pranaam* and asked him politely, "Swamiji, today is not a student's meeting day. Who have you come to meet?"

"I have come to meet a teacher," said Shaman. "Shambhavi."

The watchman checked the time. "Madam will be teaching till 8 pm. You will not be able to meet her till then. Chandrahasini Madam is very strict," he added with a shake of his head.

'Oh God…' Shaman thought. In his anticipation of meeting Shambhavi, he had completely forgotten that a fire-breathing dragon called Chandrahasini ran this place.

The watchman continued talking. "However, if Madam gives permission, you can meet Shambhavi teacher."

Shaman took a deep breath. "All right, can I meet Chandrahasini?" he asked.

The watchman looked doubtful for a moment. "Normally, I do not take anyone who does not have an appointment, but since you are a Swamiji, I will take you to her."

He called out to the lady sitting at the reception. "Hemaji, I am taking Swamiji to meet Madam."

"Bahadur," she shouted from inside. "Give him the visitors pass, otherwise Madam will kill you."

Bahadur went inside and got the visitor's pass with just *Swamiji* written neatly on the name card.

Shaman was led along the beautiful driveway. Everything was neat and clean. Large acres of undulating, manicured green lawns spread like an emerald carpet. Bushes were neatly trimmed. The heady fragrance of the Night Queen wafted all over the place as its hedges lined the lawns.

Bahadur was a talkative man. "See Swamiji, there are only girls here. The only man here is me. Madam trusts me. The girls study here…" he said, pointing to the low open brick structures that looked like they belonged more to a resort than to a school.

"7 am to 1 pm is regular school, and 2 to 8 is dance," he informed Shaman.

They arrived at a vast, octagonal-shaped amphitheatre made of stone. It had five tiers which could comfortably seat over 300 people. There were roses of every possible colour on the outer perimeter in full bloom, from the deepest red to the creamiest whites. Exotic orchids hung from baskets suspended on wrought iron posts. At the edge of the amphitheatre stood a huge golden Champa tree. The smell from its flowers was intoxicating. It reminded him of the *mala* that Shambhavi had placed on Naam Yajnananda's feet when she had come to Nagaprayag.

Shaman took a deep breath and marvelled at the beauty of the place. There was a gentle breeze blowing, spreading the fragrance all around. Peacocks walked on the lawns, dragging their long tails around like they owned the place. They looked at Shaman, but didn't look like they were scared.

Chandrahasini sat erect on a wooden bench under the Champa tree with her eyes closed. Shaman thought for a moment. 'Don't tell me she is meditating!' he wondered. She wore a light grey raw silk sari with a bottle-green border and a printed yellow silk full-sleeved blouse. A big yellow *bindi* stood out on her forehead and large oxidized silver hoops dangled from her ears. As he approached, he realized she was listening intently to something. The earphones were firmly plugged in her ears.

"Madam, good evening…" Bahadur said in a soft voice.

Obviously, Chandrahasini didn't hear him. Bahadur tried again and failed. He looked at Shaman helplessly. Shaman was in two minds. He didn't wish to offend her, but at the same time he had to get her attention.

"Good evening, Chandrahasini!" he said loudly.

She opened her eyes. Surprise registered on her face, before she instantaneously regained her composure. She removed her earphones.

"Good evening, Mr Srivastava," she said with smile that didn't reach her eyes. "Bahadur, please run along and bring a chair."

Once he was out of earshot, she turned to Shaman and said with a touch of sarcasm, "To what exactly do I owe this rare honour of having you visit my humble abode?"

"Chandrahasini, I have not come to argue with you," said Shaman and he really meant it. "As for owing honour, you owe none."

"Come to the point Mr Srivastava, or shall I say *Swamiji*? What do you want?"

Bahadur came running with a foldable garden chair. He placed it in front of Chandrahasini and looked at her for further instructions. She gestured him to leave with a nod of her head.

"Please sit down," she said to Shaman pointing to the chair.

Shaman sat down and took a deep breath before saying, "I have come to see Shambhavi."

"Why do you want to see her?" Chandrahasini asked with a raised eyebrow.

"That's personal."

"'Personal'? I never knew *sannyasis* had personal things. Shambhavi is like my daughter, I won't let her be ruined by the likes of you."

"Listen…"

"You may leave, Mr Srivastava. You have no right to see her after what you've done to the poor girl."

"I just want to talk to her once."

"You can't. I won't let you hurt her another time..."

Chandrahasini stood up abruptly to signify the end of the meeting.

Shaman was livid, but he took a deep breath and just stared into Chandrahasini's eyes for full two minutes. She was clearly uncomfortable.

"Sit down Chandrahasini," he said in an ice-cold voice.

Surprisingly, Chandrahasini sat down with some reluctance.

"I am not leaving this place without meeting her. You can do whatever you want. I am a *sannyasi* and I am not afraid of even being bodily thrown out," Shaman said quietly.

"*Sannyasi*? What kind of a *sannyasi* are you? Proud, arrogant, intellectual hustler! Don't think this ochre garb is going to influence me in any way," she said pointing to his robe. "I know what you guys think of yourselves when you throw your weight around with that robe, projecting that you are renunciants, who have given up their all for the sake of the highest truth."

"Chandrahasini...."

"Don't stop me... In reality, it's a big bag of bullshit! You guys are poverty-stricken, uneducated folks taking up *sannyasa* because you don't have the guts to eke out a living," Chandrahasini said fiercely.

Shaman was unperturbed by her accusations. "I was educated at Harvard," he said. "Chandrahasini, my ability to eke out a living is beside the point. You have no idea of spirituality and I seriously have no interest in educating you. I just want to see Shambhavi ..."

"I don't think she wants to meet you," Chandrahasini said with a ring of certainty.

"I'm sure Shambhavi would like to meet me." Shaman was

irked.

"I doubt she'd be interested," Chandrahasini said. "The girl was near catatonic when she returned from Nagaprayag. And I hold you entirely responsible for the damage you have done to her heart," she added with vehemence.

Chandrahasini closed her eyes and shook her head, as if to diminish the strength of her memory.

"I would rather ask her opinion than yours," Shaman observed calmly.

"Sure! I'll send for her and it will be clear once and for all." She called out to the sweeper who was raking the lawn, "*Shambhavi Madam ko garden pe bulaao.*"

The sweeper went away saying a '*ji*'. Both of them waited in awkward silence. After some apprehension, seeing that it may take some time, Chandrahasini asked Shaman, "What do you want to do with Shambhavi?"

"What do you think I'd want to do?"

"How do I know? You are answering a question with another," she said with derision.

Shaman ignored the second part of her question and said, "I'm as human as they get, Chandrahasini. I love Shambhavi and I wish to marry her."

"Marry her?" Chandrahasini croaked. "You must be closer to my age than hers!" She laughed. "Oh! Wonderful! What a noble idea for a *sannyasi.* I mean, aren't you the limit? Be a *sannyasi,* lure some innocent girl and get married to her. Really sharp, I must say! Do you know that scores of people have approached me with proposals for Shambhavi? Highly successful statesmen, hugely talented artists, millionaires, and scions of business empires… She has turned them all down and now *you* want to marry her?" she said with mirthless laughter.

Shaman remained unperturbed. "You ridicule the natural and noble drives in human beings."

"Natural and noble human beings don't get into *sannyasa* and stuff, Swamiji. They earn their living and marry girls without tricking and conning them. Besides, I am curious, are you *sannyasis* allowed to marry?"

"I do not wish to speak about these things with you," Shaman said, a little disturbed.

"Why? I have a right to know. After all, I am her guardian."

"Yes, but these are complicated personal issues."

"Nonsense! I think you are just being an escapist like every *sannyasi*. Do you have the guts to answer my question to my face?"

Shaman was silent.

"Are you *sannyasis* allowed to marry?" she reiterated.

"No, *sannyasis* are not allowed to marry. That is the reason I will be forfeiting my *sannyasa*."

"Forfeiting *sannyasa*? Is it a take-it-if-you-like-it, leave-it-if-you-don't-like-it kind of affair? You are saying you're giving up *sannyasa*. What if you give up Shambhavi? A person who is capable of giving up *sannyasa*, can give up anything."

"You are entitled to your doubts, but life is not always so straightforward. God tests us through complex situations and there are no straightjacket answers to life's conundrums," Shaman replied calmly.

"All I know is this, you fooled around with *sannyasa*. I don't believe in *sannyasa*, but if I did, I'd consider you a blot on it."

Shaman was too hurt to reply. Her barbs hit him in the most vulnerable parts of his already wounded heart.

"You have the luxury of judging things with enormous ease

Chandrahasini. As for me, I have no judgements, I surrender like the breeze and go wherever it takes me."

"How convenient for you, Swamiji!" Chandrahasini said sarcastically.

Shaman looked away and wondered. His life at this moment was anything but convenient.

60.

He spotted a slight figure walking towards him. It was Shambhavi. Unlike her usual gait, her step was heavy and she looked down at her feet as she walked. His heart skipped a beat as he watched her approach. His eyes drank in her image like a thirsty dying man who was at last given a sip of water. For the first time he felt nervous and unsure. The scrutinising gaze of Chandrahasini made matters worse. He sat up straight in his chair and prayed for the direct intervention of his *guru*.

As Shambhavi walked closer, he looked at her with unabashed longing. He didn't care that Chandrahasini was looking at him curiously. Shambhavi looked up when she came near. There was a flare of recognition and surprise in her eyes. Her face lit up very briefly, before it extinguished again. The shutters on her lovely eyes were tightly pulled.

She wore a blue sari with a green blouse and border, tied at a height that it skimmed just below her knees. A matching pair of blue leggings and trendy flip-flops completed the outfit. There was a light shimmer of perspiration on her forehead. It was evident she had come from an interrupted dance class.

Shaman took in every aspect of her being with a hungry yearning. His eyes slid over her like a sculptor trying to memorise the form of his muse. It was evident she had lost weight; she also had a bruised look about her.

Shambhavi didn't look at him or greet him. Instead, she directly addressed Chandrahasini. "Chandra Ma, you called for me?"

Chandrahasini held out her hand. "Swamiji wanted to meet

you," she said in a voice that betrayed no emotion.

Shambhavi took Chandrahasini's hand and walked around the stone bench. She stood behind her guardian, with one hand resting on the older woman's shoulder and the other on the backrest of the bench.

There was strained silence and a palpable tension in the air. A distant high-pitched careening of an eagle broke the silence.

Chandrahasini said, "All right, you two talk. I am going to my office."

"No *ma*, you please be with me. Whatever he has to say, let him say it in your presence. I have nothing to hide from you."

"Shambhu… Swamiji has something personal to tell you..."

Shambhavi cut in, "*Sannyasis* have nothing personal to communicate. Please wait."

Shaman had played this scenario many times in his head, but he never ever thought it would be in the presence of another person, not Chandrahasini at any rate.

Chandrahasini looked at Shaman with a question in her eyes. He nodded his head. If Shambhavi wanted this to be done this way, then so be it.

He cleared his throat and looked at Shambhavi. She was not even looking at him; her beautiful grey eyes were focussed on the distant horizon.

He took a deep breath and began, "Shambhavi, please forgive me for all the things I wrongly accused you of. I was angry and frustrated and I projected everything onto you. Of course, that doesn't justify my actions. I admit, I was terribly unfair, and I deeply regret every word I spoke to you. I had no right to speak to you like that. Please, can you forgive me?"

Shambhavi didn't answer him. Her eyes seemed like cold marbles, devoid of any emotion as she continued to stare into the horizon.

Shaman's heart sank at her silence. He tried once again to appeal to her. "Shambhavi, I know I hurt you dearly. I accused you of the vilest things. What I said was unforgivable, but please forgive me," he said in a soft voice.

Shambhavi just stood there like she was carved from stone. Shaman was deeply distressed that he was going to lose her. He felt the hot prickling of tears in his eyes. He quickly blinked them away, composed himself and prayed to his *guru*. Nothing could have helped him more at this juncture than some sign of his grace.

He then noticed that Shambhavi's hands were tightly curled around the back rest of the bench in a white-knuckled grip. He was now sure she was not as unmoved as she seemed.

Shaman stood up and walked to where Shambhavi stood. He gently pried her hand from the bench, and took it into his while she offered no resistance. Her nails had left deep half-moon impressions on her soft palm.

Lifting her injured palm to his lips, he said, "Shambhavi, I love you!"

He saw tears gather in her eyes and spill onto her cheeks.

"Don't cry… It breaks my heart to see you cry," he said pulling her into his arms.

She stood still like a doll and said, "I died every day without you. The guilt of seducing you killed me every day," she said in a small voice.

"Shh... You didn't seduce me. I fell in love with you and I just didn't have the guts to face it. You were in no state to seduce me. I should have never said something like that to you. Shambhavi, I am truly very sorry." He paused for a moment. "In fact, I want to marry you as soon as possible. Will you marry me?"

"Marry?" She looked at him in surprise. "But what about your *sannyasa*?" Shambhavi asked hesitantly, swallowing.

"I am going to renounce *sannyasa*. I cannot lead a double life. I just cannot be in robes and still be with you. Nothing is more important than you, Shambhavi. Life has no meaning without you by my side," he said, hugging her.

"Tell me, Mr Srivastava, should I turn around or will I see something too personal?" Chandrahasini asked, laughing. "

"Ma, you can turn around," Shambhavi said chuckling.

Chandrahasini stood up and turned around. "I guess I am the first person to congratulate you both." She dabbed at her eyes with the end of her sari. "You look so good together," she said, beaming, admiring the way they looked as a pair.

"But Shambhavi has not yet agreed to marry me," Shaman said.

Chandrahasini looked at Shambhavi, her eyes urging her to accept Shaman's proposal.

"I will marry you..." Shambhavi whispered, reaching up and kissing him shyly on the underside of his chin.

"I'm sorry I was aggressive and rude earlier," Chandrahasini said to Shaman. "I was afraid you were playing with Shambhavi's life. I never thought you loved her and would seriously want to marry her..."

Shaman merely smiled. "I love her very much." he said.

"Mr Srivastava, just one thing—if you hurt this child again, I'll make your life a living hell. I'm very creative, trust me!" Chandrahasini warned with a smile.

Shaman knew she meant it.

61.

When Shaman flew back to Varanasi it was as if he was walking on clouds. Shambhavi had agreed to marry him. Such was his joy that he was insensate to his immediate surroundings.

When he got off the cab outside his grandfather's house, he saw that his car was not parked in its usual place. Shaman gathered that his grandfather was out. He should have called and informed him that he was coming. But there was no place for regret in his soaring heart.

He sat on the low branches of the old mango tree that grew beside his house—a place where he had spent many happy hours in his childhood, reading, contemplating and even daydreaming. As he sat under its shade, Shaman reflected on the last 48 hours. The anxiety, frustration and angst of the last month had dropped away like a dead leaf.

He saw his grandfather's car come towards the gate. Shaman quickly dusted off the dirt, and opened the gate. As soon as Manohar parked the car, he asked Shaman, "What happened? Did you apologise? What did Shambhavi say?"

"Dadaji, I asked her to marry me…and she agreed."

Manohar was beside himself with joy. "That's simply great Shaman. That's the best thing you did."

"Actually Dadaji, to tell you the truth, I myself didn't think through this whole thing. I didn't really think that I would ask her to marry me, but it felt like it was the most natural thing to do. I only thought of telling her that I love her. And more than that, I wanted to apologise to her for my foul behaviour."

"It's the most natural progression, Shaman. I think too many things are unfolding too soon for you. That's why you are not finding the space to really contemplate upon your changing circumstances... First thing, let's call Maharaj and tell him."

"Yes, I need Maharaj's blessings."

Manohar phoned the Nagaprayag *ashram* and requested Krishna Da for a call with the Master.

"Maharaj, Shaman wants to speak to you..."

"*Pranaam* Maharaj!"

"Shaman, *Jai Guru*. Shambhavi is over the moon that you have asked her to marry you. She is saying over and over again how lucky she is to find a life companion who is as enlightened as you."

Shaman was touched, but his worry would not cease until he received Maharaj's blessings.

"You will always have my blessings, Shaman," the Master told his former disciple. "There is no bigger joy for me than to see you and Shambhavi settled and happy. Shaman, do you remember what I had told you just before you took *sannyasa*?"

"Yes, you asked me to repeat *tad ekam, tad ekam*...."

"What does it mean?"

"You told me that the ultimate truth is One, so we have to reach it through oneness. At any time you must have recourse to just one thing. One *guru*, one *mantra*, one *ashram*...whatever is dual must be eliminated. So if I am a *sannyasi*, that is all; there is no external world. This is what you told me."

"Exactly! I am again saying *tad ekam* to you. It was *sannyasa* then, it will be *grihastha* now. Once you are a *grihastha*, a householder, don't look back on your old ways of *sannyasa*.

Be true to being a householder. The *Mahabharata* has lauded *grihastha ashram* in more glowing terms than *sannyasa*. Just be true to it. Don't keep one foot here and one foot there—that is a mess. Don't be a householder and behave like a *sannyasi*. That's no good."

"I will miss you and the *ashram*," Shaman says, almost on the verge of tears.

"We will miss you too. Keep yourself firmly in your householdership. Put as much heart into it as you have put into *sannyasa*."

"Like *purna hridayam*?"

"Yes, *purna hridayam*. You have a sharp memory, Shaman! I've always told you to put your whole heart into things. The heart is an enormous ocean—the ocean of light, the ocean of consciousness. The waters of this consciousness are broken by polarizing waves. But as soon as you make a commitment to one thing, there is stillness."

"I understand, Maharaj. I will give my whole heart."

"Good! And another thing, I cannot endorse your marriage Shaman." Before Shaman could respond, Maharaj explained, "I am the head of an Order and in my official capacity, I cannot validate your actions. I cannot support the decision of a *sannyasi* to marry. So, I want you to stay away from the *ashram* and help me uphold the sanctity of the codes of renunciants. I hope you understand."

Shaman nodded his head vigorously even though the Master couldn't see it. "Yes, I understand!"

"God bless you, Shaman! Now that you have made a decision to marry, that also means you have to give up the ochre robe."

The realisation hit Shaman forcefully only after the Master had voiced it. He looked at his ochre robe as if he had earned it for the very first time.

"Yes, Maharaj. I will renounce *sannyasa.*" Shaman's voice quivered as he uttered the last sentence.

"May Ma's blessings give you strength, Shaman! *Jai Guru,*" said the Master, his voice full of kindness.

Shaman said goodbye and ended the call.

62.

Shaman rose later than usual. He was curled into a foetal position, his body stiff from the sleepless night before. It was as if he did not want to face the day. He could hear his grandfather, already awake, moving pots and pans in the kitchen. Shaman washed his face, picked up his cloth bag and quietly exited the house. He headed towards the *ghaat*.

He walked down the empty street, dragging his feet, head hanging low, kicking the stones along the way. The most spectacular colours of dawn painted the eastern sky in pinks, oranges and mauves. It was a crystal clear day. A gentle breeze blew from the Ganga. Calls of sparrows, parrots and mynahs created a cacophony of sounds.

With a heavy heart, Shaman walked to the last step leading to the water, sat there and stared at the river for a long time. He took out a newspaper from his bag and with great deliberation, laid it before him in a neat square. Then he joined both his hands in prayer and looked heavenwards.

Head bent towards the newspaper and armed with a razor, Shaman commenced shaving his head, beginning from the base of his neck. With each swipe of the blade, a part of his soul felt scraped raw. As each *jataa* fell onto the newspaper, a part of him felt amputated. It was only when his lower lip quivered and his hands began to shake that Shaman realised he was crying. He clenched his jaw, trying to control his emotions.

He took a long time to shave his head. There were cuts and smaller tufts of hair in several places. With both hands, and a controlled concentrated force, he crushed the paper into a tight ball and threw it into the dust bin, along with the razor.

A beggar, sitting near the trash can, asked, "Did someone die in your family?" Shaman ignored him.

Another beggar that sat a little distance away answered, "He is a *sadhu*. They need not shave their hair for a domestic death; they are beyond all those things. But they shave their heads on full moon days."

Both were wrong.

Shaman tuned out their voices and walked into the Ganga. Once waist-deep in the water, he threw his saffron *dhoti* into the flowing current. The cloth gracefully floated away within seconds. He then removed his *rudraksha mala,* touched it to his forehead and placed it on the water. It sank immediately. He took off his holy thread and held it in his palms, letting the Ganga take it away. Then he let his wooden *khadaus*[106], the *kamandalu* and *danda* (stick) flow away too. Shaman watched as the river swallowed his only belongings.

Stripped of his robe, he felt like his skin had been torn from him. Now he was just a mass of bleeding flesh. He stood stark naked like the day he was born, and cried like a child. Hot tears rolled down his cheeks and mixed with the cold water of Ma Ganga. The pain in his chest was so tight that he was unable to breathe. Bared of everything familiar, he stood there in aching vulnerability, looking heavenward for answers.

He simply did not know who he was! In a moment it was all over. He felt like an orphan, bereft of his identity. Shaman cried loudly trying to embrace Mother Ganga in his arms as he took several dips in her water. 'Who am I, Mother?' he asked between sobs.

Shaman continued to take dips until his tears stopped flowing and only dry sobs wracked his weary body. The first ray of

[106]Khadaus: slippers

the morning sun peeked over the horizon, and bathed Shaman in its orange light as he emerged from the water. He offered water to the Sun God and stilled his mind, a practice that now came to him naturally after long years of practice.

In a flash, he understood—robe or no robe, nobody could take away who he was. His essence, his *bhakti* and his faith would always remain with him. He remembered the words of Guru Naam Yajnananda Maharaj, "The path of a renunciant has ended for you, but your relationship does not end here, it will go on. The other worldly relationships are not of here and now, they are of forever."

Shaman stood motionless, trying to assimilate all his thoughts and emotions. Suddenly, he felt a pair of hands around his waist. He was confused for a second, but then recognised the touch of his grandfather, who was handing him the ends of a brand new white *dhoti*.

Without speaking a word, Shaman tied it and embraced the old man. Once again, his eyes filled with unshed tears, seeing his grandfather's kind thoughtfulness. To Shaman's shock, he too, had shaved his head.

"It's a new beginning for both of us," his grandfather said with a smile. The old man's eyes brimmed with tears.

Grandfather and grandson emerged from the water. The old man gently ran his hand over Shaman's head. "There are a few awkward tufts left. Let's first find a barber who will shave your head properly," he said and added in a soft voice full of emotion, "Silly boy! Slinking out of the house without telling me? You are never alone Shaman, I am always there with you."

63.

Shaman waited for Shambhavi at the Varanasi airport. It had been more than a month since their last meeting in Bangalore, when the ex-*sannyasi* had proposed marraige. Though he spoke to her for long hours on the telephone, he still felt there was so much he didn't know about her.

So much had changed in such a short while starting from his lack of *jataas* to his regular clothes. Regular clothes disoriented him, so much so that he confined himself to simple white shirts or white *kurtas* over blue jeans or trousers.

Even his familiar *khadavus* were gone; replaced by regular shoes that he wore to university. Many times, he would forget about his shaved head and be surprised by the lack of *jataas* whenever his hand ran through his hair.

His hair had grown back and was a sleek cap over his scalp. His beard was practically non-existent. Though he didn't shave, there was not even a stubble. He wondered how Shambhavi would react to his new image.

Sometimes, he missed the clean air of Nagaprayag and his time with the Master, with a sharp ache. He loved his new teaching job at Benares Hindu University. It hosted some of the sharpest minds in the country; but more than that, he got to spend time with his beloved grandfather.

He spotted Shambhavi as she came towards him. She looked more beautiful than what he remembered, if such a thing was possible. She was clad in a dark pink knee-length skirt peppered with a block prints of tiny golden mangoes, and a cream and gold short blouse. She looked fit, fresh and happy.

As soon as she reached him, Shaman went for a hug, but she bent and took his blessings.

"*Pranaam*," she said.

When she stood up, Shaman hugged her. "Your place is in my heart," he said. At that moment, an immense load lifted from his shoulders; suddenly he felt ecstatically happy.

"Yes I know my place is in your heart, but I will always need your blessings."

She studied him for a moment. "You look very young; white suits you as much as the ochre did. And the robe, the *vastra*... when did you remove it?" she asked.

"As soon as I returned from Bangalore."

"Why didn't you tell me?"

Shaman did not answer.

"I am sure it was very painful," she said, her voice sympathetic. Shaman could only give a brief nod.

Once her boxes were loaded into the car, Shaman drove out of the small airport.

"Where are you taking me?"

"Home..."

"Chandra Ma said I should not stay with you before we are married."

"Your Chandra Ma has a twisted mind. My grandfather will be with us. It is a large house with many bedrooms."

"I know all that. What she meant was that I should not be married from your house. She has booked me into a hotel," Shambhavi explained, gazing at the scenery outside.

"She's crazy! Which hotel?" Shaman asked, annoyed.

"The Taj…"

"Ostentatious. That's what she is!"

"Don't be judgemental," Shambhavi said in defence of her mentor. "She just wants me to be comfortable."

"Whatever makes you happy," Shaman said, yielding. "Shambhavi, there's an envelope on the dashboard. Open it."

When she did, she found a simple and delicate wedding card, printed in cream and gold.

- Sri Ardhanaareshwaraay Namah -

Vashishtha had a sudden bout of cough, he was running a high fever; his voice was faint.

"May I continue the lesson from here?" Arundhati asked Vashishtha as he was teaching his students at the *Gurukul.*

He was surprised, but he let her take it.

When the class was over, Vashishtha was delighted.

He said, "You've mastered the Vedas so beautifully. Now, you are truly my *ardhaangini.*"

~

I have found my *ardhaangini* in Shambhavi,

and she in me.

We are the better halves that complete each other.

But we will still be incomplete without you.

Love needs more love to complete itself.

Come with your blessings and love and complete us.

"Shaman, this is so beautiful!" Shambhavi said, tracing a finger over the embossed words. She leaned towards him and kissed his cheek.

"We'll have an accident if you pull me like that!" Shaman laughed.

"I hardly pulled you, I just came close to you. And don't worry, it's a deserted road. If you get distracted from driving, I'd be happy to do the honours," Shambhavi said teasing him. "Do you know where the Taj is?"

"I know where it is, but that's not where we are going," Shaman said. "You didn't see the envelope properly. See who it is addressed to."

Shambhavi opened the card again and said: "To Gangaji! How sweet, Shaman! How will we give it to her?"

He merely smiled. "Wait and watch."

The road leading to the *ghaat* was crowded with people. Shaman parked the car and entered a small shop. He returned with a packet covered with newspaper and placed it on the back seat.

"Shaman, now you are killing me with suspense."

"Patience Shambhavi..."

The sun was setting when they stopped at a narrow lane. He picked up the packet from behind him and said, "Bring the invitation with you."

There was a small Kali temple situated in the shade of an enormous mango tree. Shaman bowed his head and prayed briefly before walking on. The temple steps led to the river. The Ganga was calm and peaceful; they had the *ghaat* to themselves.

"People come here only during the *shaaradiya navaratris,*" Shaman informed his companion.

They walked down the last step and Shaman offered the packet to Shambhavi, asking her to open it.

It was a beautiful wicker basket, small and flat, lined with a scarlet silk. In it were a small *diya*, a small silver *kumkum*[107] box, some betel leaves, betel nuts, three tiny *motichur laddus*[108], a few fresh yellow roses, and an incense cone. A jasmine garland decorated the outside of the basket.

"We will place the card in this basket, light the *diya* and the incense, and then set the basket afloat on the river."

Shambhavi felt deeply moved. The light from the lit *diya* illuminated the beauty of the arrangement. The couple waded into the river together. They watched the basket with its tiny *diya* float onto the crimson river, as the Ganga reflected the colours of the setting sun.

Shaman closed his eyes in prayer. He yearned for Ma Ganga's blessings, for both Shambhavi and himself. They sat in silence on the steps, his arm over her shoulders, watching the Ganga as twilight gently casts its veil over the surroundings.

'Tomorrow,' Shaman thought, 'I will be married.'

---

[107]Kumkum: Red turmeric powder used for making the distinctive Hindu mark on the forehead

[108]Motichur laddu: Originally a north Indian sweet made from fine boondi where the balls are tiny and is cooked with ghee or oil.

64.

Vasant Panchami. It was Shaman's wedding day. Shaman wanted to carry out the Mahasaraswati Puja before he left for the venue. When he woke up at 3 am, he was surprised to see that his grandfather was already awake and had kept everything ready for the *puja*. He had had a bath and sat sipping tea.

"Dadaji you could have slept some more. Why are you up in this cold so early? We need to go to the wedding venue only by 6:30 am," Shaman said, feeling sorry for him.

"Yes I know that, but I also want to accrue some merit from the Mahasaraswati *Puja*. Go, quickly shower and come. I am ready. Do you want anything to drink?"

Shaman shook his head. They finished their *puja* by 5:30 am. Shaman changed into a new white silk *dhoti* and a matching white *angavastra*[109] that loosely draped around his shoulders. His grandfather wore a beige khadi silk *kurta pyjama* with a bright yellow silk Nehru jacket.

"You look handsome. Are you not feeling cold? It's still January, why don't you wear something thicker?"

"I am used to the cold. Moreover, it's not so cold here compared to Nagaprayag," said Shaman.

They drove in silence to the *ghaat*, then hired a boatman and crossed the river.

---

[109]Angavastra: a south Indian traditional white-coloured stole, worn by men as a sign of respect and pride, draped over the shoulders. It's a long rectangular cloth meant to cover the torso.

"It's so misty. I can't see a thing, Dadaji," Shaman complained.

"Don't worry. I know exactly where we are supposed to go," Manohar reassured him. "I told you I'll take care of all the wedding arrangements, so trust me."

Soon they came upon a simple but a strikingly beautiful *pandal* erected on the sandy banks of the Ganga. It had four bamboo sticks on four corners, and eight other bamboo sticks that created a roof on top. The entire arrangement of bamboos was invisible to the eye; wrapped completely in thick garlands of tuberoses and baby pink roses; arranged one after the other. The same garlands hung from all sides of the *pandal*, fashioning an effect of a room created entirely by flowers. Soft and lilting *shehanai*[110] music played from a small tape-recorder.

A red carpet was laid on the ground. On it was placed a long low stool, draped in a yellow silk cloth.

"Ram Ram," the *pundit* greeted them.

"You told me to be on time, now you have come late. Are you happy with the arrangements? See, we got everything from the lamps to the wood for the *havan* and carpet and chairs. We have put your *guru's* photo on the big throne right here as per your instruction."

A large arm chair was draped in a green brocade cloth and on it was a large picture of Naam Yajnananda Maharaj adorned by a fresh *tulasi mala*. Shaman immediately paid his respect to the picture. How he wished he had the blessings of the Master on this day of his life!

"The bride and groom will sit here…" the *pundit* said, pointing to the low stool.

"Shaman, do you like it?" asked his grandfather.

"Dadaji, it is incredibly beautiful!"

---

[110]Shehanai: a north Indian oboe, a quadruple-reed instrument, played on auspicious occasions, such as weddings and temple festivities

"My nephew Madan is the wedding expert here. Madan, come here and do *pranaam* to Manoharji."

A lanky bespectacled man in his mid-thirties emerged from behind the *pandal*. He seemed educated and enthusiastic.

"You have done a very good job," Manohar praised him.

"Thank you. I am doing these little weddings for a lot of foreigners here. Simple, sweet and romantic— that's what they want. Behind the *pandal* I am setting up a few chairs and tables to serve breakfast after the wedding. We are a team of five. If you need anything, just shout out to me, the caterer is organising breakfast."

The *pundit* had already kept everything ready for the *havan*. He looked at his watch and said, "Shamanji, you should be seated. We'll begin the *puja* in another fifteen minutes. Where is the bride? Manoharji, you said she would come by 7 am."

"It's only 6:30 now," Shaman's grandfather replied.

"I know you said that, I was just wondering where she was."

One boat slowly glided up, but it was too misty to see who had come. It cleared just enough for Shaman to make out the forms of Madhusudan and Vedavati.

Vedavati was a thin blonde woman in her mid-fifties. A friend of Madhusudan, she was a German national who now resided at Rishikesh. She was an ardent devotee of Naam Yajnananda Maharaj and also known to Shaman very well. Shaman remembered Madhusudan mentioned that Vedavati would be coming to Varanasi.

"I invited them," said Manohar. "It's your wedding; you need your well-wishers around you. Your parents tried very hard but couldn't make it…"

"That's okay, Dadaji. You are with me. That's all that matters!"

"Hey, Shaman. You look good!" said Madhusudan hugging

him.

"What a handsome groom!" Vedavati said, "We are honoured to be here. It was so kind of your grandfather to invite us."

"I am so glad that both of you could make it."

"Where is the bride?" asked Madhusudan.

"She will be here soon."

"Shaman, please come and sit here. It's time to start the ceremonies," the *pundit* informed them.

Shaman's mind was restless. Why had Shambhavi not come? He had told her the previous day that coming on her own was a stupid idea. He had offered to pick her up, but she had insisted that she needed to get dressed and that she would come on her own. Now he felt he should have sent Madhusudan to bring her.

He checked his watch for the umpteenth time. It was 6:55 am. There was still five minutes left.

"Where is the bride?" asked the *pundit*.

"You said 7...it's not yet 7, she will come. You continue with other things," said Manohar.

The *pundit* nodded and got down to business.

Shaman's eyes worriedly glanced acorss the room. Why was she late?

At that moment, a boat arrived. The thick mist still hung on the river like a heavy veil, making it impossible for Shaman to make out who had arrived. The last two boats had Madan's men come with tables and some catering items.

Five little girls, ranging from six to eight years of age, walked towards the *pandal*. They wore identical purple and pink *ghagra cholis*. Two of the girls carried a large picture of Naam Yajnananda Maharaj. Behind them came Chandrahasini, and along with her, Shambhavi.

"Keep the photograph on the decorated chair," Chandrahasini instructed them. She was dressed in a dark green *kanjeevaram* sari with a gold temple border. She wore gold *jhumkas* and a thick gold mango *mala*.

Shambhavi was dressed like a typical South Indian bride though she wore a heavy burnt orange and gold Benares silk sari. She wore large uncut diamond earrings, a lovely matching necklace and a gold *kaasumala*[111]. Her long hair was braided with jasmine buds while innumerable orange glass bangles lined her wrists. All in all, she looked strikingly beautiful. Even Madan and his men tried to sneak a look while working and were dumbstruck by her beauty.

Manohar whispered into Shaman's ear, "Now I know why you fell in love. Shambhavi is stunningly beautiful..."

"Happy?" Manohar asked the *pundit*. "There comes the bride!"

"She is like a Mahalakshmi," said the *pundit*. His mouth was slightly agape as he directed Shambhavi to sit on Shaman's left.

"That would be a first. A grey-eyed Mahalakshmi..." Chandrahasini mused out loud.

"Hi! I am Chandrahasini," she introduced herself to Manohar. "And these little girls are Shambhavi's students. They came to my office the other day and tearfully begged me to let them attend their Didi's wedding. I just didn't have the heart to refuse these little ones."

The girls sat next to Shambhavi. "This is Shaman Dada!" Shambhavi introduced.

In one graceful motion that only a dancer could possess, the five girls joined their palms together and greeted him with

[111]Kaasumala: a traditional long necklace from the State of Kerala, comprising a collection of little coins in precious material

'Pranaam'.

"*Pranaam* to you, little angels," Shaman said.

"And what about saying hello to the Devil?" laughed Chandrahasini.

"Hello, Chandrahasini. Very kind of you to come."

"I wouldn't miss Shambhu's wedding for anything.... And I must say, Shaman, you look quite dapper in a silk *dhoti*. Quite a change in your appearance. Thank God, those *jataas* are gone!"

"Chandra Ma! You promised me!" Shambhavi said softly.

"Yes yes...I promised Shambhavi, I will keep quiet."

Shaman's grandfather stepped forward to introduce himself. "I am Manohar. Shaman's grandfather. Even I am glad that the *jataas* are gone... Madan, one round of *pista* milk for everyone."

As they sipped on the warm *pista* milk, Manohar introduced everybody around and made sure everyone was comfortable.

"Madhusudan, could you please click some pictures," Chandrahasini asked, as she handed him a small camera.

"It would be my pleasure," said Madhusudan.

"May I call you Manohar?" Chandrahasini asked the grandfather.

"Of course you may."

"The *pandal* is looking so beautiful. When we saw it from the boat, it seemed like a surreal painting. Great taste, Manohar! It looked like part of a dream sequence in a movie – the mist, the river, the *pandal* created entirely out of roses... How romantic!" Chandrahasini gushed with genuine admiration.

"Padmini and Supriya, collect all the glasses from everyone," she instructed two slightly older girls that stood beside them.

They obeyed instantly and collected the glasses and went away to give them to the team.

"I want the *mangalsutra*[112]," declared the *pundit*. Chandrahasini took it out of the jewellery box. But before she could give it to him, Manohar stopped her. "Chandraji, please wait, I have something to give to the bride and groom."

He handed the couple an envelope.

When Shaman opened the packet, a note fell out. It read, '*With all my blessings*!' He instantly recognised the Master's handwriting. There was also a box that contained an intricate gold *mangalsutra* strung in black beads.

Both Shaman and Shambhavi had tears in their eyes. Chandrahasini sat next to Shambhavi and gently wiped her eyes.

"Don't cry my child, it's a happy occasion. You were so sad this morning that you had not taken your Baba's blessings. See, now everything is perfect!"

She handed over a tissue to Shaman. "No pictures Madhusudan, till she stops crying. All right, Punditji, why did you stop? Please continue…" Chandrahasini urged before turning back to the tearful girl. "If you cry more, all your eye makeup will become a mess… Yes, that's better. That's my girl!"

Shaman placed the *mangalsutra* around Shambhavi's neck. They were showered with red rose petals and yellow rice when they exchanged garlands. Manohar wiped his tears and said, "I'm so happy! I never thought I would see this day!"

The bride and the groom approached Manohar for his blessings. Next, Shambhavi came to Chandrahasini and the old lady hugged the two newlyweds. "Keep her happy, Srivastava. She is my precious princess!"

---

[112]Mangalsutra: Literally, 'sacred thread or cord'. A symbol of marriage, tied around the neck of the Indian bride by the groom during the wedding rituals.

65.

After being treated to a delicious breakfast at the wedding venue, the couple and the guests performed a *darshan* of Vishwanathji at the *ghaat*, and headed to Shaman's home in his car and two additional taxis.

Madhusudan and Chandrahasini sat in the same car as the newlyweds. "Congratulations, once again," said Madhusudan. "By the way, I am asking this out of curiosity, were you dating each other when I met you at Nagaprayag?"

'No, no,' the couple replied in unison. "At that point, there was nothing between us," Shambhavi clarified.

"I was just teasing the two of you," Madhusudan said, laughing.

"Good that you are not being judgemental," said Chandrahasini.

"Life is ever-changing. I know that better than anyone else." Madhusudan then pointed to Shaman and Shambhavi and added, "These two people are among the nicest individuals that I have ever known. I want them to be supremely happy always."

"Thank you, Madhu Da," said Shambhavi.

Shaman's old house was beautifully maintained and in pristine condition. Several mighty mango trees dotted the open ground outside the house. It was a large house of five bedrooms and a spacious square open to the sky, with a sunken central courtyard with steps on all four sides. A large healthy *tulasi* bush grew in the centre of the courtyard. The house had high ceilings and large windows that filled the space with natural light and air. All the rooms opened to the courtyard. A large photograph of a youthful Naam Yajnananda Maharaj hung on one of the walls in the drawing room.

When Shambhavi was about to enter, an old woman came running and performed an *arati* to the newlyweds.

"That's Kaushalya, she has been working with Dadaji for many years," Shaman supplied.

Kaushalya was a small bird-like woman with a bright smile and oodles of energy. "She used to look after Shaman when he came to stay with me. He was about three years old then. She is a child widow, she must have been fifteen or sixteen at that time," Dadaji added.

The *pundit* who had also come with them in the car said, "I need half an hour to set things up. Manoharji, show me where you want to do the Satya Narayana *puja*."

"Next to Tulasiji."

"Okay, I will set it up there."

One of the young girls asked, "Didi, which is your room?"

Shambhavi looked at Shaman. "Come, I will take you around," Shaman said.

"I'll sit with Chandra Ma. You take the girls and show them around the house," Shambhavi informed him as Kaushalya served them tea.

The girls soon returned with Shaman after the tour. "Didi, they have made one bedroom into a books room!"

"Library," an older girl corrected.

"And we can see Gangaji from your room. It's so beautiful!"

Shambhavi told them that even Shaman's room at Nagaprayag

had a breath-taking view of the *sangam*.

"Do you miss it?" Shambhavi asked him.

"Sometimes I do. More than the visual, I miss the sound of the crashing river."

Manohar came with a set of keys and an ornate-looking box. "This is a gift from Shaman's parents, and this is a gift from me," he said giving her an old jewellery box.

Inside it was a lovely old ruby diamond necklace with delicate matching dangling earrings.

"It belonged to my mother. It may not be worth much monetarily, but it has sentimental value!"

"It's beautiful, Dadaji... I will always cherish it. In fact, I will wear it right now."

Shambhavi took off the uncut diamond necklace that she was wearing and replaced it with the set Manohar gave her.

"It looks even more beautiful when you wear it, Beti," the old man said affectionately. "You have made this old man very happy today."

His gesture struck a chord with Shaman.

Chandrahasini studied the necklace, saying, "It is a fine piece, it has a huge antique value. You can't buy sets like these anymore."

It took two hours for the Satyanarayan Puja to conclude. By then Madan and the gang had set up a buffet under one of the mango trees outside. It was a beautiful winter afternoon in the open.

Shambhavi was about to put the jewellery box in her room, when she noticed the keys that Dadaji had given her along with it.

"Shaman, what are these keys?"

"Ask Dadaji."

"Dadaji, what are these keys? I completely forgot to ask you."

"Shaman, show her the gift your parents have given their beautiful daughter-in-law."

The girls got up. "Shaman Da, may we also come?" they asked politely.

"Of course."

On the other side of the house was parked a brand new black Ford Ikon. A huge red ribbon was tied across its windshield.

"It's all yours!" Shaman said to his other half.

"Oh my God... This is such a lovely gift!"

"Didi! What a car!" The girls exclaimed.

Two of the girls called to Chandrahasini excitedly and soon, everyone came to look at what the commotion was about.

"Good you are keeping our girl in style, Shaman," said Chandrahasini, nodding her head vigorously. "It's a neat car."

"But how can I accept something so lavish?" asked a guilt-ridden Shambhavi.

"Beti, my son and daughter-in-law are both highly successful cardiac surgeons in America. Trust me, they make tons of money. Shaman didn't need money all these years. So all of it is there only for you. Please accept it; it will make them very happy. They also have no one but Shaman."

"When we speak to them later, you can thank them," said Shaman.

'Didi, take us for a ride…' the young girls pleaded repeatedly.

"Later after lunch…" Shambhavi said laughing her heart out.

66.

Later that night, when Shaman woke up, he found the space next to him empty. He saw Shambhavi standing at the window and watching the Ganga. Groggily, he went to her and circled her waist with his arms.

"Shambhavi, why are you awake? Is something bothering you? Or is it that you are unable to sleep at a new place..."

The young dancer smiled, touched by the worry in his voice. "No Shaman. I am so happy, that's why I am unable to sleep."

"By the way, what are you wearing?" asked Shaman.

"Your *kurta*..." she said, laughing.

"My *kurta*?"

"I was just too lazy to unpack my things."

"Just my flimsy *kurta* is not enough protection against this sort of weather. It's cold near the window, come sit on the bed and cover yourself in the quilt. Let's just talk..."

She sat on the bed and took both of Shaman's hands into her own. "How much *japa* would you have done on these hands?"

"Well... I'm not exactly sure how much, but lots of it."

She put both his hands on her head and said, "Okay Shaman... Now bless me with the power of all the *japa* you have done that I should always be a strong pillar of strength in your spiritual journey. I should never ever be an impediment on your spiritual path."

"I bless you!"

"Now I am happy."

They lay on their bed, staring into each other's eyes, before Shambhavi spoke up again, "Shaman, another thing. As you know, the Kumbh Mela is going on in Allahabad. I want the two of us to go for a dip…"

"Sure, that is easily possible, in fact Dadaji went for the *shaahi snaan*[113] on Makara Sankranti. He had asked me to come along, but I wasn't interested..."

"Let's check when the next *shaahi snaan* is and go for it…" she said. "Shaman, I feel... if there is any sin you incurred by going back on your *sannyasa* vows, it can be wiped out by the holy dip. I don't want any sort of negativity to come to you."

"You are the best thing that happened to me, Shambhavi. I am so happy when I am in your company," he assured her. "Anyway, a holy dip will wash away every bit of curse on our path..."

"Okay, come, let's sleep now. If I oversleep in the morning, what will Dadaji think? It will all be your fault."

"Hello, you were the one who was awake at 2 am, not me. As for Dadaji, he is really cool, you are free to do what you want."

"I am beginning to like him a lot," said Shambhavi.

"I think the feeling is mutual." Shaman kissed her. "You are easy to like."

---

[113]Shaahi snaan: refers to the holy bath taken by the saints and their disciples and the members of the Akhadas (Orders) in the holy river during the auspicious dates such as January 14 (*Makara Sankranti*) at the start of Kumbh Mela that happens once in twelve years.

67.

A few days after their wedding, the weather took a sudden turn. It became extremely cold and windy. Shaman didn't have any lectures scheduled for the morning, so he decided to go to the university only after lunch.

As he sat on his bed and read the new Sanskrit journal that had just arrived, Shambhavi emerged from the shower and stood in front of the mirror, draping her sari.

She saw Shaman looking at her in the mirror and blushed. "Shaman, stop staring at me!"

"Now even looking is a sin? Why are you wearing a sari in this cold?"

"Well, it was your idea. You said you'd take me to the Vishalakshi Temple. And you told me that wearing a sari to a temple is good."

Before he could reply, someone knocked on the door.

"Shaman, please see who it is," she called.

"No, you open the door."

"How can I open the door? I'm in a blouse and petticoat."

"The person knocking has come for you and that person can see you just the way you are," he said with an air of mystery.

"Chandra Ma has come?" she asked, smiling.

'God forbid!' Shaman thought. The knocking resumed.

"Go on, see who it is," urged Shaman.

Shambhavi quickly draped her sari and opened the door.

"Shambhavi Didi!"

"Chandni! When did you come?" Shambhavi enveloped her in a hug.

"You got married and didn't tell me," the shorter woman cried. "Shaman Dada told me... He called me at the Lala's shop and spoke to me. He asked if I wanted to come and be with you. I wanted to pack my bag and come immediately, but I didn't know how. I've never left Nagaprayag. Then Keshava Da and Madhava Da were coming to the Kumbh Mela, so I came with them."

"They are here as well?"

"Yes, they are talking to Shaman Da's grandfather."

"Shaman Da, I'm so happy to see Didi! Thank you for calling me here."

"But where is Balvir?" Shambhavi asked Chandni. "If you are here, what happens to him?"

"I left him."

"Left him? Why?"

"Usual story, Didi. He wants children and I can't have babies; the village people started calling him a eunuch. And then he started getting drunk and beating me."

"Oh Chandni..." Shambhavi gave her a comforting hug.

"Now that I am with you, I don't need that stupid Balvir. Didi, you have become so thin. You are looking like a boy!"

'Once again, from which angle does Shambhavi look like a boy?' Shaman thought.

"I am not thin, I am slim. You always think I have lost weight.

Come have some tea."

"I will have tea later, your hair is wet. Where is your hair drier? Let me dry it first."

"Are you sure you don't want tea now?"

"Yes. We had tea at the station before coming here."

Shaman was thankful that Chandni was there to look after Shambhavi. He went out to check on Keshava Da and Madhava Da, leaving the girls to catch up with each other.

One of them had left to have a bath and the other was eating breakfast that Kaushalya had served him.

When Shaman returned, he heard Chandni and Shambhavi talk in the bathroom.

"There is no electricity, let me wipe your hair with a towel. You sit on the stool here, otherwise I won't be able to reach your head. You have such beautiful hair – thick, straight and long," Chandni said as she dried Shambhavi's hair gently.

"And Didi, this is such a big bathroom. It has a tub too! Like they show in the Lux advertisement!" Shambhavi laughed.

"Didi, tell me one thing, you married a *sannyasi* like Shaman Dada. Does he know anything at all?"

"What do you mean by 'anything at all'?"

"I mean is he any good in bed?"

"Shh Chandni, he will hear you!" Shambhavi hissed, her face flaming with embarrassment.

"I worry for you, Didi. These *sannyasis* are odd people. They take all kinds of oaths."

"You don't have to worry on that count; everything is fine. Now, that's enough."

Shaman wanted to laugh at their conversation. 'Women are

strange creatures,' he told himself. They discus all kinds of intimate things with ease like they were discussing potatoes or movies.

When Shambhavi came out of the bathroom she looked breathtaking.

"Hi Shaman… When did you come inside?" She asked.

"A long while ago. Keshava Da is showering and Madhava Da is having breakfast."

"Come Chandni… Now have your tea."

"Okay, Didi… I am coming, tell me where to dry your towel."

Chandni took the wet towel and followed Shambhavi out. The young dancer returned to the room a few minutes later. "The *sannyasis* want to see you."

"You come here first. I heard you talking to Chandni. Why didn't you tell her that my husband can't keep his hands off me?"

"If I told her that, Shaman, then I should also add I feel the same about him."

"Ahhh…that's an interesting learning!"

"Okay, let's talk about this detail in the evening when you come back." She kissed him on his nose. "Come out… They are waiting for you."

Keshava Da and Madhava Da were ecstatic to see Shaman. They took his blessings.

"No need to take my blessings," said Shaman.

"Nonsense. Robe or no robe, you will always be our Shaman Dada."

Shaman was moved by this statement.

"The *ashram* is not the same without you," Keshava Da said.

"There is no charm left… We all miss you, Dada. The villagers keep asking for you every time one of us goes to the market. They just cannot understand why you left. They wonder how getting married can be a crime."

"The other day, Dr Sudarshan came to have *darshan* of Maharaj. He enquired after you," Krishna Da said. "He was most stunned when Maharaj informed him that you had left the *ashram.* He was even more stunned that you left because you decided to get married. He kept repeating, 'What's wrong in marrying another consenting adult…?' He just couldn't figure out why you had to leave the *ashram*. There have always been more number of married saints than unmarried ones, he said. He felt Maharaj should be really happy that Shambhavi Didi has such a worthy life partner."

There was silence for a few seconds.

"And the person who misses you the most is Maharaj," said Madhava Da.

"Earlier, we all felt so proud. Nagaprayag was the jewel amongst all our *ashrams* and as the resident *sannyasis* of Nagaprayag, we always felt superior, like we had both the king and the crown prince in our personal kingdom… Now that feeling is gone," Madhav Da observed ruefully. He stopped talking and seemed lost for a minute. Then, coming back to the present, he said, "We are very happy to see you and Didi. We will take our leave now. Tomorrow is the *shaahi snaan* of Magh Poornima[114]. If we don't leave now, they will shut the Kumbh Nagari."

"At least have lunch and go," Shambhavi said as she emerged from one of the inner rooms.

"Another time, Didi. They will shut the gates by afternoon," said Keshava Da.

[114]Magh Poornima: full moon day in the Hindu month of Magh (January–February).

Chandni came out to bid them good bye.

"Chandni, do you want to come with us to the Kumbh Mela?" asked Madhava Da.

"No, no. I have come to Didi; that's enough for me. You people go have bath," she replied.

Shaman quickly had his lunch and left for the university.

68.

On a cold day like this, attendance was dismal. Shaman sat in the library and finished preparing his notes for his upcoming classes. He set the question papers for the second batch of internals that were scheduled to happen the following week.

When he drove home at 5 pm, his heart was beating fast at the prospect of seeing Shambhavi. The thought that she was his wife thrilled him to no end. As he parked the car and walked into the house, he heard his grandfather laughing and Shambhavi complaining, "That's cheating Dadaji…"

He found his grandfather and Shambhavi playing cards.

"Shaman! How was your day?" she greeted him joyfully.

"All good... I see you're playing poker."

"Oh, you know poker?" she asked in surprise.

"Know poker? You are insulting him. He is an *ustaad*[115] at it," Dadaji said.

"Really!"

"Yes," Manohar declared. "To the point that once, when he was a student at Harvard, he called me at some ungodly hour and said. "Dadaji, thank you for teaching me to play such good poker, I am the only one left without losing any of my clothes on poker night!"

"Shaman, you were playing strip poker?" Shambhavi asked, scandalized and intrigued at this new side of him.

---

[115]Ustaad: an expert or highly skilled person, especially a musician.

"Ohhh that was when I was a student nearly two decades ago."

"Dadaji, tell me more. There seems to be a lot that I don't know about Shaman."

"Shaman was quite popular as a student. When his friends from Harvard visited us, they had some really funny stories to share about him. I will tell you all of them when he goes to the university. As for you Shaman, Shambhavi has been home all day. Take her out. You promised her you will take her to the temple in the morning. What happened to that plan?"

"Dadaji, Chandni came in the morning and they got chatting. I was willing to take her, but she refused to come out. Now where will I take her..?"

"Take her to all those quaint cafes by the side of the Ganga you took all your friends to. What did your friend Christie say, 'Oh Shaman, I love those coffee tarts, they are to die for!'" Dadaji said in a perfect imitation of an American accent.

All three burst out laughing.

"Okay let's have dinner and the three of us can go out."

"No, Shaman, I just want to sleep early. You take her and go."

"How is Chandni settling in?" asked Shaman.

"She is very happy; currently ironing my clothes," replied Shambhavi.

69.

After dinner, Shaman took Shambhavi to the *ghaat* through a short cut. He turned into an alley that led to a series of small cafes populated almost exclusively by foreigners.

"Really exotic names Shaman… *Purple Dreams, Coffee n Gossip, Love My Latte*… very off-beat," Shambhavi said as she read the neon-lit sign boards.

Shaman took her to a cafe called *Bake My Day*. It was a small neat café which had its seating arrangement on the floor. Brightly coloured large mirror-work cushions were arranged around square-shaped low tables. On each table was placed a candle inside a small glass dome. When they walked in, Shaman noticed that the place was primarily packed with Americans and Japanese people.

The man at the cash counter was a big blonde Texan with dreadlocks and a large dragon tattoo on his right arm. He wore a tight black sweater and blue jeans. "Hey Shaman," he greeted him. "How are you man? I see you have changed your hair style! The dreadlocks are gone!"

"Hi Mike, how are you doing?"

"Shaman, did you find that dude Gopal? You were looking for him, right?"

"Yes Mike, thanks. I found him…"

"Who is the lady? Not going to introduce me?" Mike asked.

"This is my wife Shambhavi."

"Your *wife*? Wow! I mean, really, wow! I thought she was a

movie actress!"

Shambhavi was dressed casually in a pair of black skinny jeans and a cobalt blue full-sleeved top that hugged her curves. She had left her beautiful hair down.

"Hi! Mike," she greeted him excitedly.

"Sorry for mistaking you for an actress. You just look so pretty!"

"Shaman, I thought you told me that you wouldn't be hooking up with a woman because of an oath you had taken."

"I made him change his mind!" Shambhavi joked, smiling.

"I bet that wasn't too hard. Now, let me find a place for you guys…"

He called to one of the servers, "Das, open the balcony and let them sit there. What would you like to eat? We specialize in bakes and desserts. And all of our food is eggless and vegetarian."

Shambhavi looked at the neat display counter—cappuccino mousse, tiramisu, espresso brownies, chocolate walnut cakes and many more.

"Shaman, what will you have?" Shambhavi asked.

"I still have to get used to eating outside food," he said.

"Try our sweetened Greek yogurt, it's just sweet curd. *Mishti doi* as Das calls it."

"All right. I will have a cappuccino mousse, and let him try the Greek yogurt," said Shambhavi.

They sat in the balcony with a view of the river that glittered like a silver ribbon. They were just a day away from the full moon.

"How do you know Mike?" Shambhavi asked.

"I grew up here. I used to visit all these cafes. Mike must be old; he has been here for forever. He just doesn't look it…"

Soon, their food arrived. As they savoured the delicious mousse and sweet yogurt, they admired the breath-taking view.

"Just look at the river, Shaman. It's like flowing molten silver."

"Yes. Ma Ganga is so beautiful. Sometimes I stay awake the whole night, just watching her."

Mike came up to where they were sitting.

"Shaman, someone gave me these two passes to have the holy dip at the VIP *ghaat* at the Kumbh tomorrow. Would you guys be interested in going..? Tomorrow, I believe, is a big day for the dip."

Shaman looked at Shambhavi. She nodded back eagerly.

"But Mike, the city will be shut from this afternoon itself. How will we enter?"

"That's exactly what I asked the guy who gave me the passes. He said if you show these passes at the check posts, they will allow you to drive through."

"Thank you, Mike," Shaman said gratefully, taking the passes.

Mike refused to take the money from them for their desserts.

"It's on the house, Shaman. It's not every day that such a pretty lady comes to my cafe! And congrats, you make a lovely couple!"

They thanked him and walked to the car in the chilling weather.

"Are you warm enough?" Shaman asked.

"Yes. I also have my shawl in my handbag. What do you want to do?"

"Do you want to go for a boat ride if I find a boatman? But we must wake up early to drive for the *snaan*."

"Yes, yes sure."

"There used to be guy called Kabir here," said Shaman.

As they walked close to the water, they found a man warming his hands in front of a small fire made from some waste that had been lying around.

"Kabir, is it you?"

"Sharananandaji!"

"Yes."

"Can you take us for a ride?"

"Sure, Swamiji. No business today—it was windy throughout the day…" Shaman didn't bother correcting him that he was no longer a *sannyasi.*

The ex-saint carefully helped Shambhavi into the boat after he got in himself. They sat opposite each other and the boat smoothly glided along the glittering silver waters of the Ganga.

"Swamiji, did you find Gopal?"

"Yes, I did find him."

The boatman's face immediately lit up as he started humming a tune softly. But for that soft humming and the rhythmic striking of the oars in the water, the rest was just tranquil silence.

"I want to sit next to you," Shaman said softly.

'Don't… Shaman, the boat is moving crazily," Shambhavi said holding onto the sides of the boat.

"Just relax. I am walking slowly to you. What's the point in me sitting five miles away from you when it's so romantic around us?"

"Yes, that makes sense. But walk carefully."

Shaman sat next to her without rocking the boat too much. He put his arm around her as Shambhavi moved close to him.

"Thank you for bringing me on this boat ride. I will never forget this night."

"Is there anything you miss from Bangalore? Do you want anything?"

"Nothing at all Shaman. I am perfectly happy. If at all, I miss the *rudraksha mala* you used to wear…"

"You know Shambhavi, that night at the cave, you held my *mala* and slept. That one act of yours alone made me feel so tender and protective towards you."

"I must have done it involuntarily."

"Yes, it was involuntary."

"Let's buy another *mala* for you. Which one would you like?"

"Your choice Shambhavi."

"All right. Let's go back. It's now past 11 pm," she said.

70.

When they reached home, it was past 1.30 am. Shaman could see the light in his grandfather's room. He assumed that he was reading as usual. Shaman went into Manohar's room. His grandfather was engrossed in solving a Sanskrit crossword puzzle. He didn't even glance up when Shaman came in.

"Dadaji, you claimed you were going to sleep early. That's why you didn't come with us."

"That was the plan, but then I saw the new journal and you had solved half the puzzle, so I was caught in the temptation of finishing it."

"Someone gave me two passes to have a dip at the VIP *ghaat* tomorrow. I will take Shambhavi and go," Shaman told him.

"That's nice, Shaman. Magh Poornima is an auspicious day. Go early, try to be there at the *sangam* by 4:30 am. It will be very crowded."

"How long will the drive take? You just went on Makara Sankranti."

"The road is steady and the distance is about 130 km. So say about two hours; but that will mean you will be driving at night. Be careful at the *mela*. Keep Shambhavi by your side always, crores of people will be there."

"Okay Dadaji, good night. We will leave at about 2:30."

"Drive slowly, in case there is mist."

"Yes, Dadaji.

71.

"Shaman, let me drive. I don't want you to miss your *nitya japa*. It's almost 3:30 am."

Shaman over the wheel to Shambhavi and closed his eyes to begin his *japa*.

When he opened them again, they were just outside Allahabad. It was nearing 4.30 am. Shaman showed their passes at the checkpoint and, just as Mike had said, they were allowed to drive through.

They parked at the sprawling parking lot outside the Kumbh Nagari where thousands of buses and cars were parked. They hired a cycle rickshaw and went to the *sangam*. The gates had just opened. They joined the teeming millions walking towards the *sangam*.

Shambhavi held Shaman's hand and walked close to him.

"My God Shaman, I have never seen so many people together in my life."

"Yes. This is the only congregation other than the Great Wall of China that can be seen even from space!"

72.

They had finished their *snaan* and were on their way back with Shambhavi in the driving seat.

"I am still speechless Shaman! What a magical experience. How many *sadhus* were there! Some of them seemed so ancient, I am just so blown away."

"Yes. We were extremely lucky to see so many saints. In fact, there is this belief that many Gods also come disguised for a dip. This Kumbh Mela was a Mahakumbh. It's a very special one – happens only once in 144 years," he said.

"I feel so happy that we can start life afresh without having a nagging feeling of guilt in us."

"Yes. It's pretty liberating."

"Shaman, I'm very hungry. You didn't let me eat the yummy *puris* they were serving at the *bhandaras*."

"But you had just eaten two plates of *kesar jalebis* and milk."

"I was still hungry. Actually, I'm famished."

"Shambhavi! You're too much! And that milk you had with the *jalebis*, it was more of a thick cream rather than milk. I couldn't drink even one glass. And why are you driving so fast?" Shaman asked.

"So that we can go home and eat..!" said she.

Shaman paused for a moment and asked. "Shambhavi, do you miss your life before Maharaj brought you to Nagaprayag?"

She was silent for a few moments as she considered his

question. "Frankly Shaman, I don't remember any of it. I think at some level, I have blocked it out. Even though I was almost fourteen when I left, I barely remember anything. Sometimes, I vaguely recall endless vistas of yellow sand dunes stretching as far as the eye can see and I remember the feel of cool marble interiors inside my room there. But it's all very hazy. So, in answer to your question, I can't miss what I cannot remember. Life, for me, began at Nagaprayag."

Shaman felt sorry for her, but didn't say anything—he just kissed her cheek.

"You always smell so good," he said.

"Not like sin?" She asked, laughing.

"No, not like sin. You smell just right."

"I was just thinking the other day about the huge argument we had regarding your beloved Jayadeva. And I realised I have become just like him. I gave up *sannyas*, got married and I have become totally enamoured of my wife."

"It's not a bad thing to be enamoured of one's own wife, is it?" Shambhavi teased, giggling.

"No, no…I am not saying that. I am just saying it's such a different calling. Look at me. As a *brahmachari* and as a *sannyasi*, home and family and such things were always a distant movie to me; a thing that happened to other people. When I used to look at householders, it was like looking at some strange tribe. Somehow the whole wrench of worldliness seemed so remote and unbecoming. And women and marriage seemed like dangerous pitfalls. You know Shambhavi, a *sannyasi* feels a sense of pride in not having anything to do with women. It's similar to the sober person who has a condescending attitude towards those who drink."

"Did *you* have a condescending attitude towards householders?"

"I won't lie to you. Yes, I was smug and I thought I was

higher, above the common run. Many *sannyasis* actually have a condescending attitude towards the householders. I had that problem. That's why I couldn't buy into Jayadeva wanting to marry. Why would anyone in his stage of evolution wish to marry and ruin oneself? I just didn't get it. But the same thing happened to me. I had thought Jayadeva had fallen by falling for a woman. I too felt I had fallen by falling for you. I suffered. I found myself sinking into a dark and endless tunnel of guilt."

"Do you still feel guilty for becoming a Jayadeva so to speak?" Shambhavi asked looking at him pointedly.

"No Shambhavi, I don't feel any guilt now. All this condescending and looking down upon the so-called unevolved, and the holier than thou attitude is a curse of separateness."

"What do you mean?"

"The thing is, no one is above, and no one is below. The humble are exalted and exalted humbled. In my case this has been a humbling experience. I was stubbornly anchored in false unworldliness. And in one go, I made peace with the whole world.

"I no longer hallucinate an austere and foolish paradise of the non-inclusive renunciants. It's ironic, but the same thing which I considered as a malaise of worldliness became, for me, a medicine for false spirituality. Shambhavi, I can't thank God enough for bringing me down to earth and giving me the scent of the earth which carries the aroma of true spirituality. One should not judge Shambhavi, one should never spurn others thinking that one is inviolate. What we hate will actually creep into us. It all comes back to us. I spurned Jayadeva and I became Jayadeva.... "

"You sound as though you regret it?"

"No, not at all. I don't regret becoming Jayadeva, I regret having spurned him. We never know what it is to be another.

And that's the whole curse of judging. Like Jayadeva, I have renounced renunciation..."

They stopped at a railway crossing.

"Your parents are coming next week. You hardly speak about them. Tell me about them..." Shambhavi implored.

"Ahhh, my parents! Sudha and Vishwanath Srivastava! I share a good relationship with them. But we have nothing in common. They met when they were studying for their MBBS, fell in love and got married while still in college. My mother's family lived in Delhi; now her parents are no more; like my father, she is also a single child. Both my parents were brilliant students who went to America to do their post-graduation. And during that time, I was born. You know how difficult it is for two students to raise a child in America... So when I was about three, my grandfather brought me to his house and raised me. At first my parents believed I will join them once I got older, but then I became so attached to Dadaji that I didn't want to leave."

"Do you resent them for sending you away?"

"I was too busy having a great time with Dadaji, so the thought never occurred to me. The thing is, while I feel great affection for my parents, the texture of that affection is what you feel for a favourite aunt or an uncle. You will like both of them, especially my mother. She is kind and gentle. My father is a bit absent-minded and introverted. My parents have a happy marriage. They are passionate about their work and both of them are highly skilled and respected in their professional field.

"But I do know that my parents, especially my mother, feels a certain degree of guilt that they left me with Dadaji. They send lots of money which I don't need; sometimes I use some of it just to make them happy, for our *ashram*. They maintain the house for Dadaji beautifully. In fact Dadaji just visited them a few months ago. He keeps visiting them though he doesn't stay for more than a few weeks."

"Yes it must get boring for him there. His whole life is here," said Shambhavi.

They arrived at the house sooner than expected and parked the car.

"I'm glad you told me about your parents. You almost never speak about them, so I always wondered what kind of a relationship you shared with them."

Chandni was waiting, sitting on the steps outside the main door. "Didi, come; your lunch is waiting. Even Dadaji has not eaten. I told Kaushalya to make all of your favourite dishes."

Shaman thanked God for all the blessings he had bestowed on him and walked into the house.

73.

The chaos at Delhi airport seemed like it was never going to end. The ground staff had gone on an impromptu strike and so Shaman had been waiting at the airport for the last eighteen hours.

It had been close to eight months since the wedding, the happiest moment of his life. He had arrived at Delhi to give a keynote address at conference, in Jawaharlal Nehru University, on *Translating Folk Narratives from Indian Languages to English.*

The usually clean busy airport was messy and teeming with frustrated and nearly violent passengers. The ex-*sannyasi* took a deep breath and commenced his *japa*. He considered taking a cab for his return, but decided to wait a bit longer.

Two hours later, they finally announced the boarding call for passengers travelling to Varanasi. Shaman slept through most of the flight. By the time he caught a cab, he felt strangely alert, despite the late hour.

His grandfather opened the door even before Shaman could knock.

"Dadaji! Why are you awake this late?"

Manohar ushered his grandson in and locked the door. "Well, I want to sleep. But as one grows old, sleep becomes a commodity on short supply. Anyway, how was your trip?"

"Very good. In fact I met one of your students there. He is now a professor at JNU."

"Is that so? Let's talk tomorrow. Sleep now, it's very late," said Dadaji.

"By the way, Shaman," he added. "Shambhavi missed you like crazy when you were away. She hardly ate and stepped out of the house. She looked so lost without you. Her students distracted her a little, but otherwise she was just so dull. It was very difficult to cheer her up in your absence. Chandni and I tried our best, but we failed. She was especially disappointed when she realised you were not coming yesterday as per your original schedule."

"It was not in my hands, Dadaji. The ground staff at the airport went on a flash strike..."

"Anyway, try not to travel too much. That child is fairly miserable without you. She really loves you Shaman. You are very lucky."

"I understand. I will try to take her with me next time."

Shaman quietly opened the door to his bedroom. But to his surprise, he found Shambhavi sitting on the bed and writing. As soon as she saw him, she flung herself into his arms.

"Shaman! How come you didn't ring the bell?"

"Dadaji opened the door even before I could knock."

"I think he was missing you," she smiled.

"He told me *you* were missing me."

"Of course I was. It's so boring without you," she replied despondently.

"Why are you up so late?"

"I am writing a new dance piece on *Shakuntala*. Chandra Ma wants it urgently."

"What are you wearing? My *kurta* again?" he asked, laughing and holding her a little away to have a better look.

"No, your shirt. It smells of you. When I wear it and sleep, I feel like I am safe in your arms."

Shaman hugged her tight. They sat on the bed in silence. A few moments later, Shambhavi shyly spoke up, "Shaman, I want to speak to you about something..."

"Are you pregnant?" Shaman asked as he looked at her intently.

Shambhavi couldn't help but laugh despite the gravity of the question. "I really wish I was, but no, it's not that! Matangi's sister, Malati, and some of our other school friends are going to Himachal for a holiday on the 1st of next month. It will be just us girls. I don't want to go, but they are really pressurising me."

"I think you should go because on the 1st I am scheduled to go to Bangalore for two days. You will get bored here."

"Are you sure, you are travelling on the first..?" Shambhavi asked, hoping beyond hope that she wouldn't have to go.

"Yes, it's all been decided."

"Okay, then I will join them, but you know Shaman, I just don't feel like going…"

"Think about it. I leave it to you entirely, there is still time for you to decide."

Shambhavi was pensive for a second, then she said, "I got something for you…"

She opened the drawer of the bedside cupboard and gave him a small dark green silk pouch held together by a drawstring. Shaman looked at her questioningly.

"Open it. It's for you…"

Shaman smiled. "I know it's for me. I was just wondering what it was."

"No need to wonder, just open it," urged Shambhavi getting impatient.

Shaman fished out a *sphatik mala*[116] that had a two-faced *rudraksha* bead as its centre piece. He immediately touched the *mala* to his forehead.

"The two-faced *rudraksha* is symbolic of *Ardhanareeshwar*, of Shiva and Shakti. I thought it would be ideal for you. I really miss the fact that you are not wearing a *mala*. I know you must be missing it too. I remember how happy you were at the hospital when I returned your *mala* to you."

"It's beautiful, Shambhavi, thank you," Shaman said, kissing her tenderly on the lips.

"I'm glad you like it. Dadaji and I took it to Vishwanath Temple. The *pundit* placed it around the Lord briefly before giving it to us after the *puja*. It's ready, you can directly wear it," Shambhavi said with a smile.

"You and Dadaji are the ones who take care of me and think through every detail. Shambhavi, you should put this on me," Shaman bent to make it easier for her to do the honours.

She put it round his neck and said with glistening eyes, "Now you look complete again!"

Shaman hugged her. "A few days ago, I was reading up on the *Ardhanareeshwar* form of Shiva. It said this androgynous avatar of Shiva represents the perfect marriage of Shiva and Parvati. When they are together, there is perfect balance and synthesis of *Purusha*, the masculine energy, and *Prakriti*, the female energy. When Shiva accommodated the Mother Goddess as half of his own body, it is said he experienced a deep sense of completion and divine bliss. Thus when a person says you complete me, he or she is unconsciously referring to the cosmic balance of Yin and Yang."

---

[116]Sphatik mala: Pure quartz crystal rosary

"That's a lovely analysis," said Shambhavi. "In my case, Shaman, you don't complete me…I just belong to you."

74.

The bright silver moonlight streamed through the window into the bedroom. The double bed was illuminated in a surreal glow. The full moon hung low on the western horizon, so close to their window that for a moment Shaman thought it was an illusion. It must be a little before 4 am, he estimated. The silence had the soft texture of velvet.

Shambhavi stirred next to him in her sleep. He stilled himself and adjusted the quilt around her bare shoulders gently, not wanting to wake her up. Just then he felt a finger tracing a feather light path from his forehead to the bridge of his nose. He didn't open his eyes and pretended to sleep. When her finger came near his mouth, he suddenly opened his lips to nip her tracing index finger and startled her.

She gasped, "You're awake!"

Shaman pulled her closer. "I fooled you, didn't I?" he asked with a soft laugh.

Shambhavi nodded, resting her head on his warm chest. "Shaman, I want to tell you something."

"Tell me," he said, running his hand affectionately through her hair.

She began tentatively, "I used to get a nightmare. In fact a recurrent one…" She paused. "Of some people trying to burn me. Now, for the past eight months, ever since we got married, that nightmare has completely stopped."

Shaman remembered how she was shaking with fear when she had the nightmare in the cave. He also recalled what the

Master had told him about the young girl's painful past. He held her closer, wanting to protect her from her own horrific memories. Shaman kissed her on the forehead and said, "*Jai Guru.*"

"I used to be scared by it. I would wake up terrified, sweating and breathless…" She let the sentence trail.

"But it's over now!" Shaman reassured her in a soothing voice. "It's all due to the grace of Naam Yajnananda Maharaj. Even though I don't live in close proximity to him anymore, I feel his grace with every breath." He let out a grateful sigh.

"Me too," said Shambhavi, hugging Shaman closely. Her eyes were full of tears.

He returned her hug and gently wiped her tears away. "It's nearly 4. You have an early morning flight. Get ready, I will drop you at the airport."

"But I don't feel like going. I just want to be with you. I don't want to go anywhere without you."

"Okay… in that case come with me to Bangalore."

Shambhavi thought for a second and said, "Though it's tempting, *very* tempting, if I drop out in the last minute, my friends will kill me."

"It's only for five days Shambhavi, and you'll enjoy yourself. We're both returning on the same day."

"Yes," Shambhavi sighed, reluctantly slipping out of the quilt that covered them both. "I must shower and get ready."

75.

It was the third day since Shaman had come to Bangalore. The October weather was beautiful. It felt strange for him to be staying at Shambhavi's dance school and with Chandrahasini playing the gracious, almost over-enthusiastic, host. It was as if she was trying to make up for the fiery friction and altercations of their previous meetings.

Shambhavi's students were ecstatic to see him. They were all delighted to have him amidst them and told him various anecdotes of Shambhavi. She had packed personalised gifts for almost 35 people at the dance school, even Bahadur the watchman received a lovely muffler.

Chandrahasini treated him with a cautious affection. She treated him like a respected son-in-law. Right from the fresh flowers for his *puja* in the morning, to organising delicious food without onion and garlic, to arranging a picture of Naam Yajnananda in his guest room, Chandrahasini was going out of her way to make his stay extremely comfortable.

But despite it all, Shaman missed Shambhavi dreadfully. He wished he had gotten her with him. Apart from one brief phone call to tell him that she had reached safely, he had not spoken to her. The place where they were staying was remote and without telephone connectivity.

It was evening and Shaman was finished with his work for the day. He took a warm bath and sat under the towering Champa tree that grew on the green lawn outside his room. As he savoured the weather, there came a peacock that danced just a few feet away from him. Its feathers caught the dying rays of the setting sun as it twirled in gay abandon. Shaman looked on, mesmerised by its display of colours.

There was a deep sense of peace. Other than the hiss of the automatic sprinklers watering the huge manicured lawns, there was complete silence. His mind wandered to the time when he had proposed to her, right under that Champa tree and with Chandrahasini as his most unlikely audience. He laughed.

The silence was broken by the sound of hurried footsteps on the grass. He turned to see who it was and was surprised to find Chandrahasini running towards him. He was even more surprised when he noticed she was running barefoot. He immediately stood up and walked briskly towards her.

There was a look of pure and raw despair in her eyes.

As soon as she came close, Chandrahasini said in between hurried breaths, "I have some terrible news for you, Shaman!"

"Is it Guruji? What happened?" asked Shaman.

"No, it's not him..." she swallowed, trying to gain her composure.

"Calm down, Chandrahasini... Is it my grandfather?"

"No… Shaman… its Shambhavi…"

"Shambhavi?! What happened to her?"

The tears were now flowing freely from Chandrahasini's eyes. Her dark mascara spread like black streaks along her cheeks.

"She is no more, Shaman…" she said, her voice cracking towards the end.

"She was caught in a freak snow storm on her way to the Kala Bhairava temple on a peak close by. She lost her footing and fell down a cliff… She died instantly..." Chandrahasini whispered.

"She's…dead..?" Shaman asked in hoarse voice. "Are you

sure?" He asked, his eyes wide with disbelief.

She nodded, trying to keep her composure to the very end. "She has left us and gone, Shaman… Gone for good!"

Chandrahasini turned into a sobbing mess on the fresh green grass as Shaman stood there, his whole body turned into ice with shock.

76.

The flight back to Varanasi was a blur. Shaman's mind was in a dark place. He was incapable of thought or feeling. It was as if he had been left in a vacuum – breathless and devoid of light. Long deep breaths left a tightness in his chest that threatened to burst. Images of Shambhavi flashed through his mind like lightning that illuminates the surroundings for an instant before the coal blackness consumes everything in its gaping maw.

Chandrahasini sat beside him, trying to keep an iron-grip on her emotions. But the tears flowed down her cheeks despite her best efforts.

Many of Shambhavi's friends and colleagues were on the flight with them. They had plunged into deep misery as they heard of the demise of their beloved friend. News of her death had shattered everyone at the institute – the cooks, the sweepers, the gardeners, and most of all, her tiny students, who were perhaps dealing with death for the very first time.

Many people spoke to him, many hugged him, but Shaman felt nothing. It was as if he had turned into dead wood – unfeeling, disconnected and immune to his surroundings. Later on, he realised that it was sheer shock that had cocooned him to give him the strength to deal with the worst phase of his loss.

He became aware of his surroundings only when he entered his house in Varanasi. All of the lights were on and the house was bustling with people. And yet, despite their presence, there was a strained hush and an unpleasant silence.

Chandni came running and fell at his feet, sobs wracking her body.

"Dada, tell me it's not true... It cannot be true!" she cried incessantly.

Shaman helped her to her feet, but didn't speak a word. He heard faint snatches of conversation that penetrated his numbed consciousness.

"She didn't suffer at all… Death was instantaneous," someone said.

"Poor thing was so young!" another voice whispered.

"Good they don't have children."

"Unfortunate that Manoharji is facing such a loss."

His grandfather sat in the corner of the room. He bit down hard on the corner of a hand towel in an attempt to quieten his sobs. As soon as Shaman sat next to him, Dadaji held his hands in a tight grip. A few moments later, Shaman moved to sit next to the *tulasi* in the central courtyard.

He heard a vehicle drive into the compound and within minutes, men entered the premises, carrying a box.

Dadaji heard the commotion and went to the door.

"Body *kahaan rakhnaa hai*? (Where should we lay the dead body?)" One man asked Dadaji in a low and respectful tone.

He gestured towards the *tulasi*.

Soon, Shambhavi's dear friends, Matangi and her sisters, arrived at the house along with their father, Mr Kanoria. Shaman immediately got up and went to his room. He wanted to be left alone.

A few minutes passed before he heard a deep heart-wrenching cry, "Oh my child... Oh my child…"

Shaman didn't recognise the voice, but the raw emotion cut through his wooden state and forced him to emerge from his room.

Chandrahasini had lifted the limp lifeless body of Shambhavi from the ice box. All Shaman could see was the cascade of her long dark hair now caked with blood. He shut his eyes immediately.

Blindly, he jostled through the crowd and sprinted out of the house. He couldn't handle it anymore. Seeing Shambhavi's lifeless body had ripped apart his protective cocoon of shock. He felt as though a thousand nails were being driven into every millimetre of space on his body.

Shaman walked for what seemed like several hours before he finally ended up in Manikarnika *ghaat*. He sat down and stared at the flames of the burning pyres.

"So, this is death… And this is how it feels to lose someone you love," he said out loud.

A show reel of all the days spent with Shambhavi started to play in his mind in slow-motion. Their first meeting, their first fight, their first kiss, their wedding…

Unlike some couples who had spent a lifetime together, for Shaman, the memories were exceedingly fresh, and even more agonizing – they had had such a limited time with one another!

The sun was just rising when he felt someone tap him on his shoulder. It was Madhusudan. "Come Shaman, let's go home. You are needed there."

On auto pilot, Shaman walked home with Madhusudan.

77.

It had been 61 days since Shambhavi had left the mortal world. Shaman lived life in a vacuum after her demise. He felt her absence in every breath and every passing second. It felt as though he had swallowed a sharp razor blade. The immense effort it took to swallow the hard lump of misery had left a perpetually raw wound in his throat. The effort it took to motivate him to breathe made every single breath painful.

He recalled the Master's quoting from *Yoga Vashishtha*—if one could think of God with every breath, even for a single day, that day itself God would surely appear. Shaman wished Shambhavi could appear, even just for a glimpse.

He longed for her with the simplicity of a child longing for its mother. It was an existential longing. The days refused to turn into night and the nights refused to turn into day. Misery prolonged time much beyond its physical limits and time crawled along painstakingly on broken knees.

He tried to continue his life in Varanasi, but could not do so without noticing Shambhavi's unique fragrance in every nook and cranny of the house. He felt suffocated; her memories dwelled in every room. He heard the faint residues of her laughter in their bedroom and the haunting echoes of her anklets in the halls. It entangled him in a web of loneliness so dark that he left the place as soon as the *chautha*[117] was over.

---

[117]Chautha: A post-death ceremony in Hindus. On the fourth day, called chautha, the ashes charred bones of the deceased are collected and subsequently, immersed usually in the holy Ganges at Haridwar, (U.P.) in the presence of a priest.

He moved into a small shack near Gangotri with an old *sadhu* named Radhanath. It suited Shaman just fine that Radhanath was immersed in his own *sadhana*. They cooked once in two days while Shaman barely ate.

The unforgiving weather of November left the place bitterly cold. Trees were shorn of every leaf, turning the area into a stark landscape. Shaman felt the barren view reflected his state of being perfectly. The harshness of his environment coupled with the biting cold made life unbearable, but Shaman wanted Nature to punish him; he wanted to be punished for staying alive.

He had bottomless depths of anger and pain, for his sadistic twist of fate. He reflected several times; he had been fine being a *sannyasi*, then he met and fell in love with Shambhavi, and then, even before he could relish their life together, she was snatched away with a callous abruptness, leaving him in a place worse than where he had started – all alone!

Just as how one gets disoriented when the spotlight is switched off and the room is plunged in sudden darkness, so Shaman had returned to the same spot, before his meeting with Shambhavi, but aware of the sharp aching loss of losing a loved partner.

'I never knew it was possible to feel so much pain and yet have no external manifestation,' he thought as he looked at his reflection in the lazy waters of the Ganga. He was amazed at how he was still alive despite being reduced into a ball of sheer misery. He lived his life willing himself to die. He knew he shouldn't take his life, so he didn't, but he didn't do much to stay alive either.

He continued to ask himself, "Why am I alive? Why am I not dead?" Shaman barely slept and hardly ate. The last two months had aged him considerably. He had lost tons of weight; his hair was now peppered with grey, his eyes were vacant, and his burning zest for life had been snuffed out. Now they were just pits of vacuous emptiness; his dreams had been snuffed out by the cruel heels of fate. The only thing he seemed capable of was prayer, which he did for many, many hours a day and sometimes through the night.

Shaman stood praying in the freezing Ganga for several hours. He welcomed the lacerating cold of the freezing waters, as he stood motionless in the waist-deep river. He fasted for several days at a stretch, subsisting only on a few sips of water, and walked long distances in the harsh barren Himalayan landscape, singing the *Hare Krishna naam* loudly. Sometimes he observed strict *mauna*[118] and didn't speak for weeks on end. The intense and physically punishing prayer just about delicately held his sanity together. Memories snapped like the gaping jaws of vicious hounds at the edges of his consciousness when he meditated. Nonetheless, they didn't dare to step into his mind when he prayed. But the second he opened his eyes, they tore at him with violent abandon. His eyes had no more tears in them. Instead, they burned with pain and loss.

He remembered Shambhavi on their wedding night as she asked him to bless her, so that she may always be his spiritual strength. She had wished to never be an obstacle to his prayers. In life, her presence had encouraged him to pray with full vigour; so much so that, even after her death, her physical absence did not restrain him. Ironically, her strangulating memories compelled him to pray with greater intensity.

~

It was evening. The weak sun hung low on the horizon; even the melodious calls of the birds failed to touch Shaman.

As he walked on, he spotted a large brightly coloured bird—a Monal! Its iridescent rainbow-coloured feathers, along with its wiry, metallic green head-crest were illuminated under the dying rays of the sun. Its head was bright green, its eyes ringed by a vibrant blue and its neck, a dull reddish brown. Its

[118]Mauna: A vow of observing silence

body had a deep purple plumage that glittered like expensive amethysts in the slanting sun's rays. 'You too seem to be alone. I wonder what happened to your mate...' Shaman thought to himself as he passed by the Monal.

The stunning beauty of the flowing Ganga didn't register in his mind. Instead he sat on the smooth boulder and kept his hand in the freezing water till he could feel his hand no more. He wondered if there was a similar method to numb his mind. He whispered to Ma Ganga, 'Mother, why did you allow fate to play with me like a savage puppeteer? Why didn't you save Shambhavi? You could have, if you wanted to.'

The bitterness of his loss, the absolute pointlessness of his life, sometimes filled his being with red hot coals of anger and sometimes with ice blocks of misery. Why, he wondered, why did he have to fall in love and suffer the pain of separation like this?

He saw a small *linga*[119] by the side of the river. He now understood the loss of lord Shiva when Sati left her corporeal frame, and why he walked the three worlds, clutching onto her mortal body.

He remembered how the mortal remains of Shambhavi had been placed on a pile of sandal wood. A large red *kumkum bindi* adorned her forehead and her slight form had been wrapped in a red Benaras silk sari.

Shaman's soul screamed when the greedy tongues of the blazing fire he had lit devoured her beautiful form. He wanted to scream that she was petrified of fire. The nauseating smell of charring human flesh—not any flesh, but the flesh and blood of his beautiful Shambhavi—made him want to put out those flames immediately. But in the end, he watched on, like

[119]Linga: Literally a "form" or "symbol." It is the first and final form at the time of creation, perfect ellipsoid, and a main tantric symbol for Lord Shiva who is the destroyer and restorer, as well as the "God of yogis."

a mute spectator. The Gods seemed to understand that, and summoned a bout of torrential rains that almost doused the flames of the funeral pyre. He knew Gods accepted food from fire, and yet, despite the rain, they claimed her. Shaman did not want to give his beloved Shambhavi to them.

'They snatched her away from my arms,' he thought.

What remained was only an urn of ashes. Shambhavi's stunning form, her soulful eyes, her luscious lips, her long hair, had all been reduced to just a small pot of grey ashes. He didn't have the will to throw her last remains into the Ganga. He wanted some physical part of her to remain with him, but alas, he had to immerse everything in the river. He watched helplessly as the ashes floated away on the rolling waters.

Shaman only wore white clothes since the funeral. But now more than ever, he wished for the comfort of his saffron robes. He knew she was reborn and he wished he could just see her one last time.

Suddenly, vast plumes of dark clouds loomed ahead and a bitter icy wind tore everything in its path. Shaman welcomed its biting force as it almost laved off the top layer of his skin. Slowly, he made his way to the small shack nestled close to the hillside. The old *sadhu*, Radhanath, bundled in several layers of clothes, had been waiting for him outside.

"I was worried about you, Shaman Da. The wind is very strong here. I was about to come look for you. It's been hours since you went out."

"*Jai Guru,* Dada," said Shaman, bowing his head apologetically. "Sorry to have worried you."

"You are coughing a lot these days and it's only getting worse. I think you must have yourself treated."

"I'm drinking the magic potion that you are so kindly brewing for me."

The old *sadhu* shook his head and said, "I think you need

something stronger. Come inside, I have made some food; eat it while it's hot."

"I'm not hungry Radha Da, you eat."

"It's been two days since your last meal. You must eat... I insist," replied Radhanath, going in.

Shaman followed him into the small, neat shack. Radhanath had cooked a simple meal of *khichadi*[120]. He noticed the *sadhu* had already offered it to the Gods. Shaman served himself a paltry portion and sat near the fire Radhanath had lit to stay warm. They ate in silence. Shaman stared at the leaping flames. Suddenly, he saw Shambhavi, holding out her arms to him.

"Shaman Da!" The sharp call of his name broke his reverie. "Don't touch the fire, you'll get burnt!" warned Radhanath.

After that, the food turned into mud in Shaman's mouth. *Anna* is *poorna brahma*—the Upanishadic belief that food indeed was the all-encompassing spirit of the universe made him eat without wasting it. But to swallow each mouthful was an ordeal that almost made him retch.

Pain and anger masticated his psyche into a pulp of delusions, hallucinations and memories. When he lay down to sleep after hours of prayer, he heard Shambhavi's voice whispering his name in the darkness, as if she were lying beside him. Sleep eluded him for weeks in succession.

The screeching wind outside stopped abruptly and an unnerving hush followed. He looked out into the dark night and watched dainty snowflakes fall like silken feathers from the heavens. He went out of the hut, caught a snowflake in the hollow of his palm and watched its pretty form melt away.

His mind wandered to the night he had watched another snowflake melt.

---

[120]Khichadi: a dish made from rice and lentils (daal)

78.

It was snowing outside, and though it was only 9 pm, the weather felt bitterly cold. The biting chill had forced the occupants of the *ashram* to call it a night by 7 pm. Shaman had dropped Piyali Bose, the Bengali translator, at the bus stand and was on his way back to the *ashram*.

There was an unearthly silence as the soft flakes continued to fall slowly, layering everything around him in a soft white cloak. They fell like dainty white confetti that drifted downwards from the heavens. He quickly parked the car and walked to Shambhavi's room. He hoped Chandni had not returned from the village; if she opened the door, he would have a lot of explaining to do. He pushed the door to see if she had kept it unlocked, but it was firmly latched. He knocked on the door gently.

A muffled voice came from inside, "Go away!"

"Shambhavi, I'm dying in the cold. Open the door quickly."

"You can die if you want, but I am not opening the door."

Shaman knocked again and again, but Shambhavi refused to open the door. Eventually, he retreated to his room, disheartened. But his mind was constantly on Shambhavi; he desperately wanted to be with her. After 15 minutes of restlessly pacing in his room, he returned to Shambhavi's room to try one last time.

"Shambhavi, please open the door..."

"Where were you the whole of last night?" she asked.

"Shambhavi, open the door. Only then can I explain everything to you."

He deliberately made a sound like his teeth were chattering. And a few moments later, he heard the sound of the door being unlatched. He pushed the door and rushed inside.

The electric heater was running on high. Several brass lamps burned near the Nataraja idol and the fragrance of tube roses filled his nostrils. A vase full of white tube roses stood on her dressing table.

Shambhavi was sitting on her bed. When Shaman moved to hug her, she turned away. "Stay away from me..."

"And where will I go? Without you, I have no place to go in this world," Shaman declared sitting next to her. "See, I got your favourite *gulab jamun*[121] from Brijamohan's."

"You can go to Piyali Bose, and give her the *gulab jamuns* or maybe you have already fed her with your hands... Now move away and sit on the window sill."

"It's cold there, Shambhavi. Let me sit next to you," Shaman pleaded, setting the sweets on her bedside table.

"All right, you sit on the bed and *I'll* go to the window sill," Shambhavi said, walking towards the window. She wrapped her shawl tightly around herself and continued, "Now, tell me, where you were last night?"

"Shambhavi, you know I was working with Piyali. She is working on Maharaj's book. She needed a lot of clarifications, so I thought if I worked with her through the night, the work will finish quickly and then I can be with you."

"Why was she with you in your room the whole night?"

---

[121]Gulab jamun: A classic Indian sweet or dessert that is very famous and is enjoyed in most festive and celebration meals. They are berry-sized balls dunked in rose flavoured sugar syrup.

"See, that lady smokes and she could not work without smoking. Now, my room is a little away from the rest of the *ashram;* I thought it would be the best place. That way, she would not be offending anyone."

Shaman sat next to her and kissed her cheek. "Yuck, Shaman! You reek of cigarette smoke. Get away from me. Did you also smoke with her?" Once again, Shambhavi moved away and returned to her bed.

"Don't be silly. I have never smoked... Ever."

"Well, there is always a first time... How close was she sitting to you? You smell like an overfull ashtray!"

"Shambhavi, how do I explain this to you? See, in a closed room, cigarette smoke will cling to everything. And Piyali smokes a lot."

"You seem to know her rather too well! Why did you choose her to do this work?" Shambhavi's anger increased with every answer.

"I didn't choose her, Maharaj did..."

"Don't lie to me, Shaman! Maharaj mentioned that you said that she is the best."

"But he was the one who selected her," Shaman countered.

"Selection will come into play only if there's a choice of more than one. Did you suggest anyone else?"

"Shambhavi, you are getting unnecessarily jealous..."

"Did you recommend anyone else or was hers the only name you gave to Maharaj?"

"She is the best...and that's the truth."

"So you didn't think anyone else is capable of doing this job."

She took off her *nathani*[122] and threw it at him.

"What are you throwing at me?" asked Shaman. He picked up the big round nose ring from the ground and examined it.

"You told me the other day that you wanted to see me wear the *nathani*. Here I was, wearing it and waiting for you, and you didn't even notice! You have eyes only for your Piyali," she said angrily.

"It's dark in here. I couldn't see you properly… You are not even allowing me to sit next to you," said Shaman, trying to placate her.

He sat next to her and said, "Shall I make you wear this beautiful *nathani*? I want to properly see you wearing it."

"No need," Shambhavi said, looking away. "You missed your chance."

"Why don't we forget Piyali? Why are we wasting our time talking about her?" Shaman asked.

"No Shaman, I want some clarifications. Why were you holding her hand when you went to the Prayag?"

"She was going to fall on those steps! It's not everyone's cup of tea to walk down those steps."

"Then why did you take her there? You can be so curt when you want to be."

"Shambhavi, she's a middle-aged woman, 45 years old."

"She doesn't look 45. I think you are lying."

"I'm sure she'll be flattered to hear that. Anyway, she wanted to see the Prayag up close. The book contains long passages on it and she told me she needed 'first-hand experience of the dancing waters' – that's what she called it."

"Now you are quoting the woman?"

---

[122]Nathani: traditional Indian nose-ring worn by Indian women

"Listen, I am sorry, but what choice did I have? And how did you know I was holding her hand…?"

"Obviously, I was watching the two of you. Both of you were talking non-stop! Another thing, why did you take her to the market in the village?"

"Oh, that! She had one flimsy shawl with her. Without proper warm clothes she would have died in this cold."

"May be you should have taught her your trick of living in the snow with no real warm clothes," Shambhavi replied, still a little miffed.

Shaman hugged her, but she was stiff in his arms.

"She is agnostic. There is no question of teaching her any trick."

"You then went to Café Moon Beams and sat with her for hours. Why? Why did you hang around that cafe?"

"You were really spying on me!"

"Answer the question, Shaman," the young dancer insisted.

"Piyali likes to drink coffee and smoke at the same time. Now, that kind of thing is not possible here in the *ashram*. Without caffeine and nicotine, her brain just doesn't work. It was taking forever to get the job done, so we sat in the café and completed a major portion of the work."

"You seem to have an explanation for everything that I ask you."

"Shambhavi look at yourself." He led her to the mirror on the dressing table and pointed out her own reflection. "Will I even look at anyone when I have you looking like a Goddess?"

Her eyes met his in the mirror and she smiled. She giggled when Shaman started to kiss the back of her neck. "Don't do that. It tickles!"

"I know."

"How do you know that…?"

"I heard you say that to the fawn at the temple."

"You devil! You were watching me?"

"Many people have called me many things, but 'devil' is a first. You are going to pay for that, and for all the false accusations you made in the last hour."

Shaman caught her in his arms, trapping her, and continued to kiss her in that ticklish spot till she collapsed in a heap of helpless giggles.

"Shh… Someone will hear you…"

"Leave me, Shaman… Otherwise I will die laughing."

He hugged her tight. "I missed you every moment I sat with her."

"I hated her and you, collectively! You know what your Piyali said when Baba introduced me to her? 'Oh what a pretty porcelain doll!' I just hate being called a doll."

"She got everything wrong, Shambhavi; not just the doll part. You are not pretty, but ravishingly beautiful. You are not porcelain, but a warm flesh-and-blood woman!"

Outside, it started to snow heavily; the snowflakes fell faster and thicker, adding thicker layers of snow to everything in its path. Shaman said, "Look at the falling snow; it's so beautiful. Have you ever felt a snowflake melt in your palm?"

When Shambhavi shook her head, he moved to open the window.

"It's too cold to be opening windows," Shambhavi protested.

"Just for a second…"

He opened the window and gently guided her hand outside. A snow flake fell on it immediately.

"Now watch it melt..." he whispered. "Do you know that every snow flake is unique? There are almost no replicas. Imagine that! So much snow and each flake is different..."

"God's creation is humbling," said Shambhavi with awe. She hugged Shaman and tucked her face into the hollow of his neck. "I crave for the alone time I get with you."

"Me too. And you can't imagine how much!"

"Shaman, I'm sorry I didn't open the door for you the first time. I was just very angry."

~

Radhanath found Shaman lying in the snow the next morning. The ex-*sannyasi* was burning with high fever. He woke Shaman and helped him inside. He then went to the village and called Manohar.

79.

Shaman was surprised to see Madhusudan sitting next to him when he opened his eyes. He thought his friend was part of his delusion until he helped Shaman sit up.

"*Jai Guru*, Shaman," Madhusudan greeted softly.

"*Jai Guru*. How come you are here?"

Radhanath, who was sitting nearby, said, "I called your grandfather and he sent Madhusudan. You are gravely ill, Shaman Da. You have a high fever. I was very worried."

"Let's get you to a hospital," Madhusudan said.

"It's just a fever; it will settle," Shaman said, brushing off their concern.

"No, Shaman, this is serious. You need medical attention. Just look at yourself! You are mere skin and bones. You have a bad cough, too," Madhusudan countered.

"I have packed your things. The taxi is waiting outside. Madhusudan will come with you. Shaman Da, please go to the doctor in Gangotri. Your grandfather is deeply worried," Radhanath said.

The mention of his grandfather prodded Shaman into agreeing, but the moment he stood up, the world spun around him and he almost blacked out. Madhusudan immediately held him up and steadied him.

"You're awfully weak, Shaman Da. Come, let's go to the cab."

The doctor at the clinic was a young lady who diagnosed that there was nothing wrong with Shaman. He only needed nutritious food and rest, and prescribed a basic round of antibiotics. "Exposure to the cold has given him a bad cough and phlegm, leading to a fever," she explained.

Shaman hated his naturally robust constitution. He just wanted to pass away into oblivion. But nothing of that kind happened. He should have died when the snake had bit him. That would have been perfect, he concluded.

Once they got back into the cab, Madhusudan said, "Shaman, Maharaj wants to see you."

"Maharaj wants to see me? How will I see him? He forbade me from entering the *ashram,*" Shaman said with a deep twinge of sadness.

"He asked me to bring you to Nagaprayag *ashram.*"

"All right. If that's the Master's command, then let's go."

After a few hours of driving in complete silence, Madhusudan offered Shaman some biscuits. The malnutritioned man shook his head and said, "Not hungry... Actually, now I hate food. I find it hard to swallow anything."

"But you must eat something, Shaman. You've become half your size. To tell you the truth, I almost didn't recognise you back at the shack. You look a decade older."

"I just don't feel like living," Shaman said ruefully. "Living has become like a fine torture. The great part of each day is that it's taking me closer to my death. I am just waiting to die. I can't tell you how much I miss Shambhavi. I can't understand why I have not gotten some terminal illness. I am sickeningly healthy!"

"Losing a partner is painful, Shaman Da. But you are an evolved man. I have nothing to say to comfort you that you already don't know, but I have to repeat the cliché—time is a great healer!"

Shaman continued to speak as if he hadnt't heard Madhusudan's words. "I now understand fully the sheer hatred Gopal had for his lonely life bereft of his wife. To live with no meaning, to just exist, so that one can die naturally. I more than understand why he threw us out when we tried to offer him money." Shaman smiled sadly as he recalled Gopal's frighteningly empty eyes.

Taking a deep breath, he continued, "You know how it is…like a song that is over, but the melody is stuck in your head and keeps playing in your mind. Madhusudan, tell me, why did I ever have to fall in love and marry, only to lose her? Anyway, let me pray. Otherwise I'll just crumble to pieces."

~

It was past 6 pm when they reached Nagaprayag *ashram*. Shaman got out of the cab. When he saw the steps leading to the *ashram*, he remembered the first time he had touched Shambhavi – when he had taken her hand to help her out of the car upon their returned from Dr Sudarshan's hospital. It was also the first time she had addressed him as Dada. A barrage of memories assaulted him with laser-sharp precision. Shaman recoiled, unable to bring himself to climb the steps. He ran back to the cab. 'I can't go in,' he thought in panic.

At that moment, he noticed that all of the *sannyasis* had come to the gate to receive him. They stood solemnly, tears streaming down their cheeks. Venu Da, Krishna Da and Keshava Da cried openly. Partha, the priest, was trying his best to contain his emotions. A sobbing Madhav Da took Shaman's blessings and walked with him up the stairs.

Shaman clenched his teeth, trying not to let the tears spill over. When the *sannyasis* bent to take his blessings, Shaman stepped back. The short Venu Da hugged Shaman and cried like a child in his arms, his plump body heaving with uncontrollable sobs. "How could this happen Shaman Da? How could this happen?" he lamented, distraught.

Shaman's throat constricted as he tried his best to control his tears. He remained silent, not trusting himself to speak.

Leela was the next to fall at Shaman's feet. Silent tears streamed down her despairing face. "Dada, how are you managing without Didi?"

"I am not able to manage," Shaman said in a choking voice.

Krishna Da cleared his throat. "Maharaj is waiting for you."

Shaman walked towards the Master's chambers. He caught a glimpse of the *sangam,* and immediately fell to his knees and prostrated to Ma Ganga. The leaping waters joined each other in a turbulent union of spray and froth. The familiar roar struck a chord of longing deep within Shaman. Tears flowed unbidden from his eyes. He remembered asking Shambhavi under the banyan tree, whether they would meet briefly like the rivers at the *sangam,* only to swiftly part ways again.

It was as if a sharp stake had pierced his heart when he recalled how horrified she had been by his question. Her words rung clear in his ears, 'I belong only to you, Shaman.'

But, in the end, she didn't belong to anyone, Shaman thought as he slowly made his way to the Master.

80.

When Shaman entered Maharaj's room, the old *guru* was seated in his usual chair. An unexpected bolt of pure joy struck Shaman as soon as he saw the frail luminous form of his *guru*. The mere sight of his Master had the power to lift him from the darkest depths of misery, even if only for a moment.

Shaman fell at his feet. "Maharaj..." he sighed. "It has been nearly eleven months since I last saw you..." Spontaneous tears of *bhakti* poured forth from his eyes as he gently touched the Master's bony feet.

Maharaj drew the sign for *Aum* on Shaman's forehead with his ring finger. "*Jai Guru*, Shaman. Yes, I know it's been eleven months. This *ashram* has not been the same without you."

The Master touched Shaman's forehead and added, "Shaman, you have a fever. You must look after yourself. Look at the amount of weight you have lost. You are just a skeleton now."

Shaman looked at the Master, and asked piteously as hot tears trickled down his cheeks, "For whose sake, Maharaj, should I keep this body and soul together? As you know, I left you and this *ashram* to be with Shambhavi. Now she is gone. I have neither her nor you. I am in a worse place than where I'd begun. I have burnt all bridges and I am left with nothing. Why did this *leela*[123] happen Maharaj? I feel like an orphan. I have no will to live – existing on this planet has become a huge burden for me. Why did fate play such a harsh trick on me?"

---

[123]Leela: the "divine play", the word is often used to describe the inevitable play of God's will

"Shaman, do not cry, my child. You know very well that birth, marriage and death are not in our hands."

Shaman nodded, and after a pause, said in choked voice, "Knowing this intellectually does not provide me with the strength to deal with my current situation. I am completely broken inside. I don't know who I am, nor where I am headed." In a voice that carried his complete and utter despair, he asked, "Maharaj, please tell me! Did you know my life would be like this? Did you know Shambhavi had very little time?"

Krishna Da, who had been sitting in the corner during the exchange, wiped away fresh tears when he heard the direct reference to Shambhavi's demise.

The Master was silent for few minutes before he spoke. "Shaman, I tried my best to steer you so you would not have to face this loss. But I could not protect you. I failed. *Praarabdha*... destiny...is such a strong force. I could do nothing but stand by and watch things unfold. It was very difficult for me to witness the choices you made. You were already caught in destiny's inexorable, magnetic pull."

Shaman sighed, listening with rapt attention. "Maharaj, you say I made the choices, but you were there all the time, you could have made the choices for me and saved me."

"No, Shaman. I couldn't have done that."

"But why?"

"Because everyone must live his or her own life. No one can live it for you vicariously. In the *Mahabharata*, could Sri Krishna avert the war? Sahadeva was a great astrologer; he knew there would be a catastrophic war. He warned them all several times, but he could not stop it. The thing is, we cannot avert destiny and we should not try to. We must accept it without resistance."

The Master paused and then said, "Because destiny, as you

know, is not a stranger. It is our own *karma*."

"I know that, Maharaj, but it is so overwhelming when it comes. It feels like a monster."

Maharaj smiled. "Destiny is not a monster. It's our own kith and kin. In fact, it's another self."

Shaman's burning grief had not reduced, but he paid attention to the words of the Master.

"When you came to relate the vision you had at Varanasi, I made sure Shambhavi was there to listen to that magical account of your divine journey, to give her a glimpse of how unattainable you were. On another occasion, when you told me you had become fond of her, I told you to stay away. And yes, to answer your question, I knew she had little time. That's the reason I was acutely sensitive about her health. When she fell, I was anxious and insisted she be taken to Dr Sudarshan's hospital. Even when she overslept, I feared she was ill. That's why I told you to be the most ideal husband possible. I knew you had very little time together."

"Maharaj, I may sound like an ordinary person and talk like all the ignorant people who come to the *ashram,* but I still revolt at the thought that Shambhavi was built into my life only to be destroyed."

"Shaman, you yourself have counselled so many people on how destiny is our own creation."

"Yes, it is ironic... My wisdom is unable to help me today..."

The ageing *guru* looked at him and then heavenwards. "The *Gita says, gahanaa karmano gatih*—the intricacies of *karma* are difficult to penetrate."

"Maharaj, I don't know what *karma* I have committed in my past life to have lost Shambhavi like this. Even you couldn't save me from the misery that was destined for me. Now what hope do I have? I am like a kite whose thread has been cut...

I am spinning out of control, nose-diving at a terrific speed."

"Shaman, what had to happen has happened. Can you reverse it?"

"No, I can't."

"Well, then you have to move on..."

"Maharaj, I really feel I don't have the strength nor the will required to move on," Shaman sighed. "Let it all end here. I see no point in anything because Shambhavi is no more."

"What do you mean 'no more'?" the Master asked gently. "Shambhavi's body is gone, I agree, but her soul persists. I can understand other people saying such things, but not you."

"I'm sorry, Maharaj," said Shaman, realising his mistake. "You're right, I must not say Shambhavi is no more."

"Shaman, you must accept your destiny gracefully. These are *karmic* bonds—the more you wrestle with them, the stronger they will become. These have to be endured; you can't escape them. It's better to pay off the debt than postpone it. Otherwise, you have to pay with interest."

"I will try, Maharaj. But I am broken right now. Please bless me profusely so that I can pick up the pieces and live on..."

"Good! You have my blessings always. You've been a *sannyasi* Shaman and you've been a householder. You've had the best of both worlds."

With this realisation, Shaman only felt exhausted. Sensing that, Maharaj said, "When you're overwhelmed Shamantak Srivastava, recall the *sannyasi* named Swami Sharanananda who resides in you. You're not an ordinary soul. Do not forget that...."

Tears once again trickled down Shaman's cheeks. But as he mulled over what Maharaj said, he became more reflective than sad.

"I will try, Maharaj. I will surely try," he said, feeling the warmth in his Master's words. "How I have missed hearing your voice! I already feel energised with your blessings."

The old sage smiled and said, "Our doors are open to you. You can come and go whenever you want."

Shaman fell at his *guru's* feet in *dandavat pranaam,* his being filled with gratitude. His body lay straight as a log—the ultimate form of respect.

81.

The time spent at the *ashram* was bittersweet for Shaman. On one hand, spending time with the Master was a balm to his aching soul, but on the other, the *ashram* was brimming with memories of Shambhavi. Every nook and corner, from the cowshed to the Gayatri Temple, echoed with memories of the time spent with her.

The first few days were the hardest, but strangely, being amongst the *sannyasis* who had known her since she was a child, felt cathartic. Shaman no longer felt alone in his grief and deep loss. It helped as they told him anecdotes of her girlhood. The *sannyasis* too, mourned her death. They cried freely when emotion overwhelmed them. As the days flowed into weeks, they comforted each other.

It was still painfully difficult for Shaman to eat more than a few morsels, and nearly impossible for him to sleep more than a few hours without waking, aching for Shambhavi. But eventually, he was able to smile when a funny story was related about her. It was a hard and slow journey, but the process of healing had gently begun.

Shaman still didn't have the courage to enter her room. But when the Master handed him a whole sheaf of letters that Shambhavi had written to the *guru* over a period of nearly a decade, he could read them without breaking down completely.

Her letters from school had a young girl's curly handwriting that had slowly metamorphosed into graceful calligraphy as she grew up. Maharaj had kept the letters neatly in an old file. The letters gave him fresh glimpses of her personality, her deep understanding of life, and how beautifully she had accepted her unfortunate circumstances of being orphaned and then being almost burnt alive. She had embraced every challenge life threw at her, with dignity, strength and fortitude. Her zest for life was unmistakable. Shaman respected her even more after reading her letters. He made a promise to himself that he would no longer mourn her, but honour her life and the time he had spent with her.

He returned the file carefully after the Master had finished his meditation. The ageing *guru* took the file and, as if reading his thoughts, said, "We should be able to remember her and how much affection she showered on each and every one of us, without grief. As you know, Shaman, the quality of her onward journey will suffer if we continue to grieve. It will hold her back."

"Yes, Maharaj, I agree with you completely. It's selfish on the part of survivors to cry. Shambhavi deserves better. I must set her free. Though it will be hard, I will sincerely try not to shed any more tears," Shaman promised.

"May Ma Durga empower you, Shaman. That is the best gift we can give to the departed."

82.

Apart from the gentle pitter-patter of falling rain and the almost non-existent hum of the air conditioner, there was a significant period of complete silence after Shaman had finished narrating his story.

Indraneel sat motionless, his eyes brimming with unshed tears. "Shaman," he said, "there are no words to describe the tremendous loss you have faced. And now just look at you! No bitterness, no angst, no sadness. In fact, you glow with positivity and joy. My respect for you has increased a thousand-fold." Joining his palms, Indraneel bowed his head.

Shaman smiled. "Indraneel, it was a long time ago. Besides, I cannot take credit for all this. I was completely losing it. It was nothing but the grace of the Master that kept me sane. I could not have made it this far without his blessings."

"Grace, yes, I fully agree with you on that, Shaman. But what courage, grit and determination it takes to not go down the road of self-pity and self-destruction! To tell you the truth, when Avani had broken up with me, I had been so depressed that for months on end, I just locked myself in a room and almost drank myself to death. But in your case, my God... I can't even begin to imagine the deep trauma you must have faced at the sudden death of your beloved wife."

"It was hard, Indraneel, indeed very hard. I had nearly lost my mind. I could hear Shambhavi's voice right next to my ear like she was calling to me almost all the time. I didn't sleep for months on end after her demise. I was sucked down a great dark tunnel of misery. Without Maharaj's grace, I would have died a slow painful death of neglect and starvation. Speaking of starvation, I'm absolutely ravenous. Let's go and hope we find some food. It's past 11:30 and it's a rainy night."

The younger man laughed at the quick change in subject. "I always knew you were focussed on food. Even when I wanted to discuss my deep existential angst with you, you wanted to eat first. And now, when I am still reeling from your story, you are talking about dinner!"

Shaman chuckled. "Indraneel Bhai, one has to eat and sleep. Only then can one be healthy enough to pray and meditate sincerely. And if one prays and meditates sincerely, everything in this life will be taken care of by the Almighty."

"I know that now. Okay, considering it's almost midnight, what are our dinner options?"

"Hmm...to the best of my knowledge, everything will be shut. We could try a momo vendor who does business till late into the night."

"You leave close to 2 am from the shop," Indraneel said. "I think you need to maintain more sane hours, Shaman."

"Look who's talking about sane hours!" Shaman countered laughing, turning off the lights.

"Shaman, I no longer work late into the night, especially after the girls... I want to spend time with them."

"That's good. You must prioritise them," said Shaman, locking the shop. "Take that umbrella from the stand. Though it's just a faint drizzle now, it may start to rain in earnest anytime." Thunder rumbled ominously before he could complete his sentence.

The two walked in silence along the wet, deserted road towards the Ganga *arati*. A little ahead, they could see a sizeable crowd consisting mostly of foreigners, and a few local youngsters, standing around the momo cart, eating. There was the distinct smell of marijuana in the air.

A couple of foreigners called out to Shaman and he waved to them as Indraneel ordered their momos. Even before they had paid, the brisk vendor handed them two plates of steaming hot momos. Shaman and Indraneel took their plates and sat down on the *ghaat*. The waters of the Ganga rushed by with a vibrant whooshing sound. Little crests lapped at the *ghaat*. The two friends ate silently and then ordered tea from a vendor under a tree.

"You are unusually quiet," Shaman observed.

"I must confess, your story just blew me away. I would never in my wildest dreams, have guessed that you had a past filled with so much turmoil. Who would have imagined you were once a man in ochre robes, a *sannyasi,* slated to head one of the most illustrious spiritual Orders of our times? Tell me Shaman, how did you end up with a bookstore? Nothing adds up. I always thought I was close to you and I had you all figured out. But look at us now, I have no clue at all."

Shaman took the tea cup the vendor offered and took a small sip. "After I went back to Nagaprayaga, I stayed there for a few months. Initially, I found it very difficult to live there, but slowly, especially after reading Shambhavi's letters, I made a conscious decision to no longer mourn her loss. I decided to clean my old room in the *ashram* to distract myself. Prior to that, I just slept anywhere, on the *ghaat,* in the temple... There was no specific place. If I was too exhausted to move, I would just close my eyes till my next nightmare."

Shaman cleared his throat and continued. "When I went to clean my room, I found my books. It was like meeting old friends. I started reading some of my favourite parts in certain books. And for the first time in many months, I lost track of time. Reading gave me much needed sanity. It was then that I realised that since Shambhavi had passed, I had not held a single book in my hand.

"I told Maharaj that reading gave me solace. He blessed me

and told me to find a future where books were the fulcrum. And that's how El Dorado happened."

Indraneel had been listening to Shaman with rapt attention. "What a journey Shaman! But why Rishikesh?" he asked.

"I couldn't imagine staying in Varanasi. Nagaprayag was not an option because it was too small a place for a bookstore. I even briefly toyed with the idea of a library. I had always liked Rishikesh. It has a thriving reading population and good bookstores. My grandfather wanted to be with me, so we shifted here. In fact, he passed away just a couple of years ago. Our house in Varanasi was turned into a hospital, run by a charitable trust."

"So you live here all by yourself?" Indraneel asked, finishing his tea.

"Remember I told you about Chandni? She is with me, and the girl Payal, who works at the store, is Chandni's niece. She is still a garrulous woman with a loud mouth, but I know Shambhavi would have wanted me to take care of her."

Indraneel nodded and asked, "Shaman, I'm curious about one thing. You gave up a successful career in Harvard for *sannyasa,* then you gave up *sannyasa* for a woman you loved. You lost her, and your position in the *ashram,* ending with nothing. I know you run a successful bookstore, but how do you manage to stay positive? What keeps you going?"

Shaman's reply was firm and confident. "Gratitude keeps me going, Indraneel. Plain gratitude creates a sense of joy in me. And I live in that *ananda,* that bliss."

"How?"

"There comes a time Indraneel, when the long night of pain and suffering reaches the dawn of self-discovery. The stimulating time at Harvard, the enlightening years at the *ashram,* the loveliest time I had with Shambhavi, everything was too perfect. My life, I realised, was too precious to be cast away in grief. I felt I'd be insulting my life with thanklessness and ingratitude if I were to be sad."

"Well, that's a great perspective," said Indraneel.

"That's what I live by now. You know, there's this thing the Master once explained to me. He said God is a giver, He keeps giving to all, but only a few are appreciative of what they receive in life. These grateful ones become *prasanna*—peaceful and blissful. They can concentrate their minds."

"You're absolutely right. We can't hope to live well without being peaceful and blissful."

"Indraneel, our life needs gratefulness and cheerfulness to be able to live in the present. These two release a fountain of bliss that spreads a wave of positive thinking, freshness, vigour and zest. That's what the *Upanishad* says too. *Raso vai sah,* God is bliss, and the little joys that we experience in life are but particles of that infinite bliss. We need to create a chain of awareness of all that God has bestowed upon us and continues to bestow on us every day. Once we teach ourselves to become aware of that, we begin to feel gratitude and from that feeling of gratitude, we can easily reach the summit of unlimited *ananda*."

Once again, Indraneel was struck by Shaman's profound wisdom. The eastern sky was already showing signs of turning a light grey lined with soft pink. The waters of the Ganga reflected the changing hues with quick precision.

"Another new day, Indraneel, and another brand new gift from God. I will meditate now."

Shaman walked into the river to offer his *pranaam* to Ma Ganga.

ACKNOWLEDGEMENTS

To Yashi, Swarup, Ramya, Aniruddha, Divya, Vickie and Vikas, I give due and grateful credit. Their contribution to this novel has been invaluable.

Wish To Publish With Us?

We are always keen to look at interesting content across genres. Please email your submission to: **submissions@leadstartcorp.com**

The submission should include the following:

1. **Synopsis**
   A summary of the book in 500 - 1000 words. Please mention the word count of the manuscript.

2. **Sample chapters / Poetry**
   A couple of chapters from the book; these need not be in order, just send the best two chapters of the book. Or a few poems if the same is a collection of poetry.

3. **A Note About The Author**
   An interesting note about yourself (about 200 words).

4. **Additional Information**
   - Target audience
   - Unique selling proposition
   - List of illustrative content (if any)
   - Other comparative titles
   - Your thoughts on marketing the book